HENRI

a novel of indecisions

JOHN OSBORN

authorHOUSE®

AuthorHouse™
1663 Liberty Drive
Bloomington, IN 47403
www.authorhouse.com
Phone: 1-800-839-8640

First published by AuthorHouse 8/30/2011

ISBN: 978-1-4567-6151-6 (e)
ISBN: 978-1-4567-6152-3 (dj)
ISBN: 978-1-4567-6153-0 (sc)

Library of Congress Control Number: 2011906956

Printed in the United States of America

Other Books by John Osborn

MICHAEL

SAMANTHA

DANIEL

GLORIA

SET IN 1999 THIS IS the fourth novel portraying the life of a Lord family member. Cousin to the Lord family living at Fotheringham Manor, Henri Lord finds himself struggling to decide how to live his life. Deep in debt, pilfering clients' money, uncertain about his own sexuality, and frustrated with the whole Lord family, Henri's own family is threatened by some London criminals. As has happened throughout much of his life it is sister Giselle who tries to help. Proud of his parents, who died tragically climbing top level mountaineering routes in Europe, Henri does find some personal satisfaction and peace of mind when he climbs. And it is his strong mountaineering capability that Henri uses to overcome some personal trauma and lets him try and resolve his other personal dilemmas as the millennium ends.

How did it all start?

Just as you would expect, the Oasis Club was dark, smoky, and noisy. On the stage two young girls draped themselves around smooth steel poles in a sensuous and rhythmic way that decorated the music gently reverberating around the room. Small tables supported glasses, ash-trays, and the elbows of the patrons of this West End relaxation spot. Soho has been an area of entertainment, excitement and several forms of relaxation for a long time in the twentieth century, and before that it had been a warren of mean streets given to similar but less classy night life for a lot longer. Sitting at one of the tables the threesome all had different agendas for their appearance here tonight. Buzz Haas was a photographer by profession and a pain in the arse by personality, but then to be good as a member of the paparazzi you had to be. Went with the territory Buzz said. In your face confrontations is how I earn my daily crust he would say, unless you have some more interesting parts you want me to photograph. Leslie Dauphin wrote, usually critical, scathing, scandalous and demeaning prose for whatever paper he/she could entice to print the stories. The uncertainty about the gender was a favourite ploy of Leslie. Biologically, well according to the equipment, Leslie was male, but Leslie believed in playing the odds and would dress, act, put out in whatever sex made sense for the occasion. The third member of the group was there under duress, and becoming more and more confused as the evening wore on. According to the other two bodies in the trio, Henri Lord was the bait, the trial balloon, the entry into the world that Leslie wanted to describe in words and Buzz wanted to snap. Unfortunately, Henri wasn't quite sure exactly what his role should be or even could be.

At age thirty eight, married, and with a good job as an investment consultant in the city of London, Henri was a very confused and worried man. Any amateur psychologist would not have been surprised that Henri was confused but would have been at a loss to understand what to do about it, and so was Henri. Well just think about it. Henri had been born in France in the early sixties, a year after his brother Marcel, and a year before his sister Giselle. His father Charles and mother Helene had both been brilliant mountaineers. They had climbed extensively in the European Alps, especially in France, Helene's homeland. For six years Henri's parents had climbed and scraped by with a living partly supported financially by the parents from both families until Helene's parents were killed in a road accident. The following year Charles and Helene themselves died while climbing a new route in the mountains. Suddenly, the travelling lifestyle of the three young children stopped – dead so to speak. The French world collapsed around them into a hiatus of various squabbling authorities before the land, the language and the people around them changed too; confusing, unsettling and very definitely different. Henri was five at the time and looking back he had told himself many times now that he couldn't really remember his mother or his father. What a revelation he had thought, not to be able to remember your own parents, and they had obviously been marvellous. Both of them bold, daring, non-conforming individuals who had cast aside the normal trappings and constraints of conventional life to be themselves. And I can't even remember them Henri thought to himself. I can't even remember my own parents.

After several weeks battling Gallic bureaucracy, patiently arguing with cold calculated scientific logic, and finally spending a considerable sum of money on lawyers and slow-moving French advocates, Stephanie Lord moved heaven and earth and ultimately the three children of her dead brother Charles to England. Stephanie's eldest brother Anthony and his wife Sylvia had helped, although at the time they too were struggling to establish their software development company called Brainware, and run a complex farm and forestry estate at Fotheringham Manor in Somerset. Fotheringham was the ancestral home of the Lord family.

Henri let his mind wander back. Marcel, his elder brother was already strong, out-spoken and determined to succeed. Characteristics that he has maintained and even strengthened over his lifetime thought Henri. Brother Marcel now skippered yachts in International races worldwide and competition and winning were everything. Younger sister Giselle had been four when Aunt Stephanie managed to bring all three of us together to England, and she had been quiet, thoughtful and intelligent. Now look at her thought Henri. Multi-lingual, well established with a senior position in some Government office and always looking so elegant and refined. And me, well look at me muttered Henri to himself as he let his gaze sweep around the smoky Club room. The Oasis was a night club where the performers were female and Henri still wasn't sure whether this was the right scene for him. Should I be at the gay club down the street, or the transvestite club a block over? He turned his gaze to Leslie who was looking around at the various patrons and trying to conjure up a set of words to capture the scene in a provocative paragraph. I do love him so thought Henri. He is so good. Where, when did I change, or did I ever change?

Moving to England just as he started school had been a challenging change for Henri. Although his aunt dressed him like a normal English kid he struggled for that first year with the language. Marcel had helped as Marcel's attitude and fists weren't going to let anyone bully his young brother. Like all kids Henri quickly picked up the language, and with that he found a couple of friends. Soon, on his new bicycle, and with these schoolboy friends, they were off from the outskirts of Bath, which was where Aunt Stephanie and his siblings lived, to the cliffs and gorges around Cheddar. They walked, hiked, scrambled, and soon these adventures progressed into actual early rock climbing until that fateful day when David pulled too hard on a loose piece of limestone, fell thirty feet and broke his neck on the scree slopes. Henri was eleven that day. He peered blankly over the dance floor to the stage where Sheena was slowly and sensuously sliding around poles, pirouetting on toes, shedding veils and caressing the rippling parts of her body. As she sank to the floor and the movements became slower and slower, more and more sensuous, and finally and ultimately still, the lights blanked into a black void and Henri thought about David. Still, dead still, broken, but smiling with the loose rock clutched in his hand and his mouth open for the one final gasp. His friend. His first friend. His first male friend. His first male friend with the growing hard penis, the mock battles and the pissing competitions. Who could get it further, higher, and that first kiss?

The rescue team had been quiet, efficient and smoothly wrapped David's still white body on the stretcher as they carefully carried it down the screes to the waiting ambulance. Henri could remember that all the members of the team had been male and it was a young lad, only a teenager really, who had shepherded Henri and Alan slowly down to the road and their bicycles. When the ambulance drove off to the city the leader of the team came back to the waiting teenager with Henri and Alan. They all sat down and the leader offered them something to drink Henri remembered. Shock, that was it, something to help with the shock. Were they cold? Did they want a sweet? Sugar you know – that helps too. Can you answer a few questions for me or do you want to go home first and be with mum and dad? Be with mum and dad, now that would be a challenge. Henri remembered he was all set to explain that his mum and dad were killed climbing too, and how proud he was of them when the emotions overcame everything and the death of his friend was much more real than the death of his parents and he just froze. He couldn't speak. His mind reverted to French but no words came out and the rescue team leader turned to Alan and asked him what had happened. The teenager collected the bicycles and the rescue team leader managed to fit them into his car when he drove Alan and Henri back home to Bath. Henri was silent. Later that night, held lovingly in Aunt Stephanie's arms and rocking gently in that wonderful old wooden chair she had, Henri managed to speak.

'He was my friend Tatti,' he said, 'my special friend.'

'A dear friend,' Stephanie said, 'a close friend. You will always remember him.'

'But will I Tatti?' Henri asked. 'I can't really remember mama and poppa. I can't see their faces anymore. I can't hear their voices. Will I forget David too?'

'Fix things in your mind Henri. Fix events with people and remember the good things, the happy things about people. Remember your birthday in June when you turned five. You were in Chamonix and you told me that was the first time your mother took you seriously climbing at Gaillards. You told me you were so excited after that day – better than learning to swim you said. I can remember when you first told me that story of how your mother greeted you on top of the cliff. How you kiss the leader for taking you up such a successful climb and then your mother taught you

5

to rappel. You can remember that day Henri, and your mother's face, and her voice?'

'Yes Tatti, I suppose, and that was a good day. I did well. Perhaps I should go back. The climb I was doing with David wasn't that hard. He only fell because the handhold broke. I should go back and do it again. Do it properly. I should do it for David, for my friend. Maybe I would remember mama and poppa better if I climb.'

And his aunt had kept quiet Henri remembered. She didn't say yes and she didn't say no but she did send me down to Dartmouth for the summer, away from the gorge and the climbs.

On his father's side of the family, the Lord family side, there had been grandfather, one great uncle and two great aunts. His Uncle Anthony's father, Henri's grandfather, had been Desmond Lord, a fighter pilot in the Second World War. He too had been a climber in his youth, including some time in the Dolomites like his own parents. Grandfather Desmond had died peacefully though, soon after Henri moved to England and Henri couldn't remember him at all. Desmond's next sister had committed suicide according to family history but the younger sister was Great Aunt Veronica and she had married a naval officer. G.A. Veronica was nearly sixty but she moved with military precision, dressed in well-pressed whites, down the straight garden path that led from her cottage back door to the riverside in Dartmouth.

'Walk upright,' she commanded Marcel and Henri. 'Lift the feet. Don't slouch. A little more spring in the step if you please. It is a bright breezy day and you both need to practice. Marcel, you untie the stern and you young Henri look after the bow warp. Wait until I am amidships and the ship is balanced. Right, cast off forward. Cast off aft. Move quickly now Marcel and ship that rudder. I'll handle the centre-board. Coil that painter up neatly Henri and get ready with the halliards. Commands please Mr. Coxswain or is this a silent ship?'

'We've slipped the mooring Auntie. Up mainsail Henri. I've got the sheets. Straight downriver. Keep the weight amidships please. Centreboard down?'

'Yes coxswain. Centreboard down. Fenders inboard.'

'Clear ahead in the bow?' asked Marcel.

'Aye aye sir,' replied Henri and the lessons began. And what lessons remembered Henri. Veronica's husband had been one of the instructors at the Dartmouth Navel College just down the river, and when he and Veronica retired they had bought "Riverside" cottage complete with a mooring, a dinghy and a love of sailing. Veronica had entertained several young naval trainees from the College over the years and she had sailed and taught many of them the do's and don'ts of sailing. Now she was teaching her great nephews and she taught by the book. On board ship you did things right. You spoke clearly. You repeated commands to ensure understanding, and you did things as instructed. This wasn't a place for debate, and if you were in charge you had to give the commands. Stand up and speak clearly and promptly, although don't stand up in a dinghy!

Day after day, rain or shine, calm or windy, out they would go. Practice, practice and more practice. Coming alongside, picking up moorings, working off a lee shore, dropping and retrieving rudders, and even capsizing and self-rescue on those warmer calmer days. After the first month Marcel thought he knew it all and so auntie had them out at night-time. Navigation lights, masthead lights, recognizing who was who and who had the right of way when and where? What did the buoys all mean, and are their lights flashing or occulting? Let's get the charts out and practice with the compass, take bearings, triangulation, parallel rulers, dead reckoning, tide tables. Later on, out at night again, and what do the stars tell us? The summer holidays flew by and Henri gradually forgot part of the loss of David. The pain gradually dulled as the hands and the head toughened. And auntie was full of stories. She had been in the WRNS in the war and working out of London. She told tales of battles, of single escapades, of lengthy undetected sailings and races to find the enemy. Marcel was enraptured Henri remembered. Mountaineering parents were forgotten – in fact Marcel once told Henri that he wanted to be as different from his parents as he could be, little realising that he still retained that strong Gallic competitive temperament of his mother and father. And, in keeping with his parent's unconformity, Marcel was going to be a sailor, but not a serving officer in any navy. Marcel was going to be a skipper as fast as he could and that meant racing.

Henri and Marcel came back from that summer holiday in Riverside cottage and their lives seemed to part almost straight away. First of all Henri now went to High School and Stephanie decided to send the two boys to different schools. Henri never did know why. After the death of David, Henri's old friend Alan drifted away and stopped hiking and climbing, but Henri found a new friend at school. His High School was all boys and this in itself was a little different from his Elementary School.

Somehow, despite the accident, or maybe because of the accident and maybe because Henri was still trying to remember his parents, he went back to Cheddar Gorge. With one or two friends from High School Henri went back to explore. Cautiously, rather uncertainly at first, but as he slowly felt the warm rock under his hands and the memory of his mother on that eventful first climb returned, Henri gradually persuaded his new friends to scramble and seek the steeper faces.

'Hey, do you lads know what you're doing? You should be roped.'

Henri carefully mantleshelfed up onto the ledge beside two teenagers.

'This is neat,' he said.

'And bloody dangerous the way you're doing it. Your two friends certainly aren't going to make it. The way you're going you'll get them killed.'

The silence hung in the air. Henri looked back down the face and saw David falling. He shuddered. 'I didn't think,' he whispered. 'I supposed if I could do it we all could.'

'Well mate, you may know what you're doing but your two friends aren't quite so gifted. You climbed before? If you have you should know better and use a rope, at least to protect your mates.'

'But I don't have a rope,' said Henri. 'Yes, I've climbed before, but many years ago now. When I was little,' he added.

'You two going to talk all day or is one of you going to climb?' shouted a voice above them.

'Look mate, why don't you go down and help your pals before you get them killed? Why don't we all meet up at the bottom and we can talk about this? Our leader up above us wants us to follow but he'll help get you organised.'

An hour later, after Henri had carefully but elegantly down-climbed to his two friends and safely led them down to the road, they all met up.

'Hi, I'm Ralph. Ben and Rob here say you can climb but you haven't got a rope. You lads interested in climbing 'cos we belong to the Rockhoppers. We all climb and not just here you know. Would be a lot safer for all of us if you learnt to do it properly. You know, not just have a rope but know how to use it and the rest of the gear. Why don't you come to our next Meet? We could teach you the basics - all about using the rope, the protection, and having a helmet too. Climbing here with all the loose rock a helmet's a must son. By the way, what's your name?'

'I'm Henri, Henri Lord, and these are my two friends, Roger and Darnley.'

'And the accent Henri? You're not from around here.'

'I live in Bath but I was born in France.'

'And you've climbed before Ben tells me. He certainly thinks you can climb. He was worried about your two friends though. Roger, Darnley, you two interested in learning how to do this are you? It's exciting you know, but then again we can keep it safe if we learn to do it properly.'

'Let's all join,' said Darnley to Henri. 'I'd like to learn to do it properly with you Henri.'

And so the following weekend, and for several weekends after that, Henri and Darnley joined up with the Rockhoppers. After a couple of weeks Roger dropped out as he preferred football and wanted to make the school team. Henri told his Aunt Stephanie what had happened that first day and she contacted the Rockhoppers just to make sure everything was kosher. She wasn't surprised, and although it wasn't something she would have recommended she decided she would support the idea and not try to suppress it. Talking it over with her brother they both agreed that it was in keeping with the Lord family traditions of riding, sailing, climbing, skiing – 'and blood will out,' Anthony had said.

'The boy wants to remember his parents Anthony,' Stephanie said. 'Marcel is quite independent, dedicated to sailing and tells me he wants to be different from his parents but Henri is still trying to remember who he is and where he fits in. It's quite clear Anthony that Marcel knows where he wants to go but Henri is still uncertain.'

'And Giselle?' asked Anthony. 'How is little Giselle?'

'She is a treasure,' said Stephanie. 'You know Anthony, I expected the two boys to be a handful, and so they are, but Giselle is so helpful and supportive, not only to me but to her brothers. Although the two boys are quite different Giselle loves them both in their separate selves.

She is a delight brother, although I don't know where her future lies. Did you know she found a friend at school who is French, and then another one with an Italian mother? Although she is only ten she already speaks fluently in English and French, and now she has learnt to converse in Italian. She tells me she is European. Not English, not French she says but European – a new lady for tomorrow. Quite grown up she is Anthony in some ways but still a delightful little girl in others.'

'You certainly took a lot on your shoulders Stephanie when you adopted all three of Charles's children.'

'Anthony, think about it. You and Sylvia were just starting Brainware, managing the Estate, and coping with dad and mum. After dad died look what has happened to our mother. She's gone gaga Anthony. Sad to say I know, but whatever she did in her youth has come back to haunt her and all of that is too much. I felt that if you and Sylvia could cope with all those burdens the least I could do was look after the little ones. They're family Anthony, Lord family, and we look after each other. They had nowhere else to go and I felt strongly about keeping the three of them together.'

'Well I'm not sure they will stay together,' said Anthony. 'As you say, Marcel is off into his own world. Listening to him the other week when we were all sailing down at Riverside he says he'll be off as soon as he can.'

'True Anthony and I think that might be for the best. Marcel is strong.' Stephanie laughed. 'It's a Lord family thing you know,' she said. 'Just look back on the family.'

'What do you mean?' asked Anthony.

'Well go back to the turn of the century and grandfather. He married that whirlwind grandmother of ours, precious Virginia, and between them they produced dad, a perfectly normal Lord specimen.'

'Crazy pilot,' said Anthony.

'Yes brother dear but still strong, certain about life, marries passionately and looks after the Lord family traditions. However, next we have the late Aunt Harriet and she brother dear is what I'm talking about: second child in any Lord generation. Unhappy, uncertain, restless and either lacking in direction or excessively self-centred. Aunt Harriet partied herself to death Anthony, despite all the family effort, love and affection.'

'I'm not sure any of us got much love and affection from grandmother,' said Anthony.

'No, well,' said Stephanie, 'Grandmother Virginia came from the era when they thought if you spared the rod you spoiled the child. Beat first question afterwards. Don't speak unless you are spoken to etc. It was a different world Anthony, but, look what happened with us. You were the first and just like dad you knew where you were going and you did it. You listened to advice, both from dad and Uncle Matthew, and straight like an arrow you did it.'

'Yes, well,' said Anthony. 'Just as well I found Sylvia in my path 'cos she's an enormous help.'

Stephanie laughed and playfully punched her brother on his shoulder. 'Anthony you are a walking, talking success story, and yes, Sylvia is a fantastic part of your team. And like dad, who built a team in the war and then built a team at Fotheringham, you have built up Brainware. But, running in your shadow and trying to find where he could fit in was Charles. You did everything well Anthony and you were first. This crazy family still has a strong belief in the first gets everything and that is a burden for the rest of us. You may not realize it but the second, third and whatever other Lord family children always have this handicap right from the day they are born. Just watch with your own children Anthony.'

'But Charles?' asked Anthony.

'Do you remember those three years when we were teenagers and we went to Europe? Dad was insistent that we learn to climb properly, mountain he said not just little cliffs. Because of his gammy leg and arm he sent grandmother as a chaperone for me but we all went climbing.'

'So?'

'Charles had to be better than you. Charles had to beat you at something. I can remember finding him one night talking to himself. He was so moody you remember; so given to tantrums, but really he wanted to find himself. You seemed so confident and he was struggling to find his path.'

'I never saw this,' said Anthony.

'No brother, even though you belong in a team Anthony you never saw the struggles your brother had.'

'And so you are saying that Henri is following the same wobbly path as his father?'

'Second child in the Lord family Anthony. It appears to be a ..... I was going to say curse but that is not the right word, the right thought. It appears to come with a severe handicap. Marcel is like you.'

'Geoffrey is not that clear-thinking,' mused Anthony. 'He's a little hesitant. Actually he's a little too serious for someone that age.'

'Anthony, he's seven. Give the boy a chance. Anyway, it's Michael you need to watch. Another Lord second child, and another boy too.'

'His young sister will keep him in check and look after him,' joked Anthony.

'Maybe Anthony,' said Stephanie. 'Maybe as a sister I didn't do such a good job on Charles, and Giselle's trying hard with Henri. Keep an eye on them both can you Anthony? I know you're busy but if you get the chance talk with both boys. Perhaps Henri will get some older male guidance from this Rockhopper's group. Certainly climbing can bring out some clear thinking.'

'As long as it doesn't burn you up like Charles,' added Anthony.

'A little of what you fancy does you good,' laughed Stephanie.

'So a climbing rope for his birthday or perhaps this Christmas would not be unwelcome?' asked Anthony.

'Good idea Anthony. Take him down to Cornwall and share the first climb on his rope.'

'Sylvia's probably better for that down there,' said Anthony.

'She's just had a baby Anthony.'

'That doesn't slow Sylvia down,' said Anthony. 'Knowing her she's just as likely to sling poor little Samantha on her back while she climbs.'

'Not a good example Anthony. You take Henri. You always did climb safely. Charles may have eventually climbed harder and more difficult climbs but you brother were the best leader. Henri needs a team leader right now. I know he may ultimately follow in the steps of his parents but right now he needs some bonding, preferably male bonding.'

Henri never knew of the concerned conversation between his aunt and uncle but he did learn about male bonding that next spring. With his new climbing rope from Anthony and Sylvia, and some slings with karabiners from his aunt, Henri was well on the way to becoming a rock climber. His leader, mentor and bringer of male bonding turned out to be Ralph. With Darnley, Henri attended the Rockhopper sessions regularly through the winter of 1972 and into the awakening spring of 1973. At school Darnley could keep up with his friend, both in intellect and in shared adventures together, but out on the cliffs Henri had inherited the gifts of his parents and rapidly outclimbed his young admirer. It was Ralph who guided and led young Henri up the progressively more difficult climbs and within that first year Henri could safely climb up to the VS (Very Severe) grade. Funnily enough, Henri remembered, it was both Darnley and Ralph in their own ways that furthered my education sexually. Once again Henri scanned the smoky room and reflectively sipped on his well-watered drink. Where was Buzz Henri suddenly thought?

'Leslie, where's Buzz? He hasn't gone roaming with his camera I hope. He'll get us thrown out you know. The bouncer at the door was quite clear about cameras.'

Leslie leaned over the table and held Henri's chin in his hand. He turned Henri's head to face him and brought his face closer until their lips almost touched. 'Be calm mon enfant. Buzz is fine. We'll wait for Lola and she can educate us.'

Educate us thought Henri. Yes, that is what Darnley and Ralph both did in their own way that mind-blowing spring. And what an education, wasn't it?

Spring term meant cross-country running for first and second year pupils at High School and that involved slogging through cold rain-soaked mud, occasional pats of cow shit, slippery leaf mould and misty woodlands. Twelve and thirteen year-olds clad in white singlets, white shorts, originally white plimpsoles and ever-to-be washed white socks splished and splashed three to five miles to improve their characters. According to each individual's state of mind or body they walked, jogged, truly ran or just dodged into the woods for a fag. Darnley might not be able to keep up with Henri on the cliffs but he could run. Slender, lithe, long-limbed with an easy gliding stride Darnley could cover the ground at speed. Henri carried more weight but he did have strong legs. The pair usually led the pack of white clad, white-skinned, panting youth and finished first and second. Once they came in arm in arm as a joke joint first until the ex-Army Sports Master told them this was a race and not a girl's dance. First in the showers got most of the hot water and turning to flick at Darnley with his towel Henri slipped on the wet floor. Stunned for a moment Henri lay there until he felt Darnley pull him up and the pair clinched. Darnley's arms tightened around Henri and suddenly wet lips brushed across his and then came back more strongly as hands caressed him. Henri felt himself respond. His lips pressed back on Darnley and they both held each other and felt each other respond. Loud banging on the doors as others flooded in caused the two boys to separate quickly and both found soap and vigorous self body lathering to mask any previous activity. Nothing was said.

Every Tuesday and Thursday afternoon the whole school had sports. The elder boys, form four and above played field hockey in the spring term. The only older boys who ran were those on the school cross-country team and they ran a different and longer course than the juniors. That Thursday Henri was uncertain. Nothing had been said since that previous intimate Tuesday afternoon in the showers. He and Darnley had shared lessons, along with the rest of the Remove classes. They had shared looks but had never been alone and never touched. Did I imagine it thought Henri? No, it was a shock at first but then I responded. I must have wanted it to happen. I know Darnley likes me. He's often said he is my best friend but I suppose I never thought about it that way. Not since David Henri thought. Now what do I do?

They ran that Thursday. They ran in the rain. Mist lay in the woodland valley and the track was churned up from cattle hooves. Darnley ran hard ahead of Henri. He glanced back over his shoulder but kept running hard. Henri's mind turned over. Do I want him to beat me? Do I want him to like me? Should I let him win or does he want a strong partner? Will he like me if I try to beat him? Why didn't he say something? Why hasn't he said anything since?

Henri gritted his teeth. 'Smoothly Henri cherie,' came the words of his mother. 'No struggle but float up the cliff. Elegante.' Sure mother but this is not quite a smooth rock climb you know. This is cow shit and it sucks at my shoes. It's tough being elegant in this crap. 'With style Henri, but move quickly my love. You must learn to move smoothly and quickly in the mountains.' Henri picked up the pace and slowly narrowed the gap to his friend. The final four hundred yards were over an open field where the going was firmer and moderately uphill. He was close to Darnley now and could hear the strong breathing. Legs said Henri to himself, strong legs, just like climbing. Churn now and power with the arms and surge, not float mother but surge. Henri stepped up the pace and was close to Darnley's shoulder. His friend didn't need to glance backwards as he could hear Henri's feet now and he too racked up the pace. The two boys sped up the hillside almost side by side into the funnelled finish of the course. By a short head Darnley maintained the lead through the finish line and sank down onto the grass gasping.

'Brilliant Cheevers, absolutely bloody brilliant. That's a record son, a new school record and it was only a regular Thursday run. You're a junior too.' Tommy Handley's voice rang out across the field as if he was still on the barrack ground. He stood over Darnley and clapped him hard on the back. 'Well done son. We'll have you on the school team for sure.'

Henri sat on the grass with his chest heaving. Darnley turned and looked at him and smiled. It was not a superior smile, not an "I won" smile but a friendly smile of thanks. It was a shared smile – shared between friends.

'We both pushed each other sir,' said Darnley to the sports master. 'Helps one turn on the jets if you hear someone just behind you sir.'

'Maybe son, maybe, but you won. You were first over the line lad and that's what counts. Winning Cheevers. Winning for the school, just like winning for the battalion. Off now the pair of you and hit the showers. Marvellous, bloody marvellous.'

They hit the showers and Darnley looked at Henri.

'Thanks,' he said. 'You really helped there you know.' He held out his hand. The two boys stood there, naked, with the water streaming down all over them and shook hands rather symbolically. A moment later

Darnley swung his arm around Henri and pulled him into a more heartfelt embrace. With both hands clasped around Henri's neck he kissed him and then slid his hands down the wet streaming back. Henri felt a passion arise within him and without thinking kissed back and caressed the heat and hardness of his friend. So started his love of Darnley, his boyhood friend.

'Have you got your sleeping bag Henri? Do you have a torch? What about spare socks if it rains?'

'Auntie I'm fine. I've packed everything on the list and the weather forecast is dry and sunny. I'm not sure I can get everything in this old rucksack of Uncle Anthony's.'

'Climbing boots, helmet, rope?' went on Stephanie.

'Yes, yes, and yes again,' said Henri with exasperation. 'We'll be home around seven on Sunday evening.'

'Now climb carefully Henri. You've told me they are a friendly Club and that Mr. Beckham telephoned and re-assured me he would make sure you were safe. He said he usually led you up the routes Henri and that you were good, very good he said.'

Yes thought Henri and now he has taught me to lead but we won't tell auntie that for the moment. Already Henri was leading Severes and Ralph Beckham was promising better things to come. This weekend will be special he had said. We'll do some great things.

The Club had driven down to Bosigran in Cornwall to climb on the sea cliffs there. Saturday had been a long day what with the drive, several climbs and the excitement of a new area. The exposure over the ocean was something different and Henri felt the climbs were more open than climbing in the Gorge. There was a lot of nothing behind the back he felt, but he had enjoyed the sensation. Ralph had led him up a Severe to start with so that Henri could get a feel for the rock and the type of climbing there. Steep, sharp, coarse-grained granite felt a little different from the limestone of the Gorge. Holds were different too with the smooth vertical cracks for jamming and little nubbins of crystals on the granite faces. For a second climb Ralph let Henri lead another Severe climb which had steep, almost over-hanging faces on the top pitch. Ralph made sure that Henri thought carefully about the protection he placed as this route had some traversing.

'You have to think about protecting yourself and your second Henri,' Ralph said. 'Think about the moves and the line for both of you. Think what might happen if you or your second falls off. Can you help each other? I know the leader shouldn't fall, and the positive thought is to get up, but it is always necessary to think about the team. We do this together Henri – the rope moves as a team my friend. Just like your parents you eventually learn that you literally hold each other's lives in your hands.'

Over the months Henri had explained where he came from and why he was born in France. Ralph had taken the time to research the career of Henri's parents and what a career it had been. Both Charles and Helene had been brilliant and bold climbers. They had done and even pioneered some hard routes in and around Chamonix, Helene's home town. Ralph had been impressed and he tried to educate Henri with stories of the careful planning of his parents as well as their sometimes excessively bold expeditions.

'Know when it is time to be bold and when it is time to retreat Henri. There is no shame in retreat in mountaineering my friend. There is a rather sad but true cliché that there are bold climbers and old climbers but there are no old bold climbers.'

'Mum and dad,' said Henri.

'Yes son. From all accounts they were brilliant but the mountains are cruel and very unforgiving. Our cliff climbing here is relatively safe. Bad weather and we don't climb but in the mountains you may not have the choice. It's a different game in the mountains Henri.'

Yes thought Henri, but that is where I have to go. We'll learn here. We'll get good here but it's the mountains where I have to find myself. The older members of the Club went down to the pub in the village that evening but Ralph stayed behind to cook up a simple meal and share it with his rope mate. Henri sat with Ralph after washing up the few dishes and they watched the sun slowly sink into the ocean. It was a warm evening and Henri lay on top of his sleeping bag and let his mind go back over the day's events. Sleep came easily that evening after a tiring but exciting day. Henri dreamt of mountains, of big climbs, of broad faces and being out suspended over awesome space. Teamwork, bonding together as a rope team, looking after each other. Just like Darnley and me he thought. In the racing we look after each other. And we bond, and Henri reflected on his times with Darnley after the races, in the showers and he felt his body respond to his emotions. Henri was half asleep as Ralph's hand slowly and gently slid across his stomach and lower over his pants. Henri stirred a little in his dreams and Ralph slipped his fingers under the waistband and gently massaged the quivering flesh. Henri awoke to feel Ralph's body pressed up against his back and his fingers stimulating his penis. What now? Good? Bad? Yes? No? Bonding? As he half rolled over onto his side he felt his underpants pulled down and Ralph's body pressed nakedly hard up against his. Hands moved more rapidly, legs moved and there was a new sensation. Hot, slippery, pulling, pushing, exciting. Male bonding. The sensations continued and Henri felt himself respond. His climax was sudden, new and unknown, and he felt the wetness and the release. Ralph's motions slowed and he too found release.

'Rope mates Henri,' whispered Ralph in his ear as he ran his hand over Henri's hip and up to his shoulder. He gripped the shoulder and

Henri felt the firm pressure of Ralph's strong climber's hands. 'We climb well together young Henri,' said Ralph. 'We make a good team. We can do great things together.'

Back in his bed at home that night Henri lay on his back and looked up at the ceiling. He had to see Darnley. He had to see Darnley and tell him, show him. The feeling was good. A feeling to share and Darnley was his friend. He knew Darnley would want to share.

So remembered Henri, that was what growing up as a teenager was all about. We ran, we climbed, and we learnt about love and for a while it was good. The spats and struggles with Marcel diminished as both brothers went their separate ways. Aunt Stephanie faded backwards as the ever-supportive but non-guiding safety net. At home, in the nest, the fledgling learnt to fly unsupported. But then there was always Giselle Henri recalled. Never in your face, never demanding but there on those days when he and Darnley had quarrelled, when a weekends rock climbing had gone poorly, when life seemed pointless, then, there was always Giselle to listen.

As Henri ticked off the years at school the boys around him started to notice girls and Henri could remember the conversations, the jokes, the dares and the confessions. He joined in. He shared the jokes, and like the rest of his class he attended dancing lessons, but all the time he felt confused over his own emotions. It was his Uncle Anthony who first noticed Henri's personal preferences. As he had promised his sister, Anthony invited Henri to Fotheringham and then down with the family on a climbing trip to Cornwall on the cliffs at Lands End. At Fotheringham Henri showed no great interest in the forest and its management, nor in the work his aunt did at Home Farm. The work at Brainware didn't interest Henri either, although when his Aunt Sylvia started talking about economics and the finances behind the company

Henri did start asking questions. Money interested him. Where did it come from and how could you make it grow?

'Auntie, I can see on the Estate, in the forest that you have seeds, seedlings in the nursery and then plantations and they grow into forests. Fine, I can see all that with trees but you said you did all that at University with money too. Now that does fascinate me. That's almost like a rock climb where you look to find the start and then slowly work your way up overcoming the obstacles to bring it all together at the top. The experience grows as you climb but better is that you walk away with money in your pocket.' Henri laughed as his looked at his aunt. 'And I'm always empty in my pockets at school. If I want the nice things in life like you I had better make sure I am not empty of pocket when I go to work. I think I'll study what you did; all about finance.'

Anthony took the joint families down to Cornwall for the last week of the school holidays. They were all supposed to stay in a cottage near Lands End but Marcel begged off on the way down and Anthony detoured to drop Marcel off in Dartmouth and his beloved river with its sailing boats. Veronica said she understood and Marcel would be fine. Another detour to St. Austell dropped off Daniel, who was only three, but little Samantha wasn't going to be fobbed off on her grandparents and she was going to come hiking! The convoy of the two cars continued down to the cottage near Lands End. On most days Stephanie took Giselle and Samantha hiking along the coastal path. These three made an interesting procession as it was fair-haired Samantha who charged up front carefully pursued by watchful and caring Giselle and Stephanie struggling to keep up with the two youngsters. After a couple of days Stephanie begged her brother to take over as the two little girls were running her legs off.

Henri was in his element. Now fourteen and lengthening in all directions he found he could climb certain routes just the way he remembered the words of his mother. Float up the climb cherie. Smooth elegance. A style that is so typically French. By this time in his growing up Henri had also become aware of his dress and his appearance and this too reflected his Gallic heritage. Look anywhere on the continent and the French climbers both before and after a hard route look the picture of elegance, as if they have just emerged from the shop sporting new threads and Henri portrayed this image.

'Auntie I can lead this you know.'

Now Sylvia Lord was no slouch as a rock climber. In fact she was somewhat better than her husband, although she only told him that when they were alone. She was climbing with Henri that day while Anthony slowly and carefully led Geoffrey and Michael up some beginner routes. Although not as forceful and bold as his wife Anthony was by far the better teacher for Geoffrey and his precocious younger brother. Sylvia switched her attention from Anthony with the two boys to her rope mate.

'Right Henri son, you lead. Remember the grade do you?'

'Sure auntie. I've done this before with Ralph, Mr. Beckham.'

'Who led?'

'He did auntie but I sailed up it. Really I did.'

'Okay Henri but climb safely now. Remember everything you've learnt.'

Sylvia watched critically as Henri carefully uncoiled the rope and just as carefully ran his hands back along the length of it to ensure there were no knots and the rope ran smoothly. He adjusted his harness and almost automatically roped himself in. Ensuring they were all neatly in order and to hand Henri arranged his sling of karabiners, nuts, and quick-draws. Sylvia quietly fixed her anchor, tied herself in and held the leading rope in a protective way through her belay plate. She quickly scanned up the route and then brought her eyes back to Henri.

'On belay. Climb when ready.'

'Climbing.'

And Henri did sail up it. Neatly, smoothly, using his feet and balancing with his hands at waist level Henri was a natural climber. Just like his parents Sylvia mused. She carefully paid out the rope as Henri floated up the cliff.

'Runner on. Climbing.'

'Good stuff Henri. Looking good.'

At the end of August, at the end of England, the sun shone. Blue was the sky, although peopled with white fluffy cumulus, and blue was the surging sea, although flecked with white foam. Gulls wheeled and screamed and both climbers enjoyed that feeling of living with the activity of humans versus gravity.

'Off belay. Climb when ready.' The rope snaked rapidly upwards as Henri took in the slack and Sylvia set about untying from the anchor. The rope tightened on her harness.

'That's me.'

'On belay. Climb.'

'Climbing.'

Simple words but when the wind is howling, the sea is crashing and you can't see your partner even the simple words are too many. Then it is the rope that carries the signals. As a leader you hope that your second can feel there is enough slack for that sudden upwards move, but not too much slack if you peel off. As a second you hope that your leader doesn't try and pull you up the cliff like a sack of potatoes, or leave so much slack you fall over the spare loops around your feet. Subtle. Sensitive. A lot of feeling and empathy needs to go into that rope that bonds you together.

Sylvia too floated up the climb and revelled in the sensation. She loved to climb and even after all the work on the Estate, after all of the challenges in the Company, and having to mother four children she still felt so alive tiptoeing up the small holds so delicately in balance. She paused and looked across to watch Anthony safely belayed quietly and supportively talking to young Geoffrey. Sturdy Sylvia thought, that's how Geoffrey climbs. There is no floating but slow, methodical reasoning, like it's a mathematical exercise rather than a ballet. Son Geoffrey overcomes the climb rather than joins it for a dance. And then there's Michael Sylvia noticed. Down at the foot of the climb Michael wasn't paying any attention to the climb, to his brother, or to the rope, and when it's his turn Sylvia surmised he will force it, will try and beat it into submission by brute strength and sheer bloody-mindedness.

'You climbing?'

'Yes climbing,' called Sylvia, and she brought herself back from her two boys and their approach to life to quickly savour the next twenty feet to her patient leader. On the belay ledge Henri made sure Sylvia was safely tied in before he took her off belay.

'Neat eh?' asked Henri.

'It's a challenging steady Severe Henri. Nothing too desperate with good clean rock and plenty of exposure. You still okay for the next pitch or do you want me to lead through?'

'No, I'm fine,' said Henri quickly. 'You do climb well auntie. You look so neat.'

'Well us girls Henri don't come with big muscles but we do come with big brains and we think our way up. I'll bet your mother told you that. She taught you to climb didn't she? When you were still in France?'

Henri looked pensive and Sylvia wondered whether there were still wounds there, still childhood nightmares of lost parents and no world, but then she remembered Stephanie telling her about Henri being proud of his parents, and wanting to emulate them, unlike Marcel.

'Mama taught me to float auntie, to float up the climb. You float up the climb but I find it hard. I try and keep my arms low and use my feet. I know my legs are stronger than my arms. I run you know. I run cross-country and I'm on the junior school team. I run with my friend Darnley.'

'Which is good Henri and you're right. Your legs are much stronger than your arms and the muscles there will sustain you better than any arm-pulling. Your mother taught you well.'

'She also taught me to move quickly. She said you must learn to climb quickly and keep moving. In the mountains she said you must climb fast. There were so many things to learn in the mountains auntie but she never had the time.'

'No Henri, she never did. But, there was one final lesson she did teach you and that is a very important lesson. Do you know what I am talking about?'

'Death auntie. No matter how good, no matter how careful, no matter how well-prepared the mountains can kill you. She told me rock-climbing is fun but mountaineering is a potential dance with death.'

'So let's have some fun Henri and you lead me up this pitch you young scallywag. It's a lovely day, the rock is a delight and you my trusty leader are doing just fine.'

The following day, when Anthony took over the chasing of little Miss Samantha and the attentive Giselle, Sylvia decided to take a firmer hand with Michael.

'He needs to pay attention to his climbing partner Anthony. In fact he just needs to pay attention. He wants to climb. He claims he can climb better than his brother but he needs to learn about safety: a word that is not in Michael's lexicon. I'll ask Henri to lead Geoffrey up something. Henri is good and he likes to lead. He is a safe climber Anthony and

Geoffrey is solid enough to get up some of the V. Diffs here. You go and corral little "Miss I'm first" for the day and give your sister a rest.'

Anthony looked at his wife and folded her into his arms. 'Yes dear,' he said. 'You've got everything under control and well thought out as usual. The team is organised and I'll just go and talk with the players and enthuse them about the importance of their respective roles. Henri can lead. Geoffrey can learn. Samantha can lead her band of followers and Michael can receive safety guidance. Stephanie can sit on the sidelines and rest a while.'

'And Giselle?'

'Giselle is a delight,' said Anthony. 'She is a wonderful role model for our little Miss number one but somehow I think Samantha wants to beat Michael and Geoffrey and not Giselle. She's already told me she wants to climb but I've told her one more year. Perhaps I can find a scramble for her today.'

Although he was only fourteen Sylvia felt quite confident that Henri could safely take Geoffrey out for the day. She would be climbing close by she re-assured Anthony and Stephanie. Everything would be under control and she did need to try and instil some sense of responsibility into Michael.

Henri found the experience of teaching a young person somewhat different. Before he had always climbed with older people and most of them had been as good as he was on the cliffs. Gradually, he realised that it was easier for his second if he climbed slower and explained what he was doing. He needed to be patient when his second struggled with some of the moves and Geoffrey was a plodder as Sylvia had said. Occasionally, when Geoffrey was taking extra long over some sequence of moves, Henri looked sideways to where his aunt was trying to teach safety to Cousin Michael. All arms noticed Henri as Michael pulled his way up climbs, and such sloppy footwork. His mother tries to show him edging and balance but Michael's not listening. Now look, gazing out sea and not paying the slightest attention to the rope or his leader. Dangerous. What did you say yesterday auntie about rock-climbing is fun but mountaineering could be deadly? The way Michael climbs even rock-climbing could be deadly.

The next day Sylvia told Anthony she was going to switch things round again.

'Just when I had the team organised love you want to change positions?'

'Anthony, this is not a game my love, and it is not the forest or business. This is people learning Anthony. Broadening the mind and letting young people experience as many different things as they can in their short young lives. When they get older they get set in their ways but at this age they need to broaden their horizons. Looking back I suppose you were a typical Lord and directed down the traditional path. I came from the fluid and dynamic business of china clay production Anthony, and we were always looking for new products, new outlets, even new processes.'

'So my love, my diminutive controller, what is the order for today?'

'I'm not so sure about diminutive Anthony. I know I'm small and petite and I like to stay that way, and yes, I suppose I've always been a bit of a controller. I might like dynamic horizons for young people Anthony dear but in the business you know me. Again, from my parents, the bottom line comes from control. Still, enough of that. We're on holiday and time to ring the changes.'

'Sylvia, can we get some direction sweetheart? Enough chit-chat, diminutive or otherwise, what are the orders for the day?'

'Stephanie wants to take Giselle shopping, probably in Penzance. I'll take Samantha, Michael, and Geoffrey on the coastal path to Sennen Cove, and Henri would appreciate someone to climb with to challenge him a little. Didn't your sister want you to have a "father-and-son" chat with Henri? And it's not about the birds and the bees Anthony as Stephanie has already explained all of that to the three of them. Being a vet helped there she said as she didn't have to talk about birds and bees but about real live rabbits and even her sheep on Home Farm. She said the kids all understood that really easily when it was almost a daily experience.'

Anthony walked with Henri along part of the coastal path as the cliff bent back southeastwards towards Pordenack Point and Nanjizal.

'There's a good route here Henri, just down below us. It's long too.'

'Did you bring two ropes uncle? That makes for fewer rappels.'

'No, just the one Henri, but you're right and we'll be careful eh?'

At the foot of the climb, some ten feet above the surging ocean, Henri and Anthony got themselves organised for the climb.

'Sylvia says you're good Henri. This is a VS but it's relatively straightforward and keeps its grade fairly well. Did you want me to lead it or did you want to lead through? I heard that you've climbed VS before but that was in Cheddar Gorge wasn't it?'

'Can we try and lead through uncle? You lead the first pitch and see how I do. I'd like to try you know. I led auntie all the way the day before yesterday. She said I floated up – just like my mama taught me.'

Anthony laughed and ruffled Henri's hair. 'My brother was so intense Henri. He was driven and always searching for his place in life but your mother was both brilliant and more settled. Yes, your mother would have been the better teacher and more in tune with the joys of climbing whereas Charles was unfocussed. Yes he could climb but I doubt whether he would have understood the touch or empathy needed for teaching.'

'Auntie says you are a good teacher uncle. She says you have more patience than she has.'

'Does she now? That's as maybe but we'd better see about this climb young man before the tide comes in and washes our feet. You find an anchor and I'll check the rope is clear.'

Sixty feet higher up Anthony safely tied into two permanent bolts cemented into the cliff. The area had been used by British commandos training in the Second World War and some of the climbs had been "trade routes" as part of their training. Anthony watched Henri quickly and efficiently climb the steep wall. Look, think, see it and do it muttered Anthony to himself and Henri does all that very well. He sees the route and the opportunities and climbs so naturally. Unlike Geoffrey Anthony realised, who tended to analyse every possible option before even trying one out, and even then the trying was always tentative. There was little flow and movement with Geoffrey. Yes, he would get up the climb where he was technically capable, but there was no natural smooth movement like with Henri. As his nephew joined him on the belay ledge Anthony still held him on belay.

'Well Henri. You handled that just fine. Why don't you take these slings and karabiners and see about pitch two? You've got some nuts with you and a couple of chocks. Put a runner on as soon as you can so I've got you protected with no free fall.'

'Sure uncle. Thanks. Am I still on belay?

'You sure are. Climb when you're ready.'

'Climbing.'

Within ten feet Henri found a good horizontal crack that would take two nuts cambered together. Any fall or pull on the slings holding the nuts would cause them to try and expand and sit tighter in the crack. Bombproof as climbers would say.

'Runner on. Climbing.'

Anthony watched as he held the rope carefully belayed in his hands. Paying close attention to his leader he gently eased the rope through the belay plate ensuring there was enough slack but always attentive for any possible fall and the need to protect his partner. Henri slotted another hex nut in a vertical tapering crack and further protected himself as he slowly but positively ascended. Anthony dutifully watched and paid out the rope. Another twenty feet of serious climbing brought Henri to a massive chockstone wedged in a chimney. Inside or outside thought Henri? He thought to call down to his second but decided to look a little closer first and see whether he could work it out for himself. Although everyone now climbed in rubber-soled boots, and there weren't any nail marks anymore, Henri could see where the granite was worn and scuffed. Lichen had been scrubbed clean off the rock. So if I bridge up between the walls of the chimney I can slot a nut up this side of the chockstone and then jam up in the other crack, but which way round? In most chimney climbs there is an easy way to face and a more difficult way, especially when trying to climb out of the top of the chimney. Trouble is Henri muttered to himself there are no written instructions. Probably are in the guidebook but I'll bet Uncle Anthony doesn't have one with him. So my little challenging friend which way do we do this?

All of this mind talk goes on in every climber's head and Henri did it automatically, quickly and critically. Within seconds of being bridged up high under the chockstone he had slotted a tapered wedge in the crack, clipped on, told his partner he was climbing and jammed his hands up high on the other side of the chockstone. Bringing his legs up high beneath him, and thanking God that he had grown longer legs as he straddled, Henri could work his hand jams up the crack and bring one leg out over the chockstone to wedge the toe above his precious nut runner. A quick pull on the hand jams and a swift upward lift of the second foot and he was safely on the top of the chockstone. Without any hesitative self-congratulations Henri looked up the rest of the chimney. Swiftly, using his back on one side and his feet on the other, he backed-up the chimney to easily pivot out of the top onto a broad ledge. Anchor, tie off, take in the slack, make sure the rope isn't tangled and is taut down to uncle below. Clip into the belay plate and 'On belay. Climb when ready.' Even leaning forwards against the tight rope to the anchor Henri couldn't see his second but he heard the shout, 'That's me. Climbing.'

Slowly, feeling the tautness in the rope, Henri took in the slack down to his uncle. Anthony moved positively up the wall taking off the runners and was soon under the chockstone. 'Just taking off your nut by the chockstone Henri,' called Anthony and Henri could see his uncle's hand and then his smiling face as his leaned out on the hand jam.

'Good lead young man. See you sorted out which way to go,' and Anthony pulled hard on his hands while straddling with his feet as he bridged his way round the boulder.

'Sylvia's right Henri. You do climb well and you do float up the cliff. Even when you had to use the arms you still use your feet really well. I should have had a camera down there. Great technique. Now, let's just have a couple of those slings and the two nuts and I'll finish off this little beauty.'

Sitting on the top in the sunshine Anthony shared an orange with Henri, followed by the inevitable Mars bar for each of them. 'So your brother's decided to run away to sea?' asked Anthony while smiling at Henri.

'It's his passion uncle. There's nothing else he says.'

'But I thought there was a girl in Dartmouth too?' asked Anthony. 'Didn't Great Aunt Veronica mention a girl? Marcel wanted her as crew. Was that because she was light or because she was a girl? My aunt thought she was a very pretty girl.'

Henri blushed and didn't know what to say. 'I suppose Marcel's always liked girls. Perhaps it's because he goes to a coed school and there's more opportunity.'

'So is she pretty this girl Henri?'

'I don't know uncle. Marcel won't talk about her. Wants her all to himself I think.'

'And what do you do for girl friends Henri? If there are no girls at school there must be some girls in the Rockhoppers. Good looking lad like you should have a girl friend you know. I can remember all the trouble we had at Bristol House because that was a boys-only school too. Geoffrey goes there and Michael started this year. It was always a problem finding girls though. We used to raid the neighbouring girl's school and when we were seniors we used to play them at hockey. We split the teams up with forwards and defence but we had to play to girls' rules. Does your cross-country team race against any girls Henri?'

'No uncle. Wouldn't be fair though would it? We're stronger than they are. We'd always win. Suppose we could give them a handicap.'

'I wouldn't talk like that with your Aunt Sylvia Henri, and my little Samantha would be spitting bullets at you with those comments. She believes she can be first in anything. Girls can be strong Henri and often have more stamina. If we come back to the mountains for a minute there are lots of stories about female climbers who have survived where the men didn't. Don't sell women short young man. Anyway, you still haven't told me about this girl friend you have in the Rockhoppers,' Anthony teased.

'I prefer boys uncle,' said Henri. 'Darnley is my friend, my real best friend I suppose. He's the best junior runner. I rarely beat him.'

'Didn't he climb with you and join Rockhoppers?'

'Yes, but he is not such a good climber. Now I climb regularly with Ralph, with Mr. Beckham. He's a really good climber and a good, what do you call them? Mentor, yes that's it, mentor. He's taught me a lot of things and not just about climbing. Given the choice uncle I think I prefer to be with men. I wouldn't know what to do with girls.'

Once again Henri paused in his reflections. 'Another drink Leslie? Is Lola supposed to come to us or do we have to go and find her? Actually, why am I doing this? Why am I looking to find Lola?'

'Henri my sweet, get me another drink, and one for Buzz too. Why don't you go and talk with Gloria and explain we're getting antsy. If Lola doesn't show we'll have to come back tomorrow evening. Here's Buzz. Buzz, Henri's about to get another round of drinks in. You have any luck?'

As Buzz came back to their table Henri picked his way carefully across the crowded and dimly lit Club room and walked to the rosily-lit bar to tap Gloria on the shoulder. The reaction surprised Henri and caused Gloria to giggle because she spun round so quickly and flung her arms around his neck, wriggled herself up the whole length of him and caused him to react before he knew what he was doing.

'What a gorgeous man you are Henri. So strong and suave: so handsome and so manly,' and Gloria slid her hands down Henri's chest to his waist and then lower. 'So strong,' she whispered in his ear as she pressed her breasts against his chest. 'And yet you're not sure whether you're manly or not are you Henri dear? Not sure whether you prefer me or Leslie. Are you in the right Club Henri?'

'Where's Lola?'

'Want two of us do you - Lola as well as me, or is it Lola as well as Leslie? Lola can swing every which way you know Henri but she really does prefer people with stamina. Have you got stamina Henri? Could you stand up to Lola? You've certainly got something that is standing up Henri.'

Gloria giggled and turned away. Henri blushed, reflecting the rose-coloured lights diffusely spreading good cheer around the bar. Who did he prefer? It was easy and straightforward when I was young. Then everything was easy and straightforward. What I learnt from Ralph

I shared with Darnley and Darnley was so good. The friendship had developed as their cross-country running prowess had improved and by sixteen both boys ran in the Senior School Team, ran competitively against other schools. In the Fifth Form Henri and Darnley both sat for their G.C.S.E. examinations and like everyone else in their class they waited the anxiety-ridden weeks for the results.

'I passed, I passed,' shouted Henri as he greeted Darnley at school. 'Everything, all of them, including History which I hate. What about you?'

'Me too Henri. Fabulous isn't it. We must celebrate. Look, come back to my house this evening and I'll find a bottle of something. My parents are away and there's only my sister looking after me. Phone your aunt and tell her you're staying over. Won't be a problem will it?'

No remembered Henri, that wasn't the problem, not the phone call. His Aunt Stephanie agreed that celebrating with his friends made sense and that she would expect him the next evening. She too had planned a celebration dinner for Henri and she said his sister was all excited for him as well. That wasn't the problem either remembered Henri. The first bottle they shared went down quickly and Darnley was so excited he decided they should try something stronger. Henri had drunk wine before, for some years now as Stephanie thought a little red wine with dinner was good for the constitution. She had joked about some of the elegant and yet homely ideas that came from France and wine with dinner was one she said. Darnley reverently set the empty wine bottle aside and flourished another dark bottle from behind his back.

'Look what I've found Henri. This should warm the cockles of your deep-down Gallic heart my friend.' And it did. The bottle of brandy warmed both of them. They toasted each others success in the exams. They toasted each others success in running. They toasted their friendship. Darnley took the bottle and led Henri into the bathroom.

Carefully, and somewhat tipsily he balanced the bottle on the counter and slowly both boys undressed. The warm shower sluiced over both of them. They shared the bottle taking alternate sips. Clean, warm, drowsy with drink the two young men lay together on the bed and shared each other.

'Well there's a pretty sight this early in the morning. Wake up little brother as you and your loving friend here have school this morning. Mum told me to make sure you got off to school on time and it looks like I'll have to spank you to get a move on.'

Henri sat up and looked about him. 'My head. God I feel awful.'

'But you look most beautiful my dear Adonis. I must say my brother has some stimulating friends and you do look quite stimulated. Henri isn't it? I'm Lucinda.'

Frantically, groaning every time he moved too fast, Henri searched for some clothes. He and Darnley had obviously fallen asleep naked and Henri felt his friend stir beside him.

'I'm Darnley's sister and you must be my brother's friend. His special friend by the look of it.'

'Christ Lucinda. Get out. Get out of here. This is my room.' Darnley rolled off the bed and scrabbled about with a towel half draped around him. Struggling to decide how to hold the towel, push his sister out and close the door he dropped the towel and tripped over the end to sprawl inelegantly face-down on the carpet. Lucinda smiled but she didn't laugh or giggle.

'Darnley my sweet brother, I know you are gay. I think you look quite beautiful but I believe your friend could do with some help. By the way, it's already late and school is awaiting. I'd recommend a different uniform for school boys.' She closed the door behind her as she left and the boys could hear her footsteps quietly walking away. Gay Henri thought, but was that really a problem? He knew that some of his classmates felt that way but then again some did not. At sixteen some of them didn't know what they were. At least I know what I want thought Henri.

After the celebration party at home with Giselle, Stephanie sat down with Henri and talked about his results and what he wanted to do. Then Stephanie talked with both Anthony and Sylvia. The question on the table was what to do in the Sixth Form. Which way did Henri want to go? For Henri the answer now was simple. Money and men.

ACCIDENTS HAPPEN

'THERE, NOW, YOU LOOK VERY smart and mature. I'm sure you'll be just fine.'

'Aunt, don't fuss,' said Henri. 'Mr. MacKenzie said he'd introduce me slowly into the office and he'd found someone to mentor me.'

Henri rode the bus into the centre of the city and walked the short distance to the offices of the Highland Finance and Investment Company. Two weeks previously, partly through some contacts from Aunt Sylvia, Henri had gone for an interview with Mr. MacKenzie and they had discussed some ideas and options. During the two months of the summer holidays Henri was to come into the offices and learn about the world of money. Learn how to make it work for you Mr. MacKenzie had said, and for the clients of course. During the Second World War three young Scotsman had banded together in Glasgow and accumulated some capital and some shady business acumen. As things changed in the fifties, and Glasgow slowly folded in on itself, opportunities diminished for Duncan MacKenzie, Alan Gray and Robert Knox, and so they brought their capital and their sharpened business acumen south to the more lucrative banks of the Avon River and the elegant city of Bath. None of the three gentlemen came from the Highlands but then what do the English know about the geography north of Hadrian's Wall? They prospered. They became established. As the years passed they became respected and trusted.

Why me Sandy muttered under his breath as Mr. MacKenzie brought Henri into his cubicle? Why have I got saddled with this kid?

'Sandy, you've been here with us for nigh on five years now and you ken our ways. Don't change what you normally do but explain a wee bit as you do it to young Henri here. The laddie's interested in making money and you've done reet well at that.'

True enough thought Sandy. Learnt a lot and learnt some more that even you don't know about either you old tosser, you and your distillery mates.

As the weeks slowly passed Henri discovered that Sandy McNeil, complete with his light-coloured hair, had been christened Bert Gauge, and had been brought up in a Scottish foster home in Stepney London. Bert had smothered his baby East End gibberish to sound like a bairn from the Gorbals. Growing up in the East End Bert had quickly learnt a little of this and a little of that and become quite adept with the pen, the imaginary words, the phoney references, and the art of creative accounting. The hard-hitting, hard-drinking man that headed up his foster home worked in the City as a stockbroker, and Bert soaked up the stories and the opportunities that slurred forth from his truly Scottish foster-father. It was a chance encounter when Duncan MacKenzie visited the City of London to discuss an investment opportunity that he should lunch elbow to elbow with Neal McNeil, and that they should both notice they favoured the same single malt. Mr. McNeil was ever interested in unloading his talented but becoming expensive foster child and for an agreed-upon sum Bert got traded west to Bath as Sandy McNeil and prospered. Mr. MacKenzie thought he had got the best of the bargain as Sandy quickly demonstrated some innovative and quite modern techniques for making money. Moreover, Sandy still had some useful connections back in London and the Highland Finance and Investment Company often offered some new, never-seen-before opportunities for people in Bath to make money.

Henri proved to be a quick learner and he discovered early on that he could absorb more from Sandy by observing than by asking questions. Sandy didn't take too kindly to questions and chit-chat. The two months of summer sped by and Henri took his experiences back to school to study political science, finance and applied mathematics. All looked good on the education front as Henri entered the sixth form.

As a climber Henri started to lead some of the hardest routes around. He put up two new routes in the Gorge and inevitably progressed to pitons, nuts, etriers and the slow but strenuous world of artificial climbing. He talked of going to the Alps after his final year at school and would Darnley come too? But Darnley couldn't. Darnley had other plans.

After two years in the sixth form it was finished, school was finished. Exams were over and both he and Darnley would go on to Bristol University. Still together. They would run at Uni – both get on the harrier's team. Both get University colours. Let's celebrate.

A mass of humanity packed the Satyr Club that night. Loud rhythmic pulsating drum-based music drove the dancers to jump, twist, and twirl as the strobe lights flashed shimmering blades of colour across the frenzied faces. Open mouths, gasping voices, heaving chests, naked with sweat and coloured braces that snapped to hip-height jeans. They spun apart. They came back together. They kissed and the room floated around them. Henri had found some drugs. Just a small pill he told Darnley. Makes you feel great. Makes you feel on fire. Tingle in the fingers, tingle in the lips. Kiss me Darnley. Kiss me. Flooded with love and emotion Henri and Darnley walked out of the Club with their arms around each other. Lost in their own world they didn't hear the shouts: didn't see the five men who suddenly screamed at them and started kicking the shit out of them. Henri was strong, and freeing his arms he set about fighting back but there were five of them. Half-stoned, emotionally drained, Henri and Darnley never stood a chance.

Light slowly filtered through to Henri's eyes and he suddenly realised that he couldn't see anything but the white light.

'Lie still young man. Just lie still.'

'Where am I?' seemed an obvious question. 'Why can't I see?' and Henri tried moving his hands and arms. He felt restrictions on his arms. He tried to lift himself up. He felt a hand on his shoulder gently restrain him and hold him back wherever he was lying.

'Rest please. You're doing fine but let's rest a little shall we?'

'Yes Henri, rest my dear.'

'Auntie. Auntie is that you? Where am I and why can't I see?'

'Henri you were in a fight love. The police found you and brought you here. There are bandages around your head Henri and that is why you can't see. Just rest love. The doctor says to rest. You'll be fine Henri. You've had concussion and a mass of bruises but the doctor says you'll be fine.'

'I'm here too Henri,' said Giselle. 'I'll sit here. Would you like me to be quiet or shall I read to you? Everyone's sent you cards when they heard. Do you want to hear what they've written?'

Henri lay there. He felt like shit. He felt like he'd been run over by a steam-roller. He moved his arms but again felt a hand restrain him.

'Lie still Henri. They've got a drip in your arm,' said Giselle. 'Auntie I'll stay. I know you've things to do. I'll stay with Henri.'

Later in the day, after some more sleep, the doctor was back and checking Henri's eyes. The bandages came off and Henri could see the pale blue walls, the light streaming in through the window and the quiet figure of his sister watching him.

'What happened Giselle?' Henri asked. 'How did I get here?' Suddenly he started and tried to sit up but the pain forced him flat again. 'Where's Darnley?' he cried. 'I don't see him. Is he in the next room? Giselle, where's Darnley?'

'Mr. Lord, can we have a quiet word please son? I'm Constable Rankin by the way and I'd like to ask you a few things. You can stay Miss. I understand you're his sister. You just stay seated my love. Now Mr. Lord, the doctor tells me you are on the road to recovery and I'm pleased for you. Took a shit-kicking you did by the look of you when we brought you in. I'm glad to see we got you into good hands.'

Shit-kicking thought Henri.

'We were attacked, jumped I suppose,' stuttered Henri. 'We didn't see them until they were on us. Four, maybe five with fists and boots. Christ the boots,' and Henri gritted his teeth when he remembered the boots.

'Son, can we take it slowly and start at the beginning like. You went out last Saturday night to celebrate finishing school your aunt told us: you and your mate, Darnley Cheevers. That right?'

'Yes officer. We went to the Satyr Club. Great it was – real fun place and everyone was having a ball.'

Quite likely thought the constable, quite literally seeing as the Satyr Club was a gay venue but live and let live he thought.

'And what happened after that sir?'

'We left.'

'And went where?'

'Out into the street. We were just walking down the street. We weren't doing anything, just walking and talking. We were talking about going to the alps.'

'You mean the Adonis, the Club round the corner? You were walking to the Adonis?'

'No officer. We were talking of going to the Alps, the mountains, to go climbing. You know, mountaineering, rock climbing.'

Police Constable Rankin played prop forward for the police rugby team in his spare time and so mountaineering and rock climbing didn't register too clearly in his world but he dutifully wrote down what he'd heard.

'And?'

'They hit us. One of them had a stick, maybe a baseball bat I suppose. Another one was holding a bottle I think. It all happened so quickly. We fought back. We both climb and we both run so we're fairly fit constable but there were too many of them. Was hardly fair.'

No son, it wasn't fair thought PC Rankin. Queer bashing isn't fair. There's usually more of them than you son.

'Remember any of them would you Mr. Lord? Anything distinctive about any of them? Tall, short, red-haired, scars anywhere?' he offered as suggestions. 'How about tattoos?'

Henri shrugged and the pain rippled down his body and his face curled into a wince of agony. 'No officer. It happened so fast and next thing I knew I couldn't see.'

'Okay son. I'll leave it there. If there's anything else you might remember I'll give your sister here my card and you call me. Anything at all remember. You rest and I hope you're out of here in quick time. Maybe go to those Alps of yours or whatever eh? Rest up a little – sort of recuperation in the mountains. Isn't that where people used to go to get better? Convalesce like?'

Walking slowly with a heavy measured tread PC Rankin left the ward and quiet fell on the blue-walled room. 'Has he gone to talk with

Darnley Giselle?' asked Henri. 'He won't know any more than I do. It all happened so fast.'

Giselle sobbed quietly and reached out to hold her brother's hand.

'What Giselle? What is it?'

'Henri I'm so sorry. He was your friend. He was your best friend. I know you loved him and I know he loved you. You were both so happy, so happy together.'

Clasping Henri's hand tighter in hers Giselle whispered, 'He's dead Henri. I'm so sorry. He must have hit his head on the road or on the kerb. His head........'and Giselle couldn't continue. She tried to smother her sobs and rested her head on her brother's bed.

Dead thought Henri. My friend is dead. Not climbing, not running, not an accident but killed, murdered. The emotions ran up and down Henri's body. His mind flashed back to the long lost memory of David and the fall. His first friend. And now, and now Darnley is dead. Henri felt the tears well up in his eyes and slowly, warmly, course down his cheeks. His chest heaved as the lungs struggled for air and he blew a great exhalation of anguish out into the calming blue-walled room and cried for his friend. Giselle squeezed her brother's hand tighter but Henri had already lost all sensation to the outside world as he grieved for his dead friend. A sorrowful quiet fell over the room.

By October of that year Henri settled into First Year University. There were lots of courses, lots of reading, lots of papers to write and the need to get the brain in gear. After the first month Uncle Anthony dropped in to see his sister and speak with his nephew.

'Henri, how about a brief weekend away from the books? Sample a breath of fresh Cornish air? My sister tells me you have immersed yourself in studies and I know from experience that variety is the spice of life. Actually young man, I need a favour if truth be told. I need your experience and skills to help me a little. Can you spare the weekend after next?'

As was his way Anthony turned the effort of getting Henri "out of himself", and having too much self-pity, into making Henri appear to be doing Anthony a favour so that Henri felt good about the idea. From talk with his sister Anthony knew that Henri had stopped running – the memory of running with his friend Darnley was just too painful. However, Henri still climbed and had joined the University Climbing Club said Stephanie. Fine thought Anthony, then we will lever young Henri into helping me with my exasperating offspring. Sylvia and I seem to be having our hands full of late and maybe a session on the cliffs will do all of us some good. Anthony was right, and Henri found he could leave some of his grief behind out on the cliffs. There he had to concentrate on the here and now, especially as Anthony wanted Henri to climb with Daniel.

Daniel Lord, Anthony and Sylvia's youngest child had just turned five, and was a little unsure what was expected of him. Daniel's eldest brother Geoffrey was fourteen and already somewhat distant. Michael was ten believing he was going on twenty and so full of himself with his cocksure attitude that Daniel was either someone to ignore or someone to bully. Sister Samantha might be only two years older than Daniel but she was determined to be better than her two older brothers and never looked backwards at youngest Daniel. When Sylvia had given birth to Samantha she was delighted that she now had a daughter to nurture but Miss Samantha was no lady to fuss over. The problem baby grew up to become the ever-aggressive driving force who had to be first in whatever she did. Already she could out-ride Michael and she scorned the plodding efforts of Geoffrey. Although she had only been climbing twice before she was a natural and on any delicate balance climbing she could outdo Michael's arms-only approach. So who am I thought Daniel?

'On belay. Climb when ready,' jolted Daniel out of his reverie as he stood at the foot of the climb with the rope already tugging at his harness.

'Oh yes. Climbing Henri. I'm climbing.'

Henri sat belayed at the top of the easy pitch and carefully tended the rope down to his cousin. Daniel slowly and somewhat timidly tested holds.

'Up right Henri?'

'No Daniel, straight up. There's a left hand hold up high. Move your right foot up onto that ledge.'

'But it slopes. It will fall off. I'll slip.'

'Lean to your left with the right hand and then the foot will push itself into the hold and you can reach up high to the left,' said Henri patiently. He pulled in all the slack so the rope was firm down to Daniel. 'Right. Well done Daniel.'

Slowly, patiently, Henri guided Daniel up the climb and it was as absorbing and therapeutic as Anthony had hoped. Daniel joined Henri on the belay ledge.

'That was neat,' Daniel said with a smile on his face.

'Exhilarating isn't it?' asked Henri.

'Er yes,' said Daniel, although that wasn't the word he would have used.

'You climb a lot more sensibly than your brother,' said Henri. 'There, look at Michael over there. Be aware. Your brother is dangerous Daniel.'

'Mum will sort him out Henri. Mum doesn't take any bullshit – oops, messing about on the cliff. She's quite strict, but she says this is fun.'

'Yes,' said Henri, 'but she also says this can kill if you don't pay attention. Still, it's a marvellous feeling Daniel – a wonderful experience when you dance with the elements. You float up the rock, searching from hold to hold and you can feel the air all around you.'

'Yes,' said Daniel with a worried look on his face. 'I could feel the air all around me coming up that pitch. It felt open, exposed, scary; a lot of nothing.'

Henri laughed and tousled Daniel's hair. 'You're right. This is exposed but that is part of the joy, the feeling of freedom. There is the challenge to learn to feel comfortable in this space, and then the sheer delight when know you can live with the mountains: when you realise that this is your world. This is a world to play in and have fun.'

'Wow,' said Daniel. 'I don't feel that.'

'It will come,' said Henri, 'and then again maybe not. I suppose it's not everyone's world. Still, part of the Lord family tradition young man. You know your father's attitude. We all ride, we climb, we ski.'

'And we sail,' added Daniel. 'We were all down at Riverside earlier this year and we all sail.'

Henri looked out from the belay ledge over the ocean and thought about Daniel's comments. Yes he thought, we all sail and visions of his brother swam through his mind and they weren't all that friendly visions. A sudden flash on the cliff suddenly jerked his eyes away from inward looking and he focussed on Michael dangling on the end of the rope angrily claiming 'this is stupid.' A lesson thought Henri and he turned to Daniel.

'Did you see what Michael did?' he asked.

'He fell off Henri.'

'Yes Daniel, but why did he fall off?'

'The climb was too hard for him.'

'I don't think so Daniel. Your mother took Michael up there for a reason and it wasn't to try something too hard. I know the climb very well, and you could climb it, but you have to watch and learn how to climb it. It is a climb where you have to look and think first: think before you try and climb it. Michael never bothers to look and think. He assumed your mother would lead him up something she knew he could do, but he didn't watch what she did or where she went. Just where he fell off Michael tried to go straight up and the route goes left. It looks hard to go left as it is exposed and it is a balance move along small footholds. There are no large handholds and Michael climbs with his arms. Knowing your mother she would have explained what to do but Michael doesn't listen either. Always knows best does Michael. Watch him Daniel. Be careful around your brother.'

'But he's my brother, and I love him,' Daniel said supportively.

'Love him Daniel. Yes, love your brother but just be careful around him. Your older brother Geoffrey is a better role model. You understand role model: someone to try and be like?'

'But Michael's more fun Henri. Geoffrey is too serious whereas Michael is full of tricks and jokes.'

Henri decided that he had said enough about brothers and he stood up and scanned the next pitch.

'Want to lead this?' he asked Daniel.

'Me? Me lead? No thanks Henri.'

'You need to learn sometime Daniel.'

'Not today Henri. Let me learn with you please. You're a good teacher, like dad.'

And like my mother Henri thought. A good teacher. Maybe I should be a teacher. Should I change what I am doing at Uni? Could I really teach?

'You want these runners?'

Daniel's question brought Henri back to the here and now. 'Yes please. The route goes straight up towards that white scar about thirty feet up. I'll put a runner there, and another couple before that as well to show you how they go in. From that point we climb left before we go up again. I'll be able to see you from the top and so we'll be in contact all the time. Am I on belay?'

Daniel conscientiously checked his anchor, the free coils away from his feet, and the rope to Henri safely through the belay plate. 'On belay. Climb when ready.'

Smiling at Daniel to show he appreciated his pupil was learning all the safety procedures Henri turned and slowly but so easily sauntered up this beginner's climb. He placed runners so Daniel could learn how and where they could go. Patiently he explained why and the implications of each runner. At the white scar he left a very long sling so the sideways drag was minimised. Daniel watched carefully. Is this my world he thought? Dad says I should learn. Said it teaches me all sorts of things – not just about climbing he said. About life too - about making decisions. Strange you are at times dad. The rope went taut.

'Taking in. On belay. Climb when ready.'

Somewhat flustered because he hadn't been paying attention Daniel quickly and clumsily untied the anchor and slid the sling over his small shoulders. The karabiner swung under his feet and he had to double up the sling before he fell all over it. Slowly now Daniel he muttered, and nipped his tongue between his teeth in his decision of what to do next. Yes, make sure I've left nothing at the stance.

'That's me. Climbing.'

The weekend had been a success and the Lord family drove home to Fotheringham. Stephanie had spent the weekend at Home Farm explaining some of her work to Giselle but Giselle too had ideas of her own.

'They're all so different,' Stephanie said to Anthony.

'The sheep?' asked Anthony, whose mind was somewhere else.

'No brother dear. Get your mind back into the here and now Anthony.'

'Sorry. I was thinking about some of my concerns for tomorrow.'

'And so am I Anthony but I was talking about the young people. Marcel is away at Cowes and talking of crewing on some yacht going to the West Indies. I never see him Anthony and now Giselle was off much of this weekend. I thought I'd interest her with my work here on the farm but she has spent most of the weekend with Antonio and Enrico. You know she's taking Spanish at school? Wants to learn all the Romantic languages she says and she's still only seventeen.'

'Well Henri seems fine Stephanie. I think he had a good weekend with us. He really helped with Daniel, and Sylvia and I thought Daniel would benefit from having someone other than his parents teaching him.'

'That was good Anthony. Henri seems to be settling down after that traumatic accident. Climbing has always been a strong element in his life. Out of the three of them it is Henri who still thinks about Charles and Helene. I think he wants to prove worthy of his parents and emulate their capabilities.'

'Fortunately he is less fanatical than Charles was,' added Anthony, reflectively thinking over words and arguments he had had with his brother.

'But he does have this growing passion about money Anthony.'

'Well,' said Sylvia, as she breezed into the room, 'that's not such a bad thing to have a passion about. We might run the company and the forest but it is money that underpins it all.'

Anthony laughed and hugged his wife. 'There Stephanie, ever the bottom-line pragmatic controller is our Sylvia. No talk of the mental excitement of new software breakthroughs, new technologies and opportunities, or the joy of walking through our diverse woodlands. I believe my lovely wife sees pound notes not leaves on the trees.'

'Anthony you're full of it. Obviously you've had a good weekend husband.'

'Breath of fresh air and the family all together,' said Anthony.

'Auntie, we'd better get going. Henri says he's some books to get organised. Thanks for a lovely weekend,' Giselle said as she turned to Anthony still hugging Sylvia.

'No hablo inglese,' muttered Anthony.

Giselle laughed. 'The words are good uncle but the accent is awful.'

'No hablo inglese,' repeated Anthony and Sylvia slipped out of Anthony's arms and held out her hands to Giselle. 'My peasant esposa thinks you are wonderful and hopes you will have a wonderful life with a tall dark stranger.'

'Auntie, you're as nutty as your esposa,' said Giselle laughing. 'This is a crazy family.'

'Stephanie says you want to study languages at Uni,' said Sylvia.

'I'm going to open all the doors in southern Europe,' said Giselle. 'I'm going to open sailing club doors for Marcel and bank doors for Henri. I'm going to be their language key. I'm going to support both my brothers.'

'Well this brother needs to be back in Bristol pretty soon.'

'Come on auntie. The sheep are fine. Goodbye crazy Lords,' and Giselle linked her arms through her brothers and her aunts and wheeled the three of them out to the car.

'And our children love?' asked Anthony as he folded Sylvia back into his arms.

'Just as Giselle said Anthony. We are all crazy Lords.'

'Money, money, money,' yelled Henri. 'It's a gas, and then something about keeping your hands off my stash.' His ears jingled like the coins in the Pink Floyd number. He twisted, spun and weaved his way in the smoky Club to the pounding of the talk-defying music reverberating off the walls. Arms high in the air, mouth open gasping, smiling, grinning and suddenly holding his partner in a hot, sweaty embrace. Mouths pressed together and Henri slid a pill from his mouth into that of his partners.

'Be happy, be wild.'

As the clock turned into the 1980s Henri's world revolved around University, which cost money; and around drugs, which generated money; spun into climbing wherever and whenever, and then turned back to part-time learning at the offices of Highland Finance. It was a whirl, a gas, exhilaration and exasperation all rolled into one kaleidoscope of life. Money came in and money went out. Friends came in and went out. Bringing his eyes back into focus Henri looked at the almost naked mass of male humanity around him. Bright eyes enlivened by chemicals. Arms and legs in jerky motion and a pulsing heaving corps of naked torsos celebrating this male togetherness. Forget this is a mid-week madness thought Henri, just live for the moment.

Sitting at a desk in the lecture room the following Thursday morning Henri's mind flickered back over last night's thoughts. Live for the moment he recalled and he tried to bring his mind back into this particular moment's action. Dr. Grange was not a boring lecturer and the intricacies of investment opportunities were an essential piece of making money, and making money was today's, this moment's piece of his life. Henri fought to bring his mind into focus and concentrate. Wasn't this similar to what Sandy had been doing just last week, but then Sandy hadn't told the clients all of the risks side now had he? Concentrate Henri – this is the art of making money. At Highland Finance Henri slowly and discreetly built a personal portfolio funded from his low level drug distribution enterprise. At home Aunt Stephanie was paying for his

University education and there Henri pleaded poverty as he really had no money of his own. The wages at Highland Finance for the few hours he attended during term time were a pittance and so Auntie was there for the expenses of climbing gear and the costs of travel. Ah yes, the costs of travel, and there were costs, even when piling six blokes into a small van crammed with climbing gear, sleeping bags, tents and whatever on the road across Europe to northern Italy and the Dolomites.

'We could have stayed in the Hut you know,' complained Tony.

'Just eat some more pasta Tony and put some meat on those bony hips of yours.'

'There's no meat in pasta.'

'Then blow up your lilo a bit more. You know, less yap on the hill and more puff in the bed.'

'I don't want no puff in my bed,' said Tony. 'Come on, the hills are waiting. Sun's shining and we should be up on the cliff. Coming Henri?'

An hour later Tony was leaning backwards and gazing upwards as the streaked limestone walls soared up and outwards above him. Held by the tension on the rope through the karabiner in the piton in front of him Tony leant out to see where to go next. Sixty feet below him on a tiny ledge Henri held the two ropes carefully belaying his friend.

'Where next Tony?' called Henri.

'Buggered if I know. What's the good book say?'

'Up,' said Henri. 'Actually it says a lot more than that but it's all in Italian. I had my sister translate parts of the climbs we wanted to do and all she has written here is "up, with lots of open space".'

'Could do with your sister up here,' muttered Tony, half to Henri and half to himself. She's a good looking girl he thought but let's get our minds back to the problem at hand. Up the man says. All right for him 'cos he's not on the sharp end. Tony leant back and looked up. Okay, up it is.

The angle eased back some hundred and twenty feet above Henri and Tony found two old pitons securely pounded into the fissured limestone. He tied off and looked about him. Lots of open space he noted and there was. Three hundred feet up the Cime Grande di Lavaredo, the biggest of the Tre Cime cliffs, there was a lot of open space. Below his feet Tony could see the scree slopes and the small people walking along the path. Above him the cliff continued to soar upwards in a vertical wall. Tony carefully hauled in the slack rope down to Henri until he felt it was tight. He belayed Henri as his partner collected the karabiners and slings off his anchor and shouted up that he was climbing.

And what a climb thought Henri as he slowly advanced from hold to hold. After the initial thirty feet there was this steep, somewhat overhanging twenty feet of artificial climbing. Up with the etriers and open the awkward tape step. In with the foot and brace the leg underneath. Retrieve the lower etrier and clip into the next piton up above. Step up and repeat. Don't forget that karabiner. Shit, the gate's the wrong way round. Ease off on the tension and turn it. There. 'Up rope Tony.' Slowly upwards until the next bit of free climbing. That's better. Henri could see Tony now and he looked up and grinned. 'Piece of piss really,' he joked. 'What took you so long? Said it was up didn't I?'

'Your turn on the sharp end mate. Going up are you?'

Henri and Tony shuffled awkwardly about on the tiny ledge as they exchanged slings, karabiners, nuts and pitons. Carefully Henri slid the two sheets of paper out of his pocket. His sister's neat writing curtly stated go left at the yellow ledge for thirty feet and then up.

'And what does the good book say now?'

'Don't know about the good book Tony but Giselle says turn left at the yellow ledge.'

54

This is the life said Henri to himself as he boldly traversed left along an intermittent ledge with a variety of handholds. From a distance Henri would have looked like an insect walking over this yellow blank surface – a surface that was vertical! The situation was dramatic. Walking on a slight bulge in this vertical surface Henri could look straight down to the ground, right between his feet. The wall stretched sideways both ways in a great yellow face. A promising crack appeared and Henri looked up as the fissure continued to crack this vertical plane. Sure, about thirty feet Giselle Henri thought. Makes sense. The rock was warm beneath his hands. Almost like the Gorge Henri thought. Warm limestone. Look, can even see fossils. Just think. It was all under water at one time and now these cliffs stand as lofty sentinels overlooking the valley. The joy of climbing Henri sang. Freedom, absolutely bloody marvellous and he confidently balanced his way up the fissure. Float up mother had said. Smoothly, but quickly Henri. A smooth and fluid movement cherie. Elegant. Yes mother thought Henri. You taught me so well and he continued to float upwards. Hours later Tony and Henri sat on top of the climb and munched on grapes and gorp.

'Good that mate, bloody good. You seemed to run up the last two or three pitches. Someone turn your switch on?'

'No Tony. Suppose I suddenly felt real good. Was thinking about my mother actually.'

'She was a climber too wasn't she? Didn't I hear Diane say both your parents were climbers?'

'Yea. They both were. Good too. Brilliant really by all accounts. My dad's brother told me all about them when he first took me climbing. He wanted me to know who they were and how good they were. My uncle climbs too, but he said he was never as good as my dad. Funny really, us being here.'

'How so? What's funny?'

'My family, the Lord family. If I think about it the family has climbed here in the Dolomites through several past generations. Before the First World War my Great Grandfather George and his wife climbed around here. Then, because he knew the area and could speak Italian he fought with the Italians in this area. Sometime in the thirties George's son, my Grandfather Desmond and his brother and sister came out here to ski and to climb. That carried on because my Uncle Anthony and my dad were out here climbing in the fifties, and now we're here.'

'And your sister speaks Italian too,' added Tony. 'Looks good your sister does.'

'She's too good for the likes of you mate,' laughed Henri. 'She'd run rings around you. Speaks French, Italian and Spanish now, not to mention English of course.'

'So we could take her with us to go climbing through all of southern Europe and not get lost,' suggested Tony. 'We would have our own personal guidebook.'

'Talking of guidebooks, let's see whether we can get off this hill without getting lost first mate. The going up part might be easy but the getting off part is often a bloody nightmare. You know, the so-called "Easy Way Down" usually isn't.'

But, despite Henri's experienced comment about descents they had no problem and were soon relaxing with a jug of cheap wine. For Henri this climbing and its camaraderie were the essence of living and he felt good. During the four years from 1979 to 1983 Henri Lord learnt Economics and Finance sufficiently well to attain a second class degree. He also took his climbing to new heights as he progressed from a good rock climber to an experienced mountaineer. Summer trips in Europe progressed from the sheer rock faces of the Dolomites through to the mixed routes on the glazed granite around Chamonix and finally over to the snow and ice of the Brenva face of Mount Blanc. Perhaps not with quite the brilliance and panache of his parents Henri was still a strong and controlled mountaineer and he even ventured onto two of his parent's routes on the Grandes Jorasses.

Running behind these positive developments was another facet of Henri's life as he financed his other after-hour's life with borrowed money and drug peddling to a ménage of gay friends. The four of them drove up the M4 to the bright lights of London. Ferdie, Blair, Rupert and Henri squeezed themselves into Blair's car for a long weekend in the Spring term. Finals were getting close for all four of them but what the hell. You're only young once.

Now Ferdie had a friend, who had a friend, who knew some people in Earls Court, and so they all crashed there. That's what friends are for explained Ferdie. Bodies of all sorts and sexes were scattered helter-skelter around the extensive flat. Grass, hash, ecstasy, coke and whatever else anyone could find spread themselves over, or more usefully into the sprawl of people. Music played. Smoke filtered through the dim lights. Bottles clinked.

'Let's go clubbing,' whispered Ferdie into Henri's ear. 'Maybe we can find some new friends? You know, one night stands. Unknown. Adventure. Exciting and soon forgotten. What do you say?'

Ferdie and Henri slipped out to find the brighter lights. He looked older Henri thought. In the Club he looked older. They had gone up to Soho and toured some of the Clubs. Everyone was up there – streets were crowded. People jostled, shouted, linked arms, danced around lampposts. Lights cast shapes and shadows over people's faces as they twisted and turned in the maelstrom of young people at play. Picasso's blue period, pink period in living motion. He was sixteen, or so he said. Henri didn't ask how long he'd been on the game. 'Rubbers mate. Don't where you've been do I? Twenty quid.' Not the same Henri realised. Not the same as with a friend, a real friend. Not the same as the comforts of bed, slower foreplay, togetherness. Henri quickly paid and made his way back to Earls Court on his own. He found a bathroom and washed – all of him. Looking in the mirror he wondered who he was. Downstairs in the kitchen he found a bottle without any label and swigged viciously. The raw spirit just swirled the drugs in his system round and round in a more violent dance. He grasped the edge of the sink. He gasped.

'You okay there sailor?' said a soft voice.

Henri turned. The youth was fair-haired, wearing a tight T-shirt telling the world to "Love your Mother" and old-fashioned teddy-boy trousers. The sight was such a mixture of this and that Henri looked twice as he stood more upright.

'Come,' the youth said, and holding Henri's hand he led Henri further through the depths of the extensive flat into a small room and sat Henri down on the edge of a bed. By the head of the bed the youth opened a small table and brought out a glass jar. A bowl followed and then a spoon. From the jar the youth carefully lifted out two and then three half fruits. Peaches Henri thought.

'Eat. Enjoy.'

The peach halves were beautifully soaked in brandy and the sweetness, the flavour, the syrupy feeling of them slipping down his throat was nectar. The bowl disappeared, the spoon was taken from his hand and his syrupy lips were tenderly wiped with the youth's finger. Lying back on the bed they kissed. Sweet, soft, moist and sensitive lips caressed his. Hours later Henri woke and saw that it was still dark. Rolling over he embraced the youth beside him. He felt at peace. Last night had ended so wonderfully. Caressed, embraced, the youth's mouth had felt so wonderful on his body. He remembered the final thunderous orgasm with his hands holding the youth's fair-haired head to his groin and then sleep overcame him. Tenderly he slid his fingers down the youth's back and over his buttocks. The body beside him stirred and he felt the youth's buttocks push back against him. The thighs parted and Henri slipped himself between them. In slow motion Henri moved his hand over the hip to the youth's stomach and downwards. He could feel the pressure against him from the youth's buttocks; yearning for him. Penetration, shock and realisation all came at the same time. He wasn't a youth. He wasn't a he. He was…..

Henri pulled away and sat up.

'You're not. You're not,' he repeated somewhat stupidly, and somewhat obviously.

'Does it matter lover?' the youth said as he/she rolled over languidly. 'Just hold me. Go back to where you were. We'll vary it to suit you. Just hold me. Close your eyes and remember. Dream your dreams and just hold me. Nature will take over.'

'I can't,' said Henri. 'I've never, I've never, you know, with a woman.'

'But you didn't think I was a woman. We had a delightful time last night and I was who I was. I am who I am now and you still want me so stop thinking with your head and let your body think for you.' The youth folded his/her fingers over Henri and caressed him back to life. He/she pushed Henri back flat on the bed and spread his/her body over his. Gently closing the eyelids they kissed and Henri thought with his body.

'You're very quiet Henri,' said Rupert on the drive home.

'Where did you go?' asked Ferdie. 'I saw you going out of the Club with that gorgeous redhead. He looked a real lover.'

'You two went to a Club,' moaned Blair.

'Man, you were out of it when I last saw you,' said Ferdie. 'You couldn't have crawled let alone walked.'

'And you too Rupert?' asked Blair.

'No Blair, I found a friend who lived in the Barbican and we spent the weekend looking at his etchings.'

'Jesus Rupert. That's up market you know, in the Barbican.'

'Well my boy, I do come from landed gentry you know and one must move in the right circles.'

'And you Henri? Did you move in any right circles? Tight, comforting, all-embracing circles my friend.'

Confusing Henri thought. Did I move in the right circles? Do I know who I really am? I thought I did. It was so clear. Flashing through Henri's mind were pictures of David, of Ralph, of Darnley and now Andy. So what happened this weekend? A girl, a female, but dressed up to look like a boy. He/she said they wanted to be a boy but had a girl's body. They dressed like a boy. They acted like a boy. They wanted to be with boys. But he/she wasn't, remembered Henri. Different, yet was it? He had liked it. Who was he?

'Henri, you still with us old friend? Lost yourself on some climb now have you? Back to reality old son. Great weekend but now the final dash to the examination line. The oh so final of all finals; the great leveller. The ultimate reality test Henri and you look like you're on some other planet my friend. Jesus, that redhead must have blown your mind as well as your …..'

'Sure Ferdie. It was a blast. Tell that friend of yours who has a friend etc. that his/their flat whatever is a great place to party. A weekend to remember.' Henri turned to look at the other three blokes in the car and he grinned at each of them. 'I won't forget this weekend. Quite an education Ferdie this weekend.'

Henri graduated and Stephanie decided to take Henri and Giselle down to Dartmouth for a family celebration. Great Aunt Veronica had invited her brother Matthew down from London and the new family member who lived in Dartmouth. Three years ago now Marcel had married Marie and they had a small cottage on the outskirts of town. They also had Jean, who was nearly two, plus young Philippe, the baby. Henri had known Marie on and off for some time now, as she had been Marcel's girl friend when they were teenagers, but now Henri looked at Marie in a different light. That memorable weekend up in London just before the Finals had kindled some new fires and emotions inside Henri. Perhaps he swung both ways. Marie was comely and obviously female. Do I feel an attraction thought Henri? Should I have asked Stephanie to let me bring Justin?

'So Henri, have you decided which way to go?' asked Matthew. 'Marcel has told me he is off next week. To Spain isn't it Marcel?'

'Yes uncle. Transatlantic race to Miami.'

'Leaving Marie and the little ones?'

'Needs must uncle. Got to earn the daily crust you know. Unfortunately I wasn't blessed with the brains you had,' he added.

'Get away with you,' laughed Matthew. 'And is it brains I had or brains I have?'

'Trouble is my brother never remembers where he's put them,' said Veronica. 'Never you fret Marcel. We'll make sure that Marie knows we're here for her if she wants for anything. You know that love don't you?' Veronica asked Marie. 'I may not know much about little ones at Jean's and Philippe's ages but I've lots of friends in this town who do.'

'So Henri, what's next for you?'

'Continuing at Highland Finance aren't you Henri?' suggested Stephanie. 'That's what I thought you told me?'

'I think so. Well for the immediate future that is. Seems to make sense with my degree and being established in that firm. There are lots of challenges and opportunities there still, and old Mr. MacKenzie reckons I've got the making of a useful investment counsellor.'

'So I should think of bringing you some of the brainy thoughts I still have Henri, should I? Could finance a few of my brain cells?'

'Worth a try Uncle Matthew. You never know until you try.'

Would I try thought Henri? What would I do if any of the family came to me? Would I still invest the same way, with the same degree of risk and the same accounting procedures? No, perhaps not. Aunt Sylvia is nobody's fool and she went to LSE, and she controls all the finances of both Brainware and Fotheringham. Matthew is no fool either, for all his appearance and gestures of being an eccentric scientist. No Henri, investing Lord family money is too risky, well at the moment. Now, when I am older and smarter perhaps we could rethink that question. Perhaps we will change this stupid practice of the oldest gets everything. Perhaps redistribute the wealth so to speak. Might make some offers to Marie. Marcel can't be earning much and she has the kiddies to feed. I should go round to her cottage when Marcel has gone and see how the land lies.

It was the year of the book – 1984 that is. Perhaps Henri didn't experience quite the radical changes as portrayed in that particular book but it was a year to remember, or then again, perhaps forget. Sandy McNeil had based his life on the Dicken's character of the Artful Dodger: quite adept at not letting the right hand know what the left hand was doing and being light-fingered in the process. However, there was one character trait Sandy had that was straight: straight-laced, right down the middle, clear-cut with no ifs and buts. Men went with women and women went with men. No gays, queers, poofs, lesbians, dykes or whatever need apply. Sandy wouldn't stand for it and when he saw Justin embracing young Henri Lord it was time to take action. No questions, no explanations needed but a little light-fingering needed to be put into motion. Always thought he was a bit flaky Sandy thought to himself. MacKenzie might think he's smart but then that old man's a bit of a mystery where sex is concerned. None of the three of them upstairs is married, well not to women they ain't. Married to money maybe, and that makes sense for all of us, but what about the other? Sandy himself was married some ten years now, to a buxom lass who had come up from Devon to the big city. She may not have had the street smarts of her ex-East End husband but she could keep him happy between the sheets, and Sandy had loved his conventional rumpy-pumpy. Still do he thought, but a frown creased his face when he remembered that man wrapping his arms around Henri Lord. Christ, I thought he was a hard man. Supposed to be a strong mountaineer or somesuch. Must be a tough bloke out running up and down mountains so how could he be gay? World's going to hell in a hand basket thought Sandy but I'll fix his bloody poofy life. I think Sandy me old son we're into a little bit of creative accounting.

'Come in Henri, come in. Know it's late of a Friday my boy but I don't think this will take long.'

The three partners sat in Duncan MacKenzie's office and looked somewhat pensive.

'Sit Henri, sit yourself down lad. Will you have a dram?' offered Mr. MacKenzie. 'Alan, you or you Robert?'

'Nae Duncan. Let's away with the business.'

'Henri, we've a concern with the Weatherby Trust lad. Alan here was going over some of the transactions and wasn't quite sure where all of the dividends were going. I know it's complicated. When we drew up the terms of the Trust the original clients were quite specific about how they wanted some things hidden and some things obvious. We never did inquire where the monies came from. Not our business you know as long as it keeps rolling in. Well it has kept rolling in and in fairly substantial amounts as you know dear boy. Still, it isn't the rolling in that we're concerned about.'

'No lad, it's where it's rolling out,' added Alan.

'I just took over from something Sandy started,' said Henri. 'All I've really done is kept up the procedures and then changed a few of the investment holdings when some new opportunities came along. I always checked with Sandy and where necessary telephoned the clients.'

'Aye son. We see that.'

'And the payments lad? Where do they go?'

'Back to the client as instructed Mr. Knox. There's a detailed list of distribution procedures in the document. We've computerised all of those procedures now and the software issues cheques monthly, redistributes the agreed-upon monies back into re-investment, and moves some monies into an array of bank accounts. It was quite complicated sorting out how the software could handle all of this but we've got it sorted. Works like a charm now,' added Henri.

'Aye, computers,' said Alan Gray. 'Little black boxes. All sorts of things hidden inside those little black boxes. Not quite the same as paper and pencil. Not quite the paper trail inside those little black boxes now is there Henri?'

'No Mr. Gray, but we've done it all by hand before and after. We checked that the software did exactly as we did before. Before we had the little black boxes,' added Henri earnestly.

'Checked recently Henri have you? Seen any new deposits?'

'No Mr. Knox. It was all working just fine. The client hasn't said anything. Not to me he hasn't. Well, has he said anything?'

'No Henri, but then the client wouldn't necessarily know all the intimate details of the investments and their returns now would they? Quite specific they were about how much was to be obvious and how much was to be discreet shall we say.'

'And you have been discreet, haven't you Henri?'

'Me?' asked Henri.

'Aye lad, you. Trouble is we're not quite sure whether to fire you or promote you you see. What you've done is clever. In fact it is very clever and we were surprised you could be that imaginative. You must have learnt a few new things at that University. Suppose they can teach you the odd thing or two in a classroom. Never a strong supporter myself but then we all come from the school of hard knocks.'

The three old Scotsmen looked at each other and smiled.

'Henri, we think there is more to this than appears. We think there are wheels turning within this company and somehow you've got caught in some messy cogs. What we propose is to stage an incident. We're going to give you a public bollocking for mis-use of client's funds. We're going to have an office meeting with all the senior staff and state we've found you guilty of mistrust. That way we send a message to staff that this company won't tolerate such procedures. We keep this completely within the company and threaten sacking for anyone who leaks a word of this.'

'But I haven't done anything,' protested Henri.

'You should look a little closer lad. Look at some of your accounts a little closer. Track back through time a little and see how well off you now appear to be. Look at some of the transaction fees you have accumulated. Money into your pocket Henri.'

'But I've not done this,' protested Henri again.

'Someone has Henri. If not you then who? Within the company it looks like you have done this and we will say so. But, there is one more thing.'

'More,' cried Henri. 'Now what?'

'As I said earlier Henri, we are not sure whether to fire or promote so we will offer you a deal. We'll chastise you for the misuse and tell the company why, but, we'll explain that we don't want this going public and so we will keep you in the company. Privately we propose to pay you twenty percent over your present salary to continue what you are doing.

No-one else will know. We think you've got potential and someone has tried to shaft you.'

After that rather confidence-shattering Friday evening meeting Henri really shouldn't have gone climbing but it was all arranged. The group drove over-night north up to the gaunt grey hills of Snowdonia. Dawn found them in the Llanberis Pass as they parked the two cars by the large bivouac rocks just below Cromlech bridge.

'Look, it's too late to bother about trying to crash now and I see there's already some folk bivvying under the boulders. We'll sort out who has what space this evening but we might as well go and do something right now.'

'Hell, you're a cheerful bugger this early in the morning Dave.'

'Used to do a paper route didn't I? Up at five every morning for years. Up with the lark that's me.'

'Dave, turn down the volume. You're doing my ears in. What you thinking of doing anyway?'

Seven of the group were members of the University Climbing Club and Henri had persuaded his friend Justin to come too. 'You hike,' Henri had argued. 'You're fit and you used to do gymnastics you said. Be a laugh. Come and try. It'll be good to share a weekend together.'

The last statement persuaded Justin Tyndall. Tall, rangy with slender legs, slim build and long blond hair usually tied in a swaying pony tail Justin moved elegantly across any space. As a runner his long legs simply ate up the miles. Although Henri had stopped cross-country running he still admired people who could run and he loved to watch his friend in action. Henri had been the leader of the University Climbing Club before he graduated and in the top two or three climbers. Looking around at the group he thought about some suggestions for partners and routes.

'Why don't we all climb in the Pass today and maybe some of us will go over to Cloggy tomorrow, depending on the weather of course? Anyone got anything special in mind they planned to do?'

'Sue and I wanted to try some of the easier climbs on Dinas Cromlech,' said Harry. 'We're not super climbers you know and Sue has never climbed in North Wales. Thought we'd start on Spiral Stairs and then maybe try Flying Buttress.'

'Makes sense,' said Henri. 'Maybe we'll join you or climb alongside you. I know both climbs and Justin here is only a beginner too.'

Henri commanded respect from the entire group and soon he had everyone organised and happy at the prospects of a good days climbing. They arranged to meet sometime later in the afternoon and plan for the evening. 'Either up to the PYG,' said Henri, 'or down to Llanberis. There's beer at both places but the village has a climbing store if anyone wants to go shopping for gear.'

The month of May in England is often relatively dry for an island with a maritime climate and on occasions this no-rain phenomena spreads into Wales and the Snowdonia mountains. And so the weekend passed with bright sunshine, fluffy fair-weather cumulus clouds and a general feeling that now was a good time to climb something at the limit. Henri was really pleased about the weekend as all of the group had come together on the late Sunday afternoon with tales of success, elation at achieving good routes and a positive feeling of a bloody good weekend.

'Thanks Henri. You organised that like a pro. You got an in with the man upstairs then? Obviously someone was doing you a favour.'

It was on the drive home that Henri remembered the expression – "someone was doing you a favour". He thought back to the Friday meeting. He replayed the interview, the words, back in his mind. A public bollocking, well in front of the senior staff Mr. MacKenzie had said. And then a private rise in pay. More money thought Henri. More money for something I didn't do. Something I didn't know was going on yet it helped me. Who is playing silly buggers he thought?

The bend came at him too fast. Shaded, dark, twisty, overhung with trees and lined with stone walls the A5 highway out of North Wales is not a place to lose concentration and Henri was deep into the machinations that must be taking place at Highland Finance. So deep into what could have happened or might have happened that he didn't see the sign for a curve, or the white line suddenly veering away to the left. Despite a wrench on the wheel Henri was over the line, up over the kerb and the right fender ploughed viciously into the stone wall. The impact slowed that side of the car but the momentum whipped the left side round and it wrapped itself around a solid stone mile marker staving in the left front door. The three in the back, Sue, Dave and Harry, were packed in tight, belted and dozing until Henri veered across the road.

'Jesus Christ Henri. You okay mate?' uttered Dave who was sitting behind Henri. Stunned, shocked with his hands white-knuckled tensed on the steering wheel, Henri could only look forwards through the cracked windscreen.

'Henri, we're fine,' said Dave as he glanced across at the pale faces of Sue and Harry beside him.

'Lucky we didn't go through the wall,' said Harry as he looked at the drop to the river below the road. 'Would have made a bloody mess going down there,' he said. 'Sue you okay love?'

'Think so Harry. Suppose I was lucky 'cos I'm in the middle. Two big cushions either side of me,' she giggled a little hysterically.

Justin moaned beside Henri. 'My leg, Christ my leg.' The front door had been stove in on the stone bollard and Justin's left leg snapped on impact. Unseen by Henri their friends in the following car pulled alongside.

'Henri, Henri, you okay in there? Blimey mate, you sure made a mess of the motor. Good job there was no-one coming the other way. That would really have messed up the paint work. You all okay?'

'Terry, shut up about the car. Justin's hurt. I think I've broken his leg.'

Later, much later, when they had sorted out the ambulance, the police report, repairs to the car, alternative ways home, phone calls, and listening to the doctor in the hospital, Henri found out that he had broken Justin's leg. A simple break wouldn't have been so bad but the impact had smashed one leg against the other and made a mess of the knee-cap. A potential running career disappeared in a moment. The bloody good weekend had ended in a bloody shambles, and I still don't know who is screwing who thought Henri.

Sandy McNeil was pleased to listen to Duncan MacKenzie chastise the smarmy poofter although he noticed that Henri was already looking shattered before the dressing down. Only later did Sandy discover that the blond lover boy was in hospital. An accident apparently and Henri was to blame. Well ain't life sweet thought Sandy and he re-arranged some of the computer procedures. Accidents do happen he muttered as he looked at the opportunities lining up on his desk. Highland Finance and Investments marched through 1984 and Henri learned to live with his actions and he too looked forwards to new deals and ways to make money.

CHOICES AND DECISIONS - MONEY, MALES, FEMALES?

SANDY MCNEIL BIDED HIS TIME and watched the slowly growing antics of Henri Lord. He also watched the ageing of the partners. Towards the end of that rather interesting year of 1984 Alan Gray died and Mr. MacKenzie debated with Robert Knox what they might do in the future. It seemed a pity to have made all this money and not enjoy it he argued. Although all three partners had been raised under strict Calvinist roofs and had been ingrained with Scottish frugality it seemed such a waste just to sit on the golden hoard.

'We could quietly pack our bags and sail away to sunny shores,' suggested Robert.

'Aye Robert. That's an option.'

'Or salt the water-hole and watch the animals scramble about,' he added.

'You've a cruel streak in you Mr. Knox. We've some good animals here. We've taught a few people.'

'Aye Duncan, but they're all Sassenachs, even that impostor McNeil.'

'Let's bring in a ringer. Let's find someone from Glasgow to continue the fine traditions we've started.' And so they did.

In January 1985 Malcolm and Rory MacDonald drove south down the Motorways in Malcolm's Mercedes. Although the offer looked good the MacDonald brothers thought it wise to suss out the situation before moving house. They had a good thing going in Glasgow. So good in fact that several people were looking at them, and sometimes for them.

'Perhaps it's time to move brother?' asked Rory. 'We've made a small killing and what we've got is easily portable. Seems we are attracting too much attention.'

'Just let's see what that crafty old MacKenzie is offering first brother.'

Crafty MacKenzie offered terms and opportunities too good to be true but Malcolm MacDonald had a nose for good investments and he moved his wife and two daughters down to Bath within the month. Rory didn't have as much baggage to move and so he cleaned up any loose ends in Glasgow before settling into a flat in Bath at the beginning of March. The three dozen or so staff at Highland Finance didn't know anything about all these machinations until March 1st. when Duncan MacKenzie, ably supported by Robert Knox, introduced one of the new partners, Malcolm MacDonald.

'Mr. Knox and I have decided it was time to introduce some fresh capital and some fresh faces,' explained MacKenzie looking over the assembled staff. 'We thought a new infusion of various assets from the Highlands would help expand our opportunities. We're looking forward to a long and fruitful future.'

Didn't see very far into his own future thought Henri a couple of weeks later as Duncan MacKenzie suffered a stroke, a heart attack and ultimately a last gasp. The funeral coincided with the appearance of Rory MacDonald.

'Who's the smart dresser alongside old man Knox then Sandy?' asked Henri as they gathered around the graveside. 'Seems he's knows Malcolm MacDonald too,' he added.

'Buggered if I know,' muttered Sandy. 'Not sure this outfit's going in the right direction Henri mate. There's too many people at the top who ain't local you know. West Country folk tend to be a little suspicious of strangers I've found.'

'Well you aren't exactly local,' laughed Henri. 'At least I come from down here.'

'Sure mate, along with that froggie accent; real local you are.'

Within the week all of the office knew that Malcolm MacDonald had a brother and it was the brother, young Rory, the smart dresser, who started looking very closely at the activities of the various personnel. The company had fifteen investment counsellors and supporting them were twenty office staff handling typing, filing, telephones, reception and tea-making under protest. Rory MacDonald may have been the younger brother but at thirty two he had progressed from being a whiz kid at the Technical College in Glasgow to a lean and mean hatchet man who believed machines could replace humans. Brother Malcolm may be the man with a canny eye on the stock market and other less public places to invest but it was Rory who rigorously assessed the internal workings of Highland Finance. Within the month there was a new computer system: there was intensive training for the investment counsellors and there was a lot fewer support staff. By the end of April Mr. Knox called together the six senior counsellors and described how the company was going to operate. Well, in reality Rory MacDonald explained as Knox and MacDonald senior left right after the introductions.

'Everything is going electronic, computerised,' said Rory. 'We've got our own server. I've hired a database administrator and he'll handle backups and routine maintenance. All the machines in the office will be identical and software standardised. There will be no special personal procedures and we'll all do it the same way, my way! I personally will supervise all audits and just so there is no misunderstanding I have been in this business and in this software system for a long time. You speak with my brother about investments, risks, and finance rates but you speak with me about the system. Only Jeremy, the database administrator and I have root access. Anything down below normal user procedures you come and see me. Understood? We're going lean and mean.'

'Frugal he means,' muttered Sandy under his breath, and quietly cursed that he would have to learn some new ways to wheel and deal under this bare bones framework. 'Going to be hard to put one over this tight bastard,' he muttered.

'Henri, Henri Lord, what're you doing in here?' asked the tight bastard in question.

'Same as you Mr. MacDonald I expect,' said Henri. 'I'm about to lose my home as my aunt is moving closer to her workplace and that means I need a flat here in town. Thought I'd come and look over some options.'

'You're single then?' asked Rory Macdonald.

'At present.'

'Think you can afford a flat alone on your wages? Think we pay you enough? I hear you have an expensive weekend activity. What was it old Knox was telling me? You climb or something? Chase around Europe and run up and down hills he said.'

'True enough but we do it on the cheap. Bunch of lads packed into a van, camp and live off bugger all. Lean and mean diet helps us run up and down the odd hill or two. Did Mr. Knox tell you that these hills we run up and down are vertical?'

'Something like that he said. Roped together so if one falls you all fall. Strange the things some people do isn't it?'

And yes it was somewhat strange thought Henri when he next saw Rory Macdonald the following weekend dancing with Jeremy Cohen at the Pride Palace. Henri was there with Justin. The broken leg had healed but the knee would always be weakened. Dancing was an energetic movement around one leg kind of activity for Justin, but he loved being out with his friend. Justin was proud to "come out" with his handsome, robust partner who had quite a reputation among the in-crowd at the Palace. Folk there had heard about the things Henri could do out on the cliffs and the stories got embellished with the retelling. The building of Henri's image helped as he and Justin gradually expanded their peddling of mind-enhancing chemicals.

'Small world Mr. Macdonald.'

'Henri, yes, small world and I'm hearing even more things about you. We've only been here a couple of times but everyone I bump into seems to know about you and your friend here.'

'This is Justin, Justin Tyndall. Justin meet Mr. MacDonald.'

'Hi, I'm Rory and Henri knows this is Jeremy.' Jeremy rolled his eyes and smiled but he kept on dancing. Stoned on something Henri surmised. Wonder what and where he got it?

'Giselle, this is likely to be our last tutorial and there is something I would like to ask you.'

'Dr. Hopkins?'

'Where are you going next?'

'We've talked about this Dr. Hopkins.'

'Humour me this one last time Giselle.'

Giselle Lord looked at her tutor and wondered what this quiet old scholar had in mind as there was a smile starting to show in the wrinkles around his grey eyes. What had he found she wondered but the soft face opposite didn't offer any suggestions? She decided to start simply.

'I suppose like many young people Dr. Hopkins I want to help somehow, or perhaps somebody. I've thought about teaching and we've discussed this. I've also thought about travel. My eldest brother sails all over the world and that appeals to me – the opportunity to see new places and meet new people. Although I don't sail and climb like my two brothers I do enjoy being out-of-doors. I've even thought about trying to get a job at the European Union offices with my languages, but then I'd probably be helping some man by carrying his papers. Maybe just his coffee.'

Dr. Hopkins laughed. 'I think you can do better than that. In fact I know you can do better than that. Yes, we've talked about this a little this year and I've taken the liberty of arranging for you to meet a Mr. Dalton. Actually, if truth be told my dear, it is Mr. Dalton who requested meeting you. He may discuss something with you that could interest you and I know that you would be eminently suitable. Will you indulge me?'

This time it was Giselle who laughed. 'Dr. Hopkins you are not a fuddy-duddy old-fashioned Professor as you try to make out at times. Indulge you indeed! However, perhaps I should ask who is this Mr. Dalton?'

'He will explain Giselle, and then again he may not.'

Two days later Giselle met with Mr. Dalton in a quiet and yet intriguing interview in Dr. Hopkin's study.

'I understand you have a talent for languages Miss Lord. You speak all the Romantic languages I believe?'

'Yes Mr. Dalton, although my Portuguese still sounds like a *turista*.'

'Serbo-Croat? Russian? Any of the Slavic languages?'

'No sir.'

'But I do understand you have a love of languages. You enjoy the source, the roots and the etymology of words; a little like a puzzle or a detective story. How well do you know your grandmother?'

The sudden change of pace and subject made Giselle sit up and think for a moment.

'My mother's mother is dead sir. Has been for some time so you must mean my father's mother, Rosamund. Unfortunately she's rather not with us and I've never known her very well. My Aunt Stephanie brought us up, that's my two brothers and I, and she never got on very well with her mother so I never saw her very much. She always seemed distant, but I understand from my Uncle Anthony that she was a very talented and courageous lady. She worked for some special group in the war. My other aunt, Aunt Sylvia couldn't get on with her at all but she always admired her for what she had done.'

'She helped people you know Miss Lord. She helped a lot of people. Many years ago now I worked for a gentleman who knew your grandmother. He thought she was quite remarkable. She too had a gift for languages and for puzzles, a little like you.'

'Dr. Hopkins mentioned you might talk about things, future things that might interest me Mr. Dalton. You seem to be dwelling on the past. He said you had asked to see me. He inferred you might have some employment but he wouldn't or couldn't say what it might be. He also warned me that you might not say who you were.'

Mr. Dalton laughed. 'Did he indeed? Well, part of that is true. I did ask to meet with you. In fact I will ask you to come up to London in a couple of weeks and meet with two of my colleagues. We all work for the government, in the Ministry of Supply but that really doesn't tell you a great deal. Let's say Miss Lord that we are very interested in you and your future, and we think we can offer you an interesting job helping people.

Dr. Hopkins mentioned that you wanted to help people but you weren't sure how. I think I can safely say the work we do definitely helps people and does require someone with your language skills. We will also offer you every opportunity to learn other skills, and other languages too for that matter. Dr. Hopkins mentioned that you like to travel and see new places – well the job would involve that as well. Look Miss Lord, I'm really happy to have met you and I would really like you to come up to London for an interview. I think we can offer you an exciting future.'

Down at Fotheringham the next weekend Giselle walked around the farm with her aunt and Stephanie explained what she was doing with the sheep.

'Auntie I understand all that but it isn't the whole story is it? You can have all the breeding you like, the right genes for productivity, wool texture, disease resistance, you name it but if the sheep end up in the wrong field shit can happen.'

Stephanie laughed. 'Not sure about the description but yes my love. Life is all about a mix of genetics and the environment.'

'And I want to help people who may or may not be the top level genetic material but life has dropped them in the shit. Through no fault of their own they are on the bottom and need help. Life owes them.'

'No Giselle, not really. Life doesn't owe them anything my dear, but I think I understand you want to help people who are being constrained by a life over which they have no control: the down-trodden so to speak. Am I right?'

'Auntie look at me, or you for that matter. Marcel, Henri and I have never gone hungry. We've never had to fight, or hide, or go without really. Sure, Henri gripes about never having enough money and Marcel doesn't really see how hard life is for Marie. She was a good sailor too you know, but Marcel left her behind when he took off and she has Jean and

Philippe to care for too. But to come back to me. I've wanted for nothing. I'd like to help people who have not been so lucky.'

'And this Mr. Dalton explained that was what the job was about?'

'Mr. Dalton didn't explain anything auntie. He just hinted and danced around but he thought I would like it.'

'And he asked about my mother?'

'He inferred that the work might be related.'

'When you're in London Giselle find time to talk with your Uncle Matthew. I think Aunt Veronica is out of the loop by now but Matthew will still know people. He makes out he is a wild eccentric scientist but he is probably the most informed member of the Lord family. Try and find out more from these colleagues of the enigmatic Mr. Dalton but talk with Matthew. He'd enjoy seeing you anyway. Over the years he has given all of us some valuable advice.'

After her graduation, which she celebrated with Anthony, Sylvia and Stephanie, Giselle quietly enrolled in the government to work in an office in Bristol. The sign on the door said "Translation Services" but the work included listening, visiting, and interviewing or perhaps interrogating a wide variety of people from all over Europe and the Middle East. People smuggling and arms smuggling were the major subjects of interest and Giselle found herself helping people in ways she had never imagined. Quietly Giselle found out that not only had she been vetted but so had all of the Lord family. 'No boy friend Miss Lord? No girl friend?' and it went on. She signed the Official Secrets Act and her world changed. Outwardly it all looked like a conventional government office job where her languages were essential and valuable. Internally Giselle became fascinated with an underground world she never knew existed.

'No Henri, I might dearly love you brother but I will not share a flat with you. Anyway, you're working here in Bath and I'm working in

Bristol. You've got a good job and a lifestyle that is not mine. Now that auntie has moved down closer to Fotheringham I realise that you've got to fend for yourself but you have to live your own life. Why don't you share with Justin? He'd love that Henri. He worships you and I thought he came from a wealthy family. He must have money.'

'His parents cut him off. Said they couldn't understand him and didn't approve of his lifestyle. Christ Giselle, this is the eighties, not the fifties. Can't people understand the world has moved on? You understand?'

'Yes Henri, I understand but I'm not sure Marcel understands. No, that's not quite the right words. Marcel understands but he doesn't necessarily accept or condone. Auntie understands, and so do Anthony and Sylvia I think, but not everyone accepts Henri. Obviously Justin's parents don't. But so what? Justin has a good job. Surely the pair of you can find something affordable?'

That summer Henri had suffered several setbacks. Stephanie selling up and moving to Fotheringham was just the first. Henri becoming more dependent on his chemical products was another and now the MacDonald brothers had managed to persuade Robert Knox that the hidden bonus wasn't really necessary any more. That should have died along with Duncan MacKenzie and what was Henri Lord going to do about it anyway if we stop it? Like Sandy McNeil, Henri was finding it difficult trying to develop ways with the new software to personally benefit from some of his client's investments. Life was a bitch.

Money, now that was the key thought Henri to himself. With money all of my problems will go away but it was Justin who went away. Justin, with his sick father and the need to be home to offer support for his mother went back to the family home. Because Henri was certainly *persona non grata* in the Tyndall's household it was a lonely Henri that August weekend. Looking gloomily at his assets Henri came across his

Brainware shares. Now there's a possibility he thought. When Marcel, Henri and Giselle had that special birthday to come of age Stephanie had given each of them some of her shares. The annual dividend from these shares was nominal but the actual value of each share had increased substantially with the success of the company. Brainware had developed into a very profitable state of the art company thanks to the judicious visionary activities of Anthony and the very stable and conservative management of Sylvia re-investing most of the profits back into the company. Both Anthony and Sylvia believed people were the key to their success and they hired some very smart and technically gifted young folk. Anthony also kept his ears open for visionaries doing post graduate at the University. He offered all sorts of contract work for these producers of tomorrow. So what could he do with these shares thought Henri?

Down in Dartmouth Henri made a token visit to see his great aunt where he learnt that Marcel was away sailing. Realising that Veronica wasn't likely to offer a receptive ear or financial handout Henri took himself away to see Marie. Young Jean had just turned four and little Philippe was nearly three. Knowing that Jean wanted to be like his dad Henri offered to take the boys sailing on the river.

'It'll be a treat for them Marie. Give you a rest too,' he added. 'With Marcel away it must be a lot of work with the two little ones. Let me put these flowers in a vase for you and I'll entertain the boys on the river. We've got Aunt Veronica's boat and I know she's not using it this weekend. I've just come from there. Jean will love it and I'll make sure Philippe is okay. The weather's perfect with just a light breeze and I'll bet the two boys would sooner be out on the river. Messing about in boats is such fun. Come on, you used to do that when you were growing up. Marcel was always telling me about your early years sailing here on the river.'

Henri spun the words, just like he could when entertaining a potential client in the office. The cadence in the voice rose and fell and the arguments seemed irrefutable, and Marie felt she could really enjoy a day of relaxation. It was true that with Marcel away the boys did keep her on the go, but they were such darlings, and she loved them so.

'Henri it's a lovely idea, and thank you for the flowers. I'll look after them. Why don't you go and ask Jean and Philippe whether they want to go on the river? It's true, I would enjoy a break and I'll guess Jean will be mad to go. He keeps nagging at me to take him sailing. Just like dad he says. I want to be like dad mum.'

As Marie predicted Jean was dead keen to go sailing.

'I'll look after Philippe mum, I promise. I'll make sure he is bundled up safely. We'll keep him amidships all of the time. He'll be our supercargo.'

Marie laughed as she listened to her son spout all the right words and try and re-assure his mother all at the same time. 'You're just like your father Jean,' and Jean blushed with the praise.

'We'll take some crumbs for the birds Philippe. We'll see all the young ones on the river. There'll be lots of youngsters on the river and with their elder brothers looking after them. Just like us,' Jean added. Philippe looked at his mother and then back to his brother. 'Dad would want us to go,' urged Jean. 'He'll be so proud of us when he comes home and finds we can both sail.'

Brilliant idea thought Henri. This should put me in Marie's good books. Maybe I'll stay the night and talk with Marie after she's put the boys to bed. Marcel has been winning recently and so there's got to be some money somewhere. I'll offer my shares to Marcel or just let Marie mortgage them for a while. I just need some money to tide me over. Something will turn around this autumn. Henri persuaded himself that his plan of action was potentially lucrative but he hadn't taken into account his own personality.

'No Jean, let the head come round smoothly. Don't jerk it. Don't haul the sheets in so quickly or so tight.' When climbing, Henri was in his element, and there he could teach quite naturally. He was in empathy with both the rock and rock climbers but out on the water Henri still had a subtle and buried jealousy about his brother. The water had been Marcel's environment – the place where his elder brother could eventually run rings around him. The place where Henri would grind his teeth with frustration and think of all the unfairness in being second. Silly really but Henri never lost this feeling of inadequacy and over time it was increasing as his world spun around him. The repeated negative comments, the series of "don'ts" rather than "do" or "well done, that's right" progressively soured the day's experience on the river. The mood overwhelmed Philippe who cried, wet his pants and refused to stay still. Jean became sullen with Henri's bullying and it was a quiet and mutinous crew that tied up at Aunt Veronica's mooring.

'Had a good day?' she joyfully inquired but the looks on the faces of the two little boys answered her question without any words.

'What happened Henri? The boys look very upset.'

'Nothing aunt, it's nothing. They're just slow learners that's all.'

'But Jean is so keen Henri. We were out the other day and he was doing beautifully. Philippe's too young at the moment but Jean was very competent. We went down to the end buoy, gybed and everything. We had a grand day, didn't we Jean?'

'Yes auntie,' said Jean quietly. 'I think Philippe needs to go home auntie.'

'Then why don't we all go home,' said Veronica practically. 'I'll just put on some shoes my dears and we'll all go home. You too Henri. You too as Marie may want some explanations.'

The good idea quietly faded away and Henri faded away from a somewhat accusative household and slunk back towards Bath. The day was still sunny though and the weather lightened Henri's mood as he drove north. Fotheringham he thought. Perhaps Anthony would consider holding my shares for a fee. He might even want to buy them back. The more he thought about it the better the idea seemed and it was a buoyant Henri who turned up the gravel drive to approach the Manor House. In a very relaxed and truly English fashion Sylvia had assembled the family for Saturday afternoon tea. Quite by chance the entire family was there and Henri walked in to an animated conversation about inheritance.

'Pour yourself a cup Henri and join in the discussion,' offered Anthony. 'Staying to dinner?'

'Yes, thanks,' said Henri.

'I'll just tell cook,' Sylvia said, and she went down to the kitchen.

'Henri old chap, you're just in time to support the poor children in this family,' said Michael. 'Anyone not born first in this ancient, stuck in its dotage family has to lick up the scraps. Father is sticking to his mad traditional custom. Beats me how anyone who runs a so-called state of the art company dealing with tomorrow's challenges can possibly think like a nineteenth century aristocrat. Should we get out the guillotine? You're half French. You could relate to the guillotine.'

'No Michael, dad's English: hung, drawn and quartered,' said Samantha with a mischievous smile on her face.

'Daniel, will you defend me?' asked Anthony turning to his youngest son.

'I will,' cried Sylvia as she swept back into the room.

'Thank god for that,' Anthony said. 'For a minute there I thought I was fighting solo.'

'You've gone quiet Geoffrey,' Michael said challengingly. 'Still, you don't have to say or do anything do you? It all comes to you without you lifting a finger; next year too brother dear, on your precious twenty-first. Dad it's nuts, it's obscene. We should vote on it.'

'Michael my love, families are not run like democracies. We don't run Brainware that way: we don't run the forest that way and we certainly don't run the Lord family that way. Lesson number one Michael is that life isn't fair. We all have to make our own way in this life.'

'Sure mum and our little sister here let's everyone know that's what she always does. Trouble is she drags everyone else into it too. She dam nearly had me fall off riding this morning as "she made her way in life" as you said mum.'

'It's like sailing brother dear. I had right of way and clearly out-paced you,' asserted Samantha smiling sweetly at her brother.

'So Geoffrey, what are you going to do next year on your birthday?' asked Henri. 'You going to propose any changes as Michael here suggests? Your madcap sister may not care but I'm sure young Daniel here would like something better than scraps. Bet they feed you better than scraps at Bristol House eh Daniel?'

'Sure do Henri. Grub there is smashing.'

'Better than at home Daniel?' laughed Sylvia. 'I'll tell cook you little devil.'

'No mum, it's better than smashing here at home,' said blushing Daniel.

'So your brother Geoffrey here should share some of his extra-smashing grub?' interrupted Henri as he looked at Daniel.

'Actually Henri I agree with mum and dad. Talking with some of the other chaps at school and hearing about their families I think this one is pretty cool. Over the years we've done alright so I don't think we should change anything. Like mum says, we make our own way in the world.'

'And out of the mouths of babes and sucklings come words of wisdom,' added Samantha. 'You're growing up little brother. You going to challenge me Daniel?'

Sylvia sat back in her chair and watched and listened to her offspring. Geoffrey was still quiet, studious almost, and quite conservative. He won't change anything Sylvia thought. He may not have the exciting panache of his father but he is Lord family through and through. And Michael she mused. Oh Michael I sometimes despair of you son. We never seem to be able to talk and understand each other. Moving her eyes and thoughts Sylvia looked across the room at her daughter. Samantha is fine. We're so alike although she is wildly volatile, but then so was I at her age remembered Sylvia. No Samantha darling you will find your own way in this world without any problems. And then there is my special baby. What will you do Daniel? What will you do in this life my precious son? You love both your brothers so much and they dismiss you. Samantha doesn't see you but it is your brothers you look to.

'You never said Geoffrey?' asked Henri again. 'It'll soon be next year. The outside world jumps up pretty quickly to bite you you know. I'd make the most of the comforts of home Geoffrey 'cos it's a dog eat dog fight in the real world.'

Wonder where that came from thought Sylvia. Stephanie was mentioning just the other day that Henri appeared to be somewhat at a loss for a month or so. Giselle had been quite concerned about her brother Sylvia remembered.

'Justin is away at the moment isn't he?' she asked.

'Yes. His dad is real sick and he had to go home and help his mother.'

'Changing the subject for the moment Henri, didn't I hear that there had been a couple of personnel upheavals in your company recently?'

'That's right uncle. After one of the original partners died old MacKenzie brought down the MacDonald brothers. They're also from Glasgow.'

'True highlanders,' laughed Sylvia.

'Don't know about that but both Malcolm and Rory MacDonald are canny Scots. The elder brother knows his way around money. He's an interesting man to work for.'

'But the younger brother is more into our line of work?' asked Anthony. 'I'd heard he was mad keen to computerise everything in sight. We'd even thought of contacting him to see whether we have anything that might interest him. If he's linked everything together on company servers he'll need some good security plus a very reliable backup and maintenance procedure. That's part of our world.'

'Actually, he brought down his own package from Glasgow, and very sophisticated it is too. He also hired a topnotch database administrator and he and Rory have nailed down everything real tight. So much so it is difficult sometimes to wheel and deal to help a client.'

'But you still can wheel and deal Henri? I thought that was part of Highland Finance and Investment's philosophy and selling line. You offer trusted, long-term opportunities for people who want to invest, and that can include some rather exotic and unusual portfolios. Isn't that your speciality Henri? You're there as an Investment Analyst Stephanie told me?'

'That's true auntie. We handle financing too but I've moved over to the investing side of the company. There's some good deals out there too at the moment.'

'No Henri, no,' said Anthony laughing into his hand. 'We're not in need of investment opportunities as most of what we make gets ploughed back into the company and the Estate. You should know as you receive the dividends. You've a few shares haven't you? Stephanie told me she'd given some to Marcel, some to you and some to Giselle.'

'Precious few Uncle Anthony, and the dividends are nominal as you say.'

'Look, we'll exchange business cards and you see whether this Rory might phone me.'

'And you'll buy my shares and I'll invest the money into one of my good options? Or perhaps we'll combine my shares with some of yours and we'll make some money together?' suggested Henri hopefully.

'Boring,' said Samantha loudly putting her cup on the table. 'It's sunny. It's a beautiful evening. We should be riding. Who's coming out to enjoy the outdoors? Come on Daniel. For once you might beat me, but then again perhaps not as I outpaced my obnoxious brother here. Geoffrey get a horse for Henri. We'll all ride and perhaps the younger poor children can upseat you. We may get a new successor.'

'Samantha – don't say such things. Go and ride miss. Your horse will soon keep you occupied.'

Grabbing Henri by the hand Samantha dragged him out of the room and Geoffrey looked about him somewhat at a loss.

'Geoffrey go and sort out a horse for Henri. Samantha will probably try and find him some mount who doesn't like riders and give him hell. You know what your sister's like. Take Michael and Daniel too. At least Samantha's right about the weather, so go and ride all of you. Your dad and I need a little peace and quiet before dinner: before the extra-smashing grub.'

Looking at his two brothers Geoffrey stood and the two boys left with him.

'So is Stephanie right Anthony?' Sylvia asked. 'Henri is a little uptight. Stephanie said he's muttering about money but she's told him that he's a man now and over twenty-one. He seems at a bit of a loss without Justin. Isn't he going climbing in the Alps again this year? That should lift him up a little. He really is a good climber and he does get a real shot in the arm after those trips.'

'Stephanie mentioned she was worried that he was getting shots in his arm from something else.'

'Perhaps a change in lifestyle is needed,' suggested Sylvia. 'A woman?'

Anthony looked across the room at his wife. 'Somehow I don't think so my love. I realise you imagine that is a good "cure" for many male worries – to have a strong steady woman at your backside – but I don't think that would work for Henri.'

'Maybe not apt symbolism Anthony but women make the world go round my love.'

'And thank god there are only two in this household.'

'So we agree. Henri needs a woman.'

'I'll go and see cook about extra-smashing grub.' Anthony chuckled as he left the room and Sylvia relaxed back into her cushions. Should we interfere with Henri she wondered. Maybe I'll talk with Giselle. She's the closest.

'Henri, it's me. It's me, Justin.'

'Where are you? Are you coming home? Jesus it's lonely without you Justin.'

'Look, I can't talk much. My dad's in a real bad way and I can't leave my mother Henri. She's depending on me. Dad's only partially lucid and when he is he keeps on about the family name. The pressure is horrendous Henri.'

'Okay okay Justin. I hear you love. Just keep calm and it will all blow over. You coming home?'

'Henri I can't. I just can't,' and Justin hung up.

'Bollocks,' said Henri to the dead phone and he slammed it back onto the cradle. Looking out of the window the rain continued to fall and the excitement of another dead weekend loomed. He didn't even feel like climbing. Popping two pills and draining a bottle of brandy Henri fell asleep on the couch and felt like shit the Saturday morning when he woke. A furry tongue, a cricked neck, and the feeling of uselessness summed up his state of body. The state of mind wasn't much better. Feeling it wasn't really worth the effort Henri dragged himself to the shower and opened his mouth trying to wash the fur off his tongue. Water cascaded over the rest of his body and he looked at himself. He had good legs. He had strong arms. He had impressive pecs. Running and climbing had shaped his body and he looked good. So why do I feel like shit he thought?

'Coffee,' said Henri loudly to the mirror as he brushed his teeth and continued to remove the fur from his tongue. Out on the street the light summer rain continued to fall and Henri decided to drive into the centre of town and find a real coffee shop. 'Treat yourself and then perhaps with nothing better to do perhaps we'll go into the office,' he told the mirror.

The Kasbah was a coffee shop that had seen the world evolve from the changing fifties when expresso machines were all the rage through to the modern world of exotic lattes, crème moca and whatever permutation of Colombian suited your fancy. The décor too had changed with the times and now it was bright, stainless steel and glossy brightly coloured curved plastic shapes. Coming in from the soft grey rain it was like entering another world and Henri's spirits lifted as he walked in through the door. He sat in a window seat but turned to face inwards towards the brighter lights. Ordering a frothy concoction that seemed to suit his mood he scanned the patrons.

'Henri, Henri Lord. My but you look a smart and cheerful sight. Mind if I join you? I've been looking at the latest kitchen accessories but they've nothing compared to what I've already got at home. Thought I'd come in here to rest my feet. Sit down Henri, sit yourself down. Don't go standing on ceremony for me love. My Sandy says you're a Lord and then he laughs and says you're a lord twice over. Do you really like the stuff they serve in here? Pretty weak I think. Look, do you really want a good cup of coffee Henri? Why don't you come back with me and I'll fix you a real coffee. Sandy bought me the latest in coffee-makers from the catalogue. It's real state of the art love and makes a perfect cup of coffee. Sandy's away and so we won't be disturbed. We can have a cup of coffee and talk. Listening to Sandy I'm quite interested in you and your family. He says you also have some real dandy thoughts on investments. I know he's smart Henri, my Sandy. Smart man from the big city he is and although I'm only a poor country lass I reckon he's a winner. Away now isn't he? Gone on some course he told me. Up in the Midlands, somewhere near Birmingham he said. Still, you'd know that working beside him so to speak. You got your car close by? I came in in a taxi this morning. Come on Henri, we'll have a coffee and see what happens eh?'

Henri sat quietly listening to this somewhat non-stop monologue but his mind was half tuned out and thinking about a whole array of other things. Sure, he knew that Sandy was away for the weekend. He also knew about Alice McNeil's fantasies for having the most recent gadgetry and new furnishings. Sandy had complained several times about Alice forever ordering things through the catalogue. Trouble was every time a new catalogue came out there would be a new whirlwind of purchases. This put a strain on Sandy's finances and with Rory MacDonald's control things were a little more difficult to adjust to Sandy's advantage.

The other thing that Henri knew, or so the rumour went, was that Alice McNeil "played away". During a couple of unguarded moments

Sandy had told Henri that he was very conventional about sex. Henri had already and rather belatedly discovered Sandy's aversion to homosexual sex. However, in the heterosexual activities he shared with Alice, and she is quite a passionate country lass Sandy had confessed proudly, it seemed that Sandy was strictly conventional and only enjoyed his rumpy-pumpy in the missionary position. This tit-bit of information seemed to support the rumour that Alice herself wasn't so conventional. People in the office had seen Alice with other people and word was that Alice was a bit of a goer.

'So go and get the car love. I'll wait by the door, out of the rain like. Make you a proper cup of coffee I will. You'll see.'

Coffee from the ultra deluxe machine was followed by a tour of other household items to be admired for their newness and high price. Alice had heard about Henri's climbing and so she wanted to see how it had developed his legs, his arms, his chest and so on. Lying together on the bed Alice ran her fingers, lips and teeth over Henri's face. Slowly she slid herself down his body and the fingers, lips and teeth played with his chest.

'Pert darling, excited aren't they? Just like mine. Here feel.'

She slid lower and fingers, lips and teeth continued their pressure.

'Swollen and wet too darling. Feel. Feel me. Sandy doesn't like that. Doesn't like anything unconventional. Doesn't like me to swallow him but you love, now you seem to enjoy things.'

The hand became harder and the skin stretched. Alice's mouth was back down on him again and teeth nipped. Henri arched on the bed with the pain but he didn't move Alice's head.

'Like that do we treasure?' Her nails pressed into him and he felt her wetness against his leg. The lips enfolded him and again the teeth rasped. Her hand slid up his chest and pinched his swollen nipple.

'Christ, that hurt.'

'Yes love but you're enjoying it.' She was about to say that she did too and her Sandy would have none of this but she kept her mouth shut clamped on his swollen penis.

'Makes me wild Henri. Makes me hot.'

The hand pinched the nipple and the teeth rasped the whole length of him as Alice contracted her mouth as tight as she could. Henri's world exploded. Frustration, no Justin, no money, Lord family stupidity, Rory Macdonald's needling and now Alice's stimulating foreplay all coalesced into the need to fuck, to possess and to take it all. Justin, where are you when I need you my lover? Henri strongly rolled over from his back to pin Alice beneath him. He reached under her buttocks and held her legs over his shoulders.

'Yes,' she cried. 'Yes, yes, yes.'

Henri held his hand across her mouth and thrust between her thighs. With Justin they usually coupled as two spoons but occasionally, when particularly passionate, Henri would possess Justin face to face. It was a complete coupling with mouths, tongues and intimate male penetration. In his passion and pent-up frustration Henri thrust into Alice and sodomised her. His hand stifled any cries and there was no love or endearment in the action. It was pure sexual rage; pure male release. Alice writhed beneath him but with her legs up high and Henri's strong body pinning to the bed her contortions merely stimulated Henri to a fiercer thrust. Suddenly it was over and Henri was standing up beside the bed looking at the naked body of Alice. He looked as if he was seeing her for the first time. Bruised lips, round full breasts, swollen mount and plump thighs. Not like Justin at all.

'Bastard. You bastard.'

'Your bit of rough Alice. I'm your Lordly bit of rough with aristocratic grace. Sandy wouldn't like that either would he? Bet Sandy never thought you could do it that way. Heard you liked adventure – heard you liked to try it different ways. Well darling, I'll bet that was different.'

'Bastard.'

'Suppose we could do with a little more foreplay,' said Henri. 'Next time I'll get more involved with the foreplay so it doesn't come as so much of a shock. Quite natural you know and you'll get to like it over time. It'll be our special treat. Lots of variations there Alice. Nothing like Sandy of course.'

Alice curled up on the bed into a foetal position and sobbed. 'Bastard,' she whispered.

'But I'm not,' said Henri. 'Born the second son and well after wedlock you know. Bugger maybe but not a bastard darling. I'll just spruce myself up a little. I'll know when Sandy's away and I'll call you shall I? With a little practice and some mutual admiration I think I could learn to enjoy this. Seeing as how you can't tell Sandy we'll keep this as our little secret shall we?'

Alice continued sobbing into her pillow.

'Have a soak later darling and think on it.' Henri turned and went into the bathroom to shower. Coming back into the bedroom he found Alice sitting on the side of the bed. Silently he put on his clothes. When he was ready to go he turned to look at Alice one more time.

'Sandy said you were gay. Hates gays does Sandy. He'll fix you Henri Lord. I'll get him to fix you you bugger. Still, next time he's away we'll try again and I'll be prepared. Maybe I'll have something special for you too. Won't know what to expect now will you? Dare to come back Henri?' and Alice stood up and walked naked and proud into the bathroom and slammed the door shut.

The morning experience stimulated Henri out of his lethargy and he planned for a night out on the town, even without Justin. The crowd at the Pride Palace was jumping that Saturday night. There was a buzz in the air Henri noted. Talk ran round about a new delivery in circulation and already there was a frenetic pace to the dancing. Whirling around with a bald-headed bruiser wearing black leather pants, a torso jangling with chains, and eyebrows liberally decorated with silver rings, Henri caught the shoulder of the neighbouring dancer with his outflung arm.

'Sorry mate,' he said as he turned to see who he had hit.

'Curb the passions young Lord,' said Rory MacDonald. 'Keep the brawny arms for wrapping around people not thumping them. Who's the gorilla?'

The gorilla growled and yanked at his chains. He advanced towards Rory. Henri gently seized the chains and pulled the gorilla round to face him. 'He's only a wee Scottie now Dan. Not worth the trouble and it isn't an "excuse me" dance.' Henri giggled. 'Here, have a pacifier,' and he handed the gorilla some E. The gorilla growled again, popped the pill and ambled away into the crowd.

'Where's Justin?'

'Where's Jeremy?' and both questions flew across the space but most of the sound was swallowed in the room's noise. Henri was about to repeat the question when another couple of dancers pushed him sideways and he fell into Rory's arms.

'Christ Henri. First you thump me and now you're trying to embrace me. Do all you Lords act in this way? I may be only a wee Scottie as you told the gorilla but I don't need the English rape and pillage mate.'

'Sorry Rory. Gets a bit crowded and wild in here. Want to grab a drink? So, where is Jeremy? You didn't say.'

'Sick. And your better half? He is your better half isn't he by the way? Sandy McNeil was muttering away at me some time ago about this long-haired blond wrapped all around you and how it disgusted him. Took me a while to realise that the blond was male. Still, Sandy is amazingly straight-laced given his background. Fortunately it doesn't apply to his work. Enough of that. Let's find a quieter spot.'

Lights were low in the adjacent lounge with its plush narrow seats that let patrons press the flesh as the mood struck them.

'So, while the cats away the mice can play Henri, is that it? Although I would expect you are the cat in your relationship. Isn't Justin Tyndall the son and heir of Lord Tyndall, past High Court Judge?'

'Yes,' said Henri as he twirled the drink around in his glass. 'Yes, Justin is the passive adoring mouse and that is only part of the problem. His dad's gasping his last apparently and Justin is holding his mother's hand.'

'From what I've heard about Lord Tyndall he's probably not happy with his son and sole heir tripping the light fantastic with another Lord, especially a male lord.'

Henri laughed and clinked his glass against Rory's. 'Difficult trying to get progeny and successors to the line,' he laughed. 'Fortunately I don't have to worry about all that. My older brother has taken care of that responsibility.'

'So this cat is prowling solo? Looking for other nobles of the landed gentry or just bagging gorillas? Actually, talking of landed gentry, doesn't your family own some property of renown?'

'True. My uncle was asking the other day after you too.'

'Me, or Highland?' asked Rory.

'Well a bit of both I suppose. My uncle and aunt run Brainware, and they produce commercial software including security and maintenance routines. They asked whether you would phone them in case they have some products which may interest you. Here, here's their card.'

'Could trade Henri. Did you offer a quid pro quo?'

'You bet. I offered to interest them in several opportunities we have – good places to invest. Told them we'd keep the Lord money in the family so to speak if I was their investment counsellor.'

'Good line Henri. I may call, or rather I may let Malcolm call. He's got the voice. Sell you anything can Malcolm. If, and maybe when it gets technical I might join the discussion, but you go looking for opportunities there Henri. Just remember, close family get too embarrassed to complain if things don't pan out exactly as forecast. Enough of that, it's Saturday night and this cat gots some playing to do. Think I'll avoid the gorilla and find me some deep-throated cat lover. See you.'

Henri too avoided the gorilla and he woke the next morning to find a long black ponytail lying gently over his neck. Its owner stirred and rolled over to face him. A smooth olive face with startling brown liquid eyes gazed at him from twelve inches away and the full lips slowly curled into an endearing smile.

'Well hello lover. You slept happy my friend. Fell asleep satisfied but then that's my speciality. I can predict your delights and bring you contentment, after having taken you to some great heights darling. Wouldn't you say you flew last night? Didn't I take you places?'

Henri lay dreamily listening to this soft fluid flood of words and let his mind swirl around in a half-awake dream. Gentle fingers slid over his body and he felt himself respond. The full lips stayed open and brushed over his with just the sensuous flicker of a tongue. Just when he had responded to the brushing and could feel fingers caressing at his groin the tongue surged in like a sudden penetration and a hand clenched him firmly. He gasped at the two simultaneous sensations. Reaching over with his arm Henri let his hand slide down the pony tail and on down the smooth back to the slender buttocks. The tongue in his mouth pulled in and out in a hard demanding fashion and then suddenly the olive-skinned body spun round and Henri gasped again as the hand held him wedged between the slender buttocks. A hand thrust Henri's hand down between the youth's legs and the two bodies joined. Like the tongue the buttocks pressed to and fro demanding. Henri's hand grasped the youth's swollen hard flesh and the motions became faster. Release rocked the bed and Henri cried out. The youth smiled and let his body relax back against Henri's. They slept. They slept 'til past noon and the day just ebbed away.

Doing what feels good

WHEN THE PONYTAIL LEFT HENRI felt at a loss. What was he really doing he thought? What mattered – men, women, money? No, I still get my greatest satisfaction out on the hills Henri realised. There is a freedom to climbing, and a passion. Perhaps it is the only place where I feel good. There in the hills there is none of these interpersonal emotions that seem to clutter up my other life. There is no mental struggle or question about male/male or male/female relations. When I am in the mountains I get these good vibes realised Henri. After all, I am a child of my parents, and obviously from some of the climbs that they did there was a tremendous passion, a tremendous feeling of living and internally shouting for joy. Henri thought on his parents and wished, as he had done many times in the past, that he had been old enough to really remember them. They had had none of the stresses of work but only the need to be very aware of their surroundings and each other. Sure they had to think about the next day, the next climb, the next move, but in a world that was both challenging and stimulating. There was none of the clutter and stress that Henri experienced in his everyday life. He felt he desperately needed to get himself into the hills. There perhaps, while filling his senses with the wonders of mountaineering, there he might be able to sort through and answer those questions that plagued him. That evening Henri pulled out the Alps folder and started to plan seriously for the end of the month. For two weeks he arranged to travel with three climbing friends for some serious mountaineering. And after a weekend like this one he told himself, he'd better stop procrastinating. With no Justin there had been no running and no gym workouts. He hadn't climbed for a couple of weekends and what the four of them had in mind were some serious routes.

In the history of mountaineering there were six top challenging north faces in the European Alps, and for a period of time, up to the fifties, these set a standard for top level climbing and climbers. One of these faces was the north face of the Piz Badile in the Bregaglia Group in Switzerland, first climbed by Riccardo Cassin. Although it was mostly a rock climb it had taken three days for the first ascent, complete with an unexpected blizzard and two of the five people dying of exhaustion on the summit. The famous French climber Gaston Rebuffat made the second ascent and he too took three days as well. The face acquired a reputation until people like Herman Buhl came along and solo-ed up it! Henri wanted to repeat Buhl's ascent and then his descent down the NW ridge; a sort of classic round trip from and back to the same hut.

Because Henri didn't like to climb solo he planned to make the climb with Mark. The pair left very early in the morning when the sky was just lightening with the incipient dawn. The initial slopes were easy and soon they reached the smoother slabs of the face itself. As the sun slowly rose into a pale blue sky Henri and Mark felt how the rock was dry and rough beneath their hands, and for the initial pitches they solo-ed up carrying the rope on their packs. Both were good climbers and Henri felt in his true element as he steadily and joyfully climbed upwards. Here he could leave all his uncertainty behind him. The concerns about money, about sex, about anything were all subsumed in this exhilaration of climbing.

About halfway up the three thousand foot face the pair rested and Henri scanned the cliffs above. They had successfully bypassed the small ice shield in the middle of the face and Henri surveyed the clouds that were starting to scud across the initially clear blue sky and a wind that was whipping the dust about. From the guidebook Henri knew they still had the Great Gully pitch to surmount. From his mother's teachings Henri knew that they had to move fast.

'So onwards and upwards?' stated Henri as he pulled the rope from his pack. 'The next bit is supposed to be difficult so we'll rope up here but climb together for starters. Looks like a change in the weather.'

'We'll have to move Henri but let's push on. We're over halfway up and even in a storm that ridge is not too hard.'

Mark's words were enough for Henri to tie on, arrange belays and carry on climbing. Pitch after pitch they climbed upwards and the clouds descended until both men had to put on more clothes, find gloves, curse at the wind and finally stand together on the belay regarding the swirling snowflakes.

'So much for a fine summer's day,' growled Mark.

'You know Cassin nearly got stuck on this face in a storm? He and his mates succeeded but the two guys who tagged along with them died on the top.'

'You're a cheerful sod Henri. Still, if I remember right Cassin survived because he trained hard and kept fit like we do. Look, we're only three or four rope lengths from the top and then we can scoot over into Italy down the easy way. That'll be safer.'

'But we've no passports,' said Henri.

'It's all E.U. now Henri so we're all one mate. Switzerland, Italy, France, Austria – you name it and we're all one big happy family. Not a problem.'

'But I want to go down the ridge and all our gear is back at the hut.'

'Let's get up first,' said Mark rather practically, and even as he said it the snow stopped, the sun shone and suddenly it looked like summer again, although there were still patches of slush lying about in the hollows. They raced up the last three pitches to reach the top. The positive change in the weather gave them fresh heart. After a brief snack and drink on the summit Mark looked questioningly at Henri.

'Down the ridge then?' suggested Henri. 'We can down climb and rap off any really steep bit.'

'You sure?'

'Come on Mark. It's the fastest way home.' Henri felt in his element. He felt strong and perfectly in control. Clear, decisive and at ease. Remembering faint memories of his mother he moved surely and quickly over the mixed terrain. Descending down the top of the northwest ridge the weather made another turn. It refused to stay in the summer season and after the initial four hundred feet of easy but exposed downclimbing the wind suddenly roared in and the mists descended again. Within twenty minutes it was blowing a snowstorm and the temperature plummeted. Despite all of that Henri felt good. We have done a really good climb he told himself and we're both in top form. This is what it is all about.

'Come on Mark. This is serious but we can handle this. The face was a great challenge and we can deal with the ridge. You lead and I'll follow. Anywhere uncertain I'll top rope you down and you decide whether I should climb or rappel. We'll beat our way through this.'

Down at the Sciora Hut Dale and Ben had retreated from their route and were congratulating themselves on a wise decision. They guessed Henri and Mark had had to bivouac and would be really pissed off if the face was icy tomorrow.

'Henri was dead set on doing that face. In fact he wants to try as many of those classic north faces as he can you know. Had the list all worked out Dale. Gets real meticulous does our Henri when climbing's involved.'

'Good job he does mate. That face is no picnic in these conditions. Even if they get up they'll have gone down the Italian side.'

The door burst open and two white covered bodies stomped into the hut.

'Well lads. Did we win the bet 'cos I'll guess both of you thought we were still up on the hill?'

'Jesus Henri. That doesn't look like a summer costume mate.'

'Put the kettle on for a brew you bloody northerner,' growled Mark. 'Henri and I don't believe in sleeping on the cliff when there's a nice warm hut about.'

'So that's one down Henri on your magic list is it?' asked Ben, 'or did you have to retreat?'

Mark peeled some of the snow off his cagoule and threw it at Ben. 'Cheeky sod. Went to the top didn't we?'

'Did you rap back down the whole face then? You must have left gear all over if you had to rap down.'

Henri smiled and sat down by the table. He bent over to take off his boots. Wriggling his toes he looked back up. 'Just as we planned Ben we came back down the northwest ridge.'

'Shit, that's some trip. You must have felt good. So where next?'

'We'll ask the hut guardian about the weather. If this is likely to stay stormy we could skip the north face of the Cima Grande. We've done that anyway, although I would like to do the north face of the Cima Ovest. That is supposed to be harder, even more of a gymnastic route.'

'We could consider the Matterhorn, or maybe go all the way to Cham.'

'Bypassing the Eiger?'

'I'd heard that's become looser and looser. Rockfalls much of the time.'

'Like the Matterhorn.'

'If we're all four going to make a go of it then we should try the better rock on the Dru. That's a classic north face. That's on my list you know. If that's in any condition we could also try the Grande Jorasses or the west face of the Dru. That route that Brown and Whillans put up is a good rock climb. Or the one Bonatti did on the southwest pillar.'

'Rock's certainly better there Henri.'

When he looked back on the two weeks Henri reckoned the holiday went downhill from that point in time. He had been in good form and felt really charged up after that classic traverse of the Badile. In Chamonix the weather was mixed and the four of them went up to bivouac under the north face of the Petit Dru. The walk from Montenvers across to the foot of the Dru is an uninviting hike. After traversing the tourist-infested Mer de Glace the foursome clambered up more than one thousand metres of steep grassy slopes leading to long dusty moraines. They bivouacked at the Rognon below the snow slopes. Despite the rock being better a piece of it still managed to fall off and fracture Ben's arm. After they had brought him safely down to the town and left him to convalesce in the campsite the three of them returned back to the Dru. This time they reached the prominent niche on the north face. They traversed this going from left to right towards the steep ridge separating the north face from the west face. Crossing the ice in the niche the heavens opened and virtually washed them off the face. The retreat was plagued with frozen ropes, wet and icy holds and frightening stone falls as they scampered back across the scree slopes beneath the face. It was a sullen, sodden retreat to the campsite. Despite all these setbacks Henri still felt positive and energetic.

'Look lads, if the storm's been that severe all the usual loose shit will be frozen in place. Any of the mixed routes will be safer, maybe easier. Why don't we go and do the north face of the Droites?'

'That's too far Henri.'

'The climb down from the top would be dangerous with all the fresh snow.'

'There'll be too much avalanche danger.'

Mark and Dale kept putting forward negative replies and Ben just made more brews.

'We're running out of time and so far all we've done is the Badile. I need to do something.'

In desperation Henri picked up Lucien in the bar in town but all Lucien wanted to do were artificial climbs. Henri realised that something was better than doing nothing and so he decided to climb with Lucien. The Mer de Glace face of the Aiguille du Midi faces south to catch the sun and dry the rock. The route offers bright clean granite and an exposed view down to the glistening glacier below. It also offers a really easy way off the summit because the telepherique from the Col de Geant and Courmayeur passes over the top, but first you have to get there.

'On belay Lucien. Climb when ready,' he shouted and Henri pulled on the two coloured ropes that disappeared beneath his feet under the overhang to his French partner. Slowly Henri took in the ropes and he could hear the clink of karabiners and "merde" several times. Draped with slings, karabiners, and etriers Lucien carefully ascended beside Henri and smiled.

'Eh bien mon chere. Est fantastique n'est ce pas?'

'Oui,' muttered Henri. He had forgotten most of his French. 'Mais, regarde. Pas beau temps,' he managed to say before thunder rolled across the heavens. Lucien looked out over the glaciated valley and watched the shadows of the clouds now race across the snow. Almost without warning the sky clouded over, the mist descended and the thunder bounced off the peaks.

'Will it pass?' asked Henri. 'We aren't geared up for any bivi. We'd better retreat.' Lucien understood enough English to catch the gist of Henri's quiet comments which were almost spoken to himself.

'Le sommet? Est jusque deux cent metres.'

'I don't care if it's one rope length Lucien mate I'm going down. I know I told you I wanted to climb but I also want to stay alive and that looks serious.' Henri started to organise the various bits of gear. 'We'll have to be careful how we rappel. It overhangs a lot so make sure you've got a good anchor before coming off rappel. And don't let go of the ends of the rope otherwise I'll find it hard to reach you.'

Henri looked closely at Lucien to make sure he had understood. He rethought the words translated into French and was about to speak when Lucien nodded. Both climbers were frustrated with having to retreat and Henri was feeling this holiday was coming apart every time he tried something. He was in good form. He was climbing well and felt really good but in the mountains you didn't dictate. One thing he did remember from his mother was the need to decide when to go up and when to go down, and right now Henri thought it was time to go down. Thunder reinforced the idea as it crashed not far away. Black clouds rolled over the ridge of the Grande Jorasses across the Mer de Glace.

Lucien stood on the ledge looking at the weather and looking at Henri. From the expression on his face Henri thought the man might cry. It was weird. Lucien shrugged his shoulders in a characteristic Gallic fashion but without a word he knotted the two ropes in preparation for a rappel. Well at least he understood that part thought Henri. Stowing most of the spare gear in his sack Henri checked that his belay anchor was properly arranged for a rappel and he noted where was the knot in the two ropes. Being ultra careful he also checked the knot that Lucien had tied.

'Je vais,' muttered Lucien and he was off. Sliding fast down the rope Lucien disappeared and Henri watched to see that the anchor and the karabiner were safe. Again thunder rolled around the mountains and Henri could see a band of rain sweep across the Mer de Glace. A faint cry came up from below and the two ropes moved a little. Good thought Henri. He's checking that the ropes will run okay.

Carefully Henri lifted the two ropes and feeling they were unweighted he slid them into his karabiner with rappel bars. This neat little gadget on his harness let him rappel down under control and his lower hand controlled the speed of descent. Henri even contemplated putting a prussik knot on the rappel ropes just in case. With the amount of overhangs on this climb any normal rappel could leave you swinging in space and the prussik was a safeguard to hold you in place on the rope and have two hands free to swing and catch the rock. We'll check on the way down he told himself. Only when he was sure he was safely on the rappel ropes did Henri untie himself from the belay anchor. He didn't need to remind himself that more climbers get killed going down, especially rappelling.

Over the first overhang Henri could see down to where Lucien was safely ensconced on one of the belay ledges they had used on the ascent. Carefully Henri slid down the ropes and joined Lucien. He tied into the anchor. Now comes the moment of truth said Henri to himself as he tried to remember which side the knot was on.

'Tire.'

'Yes pull,' said Henri. 'Lucien hold the red rope. Tie it off somewhere.' Henri slowly and steadily pulled at the red rope and let the blue one float into space. The ropes ran and Henri thought thank God. He watched the end of the blue rope disappear over the overhang and slowed his pulling. Don't jamb he muttered to himself. Run free. Suddenly, there was no more tension and the ropes fell from the sky. Between them they pulled in the ropes and Lucien set up another rappel. Once again Henri carefully confirmed the anchor was good, the rope ran freely and he noted where the knot was.

'You'll be free of the face at the end of this rappel,' said Henri. 'Slip on a prussik. I'm going to. We'll have to swing about a bit to find the next anchor. Remember the route traversed just below us.'

'Bien sur,' grunted Lucien but he didn't look up from what he was doing. Was he pissed off thought Henri? As the wind whipped the mist around the temperature dropped and thunder still rolled around above their heads. A thin rain seemed to dribble out of the mist and both men shivered. Having threaded the twin ropes through his rappel device Lucien dropped down the cliff face. With the mist and the overhang he was soon lost from sight. Henri looked around him. Tied to two pitons and standing on a metre long ledge that was apparently plastered onto the face he could see very little of his exposed position. Climbing earlier in the day he had felt really good, really into the climb. It was a first-class route, a classic in fact. Now it was a drag just to get off. Lucien was taking a long time thought Henri but there wasn't anything he could about it. Nice lad. Had been good the previous night. Better than the usual one night stand. Seemed to be a good climber if the chit-chat wasn't just bullshit. No, he climbed well today. Was fast enough up those pitches and neat on the artificial parts. No, no bullshit. What the fuck's he doing? The rain increased and the temperature continued to fall. Don't remember any of this in the forecast thought Henri but then again it's Chamonix so what do you expect? Henri reached for the ropes and tried to lift them. So Lucien must have found an anchor thought Henri as he could move both ropes. Just can't hear him in all this weather and the overhang. Henri slotted the two ropes through his karabiner with the rappel bars and then fitted a prussik knot above the karabiner. One last look at the anchor, take off the belay and here goes nothing. Slowly he eased himself off the ledge and down beside the crack they had ascended on the way up. Over the lip of the overhang and then feet off and swinging in space. Surreal thought Henri as he twisted gently in the mist. He slowed his descent and made sure the prussik knot slid safely but securely. Wonder whether the silly bugger kept hold of the rope ends thought Henri.

'Lucien. You okay?' as Henri peered through the mist below his feet.

'Oui. A gauche un peu Henri. A gauche.'

A sudden swirl in the wind whipped the mist away briefly and Henri could see Lucien on top of a large pillar. Still hanging in space Henri looked to see whether Lucien held the ends of the rope. Christ, thank god for that thought Henri. That'll help. He landed safely beside Lucien.

'Good choice. What's the anchor like? We're off the ascent route you know?'

'Okay,' was all Henri got in reply.

'Il y a un probleme?' asked Henri.

'Rien.'

Okay thought Henri. My loving friend seems to have gone to talking in one word answers. Just let's get off this bloody hill. Henri tied into the anchor and unclipped from the ropes. Making sure he had tied one rope to the anchor he took off the prussik and started to gently haul on the red rope. The end of the blue rope disappeared up into space again. At least we're relatively dry under this overhang thought Henri as he retrieved the rappel ropes. Again, safely free from the rappel anchor above, the two ropes fell out of the sky. We're in control thought Henri and he smiled. Bugger the weather. Bugger the climb. We're still in charge. They threaded the two knotted ropes through for the next rappel.

After three more rappels further down the climb Henri thought they must be getting to the foot of the face but he still couldn't see anything through the mist. By this time the rain had intensified and flakes of snow mixed in the rain produced a slush that started to rest on the ledges. Henri was facing the cliff and checking on the anchor when he heard Lucien cry out. He turned to see his partner frantically using both hands to hold onto the two ropes.

'Hold on Lucien. Hold on!' – which was a bloody useless thing to say thought Henri as soon as he said it because Lucien was already holding on for dear life – his life. After so many rappels Lucien had become careless and not checked he had completely closed the gate of his rappel karabiner. The ropes had slipped out when he put his weight on them and now all that held him was his hands. Again, getting tired Lucien hadn't bothered with any prussik.

Henri quickly took off his sack and rummaged around for some slings and etriers. He started to rig a series of loops down the cliff towards Lucien. If he could get an extra rope or sling down Lucien could stand in it and relieve the strain on his arms. Henri frantically tried to extend the nylon ladder down the cliff. Lucien struggled with his feet trying to find any kind of hold but the granite wall was smooth and there was no purchase. It all seemed to happen at the same time and it seemed to happen so slowly thought Henri. It was like a slow motion part of a film. The ladder of slings and etriers was short and as Lucien reached up with one hand the other hand slipped off the two ropes. Henri watched in horror as Lucien managed to grab wildly for the ropes but his hand closed around only the blue rope. His weight on the one rope just pulled it rapidly down. The red rope slid up just as quickly until the knot jammed hard in the rappel karabiner and with the shock Lucien lost his grip completely. The mist swallowed up Lucien's body in a second and Henri was alone. The snow changed from sleet into flakes and the wind dropped. Henri forlornly lifted the useless ladder of slings and etriers and methodically unclipped each piece of equipment. He put them back into his sack and tied up the lid. Automatically he slung it on his back and only then did he realise where he was. Leaning back against the streaming cliff Henri looked out into the snowy nothingness.

Henri had never liked climbing solo. He knew that several of the top climbers would go out and do something spectacular all alone but this had never been his world. Right from the start he had always climbed with a partner. The rope that joined him with his fellow climber was more than just a rope. For similar reasons Henri always preferred to climb down things rather than rappel. It was more a shared experience whereas in rappelling one got separated. You did each piece unconnected from your partner and now his partner was lying hundreds of feet below him, very unconnected. Get your act together Henri as this is you and you alone mate. His mother's words came into his mind.

'Henri, climbing is easy my love,' his mother had said. 'It's when things go wrong cherie that you must be strong. The ascent is a challenge, yes, but it is the descent when you must use your head. This is especially true when you retreat.'

Yes mother thought Henri. How right you were and now I've got to use my head all alone. All alone mother mused Henri and I hate going solo. Too bad Henri said another voice in his head. All you've got out here Henri is you. You're a climber, a mountaineer, well prove it. Henri stood on the ledge and shouted 'Shut up. Shut the fuck up,' but the snow swallowed his cry.

After three more very careful rappels, some four hundred feet or so, Henri's feet reached the steep snow slope at the foot of the face. The new soft snow slid easily off the hard old snow surface. Brilliant thought Henri. I'll just avalanche off from here into some bloody great crevasse. If I'm lucky I'll fall into the same one as Lucien's body. No, fuck it he thought. I can do this. Henri pulled down the two ropes and as the coils slithered down the slopes it helped clean off the new snow. Putting one rope inside his sack Henri tied into the second rope and coiled it over his body. Just in case we have to be heroic and practise self-rescue he told himself.

Three hours later, as the snow was easing off and visibility returning, Henri reached the terrace of the Requin Hut. He reported the accident to the Hut guardian and a radio message went out to the valley. Unpredictably the storm passed and the weather cleared. The rescue was quick and efficient and Henri accompanied the body of his friend down into the valley in the helicopter. It was a painful hike back from the police station to the campsite in Snells Field.

Two hours later four dis-allusioned climbers threw their sodden gear into the van and drove out of the campsite in Chamonix. They left behind their frustrations. They left behind many other pissed off English climbers ensconced in wet sleeping bags supping endless brews.

'Typical,' said Henri, 'bloody typical summer weather. You have to spend all season out here just to get that one day when you can do anything. Coming out here for two weeks is like a crap shoot.'

'At least you got one route ticked off your list Henri.'

Before Henri could answer Dale swore loudly and the van swerved viciously across the wet road. Wrestling with the wheel Dale managed to stop with the van still upright.

'Get out your side Mark but watch the bloody traffic.'

'Get out your own side Dale. It's safer your side.'

'Can't you silly sod. If you hadn't been congratulating yourself on getting up the Badile you might have noticed I managed to miss the bloody great poplar tree next to my door. Why the French insist on lining their roads with these sodding trees beats me. Anyway lads, we've got a flat tyre and Mark here needs to get out and we can fix it. Well I hope it is just a flat tyre and not something wrong with the steering.'

After changing the wheel, which necessitated unloading much of the wet gear onto the sodden side of the road the rain just added to their misery. Inadvertently, Ben's sack managed to roll down into the ditch alongside the road and that led to another round of words.

'I'll drive,' said Henri, as Mark and Dale continued to snipe at each other. The rain continued and the three lads lying in the back on the mound of wet gear dozed as steam rose up all around them. Henri fiddled with the radio trying to find something to keep him awake. He realised he was suffering from belated shock and overall exhaustion but he felt he was more in control than any of the others. The siren caused him to jerk back upright and once again the van swerved from side to side across the road. Like Dale, Henri managed to keep the van between the avenue of poplar trees and the police car kept a safe distance behind them until Henri had straightened up. The siren and flashing lights brought Henri to a stop. The speeding ticket added fuel to an explosive situation and when they drove onto the quayside in Dieppe the four of them staggered out of the van and howled. The sight of the cross-channel ferry leaving Dieppe put a cap on it. The atmosphere within the van became more steamy and it was four very irate tourists who finally unloaded in London. Henri finally reached his flat.

'Absolute fucking shambles Justin. One climb and piss all after that. Two weeks and god knows how many francs and one bloody climb.'

'But you said it was a good climb Henri,' Justin added supportively.

'Aye, it was that. Mark and I did okay there, storm and all. But after that it was sweet F.A. Look, I've got to unload a whole pile of wet crap and sort through the gear. After I've got that squared away we can talk. Jesus I've missed you Justin. Climbing might be one part of me but you are the other part. Come here and give us a hug you silly bugger.'

Henri slowly and methodically unpacked his gear and hung bits up to dry. Carefully he went through each rope and then each sling, karabiner, nut and etrier. Never know when your life may depend on this stuff he thought to himself. Camping gear spread itself throughout the flat and Henri slowly unwound from his two weeks frustration.

'At least the dozy Customs bods didn't find this,' he told Justin as he slid two white plastic bags out of the hollow tent poles. 'Bit of a pain repacking it into these sleeves but a neat place don't you think? Maybe we'll try some and a drink to celebrate my coming home. Let me go and shower and we can relax together.'

Henri hadn't noticed how quiet Justin had become. Coming out of the shower with a towel wrapped around him he sat down on the couch and pulled one of the bags of coke towards him.

'Got a knife Justin? Hey love, what's the matter?'

Justin was sitting white-faced and quietly sobbing into a handkerchief twisted tightly around his hand. Henri moved over and put his arm around Justin's shoulders.

'Surprised you didn't fall over my cases,' stuttered Justin. 'Surprised you hadn't noticed the books are gone and now I'm gone,' and he burst into tears.

'What do you mean gone?'

'Gone Henri, as in I'm leaving. I've got to leave. Pater says I must leave and mummy is insistent too. I've got to go home Henri.'

'But this is your home Justin. Here. Here with me.'

'Henri I'm so sorry,' and Justin sobbed. He wiped his eyes and looked at Henri. 'We can still run you know. Run together.'

'Fuck running Justin. I want us to be together. Look, let's have a snort, a drink, and a good night together and we'll talk about this in the morning. It'll feel different in the morning.'

The doorbell rang and Justin stood up. 'That's for me Henri. That's Danvers for me. Mummy said she would send Danvers so there would be no change of mind.' Justin walked to the door and greeted Danvers, the Tyndall family butler and chauffeur.

'These cases sir?'

'Yes Danvers. Bye Henri. Look after yourself.' Justin mouthed "I love you" and was gone. Henri just sat there in the empty flat. He looked around. Without thinking he picked up a knife and slit the plastic tube. Lifting a little of the powder with the blade of his knife he automatically tipped it onto the table and leant over. Closing one nostril after the other he snorted. Leaning back we waited for the reaction. Nothing. Nothing was happening and Henri leant back over the table and repeated the action. Nothing again. Absolutely fuck all and Henri howled at the empty room. The rooms seemed to close in on him and he could touch both sides. Frantically he looked from wall to wall and the graffiti shifted in and out of focus. Where am I he thought? Leslie where am I? Christ Leslie.

In a sudden clearing of the mind Henri realised where he was. He looked down and his trousers and underpants were round his ankles as he sat on the toilet. Shit, I'm in the bog. I'm in the bog at the Oasis and Leslie's outside. Leslie is probably wondering where the fuck I am. Henri struggled with his clothing and stood up. Leaving the washroom corridor he walked unsteadily across the Club floor.

'Well Henri, you know what we discussed? I thought you said you knew some of the girls here in this Club? You know what Buzz and I want to do?'

Yes thought Henri. He knew what Leslie and Buzz wanted to do and that further added to his confusion and discomfort. How much did Leslie and Buzz do together he wondered, and exactly what did Leslie and Buzz do together. Henri was "married" to Leslie, or each was each other's significant other if you like, and Henri was worried about Leslie's attachment with Buzz. Unlike Leslie, Buzz was categorically male and made sure everyone knew it. So it was Henri again who was the confused individual in the trio, because Henri wasn't sure at this time in his life whether he was male or female, mentally that is.

'Henri, this is a delight. It's good to see you are still here. What can I get you and your friends to drink? Same again is it or something special as you appear to be celebrating?'

'Hi Gloria. It's good to see you too. Buzz, you still drinking whiskey? Leslie, what about you?'

'I'll have another vodka and put some spirit in this one darling can you,' said Leslie as he patted Gloria on her derriere.

'I'll have a scotch too please,' said Henri. 'Who is here tonight Gloria? Who might I know who is here tonight?'

'Sheena will dance again later Henri. Remember her? How could anyone forget Sheena? Lola should be in later tonight too. I can get her to come over if you like but it'll cost.'

'Sure Gloria, bring her over,' said Leslie. 'Henri said we should meet his friends and we might like something special. We've all get special needs here you know.'

'I'll get your drinks and see whether I can find out when Lola will be in. I'll tell her that Henri is here.'

'And his friends darling, and his friends. Buzz and I here have some very special needs. If satisfied it would make our own lives so much better you know.'

Gloria stood by the table thinking over the conversation and the threesome. She had met Henri Lord earlier in the year when she was down in the village near Fotheringham Manor, home of the Lord family. While collecting the drinks from Rita at the bar Gloria thought back trying to remember who were the other couple with Henri? There had been the murder of Freddie Dunster in that infamous cottage on the Lord family estate and Gary Templeton had been found guilty. Although Gloria was intimately involved in the murder there was no evidence directly linking her with the crime and so she had never been charged. Neither had any of the other girls Gloria had organised into the brothel she was running in the empty cottage. Neat deal that had been thought Gloria but Gary had to get greedy and then have some scruples. Still, the stupid git paid the price didn't he, but this Henri Lord now? Where did he fit into that weird household? Gloria picked up her tray and carried the drinks over to the table. The conversation seemed to be rather one-sided and it looked as if it was Henri who was being badgered by the other two. Totting up the bill on their tab Gloria hovered trying to catch some of the words.

'So is this Lola a better opportunity Henri? We need you to open up some invitation you know. This is work Henri and not a bloody holiday. We need information. We think this is just the veneer and the action is down below. That's where you've got to go Henri. Still, you like that don't you? Leslie tells me you like that.'

And what else does Leslie tell you thought Henri. Christ, how will I manage this? 'Gloria, did you find out about Lola?'

'She'll be in in about half an hour Henri. Shall I send her over when she comes in?'

'Yes Gloria. Do that love,' said Leslie. 'We're all waiting.'

'Well watch Sheena dance in the meantime and see whether that does anything special for you,' said Gloria. 'For your special needs,' she added.

Henri Lord was a cousin of Samantha and Daniel Lord Gloria remembered. He was the son of that brother of Sir Anthony's who was killed way back, somewhere in Europe. Gloria had met all of them in the

George and Dragon pub where she had worked in the village. Christ that seems ages ago now she thought and yet it was only earlier this year. He was a rather morose sort of bugger she remembered, and always seemed to have a permanent chip on his shoulder. Suddenly Gloria recalled who one of the other two was at the table. One was his significant other and Gloria remembered the question in the George whether it was male or female. She giggled to herself. That Daniel Lord and the significant other had had some sort of argument, something about money. Yes, that's right she remembered and typically Miss Samantha sorts it all out. Jesus there are some weird people in that family. But Lola thought Gloria, Lola will sort any of them out. Male, female it won't matter to Lola as long as they pay for services rendered, and if they want Lola they will pay giggled Gloria.

Sheena's dancing was sufficiently classy and entrancing to keep half the audience entertained and Henri had a moment to watch and still let his mind wander without the incessant chatter from Buzz. Christ there were times when he could throttle that non-stop yap. At least he isn't flashing that camera in my face, or anyone else's face tonight thought Henri. I can imagine why some people would like to smash those cameras into the faces of the paparazzi. It's a wonder that so few of them get assaulted. Henri looked at Leslie and his face softened. Heaven, what a partner he thought. Full of drive and so determined, and yet gorgeous with it when we are together. Can be tender, loving, supportive and then really defensive if someone attacks. Where did I lose it? I used to have drive, ambition, even a non-conformist streak for a while. Henri smiled to himself when he remembered his years growing up.

'Thought you went to find Lola?' asked Leslie.
'Gloria said she would be in later,' said Henri.

117

'And so I am. Only a little late but then one shouldn't come too early if you know what I mean. Now Henri, my friend Gloria tells me you were looking for me, most anxiously she said. Come my friend. It's time we spent a little quality time together.' Lola extended her hand and Henri automatically took it. Suddenly Lola whisked him off his chair and was leading him at a decidedly fast pace across the floor. Leslie turned to Buzz and grinned.

'Perhaps we'll get some action at last,' he said. 'Anything happening your end?'

'Poked around a little and caught some useful words. There's a connection between this place and the Exotica and it sounds as if the Exotica is more likely to be photogenic. Want me to hang around or should I go exploring?'

'Buzz, go and have a quick word with Gloria over by the bar. If memory serves me right she worked at the Exotica. Bribe her, threaten her, I don't care but find out a little more about the Exotica before we go exploring.'

'Right Henri. Sit you down right there my lovely. Gloria tells me you are the strong silent rock climbing type, or that's what she said Daniel once told her. It is Henri Lord isn't it? It is the Henri Lord that is what, a cousin or something of the lordy lordy Lord family? That was a gas Henri, down there at Fotheringham, but then Daniel and his nosey sister had to put an end to Gloria's passion palace. Strong and silent eh Henri? We'll see about that lover shall we? Perhaps I'll tie you up and you pretend you're caught in your climbing string or something?'

'Rope,' said Henri.

'What's that Henri? You spoke. Rope was it. Okay my beauty, we can find some rope. You just rest there on the bed love and we'll do the rope trick shall we? Why did you want to find me Henri? Had you heard what I can do with strong silent types? By the time we're finished my quiet giant we might get some sound out of you. Now strong arms just tied like so and my, but look at you? Now aren't you the muscular one? And if I tease a little here?' and Lola opened Henri's shirt, stepped back and cracked her whip. She splayed the leather ends slowly across Henri's chest and watched him lift up off the bed.

'Can't stand to see a man so hot myself. I'll just slip into something cooler, something casual,' and Lola turned round and slowly unzipped the back of her dress. It slithered to the ground and Henri could see the red threads across Lola's back and a second around her hips. She turned and he gasped as she cracked the whip inches above his chest letting the spent strands slide across his stomach. Wearing little red cups that lifted her breasts Lola stood there and slowly slid her hand down from her breasts to her waist and under the hip strands beneath the red pouch.

'You look hot too honey and you're still not saying much. Thought you wanted to see me Henri. Well see me and talk to me Gloria said. Well you're seeing me but you aren't saying much Henri. Perhaps I'll have to make you talk.' Leaning over Henri she unzipped his pants and suddenly he was naked to the waist. Without any warning the whip cracked on his thigh and he tried to leap off the bed. A second time Lola snapped the ends and Henri's other thigh turned red with the impact. She slowly drew her fingers from his knee up over the reddened thigh and then did the same on the other thigh. Henri's body arched and his feet kicked.

'More rope Henri? Shall I tie up the ankles or do you want to thrash about? Exciting to see you writhe Henri,' and Lola drew the pliant whip down the length of Henri's body.

'Jesus,' cried Henri.

'No darling, just Lola, and we can't do miracles love so what did you want to talk about. By the way, the person you were with Henri. Gloria wasn't sure whether she was my type or her type. Was he a she Henri or was she a he? Personally darling I prefer "shes" as they last longer and you my love seem to have collapsed. Perhaps now you've found your tongue, or would you like me to find your tongue?' Lola stood astride Henri and started to lower herself onto him.

'No, no Lola. No, I've found my tongue.'

'And just when I was hoping I might have to find it for you,' she said stepping aside to drape her whip over Henri again. 'You know bull fighting Henri? Early on in the process, after the matador has teased the bull a little, the banderilleros place darts into the bull to stimulate it. Makes it a little wilder and more fun for the matador. Shall I get my darts Henri? Then of course there is also the picador but that is too brutal for you my love. That gets rough and is only for the strongest clients and you my strong silent man have unfortunately limped out.' Lola pulled a little chair up alongside Henri and sat astride it. She waved her whip about languidly and softly said, 'Speak Henri.'

Henri's mind was a whirl of sights, reactions, chemicals and he struggled for thought. Crack, crack the whip leapt into life and once again red marks bloomed on Henri's body. 'Speak Henri.'

'Girls Lola,' and here Henri paused as he tried to get his thoughts in order.

'Very informative Henri,' and Lola waved the whip about.

'No, no Lola. Girls, foreign girls.' He paused. 'Illegal girls.'

'I'm not exotic enough for you Henri? Want me to have slit eyes, colour my skin, speak in Hindi? Want me to use live snakes instead of my little whip? Perhaps there should be two of me, or even more, a whole fucking troop?'

'No, no,' said Henri again. 'You're wonderful, fantastic. Your whip is ......'

'Is what Henri?' and Lola cracked the whip fiercely across the room.

'I want to meet illegal girls and talk with them,' gushed Henri all in one non-stop slew of words. 'Leslie and I want to meet them. Buzz too.'

'Jesus Henri. You want this non-stop foreign girl orgy for you and your two friends and you're asking me? You're asking Lola to pimp for you? You want to offer me a finder's fee or something Henri? And how are you going to talk with these foreign girls Henri? You haven't said a lot to me love and I speak your language. I don't believe you just want to talk Henri. I think you and your friends are into some kinky orgy and the talking is a smoke-screen. Think they'll teach you something new Henri? Your friends got any more stamina than you Henri 'cos any more than one foreign girl is likely be a waste of space if they're both like you. That's why I prefer women Henri and you never said whether your friends were men or women did you? Leslie and Buzz weren't they – well that could mean anything I suppose?'

There was a silence in the room while Lola drew a breath.

'Gone quiet again Henri.' The whip came back into action and Lola leapt up astride Henri again. 'Do I need to find your tongue Henri?' and Lola slowly bent her knees and slid the slender handle of the whip under the strings on her cache-sex and started to move it downwards.

'Leslie's a reporter,' blurted out Henri as he tried to wriggle his head away from Lola's threatening crotch.

'And Buzz?' Lola stayed crouched over Henri and swayed above him to keep his attention.

'Photographer.'

Lola lowered herself all the way to sit on Henri's heaving chest and looked at his strained face.

'And they sent you to be the messenger?'

Henri nodded keeping his eyes jumping from Lola's face to her crotch on his chest.

'So this Leslie and Buzz, both guys you say must be gay.'

'No, not really.'

'Not guys Henri? Not guys and they send you to talk to me? Well, eventually you talked.'

'Yes Lola. Yes I mean they're both guys, Leslie and Buzz.'

'What girls Henri? You said foreign girls. There's no foreign girls at the Oasis. Why you really here Henri? Do I need my whip again, or shall I just…..?' and Lola eased herself higher up Henri's chest.

'Gloria had mentioned two Clubs. She told someone about two Clubs. We heard she had worked at two Clubs. Someone said there were foreign girls at the other Club. We didn't know where and I was to find out. Leslie told me to talk with you. He'd heard you prefer women and Leslie thought I was the best one to talk with you.'

'Because Henri you don't know whether you're coming or going do you darling? Sounds like Leslie and Buzz are the even stronger silent male types who like to do what I do – dominate. You're the most fucked up one aren't you Henri? Next time darling we'll change the routine a little for you. Although I prefer women I can dominate men who want to be women too Henri.'

'Where are these foreign girls Lola?'

'Now that's going to cost you Henri. Not to find them darling 'cos that's easy but if you want to talk to them then that will cost. They have some very strong and very mean friends Henri. Friends who don't want their little girls talking to anyone Henri. Those girls aren't for talking Henri. The strong friends make sure the little girls' mouths are used for other things. Are you sure, or are your friends really sure they want to go down this road? Not only is it expensive but it is a rough road Henri, and you might be a strong silent climber my love but I'm not sure about rough roads,' and Lola drew her whip down across Henri's body again. He tensed, awaiting the crack but Lola simply leant over and gently kissed him.

'Tell your friends to go and carefully visit the Exotica. Carefully mind you. I'll make some inquiries and find a possible way in. Don't you go looking for yourselves or you'll queer the whole pitch.' Lola laughed. 'Can queers queer a pitch?' she asked. 'Now my sweet I'll untie you, let you find your clothes and you can pay me for my attention. As Gloria suggested you saw me and talked to me and you talk so well Henri.' Lola laughed and watched Henri struggle into his pants and button up his shirt. 'Your wallet's still safely in your jacket darling and you just need to lighten it a little and I'll see you later. Give me a week. No, better make it two as I've got to be more than a little careful. Hasta luego mi amigo.'

REMEMBER CAROL HENRI?

HENRI FOUND HIS WAY BACK to Leslie who was scribbling at the table.

'Where's Buzz?'

'I'm here Henri. Where've you been?'

'Christ, that Lola is something else. Where did you find out about her Leslie? I know she was down at Fotheringham with Gloria but how do you know her?'

'I was in here a month or so ago and I was talking with a couple of wankers from down in those parts. You know, down where your family home is at Fotheringham. Anyway, one of the blokes was full of himself and he knew Lola. Knew Gloria too and I found out he knew most of the girls here. Well, we got him talking and I just listened. Christ he was full of knowing all the girls. Was all set to describe in intimate detail what he had done down in your forest Henri. Did you know the half of what went on down there? Still, through him I learnt about the various girls here. I guessed that the best contact would be Lola.'

'What did this bloke say?'

'Turns out he was the dad of the young kid who got charged with murder down there. Then he tried to tell me he was Gloria's dad too. Some people do run away with their mouths, and their imagination too.

Anyway, from his son he had learnt something from Gloria. Seems this lad was banging Gloria and the bloke thought it was priceless, 'cos she was his half-sister, or so this bloke said.'

'What's that got to do with Lola?'

'This Gloria had told Gary, yes that was the son's name, that Gloria had worked up here at the Oasis with Lola, with the dancer here called Sheena and another couple of birds. When they were working up here a couple of years ago Gloria had also worked at this Exotica Club and young Gary had told his dad some of the stories.'

'And Lola?'

'She worked there too for a while but she left when Gloria went down to Somerset.'

'So why didn't you just ask me to talk with Gloria?'

'She had some fright over at the Exotica Henri. No way was she going to give us an entry there love. But Lola, now there's a girl who's been around. Tough, isn't she Henri? I heard she was tough,' and Leslie laughed. 'You've come back in one piece though. What have you learnt then my little precious love?' and Leslie leant over the table and stroked Henri's cheek. 'What did Lola tell you with that whip of hers?'

'Come back in a couple of weeks Leslie.'

'Couple of weeks? Shit, that's nearly Christmas. Why so long?'

'Said it would cost too,' added Henri.

'But she can fix it?'

A week passed and Buzz was getting increasingly frustrated. Two or three times he had a tip off about some celebrity coming into town and they had turned up zilch. The telephone call came one evening when all three of them were in. Henri had answered it and he came back into the sitting room with a puzzled look on his face and explained who had been on the telephone.

'So should we go or not?'

Sylvia Lord had phoned with an invitation for a large family get together on Christmas Day. As it was family and spouses, friends, lovers whatever Sylvia had said, and would Henri bring Leslie?

'But not Buzz?'

'I don't think Sylvia knows about Buzz.'

'Fine then Henri but two things. Maybe there are two reasons for going. Knowing your family this will be another beating of the chest, rouse the family, wave the flag and decide where we're all going, and that might lead to money my love. One way or another you need to get your share of the Lord family millions.'

'They don't have millions Leslie.'

'Irrelevant Henri. They have something of yours if you play your cards right.'

'You said two things Leslie,' added Buzz.

'And the second involves you Buzz, so you're going too, but we'll keep you in the shadows. If the Lord family and the rest of that dozy lot down there don't know about you then we'll have you down there incognito. You can stay at the pub there as some tourist or travel book writer.'

'Why Leslie? Why is Buzz going?'

'Henri, what else was going on down at Fotheringham this past year?'

'Several things Leslie. Samantha got married and so did Daniel.'

'Bugger the family Henri. What happened in the forest? What was newsworthy? What would people like to read about, gloat over, get steamed up about, pissed off, you know? What do the proles like to imagine? Jesus Henri, what sells?'

'Dirt Leslie. Sex, drugs, perversion, hypocrisy and the toppling of the high and mighty. Words and photos of people doing things they shouldn't, and us suggesting things they might have done but shouldn't,' suggested Buzz.

'Buzz, what are you and Leslie talking about?' asked Henri looking at the pair of them. 'There's none of that at Fotheringham.'

'Apart from the murder you seem to have forgotten Henri there is that new innovative and much praised Education Centre.'

'There was no murder. They never found any body.'

'Still got a conviction though. Never mind all that it's the Education Centre that I'm talking about. Well it's really the lovely heaven-sent reverend I'm talking about. Remember we went looking last month. You got all pissed off about it being a waste of time. Well, my little bird down there tells me otherwise. Perhaps we can make him our Christmas present; our Christmas present to the masses. The out-spoken Reverend Gabriel Godschild touting his horn is why we're going to Fotheringham for Christmas Henri. Have you heard what he says? No matter, we can put some appropriate words in his holy horn but it is where he is preaching that is so beautiful. The dedicated green environmental back to nature Lord family is promoting one of God's chosen to teach the kiddies all about instant people to spread the word. No evolution, just instant, Biblical, in six days creation and us humans are the only ones worth saving. You've even got that aunt of yours Henri, Stephanie isn't it, who right next door is breeding animals to improve them? But back to the reverend for a moment 'cos there is more to the good Godschild than meets the eye. I've been doing a little digging. Our blessed reverend is a Mr. Alan Briggs in disguise. Chasing through old newspaper files I found he has carried his message around to several places, posing as several different people too. Some places he was sufficiently successful to entice part of his flock into private worship with sacrifices. After the so-called murder trial down there I found a useful contact who I use for information now and then. Rumour is our reverend is using two parts of the forest and it is the one away from the Education Centre that interests me most. You know, the place in the forest we were looking at earlier. Apparently you were right Henri, and it is that area around the cottage that is sacred. So my love, maybe we can get your precious relatives to give us a free dinner, pay you some dues and ultimately provide us with a Christmas story. Phone back and tell them we'll be delighted.'

'Sylvia said no presents,' added Henri lamely. He was still trying to take in all the various parts Leslie had outlined.

'Don't you worry Henri. We'll bring presents. We'll bring Buzz and he'll produce a photo collection that'll put Fotheringham on the map for your family. Make you feel any better Buzz? You said you were getting a little pissed off earlier. Why don't we celebrate? Let's get legless, snort something worthwhile and all end up in the big bed?'

The arrangement of the household at Leslie's flat was a little bizarre and Henri never knew whether it was good or bad. He was devoted to Leslie, and depended on him more and more now, but the living arrangements were strange. Buzz had been living on and off with Leslie before Henri arrived on the scene but he wasn't living *with* Leslie. He had his own flat off the edge of Fleet Street. Leslie's flat was in the Barbican Centre and it contained a large master suite with an enormous bed. It also had four TV screens stationed around the room with bedside controls. There were two other smaller bedrooms and when Henri married Leslie he assumed he would move into the master bedroom but Leslie had other arrangements.

'This is your room Henri. I work all hours. I don't want my work to disturb you. When the mood takes us we've got the big bed. The other bedroom is for guests.'

And the other bedroom had become Buzz's. Six months after Henri moved in Leslie moved Buzz in too and that started, or maybe continued a revolving series of who was sleeping where with whom. At times it culminated in a *ménage a trois* in the big bed and other times all three slept alone.

The three of them all sleeping together always left Henri feeling exhausted: and truly shagged out if truth be told. Over the years Henri's ambivalence about sex had changed from being the dominant homosexual male, through being the dominant heterosexual male to being the compliant male. Lying in his own bed the next night Henri tried to think back how this had happened because when he was living down in Bath he was in charge.

After Justin left Henri remembered going through a bad phase. He increased his use of drugs and that cost money. As he got to know the software at work he managed to steer some funds his way but Henri knew Rory was no fool. The only good things about that time thought Henri were his times with Alice. Putting one over Sandy was a bonus and Alice turned out to be a good "cup of coffee" for a while. After that initial virginal shock Henri shared some definitely non-conventional sexual adventures with Alice. However, after Alice had tried it in every room in the house, over every piece of expensive furniture and in every position she knew about, her demands for gifts, treats, and other attention wearied on Henri. The novelty drained away as did the money. Henri recalled he started to look for alternatives. As usual, at perhaps just the right time, it was sister Giselle who came to save him from himself.

'Henri I've found someone to help.'

'I don't need help Giselle. I need a friend.'

'Brother dear you need a lot of things and I've managed to find several of them for you all wrapped up in one bundle. Look, I'll come over on Saturday and show you. You're not going climbing are you?'

'Yes Giselle I am, for the whole weekend as it happens. What's so special anyway?'

'So right now then Henri? I can be over in an hour. Why not right now?'

'Okay, okay if you must. That'll give me time to tidy up a little. I've had a bad day at the office so don't be too cheerful.'

'I promise to be quiet Henri but I'll bet my package will buck up your spirits.'

Henri hung up the phone and made a serious attempt to clean up a little. He had planned to empty a bottle of wine and stare at the TV and see whether that offered any suggestions on making money. Normally neat and tidy it didn't take Henri long to make the flat appealing. He was house proud. Showering he started to feel there was hope and he took a little longer than expected to dress in something casual yet elegant. Looking in the mirror he grinned at himself. This might shock my sister he thought.

'Henri, this is Paulo, Paulo Zanetti. Paulo this is my brother Henri I told you about.'

'Henri, pleased to meet you,' and Paulo extended a slender hand. Henri took the hand in his and shook it. Holding it just a little longer he turned it over and looked at it.

'Not a climber then Paulo? Not a son of the Dolomites?'

Paulo looked puzzled. Giselle put her arm around Paulo's shoulders and said, 'My brother is a mountaineer Paulo, and the only thing he knows about Italy is climbing, but you can teach him there are other facets to Italian life.' Giselle turned back to look at her brother. 'Henri, can we all sit down because there are some things I want to explain?'

And so it came to pass that Paulo, an Italian student over to study at Bristol Uni and work part-time at the same office as Giselle, became Henri's flat mate. This helped pay the rent, helped Henri learn more about Italy and kept Henri from feeling lonely in bed. As his sister had said, it helped in a lot of ways. Suddenly Henri felt his life had been turned round again. He was enthusiastic and successful at work. His climbing improved and the drug dependency diminished. His sister had worked wonders but in 1988 several things became unravelled again.

First, Paulo graduated and despite pleas from Henri and even tentative suggestions from Giselle, Paulo returned to Italy. About the same time cousin Geoffrey married an Italian lady and Henri went down to Fotheringham for the wedding.

'Uncle, Anthony, this is all delightful, and you and Auntie Sylvia must be very happy.'

'You should be next Henri you know. What are you now, twenty seven isn't it? Marcel has been married a long time now and Michael always has girls around.'

'Not sure it's my thing Anthony. It's the usual problem and you've been through it. Where does one meet a nice girl?'

'Well I met Sylvia climbing Henri. Is there nobody in your Club who excites you? What about at work? I'd even suggest your sister's office parties but government people aren't usually very lively. Probably all that tea they drink, or is it sherry and biscuits at the management level? Never was quite sure with those people. Still, must be someone who climbs Henri? That would suit you too – something to do together in your golden years.'

'Anthony, I hope you're not inferring I couldn't keep up with you in our youth, or even now for that matter. Golden years indeed,' snorted Sylvia. 'Henri it's good to see you down here. We don't see enough of you and Stephanie has been telling me you don't get out enough. Your sister was really worried for a while but she found Paulo didn't she? She jokes about how much Italian you've learnt. Said you can even read the guidebook now for some of your routes. Have you met Christina's parents? Lovely people. Come, I'll introduce you. Perhaps Christina has a cousin or something.'

But Christina had no cousin and Henri drifted around at the wedding and the reception afterwards feeling at a loss. With his sister Henri drove back to Bristol and during the drive Giselle urged him to take stock and perhaps make a new start somewhere.

'Brother you're drifting, and that's not like you. You're good at what you do. Paulo told me you're proud of your achievements and your boss thinks highly of you. Why don't you suggest expanding your company? Why not a new office somewhere? You keep saying that Bath is boring. In your business, and now with your improved language skills, why not suggest an office on the Continent? That would offer you some easier access to the mountains too Henri. Come on brother – expand your horizons. I'm not saying be like Marcel with gallivanting all over the world but at least look further than Bath. Be like mum and dad - be bold, adventurous.'

Henri looked at his sister as he sped up the Motorway. 'You don't even remember mum and dad,' he said. 'You were younger than I was and I hardly remember them.'

'Henri I'm not saying do what they did. I'm not saying be exactly like they were. Stephanie was telling me this past weekend a little bit more about them. It just came up in conversation but she thought you had their drive. She thought you needed a push in the right direction and your hidden self would come through. She also thinks you're quite like dad but much more in control.'

'So you two have been talking about me?' cried Henri as he gripped the steering wheel somewhat tighter.

'Henri we both love you,' said Giselle quietly as she looked at her brother. 'We both feel you are stifling yourself. Somehow you need to be free. Like shedding your skin and being a new you. A rebirth or something Henri.'

'That sounds more like a genetic breeding experiment of Stephanie's,' Henri said.

Giselle softly laughed and reached out to lightly touch her brother's arm. 'No Henri. We love you the way you are. We just want you to be yourself and be happy.'

Henri never knew whether any of the family ever said anything: whether any of his aunts or uncles spoke with Highland Investments but within a week he was summoned into Malcolm's office. Rory was there too, as was Robert Knox, and it was the old man who sat in the principal chair and did the talking. Listening to Mr. Knox Henri realised that his adventures with Alice had led to Sandy being creative with client's money again. This time however, Rory MacDonald was very aware of what went on inside little black boxes and the three senior partners knew that Henri wasn't the creator of the scam. However, the three Scots were interested in knowing why this had happened. Henri looked at each of them in turn and made a decision.

'It's because I'm gay,' he said very quietly. 'Sandy must have found out that I'm gay. I've never made it a secret but then I've kept my private life private,' and he looked at Mr. Knox and not at Rory as he spoke. 'Listening to Sandy I think he finds this wrong, a sort of abomination. When he told me this I suppose I was a little more tight-lipped about myself but he must have found out somehow and he tried to finger me.'

Henri looked straight at Robert Knox. 'You may remember Mr. Knox something like this happened four or five years ago? Before Malcolm and Rory came down from Scotland and you and Mr. MacKenzie sorted it all out.'

'Aye lad, I remember it well but this time we're thinking of doing something different.' Robert Knox paused and looked at the MacDonald brothers. The three faces told Henri nothing. The silence lengthened and Henri wondered what was coming next. Last time had been a bollocking and a bonus but this seemed different. He bit his tongue and his mind raced over the previous week's activities. He dared a glance at Rory who he knew was gay and who might be on his side but Rory kept a deadpan face. It was Malcolm who spoke.

'Henri, we're impressed with your investing skills and your feel for the opportunities. You seem to have some intuition about futures, and when you decide on something you move quickly and decisively. I suppose you do much the same thing when doing this climbing thing. Sort of mixture of "Look before you leap" and 'Nothing ventured, nothing gained". Positive action after speedy analysis.'

Henri kept quiet and a silence lengthened. No question had been asked. No opinion sought. No commitment stated.

'But we like McNeil too,' blurted out Robert Knox. Henri stirred in his chair and thought about the straight-laced Calvinistic background of Robert Knox, who probably didn't know the word "gay". They were going to fire him this time, after giving him a glowing reference. They were going to keep McNeil and fire him. Not just a bollocking but the boot. Henri quietly gritted his teeth and tried to keep a neutral face as he looked back at the old man.

'How would you like to move into the big times Henri?' asked Malcolm. Henri shifted his gaze from Knox to Malcolm and realised the face was friendly and the question serious.

'Big time?'

'Henri this company is too small for infighting. We need everyone thinking and working positively at the top level. For the benefit of the company, and I might add for the benefit of our personnel, we would like to offer you a new position.'

Henri's mind raced. What was Malcolm offering? 'I'm not sure I understand,' he managed to say, and again he looked at each of the three faces across the desk. Old man Knox appeared to have gone to sleep, or at least faded from the meeting. This isn't his say thought Henri so what do the MacDonalds have in mind? I've got some hope with those two Henri realised.

Thinking back that had been a big day Henri remembered. It hadn't seemed so at the time but it had been a turning point in several ways. Rory MacDonald had phoned him that evening and explained some more of the details that had not been said at the meeting. Told him things about Robert Knox and the old man's sexual past. Told him things about the understanding between him and his own brother. Told him things about his brother's opinion of Henri's expertise. Both Macdonald brothers thought Henri would do well in London. Was there ever any new scam with Sandy Henri wondered? Did Alice ever say anything to her husband? Henri never did find out exactly how he ended up with an excellent job as a senior investment counsellor for one of the more successful finance companies in the city. And with the move to the city and Henri's rebirthing came Carol.

Henri stirred restlessly in his bed and remembered Carol Matlock. Moving to London had been like shedding a skin as his sister suggested. There were new work challenges, and benefits, plus joining a new climbing club and that led to Carol. Henri's reputation as a leading mountaineer was well known in British climbing circles and so there were several people eager to climb with him. When she learnt about his Lord family background, his position and earning power in the City, as well as his climbing prowess, Carol Matlock decided Henri would make a good catch – well at least worth a trial run to see whether he really was as good as he seemed. Carol herself came from a landed gentry family in rural Hampshire, but she had escaped the hunt and hounds country set to study at Oxford in art and design. At one time she thought of going into the fine arts auction field but decided after a couple of years there was more money in interior design for yuppies, and Carol was really more interested in spending money, other people's money, than cultivating her knowledge of fine arts. There were an increasing number of young people with money recently acquired through computer skills and e-business and these young people had little understanding of saving and constraints. They just wanted to spend and outdo their friends, and Carol was quite happy to help them spend on revolutionary artistic furnishings and fittings. The commissions came in useful too.

And could she help you spend remembered Henri. Still, then again, she could climb, she could party and she could...... Henri rolled over in his bed and thought back on those first two years in London. They were two wild and frenetic years when he had been in charge of his own destiny, well so he thought. He had had clear thoughts that he was male, in charge, the leader and with a simple goal of making money as fast as he could. Carol had helped him learn about the good things in life in London with meeting the right people and building up a network of clients wanting to invest as well as spend. Although he didn't get the chance to climb as much as before Henri still managed to go out with Carol every second or third weekend and she could climb. They did some of the really top routes in England and Wales and would come home from such weekends for a night of pent-up passion before the challenges of Monday mornings. It was life in the fast lane and Henri loved it.

After the first six months Carol privately decided that Henri was a useful asset for her future plans and so she married him. That way what he had was hers. Henri thought it was all his doing of course and he happily showed off his new wife to all the family. For a year things progressed really well until that rather fateful year of 1990. This was an unsettling and then traumatic year for the Lord family and once again Henri's mind became confused. He was accused of causing some of the trauma. The first serious event had happened in April. Michael had taken Marcel's elder son Jean sailing on the East coast. Looking after his own interests Michael had terrified Jean and somehow the youngster had capsized and drowned. Marcel flew home from Australia but Marie was inconsolable. She berated Marcel for sailing. She berated Henri because he had bullied the two boys and driven them to Michael. All in all it was a very upsetting time. Then two months later Geoffrey Lord, Henri's cousin was killed while climbing with brothers Michael and Daniel. This inevitably led to a bitter discussion within the family about inheritance but Uncle Anthony was adamant. Geoffrey had a one-year old son Peter and it was Peter who became the new Lord family heir. Adding to the unease there were two further deaths in Fotheringham's forest later that year and the family discussions over death always unsettled Henri with his memories of David, of Darnley, of Lucien. Despite Carol's good job and her numerous assignments she seemed to find a way to spend money faster than it came in. Once again Henri was short of cash and when he got stressed this way he resorted to drugs to temporarily obliterate the problem. During the winter of 1990 several things came to a head and Henri found the ground shifting under his feet again. Cousin Michael had his twenty-first birthday and he looked likely to marry into American money in the following year. However, Michael had successfully pissed of so many people over the past year that someone decided Michael didn't deserve to live any longer and he was shot in January on the Fotheringham Estate. This really shook Henri and he started to come apart in wild mood swings. The partying with Carol became more frenzied, accentuated with more drugs. Springtime brought new climbing exploits and Henri started to push his limits. Eventually Carol couldn't keep up with the extremes. Henri had started to frighten her and she resorted to find her own way of life. As Henri started to get hints about a separation he in turn tried to take Carol to new heights with the wild life in London. The drug bill mounted up. Henri tried to recoup some of his expenses and took his glamorous wife to gambolling clubs. Inevitably Henri dipped into client's money until late in 1991 Carol decided that Henri was no longer an asset but becoming a bloody dangerous liability. Tossing uncomfortably in his bed Henri remembered that fateful September – the month when his world came apart. Well it would have done if it hadn't been for his sister. Giselle had heard that Carol had walked out and when she couldn't contact Henri in London she decided to come and find him.

Henri had refused to answer the pounding on his door. He hadn't bothered with the telephone for a week. A fellow employee from the office had got no response when he tried to call but Giselle wasn't giving up on her brother. She had gone to the manager of the apartment block and demanded access. My brother might be dead she had said. Giselle said several other things as well and eventually the manager decided it was easier to comply and perhaps the lady would go away. He unlocked the door and a waft of unhealthy air drifted out into the corridor. Inside it was dark with blinds drawn and doors shut. There was no noise.

'After you Miss,' the manager said as he stepped aside. Giselle walked in somewhat cautiously and called out softly, 'Henri, Henri you there?' She turned to the manager standing hesitantly in the hall. 'That will be all thank you Mr. Ralston. If there is anything amiss I will contact you.' Giselle firmly and conclusively shut the apartment door leaving the manager standing in the hall. Turning back into the apartment Giselle turned on the lights to find her way about until she could open the blinds and let the sunlight stream into the smelly rooms. She stood in the centre of the main living room and slowly looked about her. Henri, what have you done she whispered to herself. Right Giselle, get a grip girl as this is your brother and he needs your help. Best foot forward and let's see what the silly bugger has done now.

It was later, much later that Giselle and Henri sat down to talk.

'I tried to over-dose Giselle but I couldn't even do that properly,' sobbed Henri. 'I was a mixture of fear, of helplessness, of frustration, and most of all of uncertainty. I didn't know whether I wanted to live 'cos what's the point? I thought I had put it all behind me with Carol. For once in my life I had got it right. Remember in Bath, a couple of years back, you had told me to make a new start? You told me to shed my skin and be a new me. Be forceful you said. Remember all that?'

'Yes Henri. Yes, and you did all of that and you were successful.'

'But last year messed it all up again what with Jean, Geoffrey and then Michael. It was too much like my friends. Too much like mum and dad all over again and I got lost.'

'Henri you are not lost. You've got a successful job, and from all accounts you have an excellent reputation. Through my own job I have contacts in the city and I hear good things so that is a winner Henri. Think positive. Now what about the climbing? That has always been a strong and powerful incentive for you – something to put you in charge.'

Henri sat back on his sofa and looked at his sister. He shuddered and remembered back over the last few times he had been out on the cliffs. Giselle noticed the motion and the expression. She raised her eyebrows.

'I have been rather pushing it,' said Henri. 'I suppose I got caught up with being with Carol and wanting to show her how good I was. Then there were times when I just felt invincible and it didn't much matter what happened. I just felt I had to really push and show myself that I was good, as good as mum and dad. I could hear mum telling me to be strong and powerful. I suppose I had to live up to her expectations.'

Giselle wasn't sure what to say as she had never been a climber and didn't really remember their parents in this way. Her brother just had some severe hang-up about his mother if truth be told. She decided to leave that as there was nothing positive she could think of saying so she asked, 'Drugs Henri? Drugs, gambolling, partying? I know Carol earned good money so what caused the break-up?'

'You don't want to know Giselle, really you don't.'

'Henri I'm here to help. I had to virtually break down the door to get in here and I'm not leaving until you're back fully functioning – well, I'll settle for back to work and back to living I suppose. Look, part of what I do touches a little on your lifestyle and I know it can be a downward spiral so let's make sure it isn't. Can we?'

'What do you do Giselle?'

'Nothing that would interest you brother so let's concentrate on you can we? Do you have any addictive habits? Did you need professional rehab?'

Henri slowly shook his head and looked at his sister. 'Not really. Much of it is for show I suppose. Sure it's nice to get high and see the world in a colourful way but I can do that with a good rock climb if I think about it. I suppose I use drugs to fit in, be part of the group, even be the leader on occasions.'

'But nothing you can't kick?'

'No.'

'So why did Carol leave? I thought she was a party animal. She certainly created that impression. Was it the climbing? When you started to do the hard things she couldn't get up and that frustrated you both?'

Henri laughed. Giselle looked at him. 'What did I say?' Henri laughed again and fell over sideways on the sofa in a fit of giggles. 'Henri, what did I say?' Giselle asked again. Pulling himself together Henri sat back up straight on the sofa and looked back at his sister.

'Sorry,' he said, 'poor joke.'

'What is?'

'Play on words,' said Henri. Giselle sat back in her chair and patiently looked at Henri. Eventually her brother would explain. He so much depended on other people. It seemed to frighten him to be the leader. On rock climbs maybe, but in life in general Henri couldn't stay the leader for very long. He was a follower. A supportive and quite dependable follower but he needed someone to show him the way. What had frustrated Carol wondered Giselle? Where had Henri failed to lead? Had her brother got lost again in his sexual orientation? Henri had inferred on several occasions early in the relationship that he and Carol were dynamite – almost bragging about it. Had the relationship reversed, or even collapsed? Giselle looking at her brother and she could see Henri think over what if anything he was going to say.

'Play on words Henri? I'm not sure I understand.'

'The aggressive inch stopped being aggressive,' said Henri.

'Henri what are you talking about?'

'I wasn't the hard man I used to be.'

'Henri I don't climb so that doesn't mean anything to me either.'

'I prefer men,' said Henri bluntly.

'I know,' said Giselle, 'and I do understand Henri. So was life with Carol all talk? No, don't answer that. I don't need to know. But, now that "female problem" is no longer with you what is to stop you getting yourself back into the land of the living?'

While Henri sat quiet thinking over his answer Giselle also wondered in her own mind whether there was something else, and with Henri that usually meant money. She didn't intend to ask about money because that was something where Henri easily got lost. She also thought that with his job and prospects that shouldn't be an issue. That was one subject that she and Aunt Stephanie had discussed where they thought Henri had every opportunity to look after himself. He was in the business for heaven's sake.

And Giselle had got him back into the land of the living Henri remembered. She made sure he cleaned up the flat and then she stayed until he was back on his feet at work. They had gone out to dinner and met a few of his friends. She brought me back into a new future again Henri remembered and for a while things had been good. Peering up at his ceiling Henri realised that once again his sister had set him back on the right road 'cos that had led to Leslie and that was so good.

After Giselle left, Henri had once again looked forwards and put his mind to work. As Giselle had said Henri had a good reputation and a successful job. Concentrating on his life-long ambition to make money he slowly shed Carol, shed the drug dependency and brought some sanity to his mountaineering. It was his success in the investment business that brought Leslie into his life. At this time Leslie Dauphin was a very well educated and equally well connected journalist. Having studied literature at Oxford Leslie was very skilled in the use of words but somewhere life had decided to warp young Leslie to be vindictive and spiteful. Over the years Henri never discovered what were the circumstances or the explicit cause of this attitude but every now and again Leslie's "pen" became quite vitriolic. They had met at a conference in London that was focussed on investment opportunities in Eastern Europe. Under Gorbachev the policy of glasnost, or more open consultative government had led to the restructuring of perestroika and the ultimate collapse of the old Soviet Union. The lessoning of central control and government restructuring allowed money people from Western Europe to look more openly at opportunities in the old Soviet Block. Henri had developed a nose for people who wanted to move money and assets from hidden accounts through into the more open and legal world of the west. Perhaps a subtitle for the conference could have been red money laundering thought Henri, 'cos much of the emphasis was on moving assets from the east rather than investing western money in the east, but one couldn't say that in public now could one? However, Leslie Dauphin had no such scruples, and he was interviewing people to find the right words and thoughts to support his contention. Having interviewed a few older money men, most of them Europeans from places like Vienna and Budapest, who had developed monetary skills and expertise in WWII, Leslie decided to listen to a few of the younger rising stars, and that included Henri Lord.

'Mr Lord, Mr. Henri Lord isn't it? Do you have a moment? I'm Leslie Dauphin and I've heard you are the one person here that I really should meet. I'm a financial journalist, free-lance but I write for several papers including some European ones. I really am pleased to meet you.'

Henri looked at the slender young woman who stood in front of him holding out her hand. She was Henri's height and he looked into grey, hazel-flecked eyes that seemed to sparkle at him above a curved and lightly lipsticked pair of soft lips. The lady had short, neatly coiffured blond hair and very sensuous ears Henri noticed with diamond pin studs. But the voice, it was the enticing voice that really caught his attention and that seemed to offer warmth and friendship.

'Mr. Lord?'

Henri started and rather clumsily grasped at the proffered hand. 'Miss Dauphin,' he stuttered. 'Yes, I'm Henri Lord. Pleased to meet you. A journalist you say?'

'How about a quiet drink in the bar Mr. Lord, or can I call you Henri? Seems so much easier don't you think? So much more human and intimate.'

And that was the first meeting Henri remembered, with Leslie the journalist, dressed as a lady, and that voice drawing words of wisdom out of the mouths of unsuspecting money men. Later, when they met again, Leslie explained that he/she dressed and appeared as male or female as the circumstances dictated. With a bunch of predominantly male bankers one could learn a lot more when appearing as an intelligent, attractive but definitely non-threatening female. Most men tended to relax more in female company and words came easily. Sometimes they were words of wisdom and sometimes words of confessions: occasionally of tricks played and schemes implemented. Leslie's sensuous ears gathered in all these words and his/her literary skills re-assembled these words into sharp biting prose to incite the general public to read on and look forward to the next revelation of conspiracy and culpability.

Giselle's dedication to getting her brother back on the road to recovery had been successful, and for a while Henri did concentrate on the positive things in life, but inevitably the loss of Carol, or more truthfully the loss of a partner, started to make itself felt. When he believed he knew who he was Henri inevitably started going back to the Club life of London. His friends, his climbing friends, his office friends all gradually enticed Henri back into the bright lights, deep shadows, soft voices and strident cries of the Club scene, but to start with Henri wasn't quite sure which was his scene. But then he bumped into Leslie again and it was "love at first sight" – although one should really call it second sight as Leslie was now a he and not a she.

'Henri, Henri Lord! Well fancy that. I always wondered that first time we met you know, but people told me you were a hard mountaineer or something, as well as a whiz kid with the money numbers. And now look at you. Is this really your scene? I must say you do look rather gorgeous. Doesn't he look gorgeous Tank?'

Standing nearly seven feet tall, and carrying close to one hundred and fifty kilos, Tank peered at Henri and raised his club-like hand. Henri stepped back a pace, a stride even.

'No Henri, Tank just wants to stroke you. He's quite passive for a tank, and he has the most sensitive hands my friend. A stroking from Tank is an absolute delight – a sensation to send you over the moon my friend.'

'You're Leslie Dauphin?' Henri managed to say. 'But you're…..'

Leslie laughed and lifted Tank's hand to stroke Henri's cheek. 'Henri I find I can be more successful dressing for the occasion as they say. But tonight is a relaxing occasion, and here I am dressed as you see me. But you, what about you Henri? You never did answer whether this is the real you? How come you're not clad in lederhosen or some such climbing apparel, or do you separate your own life into distinct compartments? Do you dress for the occasion Henri?'

Henri found himself quite overcome. He was seeing Leslie Dauphin in a new light and it was blinding, dazzling, quite overwhelming. The slender body, the soft blond hair, those sensuous ears and the voice, oh the voice that had originally charmed him and now filled him with warm vibrations. He almost trembled at the sound of the voice.

'Henri, are you still in their love? Knock knock Henri. Is someone at home?' and Leslie gently held Henri's arm and steered him towards the bar. Tank trundled along with them and Leslie slid his other hand down the massive naked shaven torso. At the bar Leslie turned to Henri. 'Tank here is teetotal Henri and so I know what he will have but what is your tipple? Perhaps you prefer to swallow something with your drink?' and Leslie slid a small tin out of his pocket. 'Interest you in anything mind-bending Henri or does your number-crunching brain already have enough stimuli?'

Henri was tongue-tied. Throughout that entire evening, as the threesome stayed together, Henri felt he was walking in another world and he couldn't get the voice out of his head. The three of them went back to Leslie's flat in the city and the three of them all ended up in bed together. That was the beginning remembered Henri. That was how it started – that wonderful, loving and tremendously exciting relationship with the man I love. Leslie, you saved me from an empty life thought Henri. You brought me to life and Henri fell asleep in contentment.

The dream, the nightmare, the fight and the fist in the face woke Henri. He woke to find himself face down on the floor in his bedroom with one of his shoes squashed up against his bruised nose. Slowly he disentangled his legs and feet from the twisted bedclothes and gently felt his painful nose. Christ that hurt and Henri cast his mind back to the dream and why his nose hurt. Back earlier in the summer of this year when he'd gone looking for money, his money and people had said no. Dam and blast his stupid family. Why did he always seem to come out of those decisions in the wrong place? Henri lay back in his bed and thought about those events – those oh so frustrating events that led to the present crisis.

THE SUMMER OF '99

LIFE WITH LESLIE HAD PROGRESSED and for a while Henri enjoyed the mixture of making money, climbing mountains and making Leslie happy – or perhaps making himself happy with Leslie. However, family relationships reared their heads again and as usual Henri became stressed. In the summer of 1999 he had been invited to Oxford for Monday July twelfth when the entire Lord family had assembled to share in Katya Howard's graduation ceremony. He remembered he'd even met Katya and her parents down at the Fotheringham Education Centre when he had been down there with Leslie the week before. Leslie had wanted to find out some more about the Reverend Gabriel Godschild and they had gone down and stayed in the village as Henri hadn't wanted to meet up with all the family at the Manor House. Rather unfortunately Katya had been showing her parents the Education Centre when he was there with Leslie. Typically Leslie had made some sharp caustic remark and Henri had persuaded Leslie to move on. From talk at the village pub where they were staying Henri did find out about some other changes going on at Fotheringham.

'That Mister Daniel's right pissed off with them hikers so they say Mr. Lord.'

'Well George, seems my cousin is too wrapped up with looking after his own interests.'

George Doone, landlord of the George and Dragon laughed. 'He's more wrapped up with that Miss Katya Mr. Lord. He tries to tell me she's a forester and that's why he's always taking her into the woods.'

'And where's the good Reverend Godschild in the woods George?' asked Leslie. 'I know he preaches at the Memorial Centre but isn't he offering some other services in the forest?'

'Don't know about that Mr. Dauphin. If he does he'll probably bump into that new family that've come to work on the Estate. Foreigners they are. Down from Yorkshire. Pair of 'em sure talk funny I've heard. The fellow's a good mechanic though so they tell me. His wife is something else though. An earth mother I heard Mr. Daniel say, whatever that is. You're a man of words Mr. Dauphin so what's an earth mother?'

'Who are they George?' interrupted Henri.

'More relevant George is where are they? You know, this worthy worker and his earthy other half?' asked Leslie

'Heard her ladyship decided to get Gary Templeton and young Freddie Dunster to spruce up the cottage that used to belong to Enrico and Antonio. Enrico's living at Home Farm now you know, after that stupid Idwal Ferris vandalised his place. Anyway, now we've got these Entwhistles living there. The man, Colin, I think that's his name, is supposed to be a good all round worker but the wife's a bit different. Got a nipper but she won't send him to school. Insists she's going to teach him everything and he don't need no other schooling. Bit of a fuss she made about it too I hear.'

'So the reverend will go and convert this earth mother George?' asked Leslie.

'Blessed if I know sir. Another drink is it then gentlemen?'

'Not right now landlord. We've some other business to attend to. Come on Henri, we've work to do.' Leslie bundled Henri outside the pub and into his car.

'What now Leslie? You know I can't spend much more time down here. I'm supposed to be at work. You know work Leslie? Sitting in my office in the city and making money.'

'Henri, this is work my love. Well, it's my work and we've got to find another piece of information. Actually another source of information 'cos if George doesn't know what the good reverend is doing then I need to find someone who does.'

'And who's that?'

'A greedy little snout called Tom Daley Henri and he lives just along here if I remember right.'

Going to Katya's graduation didn't interest Henri and so he begged off but he did learn of the chain of events the following week at Fotheringham. It appeared that while Enrico's old cottage had been refurnished for the new Entwhistles someone had decided to use the other infamous cottage on the estate – the infamous ex-Ferris cottage. The rather memorable scene of rape, fraternal murder, bones of young lads and then the urn of the Ferris wife's ashes mixed with gold coins. Christ thought Henri, that cottage is the scene of never-ending wonders. Henri learnt that is was the girl working in the George, Gloria Manson who was moonlighting in the ex-Ferris cottage. Although he didn't learn all the details Henri understood that Gloria and some of her friends were using the cottage for parties, paying parties apparently, but Daniel put an end to that it seems. Not quite the right kind of green revenues for the Lord family Henri thought. And on top of all that the girls were associated with the disappearance of one of Daniel's workers. One Freddie Dunster suddenly vanishes off the face of the earth and his friend is arrested for murder but no body was ever found. Henri decided his life would be simpler and less stressful if he stayed in London and ignored the family for a while but that wasn't to be.

Although Henri didn't go to Oxford he felt he did have to go to the joint wedding of his two cousins. Once again Leslie tagged along as he still felt there was a story somewhere in the Lord family that would make good telling to the scandal-voracious public. Given the number of people invited to the wedding Anthony and Sylvia Lord decided to hold the reception in the local town where they used to have their Brainware company offices. The facility where Anthony used to hold the Brainware Annual Meeting every November was well equipped to handle the reception for such a large body of guests, and there was a large body of guests. Terence Field was a popular policeman and several colleagues wanted to wish him well as he gave up his freedom to the lovely and eccentric Samantha Lord. Several knowledgeable people shook their heads and wondered who would wear the pants but one wag pointed out that the likely outspoken head of that family would probably be young James MacRae. Especially for this occasion James had promised his mother to keep quiet and behave, but he was rather surprised and disappointed that he couldn't bring Dainty into the church. He had ridden Dainty beside the carriage that brought his mother to the church and thought his horse would like to come inside and watch. Terence sat inside the church with Daniel and both men waited. Even though he could imagine the possible antics of James Terence had a good professional ability to sit, wait and listen. He was content within himself and happy that Samantha had found an answer to her worrying question of future children. After the scary birth of James, along with her pelvic inflammatory disease, Terence knew that Samantha had been really concerned that she and he couldn't have children of their own, but now that had all been resolved and they would be really together he thought.

Terence looked across at Daniel sitting beside him. Wonder what he is thinking wondered Terence, but Daniel's mind was away in the forest with his bride to be wondering how to keep the estate moving with the times. Wondering how to keep the revenues coming in and yet keep them green. Sitting on the hard wooden pews Henri was also thinking about revenues but he wasn't too worried whether they were green, red or any colour really. There was more money to be discovered and moved into my investment opportunities mused Henri and I'm sitting here wasting my time.

'Leslie, I know it's a Saturday, but let's go back to London right after the reception. I'm wasting my time down here and there's work to be done in the city. I always find these family get-togethers so stressful.'

'Henri my impatient friend you need to pace yourself a little better. Surely you don't rush up these rock climbs or whatever that you do? Actually, you don't seem to have been doing that of late. Run out of partners or run out of challenges?'

'Leslie there's money to be made. In London. Not down here and not in the mountains. For the moment there's too much going on in the money world. And yes, I will be going climbing for a couple of weeks later in autumn but right now I need to make money and not moves on any rock climb.'

'Talking of making money Henri, and perhaps money that should rightfully be yours, who will manage the books on the Estate when your ever-diligent aunt retires? You were telling me that Anthony and Sylvia were retiring now that there are two young professional foresters managing the estate – namely cousin Daniel and his American dream-girl. They won't have much time anyway you were saying as both of them play golf or something. So, my monetary friend, who will manage the books? Samantha and her detective-playing hubbie are both going to be so busy looking after their professions that they won't be around. Daniel is out pounding golf balls and as a forester he probably has little or no knowledge of money. Do foresters have any knowledge of money management Henri? Can't believe it myself as their trees grow so bloody slowly. Perhaps their renting out of that Education Centre was a dying move to stave off bankruptcy. You should investigate you own family Henri and offer services to defer the inevitable end and re-invest the few remaining shekels in something worthwhile – worthwhile to you that is. Opportunities and risks my lover – aren't they the bread and butter of your profession? No Henri, let's stay a while and mingle at the reception. I'll pursue my investigations of the good reverend as I hear he's not going anywhere in a hurry and you gently prod your relatives into revealing opportunities. Didn't you say that Christina is a possible way to influence Peter? Think about it Henri. Daniel and his precious Katya will be away for a while.'

Henri wriggled on his hard pew and thought about Leslie's comments. Looking at his friend beside him Henri thought he looked so good. It had been a good decision to get married – to be really together. They were so made for each other. He had such good ideas too realised Henri. All of Leslie's comments had been right on. Sylvia and Anthony were going to be quite busy with this latest scandal at the other cottage – the Ferris cottage. With Daniel away perhaps now was the right time to visit Christina and see how the land lies. Try and persuade her to invest some of Peter's inheritance in something personally worthwhile. Yes Leslie, good idea.

But the idea didn't turn out to be quite as good as Henri had hoped. On that Sunday, August first it was, while Leslie wanted to do some further investigations in the village about the reverend, Henri did drive to Home Farm to see Christina. Trouble was his aunt Stephanie was there with Giselle and that girl-friend of Samantha's – Janet somebody. Through Heritage Adventures – that flaky company of this Janet and Samantha – someone from Italy had inquired about family connections concerning Enrico. As a result there was a lot of excitement at Home Farm and much of the conversation was in excited Italian. Christina, Enrico, Giselle and Janet were talking nineteen to the dozen and Henri didn't know whether he would ever get a word in. The two youngsters had taken themselves off into the village to swim in the pond and Henri found himself cornered by his Aunt Stephanie who wanted to get an update on how life was treating him. She hadn't heard from him for some time and presumed that no news was good news. After a couple of hours Henri realised that he wasn't going to get a chance to see Christina privately and that she would be too wound up emotionally to think straight anyway. He left, but only after he had made sure Christina pencilled in a definite meeting for later in August.

In those first two weeks in August Henri thought carefully how he should talk with Christina and Peter. Perhaps he should go down to Fotheringham for the weekend and talk with Anthony and Sylvia first – sound them out about being the accountant and the investment counsellor for the entire Estate. If Sylvia was going to retire and Daniel and Katya were immersed in the trees part then they would need someone to look after the money end. Sylvia herself had always said that wasn't Anthony's expertise. Need to find the right approach Henri mused – point out why I am so indispensable. Trouble was things were happening over which Henri had no control.

It was hot that August and Tony had gone swimming every day in the pool above the village. As the month progressed cousin Peter had improved and become a stronger swimmer and the two of them would race up and down the line of markers that Uncle Daniel had put in the pool. It was the splashing and the shouts of 'I won, I won' that first caught the attention of Dick Gillespie. He had been sitting in the back seat of the car for most of the morning and despite the windows being open the car was hot. Dick was looking for some escape and suddenly there it was.

'Stop dad, stop please. This looks great – just what I need. Look, if you and mum want to go and look at the village just drop me here for an hour or so. You go and do your thing and I can get cool. How about it mum?'

Marian Gillespie turned to her husband with a questioning look on her face. 'He's a good swimmer Ed. We can enjoy the village and perhaps sample a pint and Dick here gets to stretch his legs. We've been in the car for three hours now and even I'm feeling a little cooped up.'

Ed Gillespie pulled the car onto the verge of the road and looked over at his wife.

'I'll be fine dad,' urged Dick. 'Just give me a minute to change and grab a towel out of the boot. There's a cold drink in mum's cooler and a couple of apples. I'll just swim where those other two chaps are so I'll be safe. Talk to them if you like and check it out. Then you can go and enjoy yourselves. Be easier in the pub without me and I know mum's dying for a pint.'

'Go on you cheeky sod,' said Marian as she turned back to look at her son but Dick saw she had a big grin on her face. Dick scrambled about out of his clothes and pulled on a pair of swimming shorts. He opened the back door and was round at the boot in a flash.

'Open up dad. Open the boot and I'll grab a towel.'

Ed Gillespie looked at his wife again and she said, 'He's hot and he's full of energy Ed. Let him run a little or he'll explode.'

'Playing that music in his ear plugs all morning would make anyone explode,' said Ed. 'Good job we bought that little portable machine for him or we'd all explode. Okay son, but play it cool or whatever you kids say now. We'll be about an hour or so. You got your watch? We'll be back around two then.'

'Be careful Dick,' said Marian. 'We know you're ten trying to be twenty son but just be sensible. The lads over there look about your age. We're not too far into the country so the natives are probably friendly and they might even speak English. A loud 'Blimey Peter, that's brilliant' rang out over the grass and Dick turned to his mother and grinned.

'Seems you're right mum. The natives speak English. See yer,' and slinging the towel over his shoulder Dick walked towards the two boys splashing about on the edge of the pool.

'Opening time Ed and I'm thirsty,' said Marian. Ed eased the clutch and let his car slowly move off the verge and into the village. It didn't take him long to drive quietly into the village and see the bold sign depicting George slaying the dragon. Pulling into the parking lot he said, 'Well ducks, seems we've found a place to slake that thirst of yours. Looks like we've found ye olde English pub aptly named. Let's see whether the ale's any good shall we?'

Naturally outgoing Dick Gillespie walked across the grassy slopes above the river towards the two boys without any concerns. New faces, new names, never worried him and he welcomed being out in front of people. As Tony and Peter were facing away from him and looking at something on the bottom of the pool Dick shouted, 'Hey, that looks pretty cool in there. Okay to jump in?'

Tony and Peter turned as they heard the voice behind them and looked at Dick on the bank. Tony held his hand up to shield his eyes as the sun was right behind Dick but only for a moment before he shouted. 'Christ! Dizzie! Now you're a sight for sore eyes.'

Dick in turn smiled, dropped his towel and apples on the bank and leapt into the pool in a mighty splash, right beside Tony. 'But we beat you this past season old mate. We beat you at Stamford Bridge and at White Hart Lane – home and away mate and so the blues are still the best.' Tony wrapped his arms around Dick Gillespie and tried to wrestle him into the deeper water. Peter stood there wondering what the hell was going on but then he decided he had better do something and he tried to get the two apart.

'Tony, Tony, hold up there. What's this all about and who is this chap?'

Tony came up coughing water and laughing all at the same time as he held Dick's arms. He turned to Peter and almost choked as he tried to speak. 'Peter, this is an old mate of mine from London, from Chelsea. From my old school.'

Tony tried to continue but the water in his throat caused another bout of coughing and Dick stepped forwards offering Peter his hand. 'Hi, I'm Dick Gillespie,' he said. 'Dizzie Gillespie to friends, and you're Peter if I heard right.'

'Yes, sure,' said Peter as he shook Dizzie's hand. 'And you're a friend of Tony from London you say? How come you're down here?'

'Fate,' said Dizzie. 'Knew this silly old bugger couldn't hide from me. Bet me he'd win last season but then he did this disappearing trick. Tried to hide didn't you Tony? Thought I'd forget all about our bet.'

Tony had stopped coughing and he looked at his old friend and grinned. 'Double or quits,' he said. 'Out to the furthest buoy and back again. You on?'

Dick quickly looked out across the pool. Shouting 'You're on' he dived and fiercely thrashed his way through the water towards the furthest buoy. Tony turned and grinned at his cousin. 'Don't worry Peter. I'll explain when I've beaten this silly sod. Thinks Chelsea is unbeatable. I'll show him,' and Tony in turn dived into the pool and smoothly powered his way through the water. Peter moved towards the last marker to see the finish but Tony was by far the better swimmer and although he was just behind at the turn he overhauled his rival and stood up first by the last buoy. He turned to offer his hand to Dick.

'Come on mate. Let's sit up on the bank here and explain to my cousin who you are. Looking at his face I can see we've been talking in riddles. Grab your towel Peter and let me tell you a short story. Then we'll let Dizzie give you a short version of his life. Short Dizzie I said 'cos we haven't got all week mate. Always full of yourself you were but you were a good mate.'

When Marian and Ed Gillespie returned to the pool they found the three boys sitting together having an animated conversation.

'Seems Dick is doing his usual thing luv. Never short of words is he?'

'Natural salesman Ed, just like my old dad. That bit seems born in 'im. Suppose we've been selling things in our family for generations. Never at a loss with people is he?'

'Dick, see you've found a couple of locals who speak the language then son?'

'Ed,' said Marian, grabbing her husband's arm. 'Do you see who it is? Look who Dick's found. Blimey, it's Tony Made. Tony luv, what you doing down 'ere? Where's yer mum then? Why did you do a runner? We was all wondering what'd happened. None of us 'eard a word.'

'Marian, Marian, hold up there love and let the lads get a word in. More than two pints ducks and you become a waterfall of words, gushing everywhere. Just sit down love and we'll let the lads tell the story.'

Just as Dick Gillespie had told Tony "fate intervened", so when the Gillespies were sitting around the tea table at Home Farm explaining who they were and how they knew Tony who should come knocking at the door but Daniel Lord.

'Christina, I've come at a bad time as you've got company. I'll call in tomorrow sometime.'

'Nonsense Daniel, come in. I've a fantastic surprise for you and it's another family thing.'

'To do with Enrico? You know, that thing that Samantha was working on?'

'No Daniel, this is completely different but just as exciting. Come on in and meet some special people.'

So Daniel ended up at the table and it was Tony who made the introductions and provided most of the explanations. The Gillespies in turn were quite fascinated with the new world where Tony now lived and it was Dick who asked most of the questions. Time sped by and tea-time stretched in to dinner and Christina bustled around happy with an enlarged cluster of people under her roof. Ed Gillespie was quite intrigued with the background and history of Enrico and Daniel found himself talking with Marian who described some of the details Daniel never knew about Tony's mother, Danielle. Suddenly Katya arrived as Christina had phoned to explain where Daniel was and that he was likely to be late for dinner. She knew Katya would be worried as she and Daniel had just returned from their honeymoon and were trying to catch up on the management of the Estate. Before they knew it they were all sitting down at the table and Christina was serving dinner and describing how happy she was to have so many people in the house. The three young lads were talking football, because even Peter now had become a little more conversant with the game that Tony loved with a passion. Christina was trying to understand the words of Marian with her London slang but as both families had been into buying and selling for generations there was a swapping of tall tales about deals above and below board. It was Katya who had asked Ed Gillespie what he did and she caught Daniel's attention with his answer. Daniel had been quietly talking some forest history incident with Enrico when Katya's voice clearly cut across the conversations and created a hush.

'Daniel, I may have found just what we need. We've talked about it often enough and when we came home we found we really did need to do something about it. Your mother told me just the other day that she wants more time with your dad.' Katya stopped, almost in mid-sentence as she realised that perhaps this wasn't the place to explain why Sylvia wanted more time with Anthony. Quickly, to overcome any chance of a question, Katya continued. 'Mr. Gillespie here is an accountant,' she gushed. 'Just what we want,' she added.

Daniel wasn't sure what to say. He looked across the table at Ed Gillespie who in turn looked right back. They'd only just met and this wasn't the place for any business discussion. It was a warm summer Saturday evening and a gathering of family and friends – well Tony's friends at least. What Katya had said was true though. Mum did want to spend more time with his dad and she had explained that Anthony's health had deteriorated quite quickly – even in the two weeks he and Katya had been away on their honeymoon. Katya and he had discussed that they both knew the forest, and with the help from the two wildlife hikers they had partnered as "forest wardens" they thought they could manage the Estate in a green fashion, but the business end was a bit of an unknown. Okay thought Daniel, we've enough common sense to manage the Estate but we need someone with mum's background to look after the money end and now Katya was publicly making a suggestion. Typical Yankee forthrightness thought Daniel as he remembered Katya's mother and he smiled to himself.

'Daniel?' asked Katya.

Daniel turned his face away from his wife for a moment and looked at Ed Gillespie. 'Mr. Gillespie, Ed,' he said. 'What my wife has just said is true but I'm not sure this is the best place to discuss it. I'm sure Christina would sooner we kept such a discussion for later. Can we defer Katya's question until later? Perhaps tomorrow if you're still here?'

'Can we dad? Can we?' piped in Dick. 'Would be neat and we could all go swimming again and Peter here tells me he's got a tree house that I haven't seen. Tony says the forest here is awesome and Peter says there are all sorts of animals. Says his aunt has some special sheep and even a couple of llamas. It's neat here dad and we weren't planning anything special for tomorrow anyway. That's right mum isn't it? Dad said you enjoyed the pub too mum. Could do that again tomorrow while I swim.'

Everyone around the table was quite caught up in the enthusiasm of Dick's entreaty and his multitude of arguments.

'They could stay here auntie,' explained Tony. 'We've got room. We could make room. Dizzie can share in our room.'

'And Dizzie really does want to see the tree-house mum,' added Peter. 'He's never seen llamas either.'

Enrico smiled at the people around the table. 'It's a delight to hear the enthusiasm of the youngsters,' he said. He looked at Daniel sitting opposite. 'Reminds me of times gone by Daniel when you were just as vocal and excited about the life in the forest. You used to drag me out to look at all sorts of things when you were Peter's age.'

Marian looked at her husband. 'Right friendly I'd say Ed. People here are right friendly and Dick's right you know. We haven't got a roof over our 'eads for tonight yet. We was planning on going on towards Exeter but there's no rush. Our Dick here 'asn't seen Tony for ages luv. What do you say to a night in the woods?' and Marian giggled.

Daniel turned to Christina. 'Would you like us to look after Mr. and Mrs. Gillespie? There's more room up at Fotheringham you know.'

'But Dizzie could stay here,' urged Tony. 'There's room for Dizzie auntie.'

And so it was settled. Dizzie Dick Gillespie stayed at Home Farm and spent most of the night talking with Tony and Peter. Daniel and Katya drove back with Marian and Ed Gillespie to find rooms for them at Fotheringham. Needless to say Sylvia was her usual ladyship hostess and welcomed them with open arms. Anthony was particularly pleased as he had always had a soft spot for Danielle and her courage. He too was interested in hearing a little more about the young lady who had bewitched his son Michael and given birth to his special namesake grandchild.

It wasn't until that same last weekend in August before Henri managed to arrange a visit down to Somerset. Two weeks previously Henri had been on a roll and after several nights of good luck gambolling he had won enough to really celebrate with Leslie. However, the good luck faltered and once again Henri found he was living beyond his means. Time to tap into the Lord money somehow Henri told himself and without any warning he drove down to Fotheringham to see Anthony. For Henri it has been a trying week, and the rat race out of London on the M4, with the hordes driving into the sun, further added to his exasperation.

'Henri this is a nice and unexpected surprise. Anthony and I were just asking about you. We haven't heard from you since the weddings. Giselle was telling us she hadn't heard anything from you either. All is well I trust?'

'That drive out of London is becoming impossible Sylvia. Why can't you all live somewhere closer – in Surrey for instance?'

Anthony chuckled as he clasped both hands on Henri's arms. 'Come in Henri come in. Sit down and have a drink. Relax. It's Friday evening and the office has gone to bed for the weekend. Down here it's peaceful and quiet and you can wind down. Sylvia here will soothe your troubled brow. You're lucky you know,' added Anthony still smiling. 'You missed all the rumpus and noise of young Peter's birthday. Although Christina had the party at Home Farm we reckon you could have heard the noise from over here. Why do young people have to talk at the top of their voices?'

'God, I forgot all about that,' said Henri. 'He must be nine or ten now I suppose. I was planning to go over and see Christina so I'd better find something in the village tomorrow as a belated present. Any ideas what he might like?'

'Henri just sit back in the chair for the moment and finish your drink. Close your eyes and count to thirty or something. Actually, there's some other news you should know about too, especially if you are thinking of going over to Home Farm. Does Stephanie know you are down?'

'No Sylvia. I came down on the spur of a moment thing and so I didn't tell anyone I was coming. Is she okay?'

'Henri she's fine. It's just there are a couple of additional people at Home Farm at the moment.'

'And we've another couple staying here too,' added Anthony. 'It's a small world Henri as the folks here now are friends of Danielle and her Tony. They're on holiday from London but they are staying the weekend. Their son, an old school friend of Tony's, is staying at Home Farm. What's his name again Sylvia – Dizzy something?'

'His name is Dick, Anthony – well that's what his parents call him but I understand he prefers to be called Dizzie by his friends. The name has something to do with music but jazz was never my thing. His father, Ed Gillespie, did tell me but I've forgotten.'

'Who else is staying at Home Farm? You mentioned this kid Sylvia but is there anybody else?'

Sylvia smiled. 'I suppose it's another example of it being a small world Henri, but also a world that now seems joined together through the wonders of computers. Actually it was partly Samantha who was responsible.'

'Not really Sylvia. It was Janet who first made the connection I think,' added Anthony.

'Who, what?' asked Henri. 'I think I'll have another drink if you don't mind as this is somewhat overwhelming. First you tell me to relax and then you barrage me with people everywhere. I came down here for some peace and quiet – and a talk with Anthony,' Henri added.

'What about Henri? asked Sylvia. 'Are you still trying to peddle your Brainware shares? We told you that talking with Rosalind Cohen might be more useful.'

'To be honest Sylvia it's about you and Anthony relaxing a little more. Now that you've sold Brainware I thought the whole idea was for both of you to take things easy. What was it Daniel was talking about at his birthday last year? He was saying you two would retire and he and Katya would manage the Estate for Peter.'

'And Henri?' said Sylvia raising her eyebrows.

'Well I came down to offer some help, some professional help. I know Daniel and Katya are both foresters, and they can look after that end of the Estate pretty well, but neither of them knows anything about money: managing money that is. With the expansion of the Education Centre and their ideas about bringing in green revenues the pair of them are going to be very busy. In fact I believe they will be quite overwhelmed with the magnitude of the task so I thought I'd offer to help. That way you two won't have any day to day worries and the Lord family inheritance will be well looked after for Peter when he comes of age. Look, I really was going to talk about this tomorrow with the pair of you but it is quite simple. I can set up some computer software here, like a Point of Sale system in a way, and Daniel and Katya can use it to enter revenues and costs. It can include a budget and spew out the usual set of managerial reports. All of that part is fairly easy and it would be useful for Daniel. I'm not sure how you handle all of that now but it wouldn't be hard to link it up with software I've got in London so that I can look after the money side. At my end I could sort out all the tax bits and pieces as well as any wise investment opportunities for surplus cash on hand.'

Sylvia looked at Henri sitting back in the easy chair twirling his whiskey glass. He in turn was looking at the glass in his hand. A few thoughts whirled through Sylvia's mind and she wasn't quite sure how she was going to play this. While thinking over the options she moved to the drinks cabinet.

'Another drink Henri? Another whiskey while Anthony and I think about the things you have just said? Sort of bombshell in a way Henri don't you think? You've kind of dropped this on us rather abruptly. Perhaps we should leave it until tomorrow to talk over in a more leisurely and complete way as you suggested? What do you say Anthony dear? Should we leave this until tomorrow?'

'But I thought we had that all settled Sylvia,' said Anthony. 'By the way Henri, did you want another drink? Sylvia offered but you never said.'

'What's settled?' asked Henri.

'Another whiskey?'

'Yes, no, well yes. Yes please' and Henri held out his glass. 'What's settled?' Henri repeated looking at Anthony

'Henri we can talk about it tomorrow,' said Sylvia emphatically. 'Look, it's a lovely evening and I'm sure a gentle ride around the forest will be good for all of us before dinner. Out there it's quiet and relaxing and you can let the worries of City life wash off you Henri. Just take in the soft greenery and the gentle swish of the trees in the breeze. I'll bet you haven't been out riding for a while Henri. Anthony, can you go and get the horses organised love while I take Henri upstairs and find a helmet that fits. Perhaps an old pair of trousers might be a good idea too Henri rather than that smart suit. Come on, it's just too nice to be inside.'

Sylvia guided the three horses down through the forest and into the clearing where the Entwhistle's cottage stood. Adam was outside playing with Storm. Ophelia came to the door as she had heard the horses walking down the forest ride.

'Evening madam,' she said. 'Beautiful evening to exercise the horses. Evening Sir Anthony, evening sir,' and Ophelia touched her forehead.

'Hello Ophelia and hello Adam. How is your mighty hound today?'

'He's champion missus thanks. He looves it here. Sit Storm, sit.'

Henri's horse skittered a bit as the Labrador had been running around him and Henri glared at Adam. Anthony leant over and smoothly ran his hand down the cheek of Gypsy, Henri's horse. Gypsy wasn't too sure about Henri and Henri wasn't too sure who was in control. Leaving the Entwhistles it wasn't long before they cantered into another clearing and here Henri pulled up on the reins. Gypsy stopped dead in her tracks and Henri had to grip tightly with his thighs to avoid pitching over the horse's neck. Sylvia turned in her saddle and looked at Henri.

'That's Samantha's horse you know Henri. Obviously Gypsy isn't used to your commands. Mark you, I suppose Samantha and Gypsy become one animal when they're together.'

'Well right now Sylvia I need to assure this beast that I'm in control,' said Henri sharply. He looked around. 'Isn't this the infamous cottage of ill-repute? I thought you were talking of knocking it down? Didn't Daniel want to let the forest revert to nature or something – or was that Katya? Both of those two seem to have this environmental green thing going.'

'Yes Henri, but the environmental green thing has led to a new friendship with some wildlife people. Two of the hikers actually who were a bit of a pain earlier in the year. Remember we told you about the damage to fences and this group wanting to re-assert some old so-called rights of way. After Daniel and Katya sat and talked with them they came to an agreement. Seems two of the group were wildlife biologists and so Daniel has made them "forest wardens". In exchange for them hiking through the area, which apparently the group enjoys for a variety of reasons, they offered to survey the forest for wildlife and make some recommendations for green revenues. Daniel and Katya both agreed that they may know the trees and the other vegetation but neither of them are experts in wildlife and wildlife habitat. They both thought they could modify the forest and perhaps some of the forestry operations to enhance the diversity and that would improve the whole area from an Education point of view.'

'So you could charge more for use of the Education Centre?' said Henri. 'If the area offered a wider array of experiences it is more valuable. And if it is more valuable then it would support a higher price to use it. So, is more money coming in? This is just the sort of thing I was talking about earlier. Daniel and Katya don't have any money management skills and here is a good example. They are missing out on a financial opportunity.'

'Hold up there Henri,' said Anthony. 'This has only just started. Daniel talked with these two lads about a month ago and nothing much has happened since. This all takes time you know. You can't change the forest overnight and the two lads have to survey the area first to assess the potential and possible opportunities. This isn't like playing the currency market Henri. Things move slowly in the forest, very slowly.'

'Yes yes,' said Henri in exasperation, 'but you could advertise this is happening, is happening right now and so the property is more valuable. And if the property is more valuable you could charge....'

'Henri take a breath,' said Sylvia. 'We came out here to relax and enjoy the peace and quiet. Give your financial cogs a rest just for an hour or so. Yes you're right, this is the infamous cottage but right now it has a reprieve. I for one recommended we bulldoze it but Katya has persuaded me to let it stand for a while. The two biologists have talked about using it as a base, a place to stay if they spend nights out here. So for the moment it remains but let's move on as it's getting closer to dinner time and cook might start wondering whether we have all deserted her.'

'So might the Gillespies,' added Anthony, and Sylvia looked across at her husband and smoothly slid her finger over her mouth. Anthony understood the message and zipped his lips on the Gillespies.

'So where are you going climbing this summer Henri?' asked Anthony. 'You usually go somewhere on the continent at this time of year,' and the conversation moved onto less controversial ground.

Back at Fotheringham Sylvia was surprised to find the house empty, except for cook.

'Madam, that Mr. and Mrs. Gillespie got invited by Mrs. Geoffrey to stay for dinner at Home Farm. Said they would be in later this evening, so there will only be the three of you for dinner here tonight.'

Sylvia laughed as she held her cook's hands. 'Mrs. Trelawney, what would we ever do without you? Nothing seems to faze you despite all the comings and goings in this crazy family.'

'You know why madam. 'Cos I'm the same as you. Good Cornish stock. Me and my long-departed husband, the dearly-beloved Mr. Trelawney, we were from Fowey and came from a china clay background like yourself. We all leant to adapt, didn't we?'

'And so it's star-gazy pie or curlew pie tonight is it?' asked Anthony as he came into the kitchen from the stabling the horses. Now it was cooks turn to laugh as she turned to Anthony. 'Sir, you know I've kept my traditional dishes to myself. Your father was never too keen on country pies. He preferred his meat where he could see it and I've cooked that way ever since. Anyway, dinner will be in forty minutes. Well, it will be if I can get all of you out of my kitchen.'

'Come on Henri,' said Anthony, holding Henri by the arm. 'Seems we are surplus to requirements here. Perhaps a relaxing bath and dressing for dinner.'

'Haven't you installed showers yet in this house Anthony? I thought Sylvia said you had refurbished this house? The plumbing here was always a joke.'

'Priorities Henri, priorities,' said Sylvia. 'We fixed the roof and we renovated the kitchen. See, look what we've done.'

'Out, out,' urged cook. 'Show him some other time madam. I've things to do.'

'Where's Daniel and Katya?'

'They've gone to visit Samantha and Terence Henri. It was James's birthday earlier this month too you know, and now the pair of them have gone over for an after-birthday quiet adult's dinner.'

'Although it probably won't be very quiet if I know James,' added Anthony with a laugh.

'There are too many kids and too many birthdays,' said Henri.

'But not a problem in your household Henri, so why don't you go and change for dinner and then you can tell Anthony and I all about your recent exploits up in the city. We'll have a quiet adult's dinner even if Daniel and Katya don't.'

As agreed, Henri kept his thoughts to himself until the following day after breakfast. He was civil to the Gillespies early in the morning but it appeared that they had a busy day planned and weren't talkative breakfast people. Daniel and Katya hadn't yet made an appearance but Henri had itchy feet. Soon after nine he decided it was time to spin his tale.

'Anthony, Sylvia, we've talked about this before. I believe I've suggested it on several family occasions but usually there's been a crowd and it's not been conducive to a real heart to heart. Now that there are just the three of us perhaps we can have a more detailed and conclusive discussion.'

'Shouldn't Daniel and Katya be party to this discussion Henri? From what little you said last night it would seem appropriate that they hear what you have to say. You seemed to be offering a complimentary service and that it would be supportive of their management of the Estate.'

'But I've got other things to do Sylvia,' said Henri. 'You told me last night about Peter and now I've got to find something for James or Samantha will throw things at me.'

'And you said you wanted to see Christina,' added Anthony.

'That's tomorrow,' said Henri sharply. 'I planned to see Christina tomorrow. By the way, who else did you say was there?'

Just at that moment Katya poked her head around the drawing room door. When she saw who was there she opened the door wider and stepped into the room. She walked across the room and held out her hand.

'Henri, this is a nice surprise. How are you? And how is Leslie? The pair of you did look smart at the wedding. Daniel and I were glad you both came.' Holding Henri's hand Katya looked at Sylvia and Anthony.

'Sorry,' she said, 'am I interrupting something? I heard voices and didn't realise Henri was here. After last night with Samantha and Terence, Daniel and I slept in this morning.' Hearing footsteps behind her Katya turned. 'Daniel, Daniel, look who's come down to see us.'

Henri let go of Katya's hand and sat back down in the armchair. Things weren't going according to plan he thought. It would have been a lot easier with just Anthony and Sylvia. I really should have been more insistent last night.

'Daniel, good to see you. I must say the pair of you look blooming. Obviously the honeymoon was a success, enjoyable, hell you know what I mean.'

'Yes Henri I do, and it was, and as my good lady said it's a delight to see you. Actually, I'm surprised to see you 'cos you usually go to the continent around this time to go climbing don't you? After those first few years you sat and worked out the best time for the weather. I remember you saying how frustrating it could be just waiting for good weather in a wet tent or a snow-bound hut. I thought you and whoever sat and worked out the optimum two or three weeks – end of August and beginning of September I thought you said.'

'Daniel my stomach is growling.'

'So can we give them half an hour Henri so the pair of them don't faint during your spiel?'

'What spiel?' asked Daniel.

'Go and eat Daniel, or help Katya have breakfast and then we can all get our heads together over Henri's proposal.'

'Sure dad. Come on Katya.'

An hour later the five of them were talking in the drawing room. Henri had carefully and slowly outlined his proposal. He had given them examples of his clients and their investment successes over the past year. Furthermore, he had provided an overview of the company and its philosophy plus the overall progress of the company and the future marketplace.

'But the key item for all of us is that it's handled within the family. Things become easier to discuss and decide. I was telling your parents Daniel that neither you nor Katya have much knowledge of my end of the business. For example, I learnt last night that you had included some sort of sleeping partners to help with the environmental side of things. Well, in a way, think of me as providing a similar sort of contribution for the monetary end of things.'

'And we would have a more elaborate computer system here?' asked Daniel, 'and it would be hard-wired to your offices?'

'Internet Daniel. Secured internet linkages. Your father knows the details. We could use our office system,' said Henri, 'and incorporate one or more Brainware security systems if you like. We could always talk with Rosalind Cohen. She'd probably be only be too glad to help. So, what do you think?'

There was quiet in the room while the five people looked at each other – all of them with some degree of questioning on their faces.

'Well?' said Henri, wondering why the silence. 'Sylvia, you and Anthony have decided to retire haven't you? I thought that was all settled.'

'Yes Henri. You're right. We have, but we haven't sat still so to speak. We recognised early on that Daniel and Katya don't have my background and so we went looking for opportunities. Recently, very recently in fact we have found someone who not only suits our requirements financially but also in a family way – well social way really.'

'Who? Who?' demanded Henri, and he turned towards Anthony. 'Anthony, we talked about this and I thought we'd agreed that I would handle the Lord family finances. Some time ago, when I was living in Bath, we talked about this and I thought that when the time came I would take over. Now that I'm living in London, and with a bigger more comprehensive company, I can offer a greater array of investment opportunities. Moreover, I know a lot more now and have a much broader network of contacts. So who is this supposed saviour?'

Again, there was a prolonged pause in the conversation but this time it was Daniel who spoke.

'Henri, I think perhaps we are talking at cross purposes. The revenues from the Estate are not large and essentially we re-invest most of them back into the Estate itself. The family here think it is better to improve the overall quality of the experience of the Estate – make the woodlands more productive, more environmentally sustainable, and ensure that the Education Centre can provide a diverse and comprehensive experience. We think we need to be specialised, perhaps unique in the products and programmes we can offer. In a way we want to be your first choice for such an experience – the place you think of first when looking for such a product. Now that idea takes time, but it also takes quality and diversity and both those two cost money. So, slowly we are re-investing in the Estate. As a result there are not really any surplus monies lying around looking for outside investment opportunities. I realise that what you are offering is both interesting and perhaps exciting, even rewarding but we don't have the capital to consider such options. As I said, I think we are talking at cross purposes.'

As Daniel was talking Henri could feel the purpose of his visit sliding away from him and he couldn't see where or how he could get any degree of control over the Lord family money.

'But is that the best use of the money Daniel? Is it the best use of your total assets? Have you thought of borrowing money with the Estate as collateral and wisely investing such a loan? Then again, have you thought of any short-term considerations? Take the monies from any lumber sale, invest wisely in the short-term to double the capital, and then re-invest twice as much back into the Estate a few months later? There's money to be made in the short-term you know. It's all about timing and that's where I'm sitting in the middle of the world so to speak. I've got all those short-term opportunities at my fingertips.'

'With all the risks that go with daily trading?' suggested Sylvia and she stirred in her armchair. 'Henri, can we all take this under advisement? You've rather sprung this on us with your unannounced visit and we'd benefit from a discussion amongst ourselves. The rather mundane book-keeping and local accounting we have under control at the moment but I think we would need to consider your ideas of investing after a rethink. However, I'm like Daniel, and I believe that the future of Fotheringham is in its uniqueness and quality of experience. I also believe in doing that slowly but surely – not in any speculative way.'

Henri realised that he was flogging a dead horse for the moment but he was determined not to let it go. If there was an opportunity he wanted to seize it and control it.

'Okay Sylvia. I hear you but I would like to commit to a further discussion within a month say. I really do think you can all do so much better if you broaden your horizons and consider investments outside this very local backwater. It's a new world out there and there are lots of opportunities. So, can we agree to reconsider my offer within the month – some time towards the end of September for instance? I'd like to be able to show how I can really help. Be able to have some positive results for you for Daniel's birthday in October if you like. What do you say Daniel? We'll have another good news story to celebrate at your birthday – a prelude to the new millennium?'

'Agreed Henri. Come down in about four or five weeks time. By then we'll have decided a few things,' and seen whether Ed Gillespie can adequately handle our affairs thought Daniel but he didn't say so.

'Right, well I suppose I had better go birthday shopping,' said Henri. Then I'll pop over to see Christina Henri thought to himself. Perhaps I'll have more luck persuading Christina that I can invest some of Peter's money.

'You'll be back for dinner then Henri?' asked Sylvia.

'No, er no,' said Henri thinking over his plan of action. 'No, I'll probably head back to London this evening thanks all the same. Still, I appreciate you listening and for the birthday updates. I'll be in touch.'

After Henri left Sylvia looked around the room. 'You were very quiet Anthony,' she said.

'What, what's that my dear?' said Anthony. 'I was dozing actually as the conversation wasn't going anywhere. Rather pushy and aggressive I thought and I had nothing to offer. Actually, I thought you had already decided what you were going to do Daniel my boy. I thought you had offered Gillespie the job and that you were just stalling with Henri. Might have been kinder to have told him to his face. If he goes over to see Christina he's quite likely to hear it from Peter or Tony, especially if Dizzie is there. Isn't Guido still there too?'

Luckily Henri had found gifts in the village for both James and Peter when he returned to Home Farm that afternoon.

173

'Hi Uncle Henri,' cried Peter. 'We're up here. No, up here. Up in the tree-house.'

Henri stopped as he walked across the yard of Home Farm and looked up into the large sycamore tree. A rope ladder was dangling down and soon Peter was descending at speed. 'Come on down Tony. You too James,' Peter urged and he turned back to Henri. 'It's good to see you again. How's smelly old London? Usually stinks in the summer, or so your sister says. She's here by the way uncle but she's talking Italian all the time and I can't understand a word she's saying.'

Tony and James stood beside Peter and looked at Henri as he stood there transfixed with Peter's flow of words.

'Giselle's here?' Henri managed to say. 'Oh, by the way, this is for you Peter,' and Henri managed to dig into his shopping bag and bring out a wrapped package. 'I thought I remembered that you liked to play cricket and hope that this is useful. Belated happy birthday Peter. Hope you enjoyed yourself. Your Aunt Sylvia said it was very noisy so I suppose you did.'

'Wow, smashing, a new ball. Look at this Tony. Thanks Uncle Henri. It's just what I need. I'll be able to spin lots of googlies with a new ball.'

'And I've not forgotten you either James as I know it was your birthday too,' said Henri as he looked into his bag again. 'I know you love to ride and so I found something special for you to groom your horse. Dainty isn't it?'

'Gee thanks Uncle Henri. Dainty will be delighted. She loves it when I brush and curry comb her coat. That's awesome. Thanks awfully. Mummy, mummy,' cried James as he sped into the house looking for his mother to describe his recent gifts at great length.

'Tony, I didn't know when your birthday was but I thought I'd find something for you too just in case. My sister Giselle has told me that you swim most of the summer. I hope these goggles might be useful. I know

174

serious swimmers wear them and hope you like them.' Henri handed over the third package to Tony who thanked Henri.

'Is your mother home Peter?' asked Henri. 'I was hoping for a quiet word. There was something I wanted to ask her. Actually, there was something I thought I could do to help her.'

'Yes Uncle Henri. She's indoors. Actually everyone's indoors and they're all talking. That's why we're out here. We were building up the tree-house to sleep there tonight. Mum said we could if we made it safe. Anyway, come inside and meet everyone.' Peter turned and led Henri into the kitchen where there was a great deal of arm waving and animated conversation. It seemed very crowded all of a sudden to Henri and true enough there were several people all talking and none listening it seems.

'Mum, looks who's here,' cried Peter. 'Uncle Henri's here!' he almost shouted and suddenly there was an incredible quiet and people froze into a still life tableau for a brief moment. It was Janet who jumped back into life first as she stepped across the floor and seized Henri by the arm.

'Henri come and meet someone from one of your favourite stomping grounds. Come and meet a true man of the Dolomites. This is Guido Tonella and he's from Cortina. Actually, he's also a second nephew several times removed from Enrico here, and that is why he's come to England. We're helping him find his relatives. Still, enough of that. Guido, this is Henri Lord, cousin to Samantha and Christina here.'

Henri suddenly noticed a suave man, about his age he reckoned, who had been standing half behind Christina. Guido advanced with his hand extended and a smooth smile on his dusky face.

'My pleasure Henri. I have been talking with Christina and your sister. It is a delight to find such eloquent Italian in this very English countryside and now I meet someone who is half French. It is a very European world we live in don't you think?'

Henri grasped the extended hand in a firm shake and smiled at Guido. 'Unfortunately my Italian is restricted to mountaineering guidebook route descriptions and not conversation like my sister, but I do love your home town. Do you climb at all? Surely you must if you live in Cortina? You live in the heart of a Dolomite paradise.'

'No Henri, no perhaps disappointing for you but I do not climb. Sure I ski. Always I have ski-ed, but the climbing is too bold, too frightening for me.'

'But he plays football Uncle Henri,' piped in Tony. 'We were playing football earlier before you came and found us up in the tree-house.'

Janet suddenly spoke to Guido in a torrent of Italian and Guido laughed as he replied and Enrico caught the cloud passing across Henri's face. Ever sensitive to people's feelings Enrico walked forwards to hold Henri's arm and catch his attention. 'I heard you brought gifts for the youngsters Henri. That was a nice thought. Young James here was trying to drag his mother away to find Dainty. He insists that his Dainty needs her coat groomed. That was an appropriate gift.'

'Too true Enrico. Thanks Henri,' said Samantha as she too gave Henri a hug, 'but we must be off,' she added. 'Christina thanks for the information and the other advice. James and I have to be going as Terence promised he will be home for dinner this evening. We'll see you all later. Janet, you can look after Guido?'

'Sure, go Samantha. Terence doesn't get to make such promises often. Take this young scallywag with you too,' said Janet and she wrapped her arms around a wriggling James.

'Ugh, kisses!' exclaimed James. 'Kisses from a hot woman,' and he rushed out of the kitchen.

'Henri I'm forgetting myself,' said Christina. 'I too thank you for the gifts. I understand you found presents for all the boys, and very appropriate thoughts too. However, please, would you like a drink of something? Enrico decided we needed some wine as Guido was coming. Can I offer you a glass?'

'It's not from Cortina Henri,' added Guido, 'but it is very smooth and pleasant on the palate.'

'And some biscotti Henri?' offered Christina. 'I made them special with Guido coming.'

'A glass of wine please Christina,' said Henri, 'but I'll pass on the biscuits as I've just come from lunch. Actually Christina, is it possible to have a quiet word? I wanted to talk to you about something special, something I thought I could do for you and Peter. It won't take long and I need to drive back to London this evening.'

'But we were all going to go for a tour of the Estate Henri. Enrico was keen on showing Guido some of the things we do here. Some of the things he and his brother have done here over the years. The boys also wanted to show Guido the Education Centre as Peter is still very excited about that. Did you know he has written a short story for the Centre Henri? It is quite clever really for his age. Giselle thinks she knows some people who might help publish it or perhaps print it.'

'Yes Henri,' said Giselle. 'Peter was very thoughtful. He worked with Stephanie and with Enrico and wrote a very interesting story about diversity – diversity in people and diversity in the forest. Even you might be interested as it shows how people need to think and act with open minds. You've always told me that your job forces you to be creative and not too locked into a repetitive way of life. Remember we talked about expanding horizons?'

'Maybe Giselle but right now I would like to talk with Christina about something quite specific. Why don't the rest of you go and tour the forest as planned and I can have a quiet word with Christina? I'm sure Guido would like to see what his long-lost relatives have been up to at Fotheringham. There's what Enrico, fifty years or so of history here?'

'Henri is this important? Are you sure it can't wait? Sylvia phoned and said you had stayed at the Big House overnight. She also said that you were planning to come down here again in a month. Is there some rush, some crisis, 'cos it would have been easier if you had phoned?'

'What are you offering Henri?' asked Giselle very directly as she looked at her brother.

'Expertise Giselle, specialised expertise and opportunities to better oneself,' retorted Henri.

'But we're quite comfortable here Henri,' said Christina. 'We have everything we need. The family is content. Guido here has found one of his long-lost relatives. Tony here has just found a long-lost school friend.'

'And we're going to form a band,' added Tony enthusiastically. 'Back in London Dizzie and I played a bit together and we've just discovered that Peter can sing. We'll be a smash. Come back later Uncle Henri and we'll play for you.'

'Later later,' grunted Henri. 'All you people think about is later. Stuck down here in the back woods you don't seem to live in the real world. I came down here to offer some real live world opportunities to Sylvia and Anthony but they procrastinated. Daniel too thinks everything is under control and doing well. You just don't realise the opportunities there are in this world – well in the bigger world, in London. Wake up people, wake up.' Henri paused and looked directly at Christina.

'Christina, you are wasting Geoffrey and Peter's inheritance. You are letting life pass you by and ruining Peter's possible future by sitting on your hands down here. You just don't know what you are doing!'

'It's not right! Henri, it's not right to talk to Christina like that,' said Guido advancing across the room. 'It's not polite. In her house too. The family here is 'appy. They are content and all is well. How come you barge in here and shout?'

'It's nothing to do with you stranger,' replied Henri angrily. 'I know this family. I know what they don't know. I know they know nothing about money and investments. It is like the parable of the three servants being given some money by their owner. They are like the one who hid his money under a stone and did nothing with it. It never did anything whereas the other two used their money and made money. That's what I'm talking about. It's a sin to just sit on it. It's a stupid waste. It's criminal. It's ignorant.'

Henri's voice had become a shout as he looked at the people standing in the room. His frustrations from the previous twenty-four hours and now this stand-off with Christina was just too much. Sod the lot of them, including this suave interloper. Bloody eyeties.

Christina sat down suddenly on her chair and put her head in her hands. Her shoulders shuddered and quickly Guido was over beside her. He crouched down and gently held her arms.

'That's enough Henri,' said Giselle. 'I think you've said quite enough. Try phoning next time before you visit rather than just barging in and upsetting people. I'll call you later in the week when you've calmed down a little. Perhaps we can talk about what you have in mind at that time but not now. Certainly not now.'

Henri looked at the faces in the room. Without another word he spun on his heel and strode out into the yard. Sod the lot of you he muttered. But I'll be back and I'll find a way to control things.

And so autumn came that eventful year

But things didn't work out that way immediately for Henri. For a while the marriage with Leslie blossomed, and Henri found the mix of making money in the city and living in Leslie's world a refreshing change. Some of the anxieties faded away and for once in his life Henri felt almost at peace with himself. However, it was a little thing that upset Henri's apparent happiness and stability. The new millennium loomed, and there was considerable speculation what the year 2000 would bring. London struggled with new innovative products in domes, wheels and bridges – all of which ran late, over budget and were topics for endless speculation. None of these affected Henri directly but the madness over computer timing did. Come the year 2000 and what would it do to the internal clock mechanisms of computers? Would they roll over into 2000 without a murmur or would there be some glitch and systems everywhere would crash or start random events? In the world of finance timing is a relevant item, and the speculation, or rather the lack of consistent answers niggled at Henri. The niggling stupidly increased and Henri became more and more short-tempered with a problem that he couldn't solve yet he thought was crucial to his world. Fortunately, Henri's mountaineering friends persuaded him to take his head out of the unknown and find peace in the hills.

'Remember last year Henri? It was good mate. We did some great things and there've been some really sensational developments to go and check out since then. You, I and the rest of the crowd have been out most weekends this year and we're climbing well. You're sounding like a broken record with this year 2K bug. Forget it – the world won't come to an end at midnight. Actually Henri, think about it mate. You're a logical bloke, so when does the new millennium actually start? Year one started at one Henri, not at zero, so when does this new deal start eh? At the end of the year 2000 really, and all this flap over the end of 1999 is a misconception – not that you could tell the masses that.'

'So climbing?'

'Yes Henri, climbing. Head out of the clouds and into other clouds – up high clouds Henri. Over 4000 metre clouds mate. Let's take four weeks this year and tour around a little, not just stay at Chamonix?'

'But there's everything there,' said Henri. 'It's home, well it is for me. My mother came from Chamonix. I feel I can really climb there.'

'Okay Henri. We'll play it by ear and we will start in Cham if that keeps you happy, but let's make it a good year.'

And so for four weeks in September Henri tried to bury his frustrations by climbing in the Chamonix area. For once the weather was unusual, was settled, was fine and Henri found further happiness in a world that he truly loved. Sexually secure in his relationship with Leslie Henri wasn't tempted or sexually distracted while in Europe. He could concentrate and really enjoy the challenges of pitting man versus gravity. The four men, all top level mountaineers, felt that this had been one of their best trips ever. Truly a time to remember and Henri came back to London rejuvenated.

However, within a week Henri's euphoria diminished as Buzz started some vindictive campaign against Henri. To Henri's dismay Leslie was aloof, almost standing on the sidelines while Buzz and Henri sniped at each other. Once again Henri's mood swings returned as Buzz was spreading rumours and hints of photographs of Henri with a variety of women.

'It was another life Leslie. It's over.'

'Where Henri?'

'Leslie it doesn't matter where. It doesn't matter who, or when, or how, or even why 'cos it's finished.'

'But why is important Henri. I thought you loved me. You said you loved me and only me. That I was your life and now Buzz is telling me about another side of you. Were you really climbing in Europe Henri? How do I know you were climbing?'

'Leslie this is stupid. Buzz is just jealous. Buzz is just trying to drive a knife between us. Why is he doing this? What has he got to gain?'

'He's looking for stories Henri. Buzz is always looking for stories.'

'I'm not a story Leslie. And I'm no threat to any stories. Buzz has no interest in mountaineering, or in financial investments. He's only interested in high-flier smut – in society or entertainment people falling off pedestals, or bar stools, whatever. Look, let's go out for the weekend? Just you and me. Didn't you want to follow up on that preacher bloke down at Fotheringham? How about a quiet weekend in the country? I'm supposed to visit Anthony and Sylvia, and Christina too I suppose although I think I'm flogging a dead horse there. But you and I Leslie? Out of the city. Out of this flat. Away from Buzz and his bloody cameras for a while. Somewhere quiet and peaceful where we can be together. What do you say?'

In early October, as the leaves had started to turn, Henri drove Leslie down to Fotheringham. The fluttering tassels on the larch trees had changed from pale green to a golden cloak and Henri thought the scene looked peaceful. He turned to Leslie as they came into the village.

'I phoned Anthony but told him we would stay at the George as we were here for R & R as well as a short discussion on finances. I also told him that you were researching a story to do with some people in Exeter and that you would be out all sorts of hours and so we didn't want to upset the household with our comings and goings.'

'Yes. Fine Henri. So we're staying in the George. I don't need to know all the explanations and bogus stories. Actually though, I will take some time to see my informant in the village 'cos I do want an update on a certain story. I'd heard that some things were heating up again, and I do want to hear whether a climax is imminent.'

'What things?'

'Henri it's nothing to do with you. Anyway, enough of all that. Let's have a slow and relaxed weekend together away from the hustle and bustle of the city. It was a good suggestion. I've had a week I'd sooner forget and the scenery down here looks sublime. The George is interesting on weekend evenings and yet quiet enough to just enjoy ourselves. Great idea Henri, great idea.'

'Christina, how are you? It's Henri, and I'm telephoning as you suggested last time I was at Home Farm. I've come down to see Anthony and Sylvia and hoped that I could come and see you and Peter. Would it be possible to see you, say on the Sunday?'

'Henri what is it this time?'

'I wanted to explain a little more about the opportunities for you and Peter Christina. I've just come back from the continent and there are several really interesting things going on both over there and in London. Talking with several of my colleagues at work I think I can describe some very exciting opportunities for you.'

'Henri I know nothing of these things. My Geoffrey used to handle all that, and Peter is still a young boy.'

'Yes I know Christina, I know. That's why I am making this offer, especially for you. I can handle these things for you. Shall we say two o'clock? See you then.'

As Henri put down the telephone and smiled to himself he turned to look at Leslie. 'You still looking for the reverend? Didn't you say he'd come back here? You stopped looking for him earlier this year. Did he leave Leslie? Anyway, I just heard that he's talking tomorrow afternoon you know, at the Education Centre. Can you drop me at Fotheringham Manor if you need the car? I'm not sure if I'll need it on Sunday though. I think I might be able to nail down some of young Peter's finances.'

'Henri I'll drop you off tomorrow and we'll sort out Sunday later. I've a little snooping to do on both days so I'll need the car. Now, seeing as we've both got our weekend's activities planned to perfection why don't we share a glass of wine, a leisurely shower and a sensual sharing of the bed?'

Henri was surprised to find his Aunt Stephanie at Fotheringham when he visited Anthony and Sylvia on the Saturday. He was even more surprised when his aunt started to grill him on his sister's whereabouts.

'Where is she Henri? I've tried her office and they tell me she is on assignment somewhere – somewhere on the continent. Do you know what she is doing? You've just come back from France.'

'Aunt, as you know the continent is a large place and I was only in Chamonix. So no, I've no idea where Giselle is or what she is doing. She translates and helps Europeans. Well, that's what I think she does. That's all she tells me she does. Still, doesn't she help refugees or people in trouble? I really don't know. Anyway, why the concern? Why do you need to see her?'

'It was something Guido said,' answered Sylvia.

'Who's Guido?' asked Henri.

'Henri don't be obtuse,' said Stephanie. 'You met him at Home Farm last month. He's that long-lost relative of Enrico. You were asking him about climbing. Still, I suppose you forgot him as soon as he said that he didn't climb. Anyway, he came back again just recently. Said he wanted to talk with Enrico again but I think he may have wanted to come back and see Christina too. She's lonely Henri, and I think she and Guido would make a good pair. Enrico would probably like that too. Could be good all round. What do you think Henri?'

'What, what did you say Stephanie?'

'Christina and Guido Henri?'

'Stephanie I don't know. I don't know this Guido. Anyway, what did this Guido say? You said he said something. What was so important?'

'When he was here Henri, when Guido was here, he had been talking with Giselle.'

'Yes, yes,' said Henri, 'I remember now. There was a great gabble going on but it was all in Italian. Christina, Janet, Giselle, Enrico and Guido were rabbiting on and all of them with arms and hands flapping all over the place – typical Italian conversation.'

'Henri!' said Stephanie emphatically. 'That was last month, when you were here. Still, I heard you were so rude to Christina that you've probably forgotten what you said or heard. Anyway, in all the animated conversation Guido said he would find out something for Giselle, something important. It was something to do with refugees like you said. Well it seems that he has but he said it was urgent.'

Stephanie stopped and looked at Henri but he just stood there. Anthony and Sylvia also looked at Henri and the silence lengthened until Sylvia said, 'So you don't know where she is Henri?'

'No Sylvia, I've no idea.'

In fact very few people knew where Giselle was, as she was on assignment as Stephanie inferred.

'Auntie, do you have any idea how best we can make contact with these people? What are we really trying to do, or perhaps, how can we best do what we got told to do?'

Giselle looked at the young girl beside her as the pair of them leant on the rail of the ferry. They were en route to Holland from Harwich. As part of her job, supposedly translating and helping refugees, Giselle was trying to discover more about a human smuggling operation bringing young European girls into England. Various intelligence agencies had slowly pieced together the various parts and procedures of the operation and Giselle's office wanted to try and fill in the details. With her young companion Giselle was travelling to Holland where some of the girls boarded for England. In this particular case the girls were thought to be from Croatia and Giselle's young companion was from Sarajevo.

'We'll be very quiet and casual,' said Giselle. 'This is just a trial run to see where and perhaps how we can make contact. We might end up speaking to them but only after we have listened a little. More likely we will just watch and listen. Watch how they are organised. See how many adults and how the adults act and talk. Also, see whether there are any other people watching the group of them. There may be other people on the ship who are not obviously part of the group but "bodyguards" or security people to make sure everything is safe and non suspicious. Sad to say Letti but this is a serious and dangerous business. These are not nice people. We will have to be very careful.'

'But what about the girls auntie?'

'Most of them, maybe all of them don't know what is going on Letti. The regular school girls are just on holiday and enjoying themselves.'

'But the others?'

'Frightened Letti, and we must do all we can to help them but we must do it slowly and very very carefully. We must find the people who are doing this and stop them. We can't help the girls directly. It will be hard. Just remember all the things you had to do with your mother. How you had to be quiet, not say anything. This trip is just to observe and learn. Can we do that do you think?'

'Yes auntie. Don't you say in English "softly, softly, catchee monkey"?' and Letti giggled.

Giselle hugged the young Croatian girl to her. 'Come on, let's go inside and look at those photographs again. Just to make sure we can recognise them if they don't speak very much. They may be quite quiet.'

'I thought the forest was supposed to be peaceful and serene Henri? Isn't this a place to commune with nature and gaze at your navel – or some such dribble?'

'And aren't you going to commune with your village insider?' asked Henri as Leslie slowly drove towards Home Farm.

'Well at least I'll do that in the quiet confines of his aromatic study,' said Leslie. As it was a warm afternoon Henri had wound down the windows of the car and the volume of noise from Home Farm was quite distinctive from several metres away. It sounded like animals in distress thought Henri.

'Are you sure you've got the right place and the right time Henri?' asked Leslie with a smirk on his face. 'Think you're going to talk high finance and slippery options with clipped coupons with that as a background? I'll be back around four. Have fun,' and Leslie slowly steered the car back towards the village and his useful village insider Tom Daley. He needed to find out some more about the good reverend's so-called angel initiation ceremony. Henri walked through the back yard of Home Farm as the esoteric music-like sounds came to a crashing crescendo and a pregnant silence fell on the place. The leaves of the sycamore tree-house stopped trembling.

'Anyone at home?' he asked, stepping over the kitchen threshold.

'Uncle Henri,' cried Peter. 'You're just in time to be our music critic. We're the DG Trio and just doing a little rehearsing but we could do with some public feedback. Did you know that Tony can play the guitar? And listen, I've improved on the drums. We all sing too. We're all good. That's why we've called ourselves the DG Trio – the Dam Good Trio. Anyway, just look, not only is Tony good with his feet with a soccer ball but he's pretty cool with his fingers strumming the strings. Have you met Dizzy? It's one of his songs we were playing. He's been playing keyboards for ever. Dizzy this is my Uncle Henri. He's from London like you and Tony. Do you want to hear the next number? It's got a real catchy beat to it – sort of rap and West Indian. Did I say that Dizzy's dad was a jazz player? That's where Dizzy learnt all about music 'cos his dad is real neat. He plays clarinet in a real jazz band – well he did up in London but now he's looking for other blokes down here to jam with. So are we ready guys? Time for "Down to Earth" Dizzy?'

Peter turned from looking at Henri to question the pianist, and Henri took in the scene before the sound hit him full blast.

'Stop! Whoa! Hold it! Hold it!!!' he exclaimed. 'Peter, give me a break.'

'You don't like it? It's got a great beat – real down to earth if you know what I mean. Step back a bit and hear the whole ensemble. You're probably too close to the keyboards and getting vibes off the amplifier.'

'Peter, where is your mother?' asked Henri.

'Out,' said Peter, 'and that's why we are practising. Enrico is not too keen on the music but he knows that we have to practice. He's really supportive and wants us to do well. We're playing for the school next month and we need the practice.'

'Where out Peter?'

'She's out walking with Enrico. They've probably gone to visit the Entwhistles at Enrico's old cottage. Enrico has carved a toy for young Adam. They're living in the cottage where Enrico used to live. Have you met the Entwhistles Uncle Henri? They talk funny but Adam's mum is really nice. They've a baby girl now and mum's over there helping a bit.'

'Did your mother mention that I was coming?'

'No Uncle Henri. Why don't you go over there and find her. It's not far. We've still got a few more numbers to try. She'll be back for tea.'

'She didn't tell you that I was coming here this afternoon to talk to you and her about investments? I told her I had some really good opportunities for you to make some money. I've just invested a considerable amount of client's money in a couple of excellent new issues and wanted to share the information. I think I can make you a very rich young man. You'd like that surely Peter? Perhaps you could invest some of the profits in buying better instruments? Perhaps I could find an agent for you, or even a record deal. I know several people up in London you know Peter. Do you have a manager? Would you like me to look after your band – help you get noticed?'

'My dad does all that,' said Dizzy. 'My dad looks after the Lord family money too. That's why we're here. Mr. Lord offered dad a job and so we've moved. We're living in the village and dad does all the accounting. He's looking after Peter's money and he knows several people up in London to help our band, if we need it that is.' Dizzy ran his fingers up and down the keys.

'That's right Uncle Henri,' said Peter. 'Remember you saw us a month or so ago and we told you. Dizzy and his family were down here on holiday and saw Tony swimming in the pool. They're old friends from up in London. Anyway, Uncle Daniel talked with Dizzy's dad and it all got decided. Grandma wanted to spend more time with grandpa and Uncle Daniel wanted someone to handle the finances. That's Dizzy's father's background and so we all teamed up. That's how the band got started 'cos Dizzy's dad thought we should all have fun. It's real neat Uncle Henri. You ready to hear the next tune? We'll turn the amps down a little if you like. You must like this music? Great Auntie Stephanie was telling us just the other day that you used to go to Clubs up in Bath, and in Bristol when you were at Uni. I'll bet you go to Clubs up in London now don't you? Auntie Giselle told us you liked music and psychedelic lights. She said you were always going to Clubs.'

Peter turned back to Dizzy and Tony. 'How about "Florida Fantasy" that you wrote for Auntie Katya?' said Peter. 'That's slow and somewhat quieter.' Peter gently tapped his drumsticks on the cymbal and started a steady rhythm on the bass drum with his foot as Dizzy picked out a sweeping series of chords. Peter smiled at Henri as Tony settled his guitar and strummed into the tune.

Henri felt an array of emotions. Part of his head was in tune with the music. The kids were actually quite good and obviously that Dizzy on the keyboards had talent but that wasn't why he was here. Shit, why hadn't Christina said? Why hadn't Sylvia said? They'd hired this Dizzy's dad. Why had nobody told me? Perhaps they did Henri thought. He'd come down here last month, no, in August he remembered with all the birthdays, and when there'd been that mass of people at Home Farm. When his sister chased him out. Yes, that's it. Henri turned back to look at the trio. Could he salvage anything here? Was this Dizzy's dad just an accountant or did he do financial planning too? Christina won't know but Sylvia will. Back to Fotheringham then thought Henri. He turned to leave the kitchen.

'Mum's at the Entwhistles Uncle Henri. Shall I tell her you called?'

'I'm going back to the Big House Peter,' said Henri. 'I'm going to talk with your grandmother.'

'You coming to Uncle Daniel's birthday Uncle Henri? We're supposed to be playing there too. It's in a couple of weeks – the twenty-fourth I think.'

'Yes, well maybe. I think so Peter. See you soon,' and Henri walked out of the kitchen as the gentle swaying and swishing sounds of Florida Fantasy reverberated around the walls.

'Did your mum forget Peter?' asked Tony, as he picked out the melody on the strings. Peter answered with brisk drum roll.

'As Dizzy said Tony, it's all taken care of,' said Peter. 'I think there was a long discussion up at the Big House and grandma decided. Now, let's go back to "Down to Earth" 'cos we haven't got a good finish to that. Weren't you working on something Dizzy – a better finale?'

The music followed Henri for quite a way as he walked in the autumn sunshine up to the Big House. Was he wasting his time he thought? Do I really need this 'cos I had that earlier windfall? But it's partly mine. Leslie told me I should get my share. Shit Anthony, get real and live in today's world.

'Henri, I thought you were going to see Christina? Now can you be quiet Henri as Anthony is resting? Of late he's become quite tired and not himself. I suppose we're all getting a little older. Can I get you a drink Henri? Daniel and Katya are out in the forest somewhere. They played golf this morning and I understand they were very successful. Daniel was muttering and Katya was laughing about smashing birdies. I didn't quite understand the joke so it must be something between them. Did you want a drink?'

'Sylvia who's this Dizzy? Or perhaps more important who is his dad? Yes, I was supposed to see Christina, but when I got to Home Farm I was greeted by howling banshees masquerading as music. Peter and his merry band were terrifying whatever wildlife is left in Fotheringham. Do Stephanie's sheep abort or have fits with all that noise? Isn't there something in genetics about mutations when animals get stressed?'

'So you didn't see Christina?'

'No, she was visiting someone, someone with Enrico I think Peter said.'

'Ah yes, the Entwhistles. They've got a new baby.'

'So, Dizzy whoever and his precious jazz playing dad?'

'Henri, we hired Ed Gillespie as the Estate Financial Officer,' said Sylvia. 'You remember, in fact I think you were here when we discussed it, that Daniel and Katya don't have that background. Anthony and I have graciously retired and Daniel decided he needed that expertise. Ed Gillespie appeared at the right time with the right credentials. I suppose it was a bonus that the son Richard, Dick or Dizzy as Peter calls him was an old friend of Tony. This has further helped Tony settle in and have another friend around so it all seemed to work out for the best.'

'Best for who?'

'For whom.'

'Whatever Sylvia, but why didn't you and Anthony tell me all this? Christina could have said but I went over there today and she wasn't around. Anyway, what does this Ed Gillespie do? Actually, what sort of experience and credentials does he have about investments? Who does he know? Who did he work for in London? Did anybody check that he is for real? There are some real slippery characters in that business Sylvia, especially up in London. You've been away from all that for some time. You're out of touch. Why don't I do some checking for you? This is serious business Sylvia. There is a lot of money at stake here. It's all part of our future. You may be getting older as you say Sylvia but the rest of the family has still got some living to do. That requires careful planning and sensible investment strategies – things I know about. Things I'm good at.'

Sylvia held up her hands to stem the flood of words.

'Henri, stop right there. This is a done deal. Ed's worked for over a month now and everything has gone very well. Just to answer your insinuations we did all the necessary checking. Ed Gillespie came with excellent references and I telephoned to verify. In addition I had some people in London do some additional questioning – not that that is any of your concern.'

'But it is my concern Sylvia. This is Lord family money, Lord family futures and that includes me.'

'Henri, we've had this discussion before and it is finished. At this point in time Mr. Gillespie is our Financial Officer thank you very much. Now, can we change the subject? On a more positive note Anthony and I would like to invite you and Leslie down here in three weeks time for Daniel's birthday. You know that it is always a great family gathering and a chance to talk about past achievements and future plans. It is a chance for all the Lord family to listen to and offer up ideas. It is a beautiful time of year here in the forest and we can all ride or drive and see some of the achievements. Daniel and Katya have slowly moved the Estate towards greener pastures and they have found some other people to help with that idea. Stephanie has been talking with the University as she too is thinking of retiring but would like her genetics work to continue. All of this opens the question of what is the long term objective for Fotheringham? Think on it Henri. Please come down. I know Giselle has planned to be here and I think Marie said that Marcel might be here too. Have you heard from him recently?'

Henri sat and looked at Sylvia. How could he turn things his way? Was there any opportunity to get the rest of the family to fight against Anthony's ideas and silly customs? Samantha always thought it was wrong. Maybe I can persuade Giselle?

'Well Henri?'

'Yes Sylvia, yes I'd be delighted. I'm sure Leslie would too. And yes, I will have that drink but can I telephone the George and leave a message for Leslie? He thinks I'm at Home Farm.'

Unfortunately for Henri the weekend of Daniel's birthday celebrations turned into another nightmare of frustrations. Sure, he and Leslie drove down to the quiet pastoral autumnal shades of gold and brown surrounding Fotheringham but inside all was not quiet. For once Daniel was quite outspoken about the new developments and future direction of the Estate and everyone was pulled enthusiastically along with the ideas. Leslie didn't make his usual pointed comments about Henri's share as Leslie was wrapped up in some village story about the Reverend Godschild. According to his source in the village the reverend was planning an initiation of the angels' ceremony and Leslie even telephoned Buzz to come down and investigate further. Without Leslie's support Henri turned to Samantha but she was fully involved in some detailed and demanding investigation for Heritage Adventures. That in turn intrigued the rest of the guests and so once again Henri lost the chance to launch any discussion on inheritance. Even the younger generation had their moments as Matthew and Veronica had heard about Peter's venture into the music world and unsuspectingly they asked for a demonstration. There was a very mixed reception to the so-called musical outpourings of Peter, Tony and Dizzy.

'Like some of your club music Henri?' asked Stephanie. 'Giselle told me you quite liked that kind of thing.'

'Can you dance to it Henri?' asked Veronica. 'It's very rhythmic. Almost like the old flapper days.'

'Dizzy's dad used to play in a trad jazz band auntie,' explained Peter. 'He taught us some of the riffs. Suppose it's a mixture of blues, rock, new age and heavy metal.'

'And that is supposed to explain it to me Peter is it?'

'Uncle Henri will do that for you auntie. Dizzy's dad says it's quite like club music. Up in the city you know. We're still pretty rough but it's fun.'

'Henri, you were looking for a sideline, another way to earn money. You were asking earlier about sharing Lord revenues. Why don't you take Peter's group in hand and find them a contract? Be their manager?'

'What's that Veronica? Manage them? No, I think Mr. Gillespie has all that in order, along with managing the Lord family revenues I should add. Don't know why I wasn't asked about that though?'

Sylvia noticed that Anthony gasped and suddenly held his chest. Trying to be discreet she immediately turned to Daniel and asked him to explain about the new advice coming in from the two wildlife experts who had been hiking around the estate. This got the group quite involved in discussing how the estate could change to accommodate a more natural environment and enhance the experience at the Education Centre. Veronica and Matthew launched into a reminiscence of how the Estate used to be before their dynamic mother got that all changed. As the group discussed whether it would be the same as before, a hundred or so years ago, Sylvia silently moved over to Anthony and without a word gently steered him out of the room. Fortunately Daniel and Katya had started quite an animated discussion as Sylvia supported Anthony up the stairs.

'Sylvia, what's happening my love? I suddenly felt faint and had this pain in my chest. Usually I don't get indigestion from cook's good food.'

'Anthony, rest a moment. I noticed you suddenly looked pale and it has been a long and tiring day. You were out around the estate with all the family today and most of the time it was you doing the talking. I know you love people about you darling but I think today was a little too much. Let the young ones take on their share. Daniel and Katya are into top gear with those ideas about "green revenues" and making the estate more diverse. They both really think it is the future Anthony. We've done our bit and we did it really well. Time for a changing of the guard my sweet. I'll just rest here alongside you and let Daniel enjoy his birthday.' As Sylvia's quiet assuring words washed over him Anthony closed his eyes as he lay on the bed and the pain subsided, the anxiety level dropped, and he fell asleep. Sylvia looked at her sleeping husband and smiled. Very gently and lovingly she leant over and kissed him. 'Rest Anthony,' she murmured. 'We've done our bit my love.' As the breathing continued peacefully Sylvia slipped out of the bedroom and made her way downstairs to the animated discussion on environmental change.

Again, money, inheritance, revenue sharing dropped out of the agenda and Henri ground his teeth with frustration. Why didn't Giselle come thought Henri. She would have been on my side. She would have spoken out about the family and changing to modern ideas. She was always keen on helping people.

And Henri was right because Giselle was away helping people – or rather trying to help people as part of her job. Although she had wanted to be at the family gathering for Daniel's birthday Giselle had to be working. Once again the ferry from Holland to Harwich battled its way through the choppy waters of the shallow North Sea. Giselle was partnered again with her young volunteer accomplice. An organised gang were smuggling young girls into England to serve in the sex trade business and Giselle was working to uncover the operation. The procedure was still relatively low key but Giselle's boss wanted to monitor the situation before trying to roll up the network. It had only recently come to the attention of the authorities, and that was through a mistake and a difficult-to-identify young body. For Giselle this particular mission was primarily delicate inquiries and observations. Both Giselle and her young friend spoke Serbo-Croat – the language of the gang and the girls. Posing as an aunt and niece Giselle and Letti wandered about the ferry looking at likely groups and chatting, trying to see who would respond to the language. If they could identify interested parties the idea was to note the size and composition of the group. They were also to try and identify whether there were other "watchers" also monitoring or guarding the group. Finally, if the opportunity arose, Giselle and/or Letti would strike up a conversation with any one of the young girls in the interested group and just generally chit-chat. Where had they come from? Where were they going? Were they going shopping, to see the sights, to hear a group, or just visiting family? Contact was to be light, no follow-ups, no future meetings, and then observe who met the group and where? How did they get off the boat and did they take the train to London? Who met them in London, and all the time was there anybody else watching from arm's length. Letti was the prime possible chit-chat contact while Giselle was to observe from afar and look for guardians. Their earlier trip had been a trial run and had not proved very successful. Giselle had argued they should try again and perhaps be a little more pro-active.

Giselle's boss had sat with his team and synthesised several scraps of information from a variety of sources. The team thought this "school group" excursion procedure was a likely method for bringing in a few girls at a time. Within an official and apparently bona fide school group would

197

be one, two maybe three girls on a one-way ticket. As the London-based gang was Serbian many of the "girls" were kidnapped Moslems from Bosnia or even Kosovo. This was a pure white slave trade and Giselle was particularly revolted by the likely fate of the "girls". However, she also realised, as did the rest of the team, that intercepting any one school group wasn't of any use. They needed to see the whole operation and determine how best to ensnare the major players. There was already a well-established partnership with the authorities in Holland and Giselle's boss was already favouring a wrap-up operation at one or more venues in London. They just needed to see where and when was the best place to strike.

'Here Letti, let's make sure you hair colouring is complete. And we'll change the head scarf. I've got on a different coat so we look different from last time in case anyone is taking photos.'

'And we've got Vladimir with us this time auntie. So we look like a full family group.'

'It's a careful role to play Letti – trying to be hidden yet trying to catch attention. Perhaps you could get "lost" on one of the decks, or hurt an ankle. Vladimir and I will see who if anyone responds to the language.'

As the ferry slowly pulled into the misty English coast Vladimir, Giselle and Letti huddled at the back of the passenger crowd and watched who went where. The party of nine girls with both a woman and man leader boarded the boat-train to London. It was hard for Giselle and her team to determine whether the "watchers" changed at this time as several people left the ferry and several new people boarded the train from the town. Overall though the operation had been a success and Giselle's group had identified the target, seen at least two other peripheral watchers and followed the group all the way into London. In the slow process of crime prevention it had been a successful week-end.

'Well that was a right useless weekend Leslie,' complained Henri as they drove back to London. 'I had talked with both Samantha and with Giselle before and they both agreed we should talk about the inheritance. When we got there Samantha was into her job and Giselle didn't even show. And if I hear anything more about Dizzy's dad I shall scream. Leslie, are you listening? You were no help either. Every time I turned round to you for support you had buggered off. Where did you go? Well say something Leslie for fuck's sake. Your face tells me you're no happier than I am. Did your snout get it wrong again? Was he too stoned out of his mind and forgot who you were?'

'Henri shut it, just shut it. Stop your fucking whining. It's money, money, money with you all the time and it's getting boring my friend. Change the bloody record. Didn't you have a winner just before we came down? I thought you told me that you'd had a winner. Came home flushed and excited. Yes you did, I remember it now.'

'Don't change the subject Leslie. Where were you? Where were you when I needed you?'

'Actually love I was trying to dig up the dirt on your precious family's support for this bogus preacher. If my intel is right I think we have found a pervert. We need to come down again Henri, some time in November and catch the dirty bugger. If what I learnt is true, and Buzz can catch the evil bastard in the act, we may have a scoop to bloody the nose of your precious family.'

'Or I could use it to blackmail them into sharing the Lord money?'

'Fuck you Henri. This is my story, mine and Buzz's. We'll publish it my friend. You'll see. Get your bloody money some other way Henri. Still, maybe if you're really nice I'll share some of the proceeds from the story with you – seeing as it's your family that we are shafting. Now don't sulk Henri. We'll come down in November, with Buzz, although we'll hide Buzz somewhere discreet, and catch this porno preacher with his pants down. Now, did I tell you what goes on at this initiation of the new angels' ceremony? Listen up 'cos Tom Daley was telling me he had heard, and learnt off the net too if I know him, that our good reverend is very keen personally welcoming new angels into his ministry. Seems the ceremony goes like this.'

But unfortunately it didn't, although Henri, Leslie and Buzz didn't know that until the end of that weekend in November. The no-show also frustrated another player, well non-player really. Winston Carruthers had just returned from an interesting and very stimulating tour of Thailand. He had filled his eyes and camera with numerous images of young girls offering an unbelievable array of services. On his return, however, after a couple of visits to the Oasis, Winston had learnt about a new venue for events worth watching. And these were closer to home – well, closer than Thailand. There were rumours, nay more than rumours, about a whole new and more natural place to go and see. Stories of sexual entertainment in the woods. Being a loner Winston had only heard whispers, snippets of conversations, disjointed phrases but he loved puzzles as much as he loved looking. Slowly he had put together who, where, but he didn't know when so he had come down to the village by Fotheringham to learn a little more.

That Saturday morning in mid-November the air was sharp and frosty and Winston walked briskly down the forest ride leading from the main road. To any outside observer he looked the part with his dark green anorak, twill pants, neat boots and the camera slung around his neck. Every now and again he would check the map and stop to sweep the binoculars towards any bird song he heard. True he did know a little about birds, and to any casual acquaintance he appeared to be a bona fide ornithologist. The cover would pass. Somewhere in this forest, somewhere in the forest of Fotheringham Estate he had heard.

'Henri, my little bird tells me that the reverend has found a new place to celebrate in your forest. Somewhere away from where he preaches. My source isn't sure whether it's a building or some magic forest grove. You know Fotheringham. Where should we look?'

'Could be anywhere Leslie,' said Henri.

'Think Henri you bloody clown,' growled Buzz. 'I don't want to go lugging camera equipment all through the bloody woods mate.'

'Peace Buzz,' said Leslie. 'Let Henri list some options. Just for starters Henri it isn't the Education Centre, and obviously it's not the Manor. Where else is there?'

'Well not Home Farm for sure,' said Henri. 'Not unless Cousin Christina has gone very non-Catholic on us. I suppose the other buildings include the office and maintenance yard and then there are the two cottages. There aren't any other buildings.'

'But didn't we see or didn't you tell me about some other new family living in the forest? Could they be involved with the reverend? Didn't you say they came from Yorkshire? No, that was George in the pub telling us. I'm sure the good reverend was in Yorkshire some time in his past. So their cottage is a possibility eh? Looking at your face Henri you obviously don't think so. Well then, what about that other new family you were going on about. Wasn't that the Gillespies or someone?'

'No,' said Henri. 'They live in the village bugger them.'

'Well who then Henri for fuck's sake. I'm cold and this is getting us nowhere Leslie,' said Buzz. 'Can't you lean on your local source Leslie or is he as useless as Henri here?'

'Not happy away from civilisation are you Buzz? Not your cup of tea out here so to speak.'

'Leslie, there's no targets for any camera out here. It's nowheresville: it's nothingville: it's dead mate. Told you this was a waste of time.'

'The cottage,' said Henri suddenly, 'the other cottage, Gloria's cottage. Could be there. Sylvia was going to bull-doze it but then she decided it could be useful for some hikers. No, not hikers but biologists. They could use it as a base.'

'Nudists are they these hikers? Biology in the buff?' asked Buzz.

'No, hold up there Buzz. Henri has a point. Wasn't this thing Gloria had going down here somewhere discreet? Must have been accessible but also out of sight. Sounds a possibility. Which way Henri?'

The three Londoners drove from the village out towards Fotheringham and Henri tried to remember the back way in. After a couple of mistakes they coasted to stop in the empty clearing around the Ferris cottage, Gloria's cottage, and now maybe the good reverend's ceremonial site. As Henri, Leslie and Buzz got out of the car to look around, and maybe investigate the cottage, people suddenly appeared from all round them. Winston Carruthers stumbled over the uneven pile of dirt filling in one of Peter Lord's soil pits of last year. He had been looking through his binoculars at a couple of noisy magpies when he lost his footing. Had he noticed the car and the other three men he would have discreetly hidden in the edge of the clearing but now it was too late.

'Hi,' he ventured somewhat feebly. 'Fascinating pair of magpies you know. Great place for birds. Lots to see. You spotting too?' His voice trailed off but his embarrassment and uncertainty was interrupted by a procession of eight noisy new people marching purposely into the clearing. Well, it was only two of them who were really noisy but their voices made up for all the other six quiet ones.

'Who are you?' demanded the diminutive young lady sporting glasses and an attitude.

'I'm an ornotho.....' started Winston.

'Not you, them!' demanded Doris, explicitly pointing at Henri, Leslie and Buzz. Somewhat surprisingly it was Henri who responded.

He'd just about had enough of Buzz and was a little pissed off about the whole deal down here.

'My family own this estate,' he proclaimed emphatically as he strode towards Doris. The other seven hikers watched. Doris let Henri come up real close and just when it looked like Henri was going to point his finger back in Doris's face she braced herself up to her full five feet and said, 'So. We've explicit permission, no, explicit direction from the Lord of the Manor to come here and help him. His Lordship himself directed us, and her Ladyship, and her resident forester. Full authority. Absolute rights. Paid-up partners.'

'Hold up there Henri,' said Buzz as he caught Henri's arm. 'That's Rupert Oldshaw,' and Buzz swung his camera into action.

'Oy,' shouted Doris. 'I haven't finished.'

Winston Carruthers turned to slip away. 'You, I haven't finished with you either,' shouted Doris at Winston's back. Winston stopped in his tracks.

'Look folks. This is much too nice a morning to get into any pissing match. How about a few introductions?' suggested Leslie – trying to defuse the situation. 'I'm sure we're all here for the good of the forest. As Henri said, it is his family's estate. He is Henri Lord by the way and I'm Leslie Dauphin.'

'The journalist,' said Rupert Oldshaw.

'And this is Buzz Haas, a photographer,' said Leslie.

'Good Lord,' said Rupert, 'the paparazzi.'

'We're here doing a story for Sir Anthony on Fotheringham Manor and just touring around to get a little background. Rupert Oldshaw I believe?' asked Leslie as he turned to the oldest of the hikers.

'You're the group that's been traipsing through here all summer?' said Henri. 'Seem to remember you pissed off my Aunt Sylvia. Didn't you go pulling down fences or something? Annoyed Daniel? More power to you,' he added.

'That's all been sorted,' snapped Doris, annoyed at being ignored. 'We're partners now. Partners with Daniel and Katya. Helping them with green revenues. Should be on a retainer but they're cheap. Cheap Lords. They paying you for this story? Do you have a contract? I could help you know. You should have a contract and be on some sort of retainer.'

'Can it Doris, just for a moment. We're just hiking through looking at the wildlife opportunities,' said Rupert. 'A couple of our group are wildlife biologists and we all have an awareness of the forest. Like you, I suppose we are helping them write a more comprehensive story of the estate – helps with the experiences being offered at the Education Centre.'

'Where the good reverend offers salvation and the means to spread the good word?' asked Leslie.

'Amen,' said two of the hikers, but when Leslie looked he wasn't sure these two would be part of the new angels' ceremony. Still, you don't know if you don't ask thought Leslie. 'I hear he offers other services in the forest. Away from the Education Centre?'

No-one reacted.

'Have any of you heard the good reverend?' he tried.

The two girls looked at each other Leslie noted. 'Yes,' said Philippa.

'And did he offer salvation? Did he suggest you become angels? I hear he is very successful at bringing new people into his flock. Has a special service to initiate novices to become his angels.'

Reaction this time was loud and fast. 'Oy! You! Who are you? What are you doing spying around here? We've got the wildlife contract so who are you?'

Doris wasn't about to let Winston Carruthers escape unscathed. She also wasn't going to let any other people trespass on her group's supposed contract, paid or otherwise.

'Just bird-watching,' stammered Winston. 'Just looking around at the birds.'

'Doris it's fine,' said Rupert. 'Let's get on. Arnold wanted to check on the escarpment. He thought there were some foxes up there; maybe a den. We've a ways to go and the days are getting shorter this time of year.'

The hikers moved off out of the clearing and Winston looked at Henri, Leslie and Buzz. He hesitated as if he was going to say something but changed his mind and slowly drifted back along one of the rides. After a moment he lifted his binoculars and scanned the tree tops.

'Well Henri? Any other bright ideas?'

'There's nowhere quite like this anywhere else Leslie. Look, rather than just traipse all over the forest why don't you go and lean on your snout. Anyway, before we do that why don't we look around here for a while and think how best to capture the scene if it was here? That would help Buzz. Wouldn't it Buzz?'

'Wonder whether that Rupert Oldshaw is caught up in this angels thing,' muttered Buzz, half to himself.

'Cameras Buzz?' asked Leslie. 'Let's do as Henri suggests for a while and then go back into the village. If this is the site as Henri suggests how would we capture the scene? Let's look in the cottage and see whether there has been any activity. Check out that area first as it might be easier if this was indoors, especially this time of year.'

'Thought you said it was an outdoors ceremony Leslie? Thought you said your village source told you this happened out-of-doors?'

'Maybe Henri, maybe for the ceremony, but the final consummation, the final initiation may be somewhere more comfortable, more discreet.'

'Well I can't think of anywhere else so let's try and be practical while we're down here. Should we come back here tonight or have you heard anything more about when?'

The three of them scouted around the cottage and the clearing and Buzz identified some locations, just in case this is the place he growled. Back in the village that evening they watched the darts match and listened to the local gossip. Leslie had gone round to Tom Daley's and Tom told them to listen at the church on the Sunday. The word on the grapevine was that the good reverend was close to welcoming some new members, if you know what I mean he added. So Leslie, Henri and Buzz mingled with the village congregation to listen to the Reverend Gabriel Godschild preach. Leslie made sure that Buzz sat separately but the good reverend embraced everyone altogether with his passionate plea for worshipping the Lord and fulfilling his message. As Tom Daley had mentioned there was a strong call to the congregation to assemble for Christmas as a special day, a special day when he Gabriel would reveal some new revelations. This would be a very spiritual day when many wonders would happen and new people would publicly embrace the true faith. He Gabriel would combine some rites of the old world in with the symbology and ceremony of the word of God to welcome new young people forever into the light. An initiation, like a christening, like a baptism, a full magnificent welcoming into the world of Gabriel Godschild.

As they filed out of the church people whispered, people chatted, people looked at each other and wondered. Was there to be a new awakening? Would the world change as the good reverend had inferred?

Was there more to be believed? Did the start of the millennium mean a new coming?

Driving back to London that Sunday afternoon, in the gathering gloom of a fog that littered the road with pools of limited visibility, Buzz thought it was all a con, and Henri agreed with him. Only Leslie was positive about the weekend. He thought the whole scene had potential.

'Look,' he said. 'Listen to the man. It's going to happen. We just need to be there when it does. It'll be a real eye-opener. The good reverend has been around for a while, parading as all sorts of people so he's a con artist from way back. Couple that with whatever ceremony he's going to perform while he's speaking to the youth in Henri's family's ultra-green, ultra-tomorrow's, ultra-biologically whatever Centre. With any pictures from Buzz it should bring the roof in.'

'So the family will need me to help them financially survive the crash,' offered Henri. Leslie gently laid his hand on Henri's arm. 'We'll do all we can to help Henri. As you've said before, it's family.'

In Leslie's flat the telephone softly rang. The three men looked at each other. The ringing continued.

'Get it Henri,' said Leslie.

'I'm in the middle of something Leslie. I'm trying to sort out my cash flow.'

'And it's not pretty I'll bet,' added Buzz. 'You've been losing at the tables and snorting to get back off the floor.'

'Piss off,' uttered Henri. The telephone didn't stop ringing. Leslie looked at the other two and slowly rose off the sofa. 'Children, children,' he mused, and he lifted the receiver. Almost immediately he held the earpiece well away from his head and looked at Henri. Henri caught the questioning look and shook his head quite firmly. Leslie slowly lowered the receiver back towards his ear. He quietly spoke into the phone in a calm and modulated voice. Once again he quickly snatched the receiver away from his ear and held it at arms length. All three of them could hear the tinny irate sound bellowing out of the earpiece. Leslie spoke briefly and gently lowered the phone onto the cradle. He looked rather questioning at Henri.

'Guess who?'

Henri sat somewhat stiffly in his chair but a perceptible shudder rippled up his body.

'Not a friend of yours Henri. Someone with a grudge by the sound of it. Someone rather demanding actually Henri. Someone with a very limited vocabulary but able to make his point quite clearly. Mentioned some large numbers Henri – large pound numbers. Made all sorts of intimidating threats too. Truly not a friend I'd want to cross or annoy Henri. I think you'd better work hard on having your family help you survive some financial crash rather than you helping them.'

'It'll have to come out of a client's account.'

'Henri, Buzz and I don't want to know any details my love. We certainly don't want to hear any solutions – especially if they're not kosher. Perhaps we'll hope for some special Christmas presents. You did say a couple of weeks back you thought something at work was going to pay off. Sounds like it had better Henri. Anyway, our Serbian friend probably thinks Christmas comes sometime in January, or whenever the Orthodox Christmas is.'

'Sure he's Christian?' asked Buzz.

'For Henri's sake I hope he's forgiving Buzz,' said Leslie.

'Give over you two. I'll sort it. I'll get it all sorted by the New Year. You'll see. Now, let's forget it and talk about something more festive. How are we going to handle this Christmas visit to Fotheringham?'

CHRISTMAS DAY

FORTUNATELY FOR ANTHONY THE BIG House was quiet that Christmas morning. All of the young people who would congregate later in the day were loudly celebrating presents elsewhere. In the local town, in his own bedroom, James was jumping up and down for joy over his new saddle. He managed to half-carry, half-drag it into his parent's bedroom while still loudly extolling its virtues and how his horse will love it. He wanted to rush over to Fotheringham to saddle up Dainty and go riding immediately. Samantha managed to persuade James to share in one of his other presents, one that Terence had thoughtfully found. Knowing James loved to hear Terence read, and now that James was convinced that he himself could read really well, they would share stories and listen to each other. With that thought Terence had found an old copy of Kipling's "Just so Stories", thinking James would love the array of animals described within. Somewhat out of character Samantha found it enchanting just to sit and watch the pair of them. Impatiently feeling the stirring of life inside her and still frightened of the possible challenges and threats ahead from a new baby, Samantha amazed herself with being able to just sit.

'I love both of you so much,' she cried out that morning as she sat in her bed looking at her two men.

'And we both love you too mummy,' exclaimed James, and then he was back into his book with Terence holding him and the book. Terence looked over James's head and smiled at his wife and mouthed 'I love you both too.'

After a few more minutes the two men had finished understanding how the rhino got his skin, and the Parsee cake in the story reminded James about his stomach. Then he remembered Janet had hinted at something special for Christmas – something he might like to eat, and he leapt off his parent's bed with a great shout.

'James. James!! You don't go running into a young lady's bedroom without knocking young man.'

'But you're a hot woman. Uncle Daniel said so.'

'Well come here then and give me a Christmas kiss before you ravish me.'

'Ugh kisses. Happy Christmas though, and this is for you.'

Janet Donaldson knelt down, clad in her rather skimpy and definitely "hot woman" nightie and smiled at James.

'Thank you kind sir,' she said. 'Can I have a hug too please?'

'No kisses then,' James insisted as he averted his face.

'And Happy Christmas to you too James,' and Janet gave James a box she had slipped out from under the bed. There came a knock on the door and Samantha poked her head around.

'See you're entertaining young men again Janet. Happy Christmas,' and Samantha came into the bedroom and gave her friend and business partner a hug.

Closer to the Big House there was young people excitement at Home Farm too.

'Look Peter, new boots. Auntie they're smashing. Just what I need 'cos I've grown out of my old pair. Super, absolutely right on.'

'We all know you're passionate about football Tony. They are black with white stripes too – almost like your team colours.'

'Fab auntie, and Spurs are doing well this season too. Beat Liverpool the other day. Four one it was. Hey Peter, that's neat.'

Peter gently lifted the microscope out of its felt-lined case. He turned to his mother. 'Mum this is fantastic. I've always wanted a microscope. I use Auntie Stephanie's whenever she lets me but to have my own is super. We'll be able to do all sorts of things for the Education Centre now: special things that we can share.'

'And in the boxes on the table Peter? What might be in the boxes on the table?'

'They're not wrapped in Christmas paper mum. They for us?'

'Read the labels son. I think they're magical gifts and more about love in this house than just Christmas only. They are family gifts. Read the names on the boxes.'

'Tony, this is yours. Wonder what they are?'

'One way to find out Peter,' said Tony, as he untied the string and started unwrapping. Inside was a brown cardboard box which just said "Winner". 'What's yours say Peter?'

'Says "Futures?", as if asking me a question.'

The two boys continued opening the boxes to find another box inside. Tony's was black over one half and white on the other whereas Peter's was all green.

'This is like those Russian dolls mum,' said Peter.

Christina sat at the table and smiled at her son and nephew. Across the table Enrico watched the two boys with a twinkle in his eye. 'Should we stop them and have them guess Christina?' asked Enrico. 'It's too easy just opening them. Perhaps there should be a treasure hunt clue for every layer.'

'Enrico when did you do this? I never saw you doing this. How did you manage to keep it hidden? Tony, what have you got? Look what Enrico has carved. That's great Tony.'

Carefully Peter unfolded the box away from the wooden figure of a man holding an axe in one hand and a book in another. Labelled at the bottom were the simple words "Forest Teacher". Tony was torn between looking at Peter and his own carving. Enrico had already carved a football player for Tony when he first came to Fotheringham sixteen months ago, and now Tony looked at his new carving. This was another football player but this one was holding a trophy, a cup up high as a winner. Tony looked at Enrico.

'You didn't paint him?'

'No Tony. I didn't want to presume. Just in case you change your mind and support Roma or Udinese,' he added with a chuckle. 'I thought I'd leave that decision to you at the end of the season. You might want to paint it in the village colours.'

'Enrico it's fabulous. After a few years I'll have a whole team. Thanks. Thank you so much,' and Tony went over and hugged the old man.

There was a bigger crowd at the Big House, but as they were all adult and Sylvia had said no presents, the crowd around the breakfast buffet was a little more subdued except for Katya. Still up in their bedroom Katya cried out, 'Daniel, Daniel, here feel. I can feel the baby. I can feel the baby moving. Put your hand on my stomach. Feel. Feel that kick. Oh Daniel I love you so.'

'Happy Christmas darling,' and Daniel slid both arms around Katya and gently hugged her.

'Shall we tell everyone? Shall we, shall we?' asked Katya excitedly. 'Samantha will be delighted. Two new babies in the family.'

'What do you mean – two new babies? Have we got twins? Did the doctor say we had twins? You never said when you went for that ultrasound scan. You never said you had twins.'

'Hush Daniel, hush,' and Katya put her finger on Daniel's lips, and then on her own lips. 'I shouldn't have said. It's still a secret.'

'Yes, I know we haven't told anyone, but twins. Really?'

'No Daniel. We don't have twins my love.'

'Then what, or perhaps who? Who has twins?'

'Don't tell anyone Daniel. I promised I wouldn't tell but now I've rather let the cat out of the bag.'

'Katya my sweet, you are being very obtuse and now I don't know which way is up. You're not having twins – right? Should I be delighted?'

'Actually Daniel, the person who will probably be the most delighted is your dad. He will be over the moon.'

'Yes,' said Daniel rather wistfully, 'in his more lucid moments. Let's get dressed and we can tell everyone at dinner tonight. Dad will probably want to share some pep talk with the family team – you know what he's like when we have a get together like this.'

'And this is the biggest get together for a long time Daniel. Even more people than at your birthday. All of the family are here this Christmas. I think I counted up to twenty people for dinner.'

Just along the corridor Henri stirred, rolled over, and asked, 'should we go and see Buzz today Leslie?'

'Henri, at this point in time my love we don't know Buzz, and we certainly don't know he is down here.'

'Well what are we going to do today then?'

'This morning Henri we're going investigating and that means church.'

'But our family never goes to church.'

'Henri, what did we hear and see a couple of weeks ago?'

'Oh, you mean the meeting in the forest?'

'Well the meeting in the forest is part of it, but think Henri, what did the godly man say a month ago about this Christmas being special? Chatting about some wondrous revelations and welcoming some new young people. So who do you think is preaching today my forgetful friend?'

'I don't know. How would I know Leslie?'

'Henri my love you would never make a reporter, a journalist. You're not inquisitive enough. You don't keep your eyes open, or your ears for that matter. Talking of eyes and ears Happy Christmas,' and Leslie rolled over in the bed and gave Henri a hug and a kiss. 'Here's a little something to help keep you awake,' and he handed Henri a small package wrapped in fancy paper. 'And now my Lord I shall go and find the bathroom in this antiquated pile of bricks, hoping it's not occupied by other members of your family.'

Down in the village things were also quite lethargic.

'Cup of tea this morning sir. Happy Christmas. We'll be a little slow this morning but then you said you weren't going anywhere in a hurry. Breakfast at nine okay is it?'

'Good morning landlord. Sure mate, breakfast at nine sounds fine. Happy Christmas to you too. By the way, remember I was asking last night if there's anything special I should note about this village, over and above the George that is? Have you had any more thoughts 'cos I've a couple of days or so here and I'd like to think I've included all of the more interesting places for folk to visit? You mentioned pies, and then you said the Fotheringham Manor Estate had some interesting history.

Maybe over breakfast, if you're not too busy, we can go over some of the better places for me to see. Ta for the tea though.'

After nearly everyone in the village had breakfast the morning moved on. Most folk went to church. It was a special day, and some of them remembered the earlier comments from Gabriel when he had spoken about new messages to come. As a result it was a packed house, standing room only for some, and the words had been spoken. An excited flock of parishioners streamed out of the church that Christmas morning. They were talking nineteen to the dozen though, as the service, well the sermon had been anything but usual. The Reverend Gabriel Godschild had persuaded the resident vicar that he should deliver a heaven-sent message as this was God's special day and he Gabriel was God's special messenger. The local resident reverend, one Peter Masters, was a man of righteous Christianity, faith in his fellow man and a distinct feeling he was listening to a new disciple and so he agreed with Gabriel. The congregation, well some of them, did not necessarily agree with Gabriel, and the ensuing conversations in the churchyard covered all the angles, including speculation on any new angels. As he had suggested, Leslie had gone to the church along with Henri.

'Need to gather some good words Henri. Some words out of the mouth of the man himself,' said Leslie. 'Good journalism Henri, good condemning journalism demands the right words. Words similar to the original words and we've just heard the original words Henri. Now we need to add some colouring to the original words. I need to apply some professional touches and add some buzz to the words. Talking of which did you see Buzz?'

'Eh?'

'Seen Buzz Henri? I need to slip him a note. My local friend tells me there is to be a meeting tonight. In fact there is to be a new angel ceremony tonight. He's rigged everything remember. With some judicious and fake emails my friend has persuaded the players that tonight is the night. We'll just have to hope the silly Gabriel keeps to a religious schedule and doesn't change his place of worship for his special evensong.'

'You think he'll hold one of his meetings tonight?' asked Henri, who hadn't really been listening to Leslie's mutterings. 'Are we going?'

Leslie turned and held the arm of his companion. He faced Henri and looked intently at the questioning expression.

'Henri, we're here to hear the good words. Here where we're supposed to be. Tonight Buzz will photograph the good deeds. The words tonight will be irrelevant. We've heard them before remember, a month ago, and now again this morning? So tonight my friend we will be nowhere near any meeting: nowhere near Buzz's activity. No connection Henri. But we will see Buzz tomorrow – quite by chance mind. Understand?'

No thought Henri but he was glad that Leslie was with him and Buzz was somewhere else. The jealousy thing was building up inside Henri. He loved Leslie and Buzz, but separately, not as a threesome.

Because it was Christmas Day the church had been packed but there were several people there amongst the flock who were not regular attendees or followers of Peter Masters. It's true that some of these smart-suited individuals had started life as Christians, very Orthodox Christians as it happens, but now they were merely followers. Under orders from on high they were following several of the other people in the church. The orders were quite explicit, and some time later, probably tonight if the rumours were true, some action would take place. During the rest of the day the band of followers split up and dutifully watched their targets.

'Happy Christmas Colin. Happy Christmas Ophelia, and you too Adam.'

'Come in my lady. Come in Mr. Daniel. Don't just stand there Colin love. Invite them in now.'

Sylvia had driven down with Daniel to see the Entwhistle family. She had brought a hamper of Christmas goodies plus some gifts for Adam. Daniel looked around him as he stood in the kitchen cum living room of the cottage. Back when he was a lad this had been the home of Antonio and Enrico Branciaghlia, and his home too he thought as he smiled seeing how often he was down here. They'd done a good job though Daniel saw as he looked at the decorations. Ophelia had adorned the room with holly, cedar sprays, and wall hangings of plaited reeds all brightened with red bunting. Painted paper chains hung across the ceiling and a small but very decorated spruce tree proclaimed it's Christmas.

'It looks lovely in here Ophelia,' said Sylvia as she slowly turned round in the room. Ophelia curtsied. 'Thank you my lady,' she said as she blushed.

'And who is hiding?' asked Sylvia looking at Ophelia. Crouching down Sylvia held out her hands. Storm, the black Labrador took this as an invitation and promptly licked the proffered hand and wagged his tail. Sylvia laughed and tickled Storm under his chin and then rubbed the top of his head. Liquid brown eyes looked up at Sylvia.

'Not you you friendly hound. Where's little Rose?'

'She's still sleeping my lady,' said Ophelia. 'She's such a good baby.'

'And I'm going to look after her,' piped up Adam. He walked round the room to stand beside the cradle holding baby Rose. Storm walked over to stand beside Adam as if to say the pair of them would look after the baby.

'Daniel, have you got that special package for Rose please?'

'Yes mum. Here it is.'

'This is a Happy Christmas gift for Rose,' said Sylvia as she handed the brightly coloured parcel to Ophelia. She turned to Adam. 'And for you you young protector, we also have something special.' Sylvia gave Adam another package in Christmas wrappings. After brief exchanges Sylvia and Daniel left the happy household.

'I said that another family could live here didn't I mother?' said Daniel as they got back into the Landrover.

'Yes son you did and I'm glad that has worked out okay. He's a good worker and Ophelia is.., well Ophelia is different let's say.'

'Mum she's just fine,' said Daniel laughing.

'And Katya?' asked Sylvia, changing the subject.

'She's more than fine mum thank you very much. She's,' and Daniel stopped himself when he remembered that they were going to tell everyone later this evening.

Sylvia looked at her son and inwardly she smiled. She already knew that Katya was pregnant but she wasn't about to spoil her son's surprise.

'Well, let's go and see whether everyone else in the family are fine shall we?'

'What's that car mum? Did you see it? There's nobody at the Education Centre today.'

'Daniel today is Christmas so forget it. Just for once Daniel let your forest rest in peace.'

'How's dad today mum?'

'So so Daniel. Anthony has his days as you know. I just hope that today won't tire him out too much. We've twenty people for dinner Daniel and you know what your father is like when all the family are together. He'll insist on speaking. Rallying the team he says. Daniel can't you persuade him to sit on the sidelines and just enjoy life?'

'Dad's never sat on any sidelines mum.'

'Just keep him away from money and inheritance Daniel. That's part of what caused the problem in the first place. You know, that stupid confrontation with Henri over the hiring of Ed Gillespie and then the brouhaha at Home Farm.'

On the drive back to the Big House Daniel remembered the two incidents and how thoughtless and irritating his cousin had become. The year before, right after his mother was killed, Christina adopted Tony and he went to live happily with Christina, Peter and Enrico at Home Farm. All went well until this past summer when an old school friend of Tony happened to come into the village on holiday with his parents, the Gillespies. The family had come back with Tony and Peter to Home Farm, met Christina and been brought up to date on Tony's life. Quite by chance I was down at Home Farm remembered Daniel when the Gillespies visited. Amazing how timing is everything thought Daniel. We wanted an accountant to relieve mum so she could spend more time with dad, and Gillespie was looking for a job away from London. Seemed a bloody good idea at the time thought Daniel. Katya and I don't have that kind of expertise and the financial side was becoming more demanding what with the money from the sale of Brainware and the accounting over the Education Centre. Ed Gillespie settled his family in the village, became the financial advisor, and his son Dick enrolled in school with Tony and Peter. The three boys got on really well and before we knew it we had a music trio laughed Daniel.

'Why are you laughing Daniel? Your dad's mind is no laughing matter.'

'No mum, I wasn't laughing at that, and I'm sorry 'cos dad's condition is worrying I know. Trouble is I hear there is no cure. A little like grandma in a way I suppose.'

'Unfortunately true Daniel although Anthony is so young.'

Daniel leant across and put his hand on his mother's arm. 'I was laughing at the enthusiasm and success of young Dickie Gillespie discovering the hidden talents of Tony and Peter. They've created a successful trio and they're all loving it.'

'Christina isn't Daniel. She says it certainly isn't her music. In fact she says she's not sure whether it really is music at all.'

'That's as maybe mum but Peter and Tony are happy and Ed Gillespie has taken over the financial work really well.'

'And put Henri's nose right out of joint in the process.'

'Dad never told us about any deal to let Henri manage the Lord family money,' said Daniel.

'And I'm not sure Daniel whether Anthony ever did discuss all that with Henri. He says he can't remember. He says he knows he talked with Henri about money but more about Henri's lack of it. He says he never promised Henri anything.'

'And Henri is bluntly adamant that dad told him he would invest in Henri's company and Henri would be the investment consultant. Henri was telling me that something similar had happened several years ago: when Henri was working in Bath. Back in the eighties I think. Didn't Henri's boss, a Mr. MacDonald talk with dad? Henri tells me there were some quite clear discussions between this Mr. MacDonald and dad. When we still had Brainware and dad was offering some of Brainware services in exchange for managing our investments.'

'Daniel that was long ago and today you know that your dad doesn't have that authority as it's no longer our company. The whole thing is very confusing and Henri's insistence is very stressful on your dad. When he heard of the blazing row that Henri had in Ed's office in the village he really had another relapse.'

'I know mum. Actually, it was the meeting before the one with Ed that really upset dad. You know which one.'

'The confrontation at Home Farm?'

'Yes mum. When dad heard about it he got really mad, which is not like him at all. Then he went to see Christina and learnt more of the details first hand. It really was a shame and Samantha feels bad about it as well. In fact she is very pissed off with Henri.'

'Why Samantha Daniel?'

'You may have forgotten mum but it was Samantha's company that Guido contacted. He knew a little bit from his parents, and they were brothers or sisters of Enrico's parents I think. No, maybe they were nieces or something. I can't remember the details. Anyway, it was Samantha who found all the links and took Guido down to meet his Great Uncle Enrico. Christina was delighted, and you know her – she gets all emotional and thought it was lovely that Enrico still had some family. Giselle was there too as it happens and in walked Henri. Insisted he wanted to talk with Christina about money – about Geoffrey's money and that he had the right to invest it properly for Peter. Told Christina he had talked this over with Geoffrey right after Peter was born and it was about time he took over. Well, of course, Christina got upset about Geoffrey and Guido gallantly intervened and everyone got to shouting and Henri even threatening some legal action. After Henri stormed out shouting he would be back Giselle managed to calm Christina and I understand from Peter there was a whole passionate mass of Italian gobblygook. Peter said he'd heard his mother talking with Enrico in Italian but he'd never heard such emotion from Giselle with his mother. One good thing that did come out of all that mum is Guido. According to my old friend Enrico, Guido and Christina seemed to have hit it off. Enrico told me that Guido asked whether he could return next summer and perhaps stay a little longer.'

'That's as maybe Daniel but your dad could do without any further stress. Just keep Henri away from Anthony and/or quiet. When I think about it it's Leslie who is just as much trouble. I'm not sure my act of Christian charity in inviting Leslie was such a good idea Daniel.'

'Maybe some of the Christian charity will rub off mum. They both went to church this morning.'

'Wouldn't have thought either of them were church goers Daniel, but then again Henri is a bit of an enigma. Giselle was telling me that she thinks her brother is becoming increasingly confused about a lot of things. She knows he's obsessed with money. She also mentioned that the company Henri keeps is not healthy. Told me she couldn't go into details but she was worried about Henri's lifestyle.'

'It's only for a couple of days mum. I'll talk with Katya, and with Samantha.'

Sylvia laughed. 'Maybe you should talk with Janet. She's enough woman for any number of men. Now that's a happier thought Daniel, a more positive thought.'

'Sure mum. Two hot women in the house should keep everyone occupied.'

While Henri and Leslie were in church that morning several of the other guests arrived. Stephanie had collected Matthew from the train station in town. Marcel had driven up from Dartmouth with Marie and Philippe. Giselle drove down from Bristol. The two "hot women" had arrived earlier when Terence brought them and young James in from their house in the town. James however just had to try out his new present and so mother and son were out riding in the forest leaving Terence to fend for himself with Janet. The group from Home Farm decided to pay their respects to the memorial in the Education Centre on their way to the Big House. Christina remembered her husband Geoffrey, Peter's father. Enrico reflected on his long life at Fotheringham with his brother Antonio, and Tony could feel sad for the mother he fought for and the father he never knew. After the four of them had stood there for a moment it was Peter who announced, 'Time to look forwards. It's Christmas and a time for good cheer. Come on mum, it's time to enjoy the family and you love doing that.' Enrico smiled as he watched Peter move his mother into a happier frame of mind. Hope Guido does return next year he thought. He and Christina got on very well. Would make a nice couple. Be good for both of them.

'Did your brother play football Enrico?' asked Tony.

'No Tony. We both worked with our hands and not with our feet.'

'Smashing,' said Tony. 'Your gift was brilliant. I was telling Peter that soon I'd have a complete team.'

'And then you'll want Enrico to carve you a guitarist I suppose Tony?' laughed Christina.

'And a drummer and a pianist mum,' added Peter. 'The whole band.'

Laughing and feeling happier than before, Christina drove the group up to the Big House.

Buzz quietly slipped the note from Leslie into his pocket and slowly walked up the main street in the village to the George.

'After all that singing landlord I think I'll have a pint.'

'Coming right up sir,' said George. 'A bite to eat is it?'

'Sure mate. One of them pies would go down a treat. 'Ow about steak and kidney?'

'Betty made some special turkey and stuffing ones for Christmas sir. Would you prefer that?'

'No landlord thanks. I'll stick to something I know. Got any chips to go with it 'ave you? Pie and chips with sauce goes down a treat you know.'

'I'll warm them up for you. With a pint is it?'

'Right on. Ta.'

Buzz ate and drank and looked at Leslie's note. Seems the gig was on. Up in his room he organised his gear. Remembering it was cold last time he was down here out in the wilds Buzz decided to don some extra clothes. After loading the car he turned out into the main street of the village. Everything was quiet and peaceful. Driving slowly he passed the main gates at Fotheringham but soon afterwards he carefully turned off the road and into the forest. Being a city person he concentrated on the forest to make sure he found the right place to turn off. As a result he was not careful enough to notice he had followers. As this particular forest ride didn't fork Buzz easily found the reverend's ceremonial meeting place. Parking on the edge of the clearing Buzz unloaded the car and slowly and carefully placed his equipment to cover the scene. He checked his cameras and timers. Just have to hope the holy man keeps to his routine thought Buzz. Leslie's snout has been pretty reliable to date. A few shots of holy holy in the woods with young angels should really excite the Sunday tabloids. Buzz settled down in his car to wait for events to unfold. He'd had lots of practice just sitting around and waiting for the big moment.

The Reverend Gabriel Godschild sat at his kitchen table and thought back over this morning's sermon. He had heard the excited discussions as the congregation streamed out of the church. Peter Masters had been delighted by the size of the congregation and the contributions on the circulating plates. And now for this evening thought Gabriel, when we embrace the little angels: when my acolytes and I welcome new sisters into God's family. Perhaps Godschild's new children will evolve from tonight's ceremony he imagined and what a delight that could be. Several people discretely scattered around outside the reverend's cottage also thought that this evening's ceremony might be a delight, but for completely different reasons.

One of the out-of-sight people outside the reverend's cottage was Winston Carruthers, and he was there for a completely different reason. At forty, single, going bald but getting richer by the day, Mr. Carruthers was a voyeur. He got his kicks from looking and he had heard that tonight should be different. Winston Carruthers had spent a fair amount of time, and money at the Oasis Club. He was well known to Gloria, Lola and to Belle. He liked to look at their entertaining of the more active clients. He was very disappointed that he had missed the antics of these ladies when they were entertaining earlier that year in the forest at Fotheringham. They had told him such stories and he had looked up their old but now defunct website. Through his internet searches and exchanges he met up with Tom Daley in cyber space and this in turn led to some useful information about the good Reverend Godschild's extra-curricular activities. Daley explained that he didn't have the energy to go chasing through the forest with any cameras but Winston enjoyed the chase as well as the kill. To actually photograph such scenes and then replay them afterwards was such a sensual delight. With Gloria, Winston had managed to enjoy several sessions of being behind the scenes, but this was even more exciting, and according to Daley tonight was the night. The man to follow was inside the cottage and Winston intended to follow this leading light of God to his other place of worship. Equipped with a video camera, still camera and flash, Winston looked forwards to an exciting and stimulating night.

In the bedroom he was sharing with Leslie, Henri leant over the table and snorted the thin white line.

'Do you have to?'

'It's Christmas Leslie. Time of good cheer.'

'Well lay off the booze then 'cos the two don't mix. I'm not sure your aunt thinks we're good company so let's behave. Just for once I won't go on about inheritance and money although you'd better do something pretty quick. You know I took that call from our Serbian friends the other day and it wasn't friendly.'

'Leslie I'm as stretched as far as I can be. In fact I've got to find over ten thousand pounds by year's end to repay my client's account.'

'You borrowing from your clients now Henri?'

'Just until my luck changes. I'll win it all back. You'll see.'

'And then you'll blow it all back up your nose.'

'Piss on you Leslie. Buzz will see me alright. He's there for me when I'm down.'

'Yes Henri, and you do go down on Buzz don't you?'

'Leslie, let's not quarrel. I love you you know. It's just this money thing. What did Tadic say anyway? That man is really obnoxious.'

'Pay up or else, in a nutshell Henri. There were a lot of other words, mostly four-letter words, but Tadic's English is limited.'

'What else?'

'Let's go down to dinner Henri and forget Tadic for a while. I haven't sat down to a family Christmas dinner for a long time: should be quite an experience. Wonder how the family will feel after they read our expose? Don't expect we'll be invited back for another dinner for some time so let's make the most of this one shall we?'

Twenty people sat down for dinner that night – all the existing Lord family plus significant others and special friends. As usual cook had risen to the occasion in her inevitable style, helped by two young girls she had hired for the evening from the village. When everyone was seated cook brought in a large tureen of soup and the two girls placed warm full bowls before each person around the table. This was followed by hot plates, hot tender meat of turkey and goose, fresh rolls, warmed vegetable dishes and several gravy boats. It was Daniel who made the rounds offering wine for the adults and fruit juices for the youngsters. Apart from James the conversation around the table was minimal as everyone enjoyed the wonderful dinner. James, who claimed that he could do more than one thing at a time, managed to tell everyone about his morning ride and eat at the same time – well, wave his fork about anyway. As was usual with James everyone listened because one never knew exactly what pearls of wisdom would issue forth from his active mouth. Samantha, sitting by James's side, had one hand semi-poised to stifle her little monster if the tales became too intimate.

'Dainty's got a lot better and she likes the new saddle grandma. She's says it helps her go faster. We almost caught up with the cars too. If mummy hadn't stopped me from jumping the fence we would have caught them. Fast as the wind we were. Weren't we mummy?'

'Yes darling.'

'What cars?'

'Don't know Daniel.'

'Remember I said that I'd heard or saw cars mum?' said Daniel.

'Christmas Day Daniel and it's a wonderful dinner. Enjoy everybody.'

'Cars on our drovers' road?' asked Anthony. 'Shouldn't be cars on that road. Dangerous for the cattle.'

'We didn't see any cows grandfather, just Aunt Stephanie's sheep.'

Speculative conversations broke out around the table about possible cars and Henri reached across the empty plates to generously fill his wine glass. Emptying it without any appreciation of bouquet or taste he drained the bottle into his empty glass.

The two girls cleared away the dinner plates and cook brought in five steaming puddings. One by one Anthony poured whiskey over the puddings and lit them.

'I'll have the portion with a silver threepenny piece grandfather,' said James. 'Please,' he added after a look from his mother.

'You'll just have to be lucky James.'

'I'll have helpings until I find one,' exclaimed James, determined to win a prize. 'And then I'll share it with Uncle Henri as he says he's always short of money.'

There was a quiet pause around the table before Giselle quickly intervened. 'Was the church crowded this morning Henri?'

'Yes, sure, yes Giselle,' said Henri, obviously with his mind somewhere else. 'Packed wasn't it Leslie?'

'Interesting sermon though,' said Leslie. 'That reverend certainly caused some consternation – made some people think. Still, I'm surprised you encourage him to speak at your Education Centre.'

'He's not in the next year's schedule,' said Sylvia with some finality in her voice. 'I can assure you Leslie that he will not be heard again at the Education Centre. We'll make sure of that.'

'Were the cars at the Education Centre Sylvia? Did you say that you saw cars at the Education Centre?'

'No Anthony dear. There were no cars at the Centre.'

'We were there auntie,' said Peter. 'Mum took us there before we came here. We all wanted to share in the memories. We wanted to remember all of the family.'

'Dad, mum, can we go to the Centre before we leave please?' asked Philippe. 'We're not up here often and I'd like to think on my brother. I know it sounds a bit shocking but I can hardly remember him and I need to remember.'

'Perhaps we should all go there tomorrow?' suggested Matthew. 'If the weather is fair then it would make a great family idea for tomorrow. We all have memories of the people's names gathered there. Perhaps a show of solidarity and a gentle reminder for the young folk about our family. There have always been strong bonds and responsibilities amongst the members of this family.'

'We'll see Matthew, we'll see,' said Sylvia. 'But perhaps we should enjoy the moment, the here and now rather than rush into tomorrow.'

'I'd like to enjoy the moment grandma. Can I have some more please: this time with a threepenny piece?'

Anthony tapped his glass with his dessert fork and the conversation dwindled away. With some difficulty, leaning heavily on the table, Anthony stood. Slowly he looked along the row of faces around the table.

'Family and friends,' he said, and then stopped. Sylvia sat at her end of the table and looked apprehensively at her husband. 'Family and friends, a toast,' and Anthony raised his glass. His other hand gripped tightly to the tablecloth.

'Family and friends,' echoed around the table.

Daniel quietly slid his chair back from the table and walked slowly round to his father. Holding his arm Daniel eased his dad back into his chair and released the tight fingers on the tablecloth.

'My turn dad I think,' said Daniel.

'Aye son, it's your turn. You've waited long enough.'

'We've all waited long enough,' interjected Henri. He too pushed his chair back from the table and stood up. 'We all wait in this family. If you're not the first then all we do is wait. But what are we waiting for? Daniel, why don't you change all of this?'

'Because it's Peter's Henri,' said Daniel very quietly. 'The future head of the Lord family is Peter and nothing will change that. The rest of us honour family traditions and serve.'

'Not me. I'll not serve and wait like some fifteenth century lackey,' and Henri grabbed his glass and downed the contents. He swayed a little. 'We need to share. We all need to share. It's Christmas dammit. Time to share.' Henri turned to look at Christina. 'I talked with you earlier

Christina. Tried to get you to understand but you had that lothario draped all over you. Share dam you.'

Giselle was on her feet and she moved to hold her brother's elbow. 'Come brother. Time to share a breath of air I think.' Quite forcibly Giselle propelled her brother towards the door.

'Always just waiting,' shouted Henri as he went through the door.

'Excuse me,' said Leslie, as he too rose and decided to follow Giselle and Henri.

'Family and friends,' repeated Anthony, who had stood again at the head of the table as if nothing had happened. Everyone's eyes swung back from watching Giselle and company exit to see Anthony topple sideways pulling the tablecloth with him. Daniel half caught his father but the unexpected weight caused both of them to topple onto the floor.

A couple of hours later the household had quietened down with Anthony tucked up in bed. The doctor reassured Sylvia that it was just a mild stroke and let him rest. Henri and Leslie were in their room and didn't want to be disturbed according to Giselle as she apologised to Sylvia. Christina had rounded up her three charges and driven everyone back to Home Farm. Despite protests from James, who wanted to say goodnight to grandpa, Terence also collected Samantha, Janet and an ever-vocal James to drive back to their home. Still apologetic, Giselle had driven away with Aunt Stephanie and that left Sylvia sitting with Katya, Daniel, Marcel, Marie, Philippe and Matthew in the drawing room.

'My brother's not getting any better Sylvia,' said Marcel. 'Marie told me he was down in Dartmouth earlier this year asking for money. He's also not looking well. When he climbed he was always fit and looking good, but now he's a bit of a mess.'

'It changes Marcel. This summer there were some lows but then again Henri had a good September climbing on the continent. He was fit for that and apparently they did some really hard climbs, even one of your mothers. Giselle has been keeping an eye on him Marcel. She's been helping where she can. She was telling me a bit more about Henri's involvement with drugs and with some people in the Club scene up in London.'

'There may be a bit more to it than that mum,' added Daniel. 'Ed was telling me something he had heard from contacts up in London. Two things actually. Because we invested some money back in Brainware Ed was talking with Rosalind Cohen and she said she had heard something. Both sources told Ed about Henri's gambling habits and that he wasn't winning. Seems Henri may have been dipping into client's funds.'

'Daniel I don't want to hear any more, not tonight. I need to go up and see Anthony is comfortable. It was lovely having the whole family here and I'm sorry the evening ended the way it has. I'll see you all tomorrow morning. Night.'

'Me too Sylvia,' said Matthew. 'Night all.'

'Should I try and find out some more details?' Daniel asked Marcel. 'It sounds a pretty sordid business but Henri is family. He was good to us, good to me at least when we were growing up. He helped me with sailing, with Michael's antics, and with Geoffrey's death. He was there for me Marcel and I would like to help if I can.'

'Daniel I really don't know. It's not my world at all. I don't like him harassing my family. It's just not on.'

'Giselle seems to be the one that knows the most Daniel,' said Katya quietly. 'She's not far away in Bristol and she has contacts in London I know. When I ask her about her job she never says much but I think she knows more about Henri's life and Henri's world than any of us do.'

'Why don't you and I talk with Giselle tomorrow Marcel?' asked Daniel. She's staying with Aunt Stephanie. 'Let's try and do something. I think Katya is right – Giselle seems to know the most and she has always been there for Henri. Perhaps he'll listen to her.'

Outside the Big House, away from the Big House, out in the forest, several people were listening. The Reverend Gabriel Godschild had assembled his small band of acolytes in the clearing close to the deserted cottage. Once the religious part of the ceremony was over the reverend was planning to welcome the new disciples into his world with a purification ceremony that was more comfortable indoors on a winter's night. The deserted cottage was ideal for such an initiation where a hearty fire kept one's naked body warm and supple for welcoming the two new angels.

Lurking in the undergrowth, already warm with anticipation, Winston Carruthers tried to keep close to the clearing and stop his breath showing in the cool air. Also encircling the clearing and muttering curses under their breath every time one of them fell over a log or scratched their face through the bushes were eight other people. They were following strict instructions, and that was no noise, no talk, and no fucking cigarettes idiot! Earlier, Buzz had wired up his night vision cameras for part of the clearing but it was inside the cottage that he planned for the best action. Tom Daley had mentioned someone had done this earlier in the year for similar antics. He'd said he'd seen some of the early video captured in this cottage but then the cops had closed the place down and he never saw anything really good. Buzz too lurked with anticipation.

It was a cool night and the reverend didn't want to stand out in the cold too long. Within the circle of hooded figures he spoke some words. Suddenly, casting his cloak aside he cried out in a loud voice and the acolytes also shed their cloaks. The naked group closed in on the two angels and slowly peeled off their smocks. Winston couldn't wait. This was too good. He raised his camera and clicked. The flash froze everyone for a moment. Buzz's cameras clicked too and Winston shot again, zooming in with the video cam. Panic, screams, pandemonium, voices, shouts, commands and suddenly the clearing was filled with people as everything went black again. Bodies were caught, thumped, dumped on the ground, and released until some order was restored. Voices and screams pierced the still night air. People violently looked for people in the dark.

'It's him.'

'Okay, away a little. You know where.'

They dragged the body away further into the bush. Several voices yelled, screamed, and then there was silence before the shouts went on again.

'Hold him still. Hold the arms.'

The axe descended. Screams again rent the air.

'Now the other bit.'

Again the axe thudded.

'Right. In the hole. Bag the bits. We're off.'

Tired, frightened, battered, successful and puzzled all of the people left the site and quiet once more fell on Fotheringham's forest. The fire in the cottage died down to red embers. The clearing around the cottage emptied. Only the call of a nightjar disturbed the night's calm as even the breeze faded away and the trees were silent. Silent as the grave.

BOXING DAY

'THIS BADGER'S GATE OF DANIELS is real neat Rory,' whispered Arnold. 'I've set the gate hinge to activate the flash. The last shots I got were quite good but I'm looking for something special. Now it's got quite cold the male may have to forage a bit more.'

'Or decide that keeping warm and staying hungry is a preferable option,' complained Rory as he pushed his fingers up under his armpits. 'You know Arnold, sometimes you get quite carried away with some of these wilderness ideas of yours, and you manage to carry me away with you. I must be mad just to listen to you.'

'Well listen to that,' said Arnold. 'That's a fox barking, and quite close too. If we sit tight maybe we'll see both of them.'

'And if we sit here much longer and much tighter maybe we'll freeze. It's a wee bit on the nippy side out here Arnold and my blood is starting to coagulate.'

'Well dilute it with some of that whiskey you brought then you tender leprechaun. Imagine you're sitting in those endless bogs of yours and surrounded with fuel. See the warmth from the burning peat and think about your singing laughing ancestors. You know, all the warm words you are always spouting about life and the great outdoors. You're always full of it so sip on the bottle and look out for that fox.'

The flash of light temporarily blinded them and the shutter whirred into life as the black and white body paused in his tracks after pushing open the gate. With a shake of his head brock continued nonchalantly down his path and back to the warmth of the den. A little way away the fox stopped too and lifted his head. No noise followed the unexpected flash. The dog fox could hear no unusual sound accompanying the sudden light. The smell under his nose continued to intrigue him and he resumed his scratching at the loose mound of dirt.

'If you've got your precious photos can we please move now?' asked Rory. 'If I don't start using my feet my toes will drop off with boredom. They're telling me they are dying of cold and can't see why they've stayed so long in this frozen position.'

'Just let me collect the camera then,' grumbled Arnold. 'But we should look out for that fox Rory. I'm sure he's close by. I'll leave the torch off so we can see him. There's enough starlight to catch him.'

'If I catch him I'll wrap his furry tail around my neck,' suggested Rory. 'My feet have passed this message to the rest of my body and all parts are telling me I'm bloody freezing. Arnold, you listening? Where are you, where….?' but Rory stopped in mid-sentence as something pushed him from behind and he went sprawling over the ground.

'Arnold, what in all that's holy is going on man? I'm eating dirt and it's definitely not going to improve the taste of the whiskey in my mouth. Christ, the bottle. Don't tell me I've broken the bottle? Ah, no, sweet Mother Mary, you're all right my lovely. Arnold, where the fuck are you?'

Rory struggled with his pockets and pulled out his torch. He flicked the switch.

'Shit. Must have broken the bulb, or else the battery is so bloody cold the whole thing has gone into hibernation. Arnold, where my beastie-loving friend have you hidden yourself, and, as an afterthought, why did you push me over? Suppose it was you pushing me over Arnold and not some phantom out of the Fotheringham Forest? Arnold, you around mate or has the cold caught up with you and frozen your tongue?'

The forest was quiet except for a scuffling grunting sound. 'Rory, Rory, I'm here.'

'Aye Arnold. That makes sense man. You're here. Good stuff Arnold, but where my wildlife wizard is "here"? If I think about it I am here too, although maybe my here is not the same as your here.'

A light suddenly shone upwards through the bare branches of the trees around him and Rory brought his eyes slowly down the path of light to its source – which was a couple of feet behind him and definitely lower. 'Here Rory, here!'

'Here Arnold, here,' echoed Rory and he peered down into the dark shadows under his feet.

'I fell in some hole. I suppose I stumbled against you and bounced down here. It smells Rory.'

'You've probably fallen into someone's old boghole,' said Rory. 'Don't think we've time for any scat analysis old man. Fortunately the bottle isn't broken, although I think my torch is. Arnold you still with us or has the smell overtaken you? Shine the light up here for God's sake and let me see where I am. Don't think I want to join you down there Arnold if it smells. I think my "here" is definitely better than your "here".'

Slowly the light slanted from straight up through the trees towards Rory's voice.

'That's me Arnold, and as you can see I'm here. Hell, see what I mean about an old boghole. Must have been the underside of this old stump I conveniently bypassed. So, no boghole Arnold but a natural uprooted giant of the forest old man. Flora as opposed to fauna Arnold so no interest to you.'

'But it is Rory, it is. I can smell fox.'

'Sure, and I can smell whiskey,' said Rory as he tilted up the bottle. 'Come on Arnold. Climb out man and let's go and get warm somewhere for Christ sakes. It's Christmas, well it was a few hours ago I suppose as it must be gone midnight by now. Why did I ever agree to come out with you this particular night? Why aren't we sitting down with friends and sharing a drink or two and a seasonal song? We should be stuffing ourselves with turkey and well-seasoned Christmas pud like any other normal human beings this night, but no you have come out and photograph the badgers. Suppose that would have been okay if I hadn't agreed to come out with you. Why Arnold, why did I come with you?'

'Help me out Rory. I'm caught in something down here.'

'Now I remember why I came out with you Arnold – to help you out of fox's bogholes. Well shine the light down there and see what you're caught on Arnold. Remember what we agreed a few moments ago? I'm here and you're there.'

Arnold flashed the light and promptly dropped it. 'Rory, Rory I've dropped the torch.'

'I can see that Arnold, or perhaps I can't see that but I'm making this great assumption that as the light has gone out you've dropped it, or merely turned it off.'

'I saw something.'

'Fascinating Arnold. Was it the fox? You said it was smelly down there.'

'It was a body.'

'Find the torch Arnold. Find the rather necessary torch and show me what you are talking about. What body?'

'By my feet. I had my foot under a leg. That's why I was stuck. I must have been standing on part of the body and trapped my foot.'

'Fascinating Arnold. No fox down there too by any chance?'

The light flashed on and waved about wildly. Finally, and somewhat hesitantly the light came back to Arnold's feet and Rory could see what was trapping his friend's foot.

'No fox I see.'

'Rory get real. It's a body, a human body.'

'Aye Arnold, reckon you're right and a male body looking where you're flashing that light. Jesus Christ Arnold. Hold the light there, no higher up. Higher! Look, look!'

The light shone clearly.

'Arnold, out of there,' cried Rory. 'Out of there right now. Here, take my hand. Pull. Fine. First things first Arnold,' and Rory quickly tilted the bottle up to his lips. 'Now you Arnold. Don't tell me you don't drink man 'cos this is shock therapy not social drinking. Another swallow.'

Arnold choked and Rory thumped him on the back. Suddenly he realised he'd better not thump too hard or Arnold would be back with the body, the headless body. Rory quickly tilted the bottle up steeply and poured some more shock therapy fluid down his throat.

'Shit Arnold, this is wildlife in the raw.'

'Perhaps the fox found it Rory.'

'Forget any bloody fox man this is a little more serious. Where are we? Somewhere near that badger's gate and Daniel Lord will know where that is. Okay, so that's the marker. Now, we've got to get ourselves out of here Arnold and find our wheels. Then we've got to go and wake up some folk, Christmas or no Christmas.'

'Rory it's three o'clock. Three o'clock in the morning. It's Sunday.'

'Arnold I don't care what time it is but someone needs to know about our little discovery. We need to find that someone and the place to start is

Daniel Lord. Now, give me the torch and let me look at the map. I know more or less where we are but I don't want you finding any more holes or any more animals for that matter. I think we've found enough wildlife for tonight, more than enough.'

Rather cautiously, with an occasional stop to finally drain the bottle of shock therapy fluid, Rory piloted Arnold back to the Education Centre. When he fell into the hole Arnold dropped both the torch and his spectacles. He had found the torch quite quickly and when they discovered the body in the hole they didn't hang about to search further for the spectacles. As a result the retreat back to the car was slow. Not quite the blind leading the blind thought Rory to himself, as he was fairly good at finding his way through the forest, but he had to virtually handhold his wilderness friend.

'Now, time to knock on doors,' said Rory.

'Why don't we just go to the police?' asked Arnold. 'There's the constable's cottage in the village Rory. It's just by the Post Office.'

'True Arnold but I think Daniel and the Lord family would prefer to know sooner rather than later, and before this day is out there's going to be all sorts of people investigating the forest. We're not going to be getting any sleep my friend and I think we should start by letting Daniel know what to expect. They've been fair with us and we've built up a good relationship. Come on Arnold, they're good people.'

'But they may have put the body there,' said Arnold.

'You think they're responsible, for that?' asked Rory.

'Well they are a little weird,' said Arnold defensively. 'There was all that talk of bodies in cottages. Remember, when we first came here? Remember how defensive the family was and didn't really want us wandering all over the forest? Told us to just keep to the rides. You remember Rory?'

'I remember us pulling down fences, demanding gates and stiles, and generally being a bit of a pain Arnold, but we've sorted all that. Daniel and Katya wanted us to help with their ideas, and we have. It's a good deal. You certainly wanted to come back here. You got really enthused talking with Katya about where and how they could modify the rides. Then you discovered that neat idea of Daniel's about badger gates and the rest is history as they say.'

'Okay Rory, let's go and pound on the door of the castle.'

'Aye, and wake up the Chief,' laughed Rory. 'Now you're back to the life in my country.'

It was Sylvia Lord who sat in the drawing room with Daniel and listened to Rory and Arnold.

'My husband is rather ill,' she had explained, although Daniel hadn't thought it was necessary to say so.

'What is it Daniel?' asked Katya, as she quietly came into the room. 'Hello Rory. Hello Arnold. Have you two been out looking for nightlife? Weren't you looking for more photographs of the badgers Arnold? Were you down by Daniel's gate?'

Arnold looked at Rory as if to say "I told you so. They're involved".

'Hi Katya.' Rory turned from looking at Katya and faced Sylvia. 'Lady Sylvia, yes, we were down by the badger's gate.'

'And got some good shots,' added Arnold enthusiastically looking at Katya.

Rory rested his hand on Arnold's arm to stem the wildlife flow and then turned back to Sylvia. 'Aye, good shots, but we've also found something disturbing, something that shouldn't be there.'

'Gross, perfectly obscene,' uttered Arnold, and he sat down quickly and looked white as shock tightened its grip on his senses.

'Arnold, you've gone quite pale. Do you want a drink, a glass of water?' Katya moved quickly and handed Arnold a glass. She splashed some water into it and Arnold gulped rapidly.

'You found something disturbing Rory?' asked Sylvia.

'What, where?' added Daniel.

'Can I start from the beginning and maybe it might make sense?' asked Rory.

'Of course Rory. Why don't we all sit down? I suppose this thing you've found isn't going to run away anywhere? There's no rush or anything?'

'No, no but let me explain.'

Rory quietly told the story of the search for wildlife, photographs of the badgers as Katya had asked, and the falling into the hole.

'Looking for the dog fox,' added Arnold. 'We heard him and we were both trying to see him in the starlight so we didn't have the torch on and I fell in.'

Rory rested his hand back on Arnold's arm and Arnold collapsed back into the depths of the couch as Rory continued.

'Unfortunately the hole wasn't empty,' said Rory. 'It wasn't Arnold's precious dog fox but another body. A body that certainly shouldn't be there. A dead body I should add. Recently dead and we'd guess death was caused by someone else as the body had no....,' and Rory's voice tailed off.

'No what Rory?' asked Sylvia and Daniel together.

'And who's dead body?' added Daniel.

'Look, we didn't hang around. When we got ourselves sorted out we realised that we had to come and tell you, and here we are,' he added rather lamely.

'Terence,' said Sylvia.

'That will mean Samantha,' said Daniel, 'and they only left here about four hours ago.'

'I'll phone,' said Sylvia. 'Terence said he was on leave but he'll know what to do. He'll phone whoever takes over. We'd better prepare for another invasion Daniel.' Sylvia turned to Rory and Arnold sitting on the couch. 'Thank you,' she said. 'Thank you for coming here first and telling us. We appreciate that. Now, as you can probably guess there will be a lot of questions and maybe some revisit to the forest. Would you two like to freshen up a little and have something to eat? We can make beds up for you if you like or you can just relax down here. I know the police will want to talk with both of you and we know from past experience that such investigations tend to go slowly and take a lot of time. Do either of you need to telephone anyone, be anywhere later today for example?'

'Mum, you go and telephone and Katya and I will look after Rory and Arnold here.'

'Let's do all of this as quietly as possible Daniel. We don't need the whole house woken up. Oh hello Leslie. I didn't see you come in. What can we do for you?'

Leslie stood in the doorway and slowly panned his eyes around the room. He walked deliberately over to Rory and Arnold. 'Who are you?' he asked sharply. 'I've seen you two before.'

Daniel moved across the room to Leslie's elbow. 'Friends of ours Leslie who help with the Education Centre.'

'Preach in the middle of the night do they? Got names. Got a name?' he said as he looked pointedly at Arnold.

'I'm, I'm ….'started Arnold.

'Leslie, if you don't mind this is a private conversation,' said Sylvia sharply. 'I'd appreciate it if you would go back to your room. Henri, please take Leslie back upstairs. This doesn't involve either of you.'

'You sure Sylvia?' retorted Leslie. 'Going to phone the police weren't you? Don't let me stop you.' Leslie stayed standing looking down at Arnold. 'You were saying?'

'Leslie stay out of this,' said Daniel, holding Leslie by the arm. 'Henri, take Leslie out of this please. We'll discuss all of this later and not in the middle of the night. Dad's asleep and I for one don't need the whole house woken up. Just go back to bed and let's try and keep this quiet.'

'Keep what quiet? I smell a story Daniel and I don't walk away from stories. We're down here for stories, and yesterday's expose was quite good for starters. I think your reverend can light up some newspapers I know, but now I hear there is another story.' Leslie walked confidently across the room and sat down very deliberately in an armchair. Daniel turned to his cousin. 'Henri, can you talk any sense into Leslie?' Henri ran his hand through his hair and shrugged. 'You know Leslie Daniel – journalist bloodhound.'

Sylvia came back into the room. 'Sorted Daniel,' she said. Turning to Rory and Arnold she walked over to the pair of them and held out her hands. 'Now why don't you two go with Daniel and Katya and freshen up in their room? You can explain your wildlife news about the Education Centre to them in peace and Daniel can arrange for refreshments away from other disturbances. I think that is everything folks. I'm off back to bed. Good night.'

Quick on the uptake Daniel walked over to Rory and Arnold and led them off out of the room. Smiling to herself about the antics of Sylvia Katya followed the three men leaving Henri and Leslie wondering where everyone went.

'I should phone Buzz,' hissed Leslie, hating to be upstaged. 'I smell a story Henri and I'm not going to be fobbed off as so much furniture by your snobby aunt. She called the police Henri and I'm going to find out why. I'll call Buzz.'

'Everyone will be asleep in the George now,' said Henri. 'It's not a direct line to the rooms you know. Goes through a switchboard and there'll be no-one there now.'

'Cell phone cretin. Gods answer to journalists. Don't travel without one, or two sometimes. Now, wake up Buzz, and get your arse in gear.'

Leslie paced around the drawing room with the cell phone pressed up against his ear. Angrily he pulled it away and looked at the screen.

'Shit. Why couldn't you have invited him here for Christmas too?'

'I thought you wanted to keep him hidden. I thought you wanted him to be somewhere in the shadows.'

And you didn't want your family to know about our ménage a trois thought Leslie. Weird family. Old, archaic, out of touch and yet Daniel and that Katya are working towards a green environment. The Education Centre was a good idea, and a good story Leslie thought. Yes, that Gabriel Godschild, the prole from Preston who preaches instant humans in a farm and forest environment is a good story.

'First light Henri. First thing we'll go and rouse Buzz. Now, how do we find out about those two animal lovers in Daniel's room? Who are they anyway Henri? I'm sure I've seen them somewhere before. Talk to me Henri.'

At five o'clock in the morning, before the first light of dawn, four sets of headlights swept up Anthony Lord's stately gravelled driveway. Frost crunched under the wheels and the front porch light shone over the opening car doors. Daniel stood at the front door and watched as Terence Field, his friend, his brother-in-law, and Regional Crimes Inspector walked across the frosty gravel.

'Long time no see,' joshed Terence, which surprised Daniel who knew that Detective Inspector Field did things by the book and was not given to jests on the job. Daniel clasped Terence's hand for the moment and quietly whispered, 'A word in your ear please before we go in.'

Apparently Sylvia must have said something to Terence over and above the brief story of Rory and Arnold because Samantha was nowhere in sight. Terence and PC Goodfellow followed Daniel into the house and into the drawing room.

'Close the door can you please constable?' asked D.I. Field. He turned to look at the assembled people, all of whom he had met and dined with some ten hours ago, except for Rory and Arnold. Terence went briefly round the room and identified everyone for PC Goodfellow leaving Rory and Arnold to last.

'I believe you two reported this to Daniel here?'

'Yes sir,' said Arnold. 'We both thought that would be best.'

'Right then, I will speak with you two and with Daniel while my constable here briefly makes notes on where the rest of you have been since yesterday evening.'

'What's this all about?' asked Leslie, 'and what did these two report?'

Terence turned slowly and faced Leslie. 'This is a police matter Mr. Dauphin and I ask the questions. Now, please excuse me. Daniel, the office I think.'

The four of them left the room and PC Goodfellow started with Sylvia. As soon as Terence had left, and before Sylvia had got passed the first two questions, Leslie stood up and marched out of the room ignoring the calls of the constable. Walking out onto the forecourt he went up to the first car and demanded to know what was going on. The sergeant looked at Leslie and didn't say a word.

'I want to speak to whoever's in charge,' he demanded again. 'I have a right to know what has happened.' PC Goodfellow appeared in the doorway.

'Mr. Dauphin, would you please come back inside sir. I need to know where you have been over the past twelve hours sir.'

'Asleep in bed you fool,' snorted Leslie. 'Now what is going on here?'

Terence appeared with Daniel, Rory and Arnold and he looked at the scene. Calmly he walked over to Leslie who was standing up close to the sergeant.

'Mr. Dauphin, do you have a problem with your hearing? My constable wants you back in the drawing room, and he also wants to know where you have been over the past twelve hours. They are both very simple requests sir. Now, if you would be so kind, go back into the house. If we need you any further we will contact you sir.'

PC Goodfellow held Leslie's arm and Leslie jerked it off angrily. 'Piss off flatfoot. Don't you touch me. In my job I eat people like you for breakfast. I'll find out, don't you worry, and I'll tell the world what a bunch of incompetent cover-up artists you are down here. Bunch of yokels trying to cover up some disaster on the Lord Estate. Just like that reverend at the Education Centre. Heresy and being allowed by the Lord family.'

'Mr. Dauphin, it is rather early in the morning for simulated histrionics and I have enough witnesses here to consider obstruction of police procedures. Do you want to return to the drawing room sir or will I have one of my constables drive you into town? Just to let you cool down a little you know.'

Leslie looked around at the police force and decided that the drawing room was closer to the action, whatever action there might be. He kicked at Anthony's gravel and stomped back into the house. Henri stood in the doorway, not knowing what to do.

'Don't just stand there Henri,' snarled Leslie. 'Find out what the fuck is going on. You're family. You should be included. It's obviously some family cover-up. Ask man, ask before you get implicated in whatever has happened.'

Silently Henri wrapped his arm around Leslie and the pair of them went back indoors.

The motorcade drove slowly from the Big House to the Education Centre and then on down one of the forest rides with Daniel leading the way. Near the badger gate Rory had said. Well, that is just down here.

'Here, somewhere near here we came out. I'm sure it was somewhere near here,' said Rory tapping Daniel on the shoulder.

'Arnold, you agree?'

'Daniel I couldn't see. I'd lost my spectacles. They fell off somewhere down the hole, somewhere near the body.' Arnold sounded even more choked up and Daniel hoped he wasn't going to be sick all over the Landrover. Stopping the vehicle Daniel hopped out and motioned to Terence.

'My badger gate is just down here a ways, beside a small dry stream bed. The badger run uses the stream bank as a cover.'

'Okay Daniel, let's keep this to the bodies of interest and that doesn't includes badgers. Or foxes,' he added over his shoulder to Arnold.

It didn't take long to discover the uprooted tree, the shallow hole and Arnold's spectacles. Police tape quickly delineated a large area around the focal point and Terence bent down on the side of the hole and looked.

'One naked male constable, and recently of this world I would say,' observed D.I. Fields. 'Still, we'll let the doctor do the initial investigating and reporting shall we?'

'Looks like he might have been dragged sir,' said PC Goodfellow. 'There's a lot of broken branches and crushed vegetation here sir. He may not have been killed here sir. Should I expand the crime scene? Tape a wider area?'

'Who's more familiar with the countryside constable? This is not my natural environment as well you know.'

'PC Meadows here sir is both local and more at home in the forest? Should we call for dogs?'

'No constable. Keep everyone else back by the cars but have Meadows and that Rory come down here. Rory will probably know where he and Arnold have walked and be observant. See whether PC Meadows can see where any dragging has happened. Ah, doctor, good morning to you. Good of you to come so quickly.'

Doctor Baird shook hands with D.I. Field and with PC Goodfellow, muttering as he did so about inconvenient times and inconsiderate places for such discoveries. Looking back at Terence he asked,' Weren't you out here yesterday evening? Don't suppose you know who this is by any chance? Is he the person who upset Anthony last night – would make things simple? Then we could all go home quite quickly you know.'

'No Doctor, as you can see the most obvious identifying features are missing.'

'Hmm, see what you mean. Anyway, just give me a hand down into this hole and we'll take a closer look.'

Back on the ride Daniel was feeling relieved. When Arnold and Rory first came to the Big House and told him they had discovered a body Daniel's first thoughts were of Mendoza. Back eighteen months ago two men from London had attacked Danielle and Tony in the Big House. There had been a stand-off in the stable yard, with the two men holding a knife to Tony's throat and threatening murder. Stanley Rogers, a business friend of Anthony's, had arrived at just the right time and disarmed the mulatto Mendoza. However, after hearing more of the story about Danielle and the two men Daniel decided to warn off the men from Mozambique for all times. Donald MacLeod, a friend of Daniel's who was staying at the Big House and who had heard Danielle's story was insistent that he knew best. With agreement from Stanley Rogers, Donald put the fear of God into Moboto by doing to Mendoza what he had done to lots of people in Mozambique. And finally, thought Daniel, we buried Mendoza here in the forest, although not exactly here and so this is not Mendoza. Daniel breathed a sigh of quiet relief because he and Donald had buried Mendoza alive, as any autopsy might show. Then Daniel had another thought. Wonder if it's Freddie Masters? After all those activities in the old Ferris cottage and Freddie's disappearance we never did find his body. Maybe I should tell Terence.

'Got any ideas Daniel?' The question came out of the blue and startled Daniel.

'Terence. Terence I've no real idea but something has just struck me.'

'Which is?'

'You know where we are?'

'Daniel, this is not the time for riddles or twenty questions. You know I'm not a country person. Explain.'

'We're not far from the infamous cottage.'

'Not again Daniel, not that place again. Why don't you pull it down or something? That place seems to attract all sorts of nefarious activities on this Estate. You think there is a connection?'

'You talking about the cottage?' asked Arnold. 'There was nobody there when we passed it but there was a smell.'

'Without a detailed explanation of various animal scents Arnold can you be a little more specific?' asked D.I. Field.

'Don't think it was an animal smell,' ventured Arnold cautiously. 'Ask Rory.'

'Male, about forty to fifty, Caucasoid, with no tattoos but an appendix scar and cause of death is not obvious but then some relevant parts are missing. Might know more after the autopsy. No, I will know more after the autopsy.'

'Time of death?'

'Within the last twelve hours Terence and I don't think he was killed where he is. There are several lacerations on the body which I assume came from dragging. Your constable is trying to backtrack but the two wildlife experts may have buggered up the trail a little. That Irishman says they wandered around a bit before settling by the badger gate. Neat idea Daniel. Clever that.'

Daniel smiled, still feeling the relief about Mendoza.

'Anything else spring to mind Daniel, apart from badger gates and cottages?' asked Terence.

'We never found Freddie Masters,' said Daniel.

'But he was young Daniel,' said Dr. Baird. 'Freddie was in his twenties and fairly fit. This is an older man I'm sure and someone who wasn't very active. No, it's not Freddie Masters.'

'Daniel I'm going to get my forensic team in to the site and see whether Rory has had any success.' Turning quickly to Arnold Terence asked, 'Smells Arnold? Any more ideas?'

'Wood smoke, yes that's it. Wood smoke.'

'Sounds like we're back to the cottage again Daniel. Why don't you and I drive there and look? Maybe we'll bump into the constables with Rory coming to meet us. For God's sake Daniel do what your mother asked and bulldoze the place.'

'Katya likes it Terence. She thinks it fits into the forest just right.'

'Bulldoze it Daniel, but after we've had a look.'

'The ashes are still warm in the fireplace. Arnold was right. Don't walk about Daniel, just stay put. Another crime scene maybe. We're going to have to tape a larger area. Hope you're not working in this part of the forest for a while Daniel. Well, what did I say?'

In the clearing beside the cottage Terence and Daniel could see the two constables and Rory just emerging from the forest.

'Been quite a disturbance all around here sir,' said PC Goodfellow. 'Looks like there was some fight or something and we've found this sir.' PC Goodfellow held up a camera in his hands.

'Gloria and her friends haven't been back have they Daniel?' asked Terence.

'No Terence, not to my knowledge anyway.'

'The camera has a name on it sir,' said PC Goodfellow, handing the camera to his boss.

'Another wildlifer?' asked Rory. 'Arnold wanted an exclusive on those badger shots. Have you talked with anyone else Daniel? You never told us there were other wildlife folks in the forest. Hey, wait up though. We met a bloke wandering through here about a month ago. Our usual group was hiking and we were doing some preliminary habitat surveys. We'd just come into this clearing when we met a whole host of people. Your cousin Daniel. I think one of them was your cousin.'

'But Henri's not any wildlifer Rory. Who else did you meet?'

'Well your cousin appeared to be with another couple. They'd come in a car I think. Yes, that's right. It was parked here in the clearing but there was another bloke.'

'What bloke? Who?' asked Terence.

'He never said. I think we all startled him. Dressed for the forest to be sure with an anorak and boots. O yes, carrying binoculars too. Looked like a birder but he didn't say anything.'

'You never asked?' queried Terence.

'Suppose not. Doris got into some slanging match with one of your cousin's friends and then Rupert realised they were a journalist and a photographer. After Rupert gagged Doris we all left. Maybe the other bloke was a wildlifer?'

'Hold up there Rory,' said Daniel. 'We've not been in contact with anyone else. We thought you and Arnold made a good team and Katya and I appreciated your inputs. We've made some changes along the lines you two have suggested. Good ideas they were too. Young Peter was....'

'Daniel, Daniel, it's just after dawn on Boxing Day, and this is not the time, although maybe the place, for discussions on integrated forest management or whatever Katya calls it. Murder is the topic under review. One dead body that is no longer wild or alive. My domain rather than yours.'

'Sorry Terence.'

Terence turned to his constable. 'A name you say constable?'

'Yes sir. A W. Carruthers according to this engraved plate,' and PC Goodfellow handed over the camera safely guarded inside an evidence bag.

'Good constable. Now lead me slowly back to the uprooted tree and let me see what might have happened. A fight you say? Let's try and keep away from the original trail and tape it as you go. Meadows, anything going on the village you know about?'

'No sir. Been quiet for a while now sir.'

'Anyone new in the village? Anyone staying at the George?'

'Don't know sir. Of course there was a crowd in yesterday for the sermon. Quite a story that reverend spins sir. Rousing stuff and the church was crowded. Lots of people in for that sir. Then there's still people coming in for Betty's pies like, especially before Christmas time. She'd done something special and my missus says they've been popular. I could ask George whether he's got anyone staying sir.'

'Yes Meadows. I'll come with you and then I'll come back to the Big House Daniel. I think we'll have a little longer talk with the occupants. Will everyone in the family be back Daniel? I think everyone who was there yesterday should be questioned – just to complete the procedures. You never know one of them might know our W. Carruthers.'

'Is that who it is?' asked Rory, 'the body I mean?'

'I don't know Rory,' said D.I. Field, 'but his name is a place to start. Daniel, can you take Rory and Arnold back to the Big House? Goodfellow will stay here to wait for the forensic team and I'll take PC Meadows back into the village and talk to George.'

'Henri, what the fuck is going on? Come on, let's get my car and go and see. You know the forest here and it can't be that big. We'll find whatever it is.'

'Leslie we can't. Terence, the Inspector made it clear we had to stay here. Told you you were interfering with police investigations.'

'I don't give a shit Henri. Tin-pot little investigation with yokels. You can outwit them surely? This could be better than the story about the reverend. It might be another story about the reverend. Perhaps he is doing more than welcoming angels in the forest.'

'Like stirring things up don't you Mr. Dauphin? In fact you're quite a pain in the arse. Waste of a good brain if you ask me.'

'Nobody asked you granddad,' snorted Leslie to Matthew.

'Henri my boy, I don't think your dad would like your friend here. In fact I know your dad would have chewed him up and spat him out. Your dad had integrity and charisma Henri. He was bold, bloody-minded and couldn't stand the tittle tattle of the media. He and your mother had some serious battles with the media you know. They did some astounding climbs, some sensational climbs together, and all the media could do was criticise. Called them sensation-seekers, dangers to other climbers and all sorts of claptrap. Your father Henri had words for them. On the few occasions that Charles and Helene spoke to the press your father had words Henri. Clear, honest, straightforward words but the media couldn't stand for that and rewrote them for that perverted world they live in. In the end your father wrote them off as the parasites they are, and you are a parasite Mr. Dauphin. In fact a rather obnoxious parasite and Henri would be well rid of you.'

'You quite finished granddad,' sneered Leslie. 'Past it you are. Archaic, like the rest of this family. Living in yesterday. The people of today want to hear about the scandals you lot all get up to. Want to learn how fucking useless you really are, or were. Learn about all the mistakes you made and we've got to live with. How you buggered up the world for generations to come. How......'

'Henri, a word if you please?' said Sylvia as she swept into the room, 'in private!' and she turned out of the room and down the corridor to the office. 'In here please.'

Shutting the door Sylvia turned and faced Henri.

'Henri I invited you down here for Christmas as part of the family celebration. I invited everyone's spouses and even friends as they are part of this family too. It was with some reluctance that I invited Leslie because he seems to manage to annoy Anthony whenever he comes here. He did last night, or rather you did after some needling from Leslie. I won't have Anthony upset any further Henri: certainly not in this house, our house. Do I make myself clear?'

'We just want our share and then we'll leave, and Leslie is working on a story. Down here he has a story and now you're trying to sit on an even bigger story. Something is going on Sylvia and we need to know.'

'Right. Here's what we do with no ifs and buts. You take Leslie up to your room and stay there until Terence gets back. He'll probably want to interview everyone again and then bring us up to date. After that, with his permission, I will banish you from this house, along with your precious Leslie. I won't comment on your life and lifestyle Henri. That is up to you but I do know Giselle is very worried about you. She has told me a little of your troubles and although I can understand I can not condone what you do. Moreover, none of that gives you the right to be so abusive and inconsiderate in this house. Do I make myself clear?'

'As crystal Sylvia.'

'Take Leslie away.'

'Fuck it Henri. I won't be dictated to like a child. Go and get my car and act like a man for a change. Jesus, this family thinks it is the Dark Ages.'

'Going somewhere Mr. Dauphin? I hope you are not thinking of obstructing the police sir. In the drawing room if you please.'

'Fuck you plod.'

Terence held Leslie's elbow and turned him round back towards the house. 'Drawing room sir. Daniel, could you telephone Samantha please and your Aunt Stephanie? Ask them to come over as quickly as possible please.'

'Terence, I've sent Katya down to Home Farm to bring Christina and the family up here. I'm supposing you want us all here, all of us who were here last night?'

'Thanks Sylvia. Yes, I'd like to bring everyone up to date and then we can let everyone go about their business without constraint.'

Within the next hour all of the people who had been at the Big House the day before assembled in the drawing room with the exception of Anthony. Peter and Tony were talking excitedly about the possibilities of bodies in the forest and James proclaimed he should be out riding with his new saddle before Dainty forgot what it was like. Terence came into the room and everyone quietened down. Standing by the dormant fireplace Terence slowly explained what had been found and what had been done to date. Tony looked at Peter as if to say I told you so. When Terence went on to explain that there was some possible connection with the ex-Ferris cottage Peter made a comment about his and Tony's discovery with the clothes last year.

'Yes Peter, I remember and that was a useful find but this is more serious I'm afraid and I don't want you and Tony searching out there again. Not just for the moment anyway. That whole area, including the

255

path around your Uncle Daniel's badger gate is all sealed off as a crime scene. I do not want to see or hear any of you in that area – that would be police obstruction. So, no amateur investigations please.'

'Who is it though?' asked Peter. 'Is it Freddie Dunster?'

'Peter it is early days at the moment and I can't answer your question. We have moved the body to the morgue for a post-mortem so there is nothing to see in the forest. I know my Detective Constable has talked with all of you and for the moment we have no reason to keep you any longer but we would appreciate knowing if you plan on any travel arrangements. We may have to contact you later.'

'Male or female Inspector?' asked Leslie. 'At least you can tell us that much. I suppose this is murder?' he added.

D.I. Field frowned as Leslie used the "murder" word with young people in the room. He could do without the journalist's sensationalism.

'Male Mr. Dauphin and he didn't die of natural causes. That's all for now and thank you for your time and attention.'

Terence turned and left the room and the house to make his way back to his constable at the crime scene.

'Get the car Leslie. Get the car and we'll go and find Buzz. He should be with us. We've got to leave anyway. Sylvia made it clear that we're not wanted and so we should go and find Buzz. You've finished here anyway, haven't you, with your story? Buzz will have the photographs and so we can go back to London.'

'Yes Henri. You get our things and I'll get the car. We might do a little tour of your forest on our way to find Buzz though.'

'Inspector Field said no amateur investigations.'

'But we're not amateurs Henri. We're professionals my friend, real professionals and there's still more to this than your family friend is telling us. Wasn't that the same cottage that was in the news a year or so ago? And wasn't that where Gloria was operating her "house of pleasure"?'

'Yes, but so what?'

'Well Henri my love, that is where my source told me to look a little closer, and that is where our good friend Buzz was going to get his photographs. So, I think we should drive to the village via that rather special cottage. Get the bags Henri and we're off out of here. There's nothing else here for us. We'll let the family sink back into apathy before I wake them up with a newspaper story that'll really piss them off.'

'But what about my money, my share?' moaned Henri. 'Leslie, my friends back in London are demanding some payback. They told me the end of the year or else. Shit Leslie, this is serious. Serious money.'

'How much really Henri?'

'Over one hundred thousand and I've still got to get some money back into the client's accounts that I borrowed.'

'You really do like to live dangerously Henri. I'm not sure our friends in London are going to love you. Perhaps we shouldn't send that other story we had about illegals to print but use it to threaten, or maybe to barter. Might reduce your debt Henri.'

'Could you? Would you?'

'Wouldn't want you to loose your balls now would we Henri? Just the sort of thing that lot might consider doing if you haven't got the money. Crude and vicious they are Henri. Get the bags.'

Henri managed to guide Leslie around the forest without getting too lost. Stopping by the police tape Leslie got out and looked down the ride towards the cottage in the clearing. A constable walked towards them.

'Area's closed sir.'

'What's going on constable?'

'Police investigation sir. You'll have to go back to the Education Centre and out that way sir.'

'Murder I hear officer.'

'That's as maybe sir but you'll have to go back the way you came.'

'Several bodies I heard. Some kind of orgy, holy rollers or something. Black mass and sacrifices.'

'Just reverse sir if you don't mind. We've a job to do.'

'And so have I officer, a responsibility actually, a responsibility to the public. I'm a reporter,' and Leslie flashed his press card.

'Is that so sir? Well, I understand that D.I. Field will be having a press conference later today or maybe tomorrow morning. You'll have to contact their office to find out the details sir. Now sir, back please.'

Leslie looked past the constable and there were several people looking around the scene and occasionally collecting some bits and pieces. A photographer was also prowling around from place to place as requested.

'Buzz,' said Leslie.

Henri turned the car around and drove back to the village via the Education Centre. He stopped the car in the George parking lot and turned to Leslie.

'We going to stay here any longer or just pick up Buzz and head home?'

'Depends,' said Leslie.

'On what? I've still got to find some money.'

'And we've got to find Buzz Henri and he's inside tucked up asleep I'll bet. Come on; let's see whether Buzz had some success last night.'

INTERVIEWS

'INSPECTOR, WE SEEM TO KEEP bumping into each other,' said Leslie as he walked into the public bar. 'Bit early to be drinking on the job isn't it?'

Leslie turned from Terence and looked directly at George. 'Where were you last night landlord? Not poaching on the Estate I hope? D.I. Field will want a full explanation of your movements you know, and probably everyone else in this shitty village. Strange goings on up at Fotheringham landlord. Infamous that place is with murders every month of the year. Well, what do you expect with ancestral homes, collapsed businesses and old-fashioned ideas? Decadent and that means murder and mayhem landlord. Still, be good for you though with more gawpers and nosey-parkers. More people to come in and tittle tattle, and drink when their throats dry. Good for you landlord. Mine's a pint by the way. What about you Henri? Thirsty work this investigating.'

Terence waited quietly while Leslie ranted on. Listening he thought, and he smiled as he remembered Samantha's observation about how he listened. Useful part of the job. He turned back to George.

'To continue George.'

'Mine's a pint landlord, or didn't you hear me with all the other voices in here?'

'We're not open yet sir. I can get you a coffee or a tea sir.'

'Like I said Henri. Shitty little village living in the past. Not yet opening time. This is England landlord, and the end of the twentieth century. Not yet opening time! Christ, you live in another world from real life.'

'Buzz Leslie?'

'Is Mr......?' and Leslie paused as he couldn't remember the name Buzz had used when booking to stay here.

'Who Mr. Dauphin? Who are you looking for? Would it be a Mr. Carruthers?'

Leslie turned to look at Terence again.

'Who wants to know?' he asked.

'I do. I was just asking George here who was staying when you rudely intervened. So, this Mr. Carruthers is a friend of yours, an acquaintance?'

'That's not the name Leslie,' said Henri. 'It was Mr. Black. Bernard Black Inspector, a friend of ours from London. He's a writer you know. Our company funded part of his research, his new book. That's how we know him. Not this Carruthers but Black,' Henri trailed off lamely.

Leslie looked at Henri and it wasn't a friendly look Terence noted.

'Mr. Carruthers is here,' said George, 'but I don't know about Mr. Black. Said he was going out to see some friends and would be late. I lent him a key so he could let himself in like 'cos I was going to bed.'

'Mr. Carruthers is in his room then George?' asked Terence.

'Suppose so,' said George. 'He came in last night. Late he was too but he came in 'cos I was up and about when he came in. Saw his car lights and checked who it was. All flustered he was and looking rather bedraggled. Saw his face in the light though and so I knew who it was. Looked like he had been in a fight but he went to bed without making any noise and so I went to sleep. Perhaps he fell over in the dark while out bird-watching. That's what he said he did.'

'So where's Black, where's Bernard then landlord?'

'Don't know sir do I? Went out and never came back. Well not yet he hasn't as far as I know. Hasn't paid though but I haven't checked his room. Should see whether his gear is still there. Had a couple of cameras with him he did. Said he needed some special photographs for his book. Was talking about architecture but I couldn't think of anything in the village of any special interest.'

'George, I think we need to see Mr. Carruthers and we need to look in Mr. Black's room. Maybe Mr. Black came in while you were sound asleep?'

'Sure Inspector.'

'My coffee landlord! Service is important you know. My friend here and I both want a coffee, pronto. I'll just use the toilet while you're getting them, the coffees. This way is it?' and Leslie walked further into the building.

'A moment Mr. Dauphin, a moment if you please?'

'Christ, a man can't go for a piss now without police permission.'

'The toilet isn't upstairs and I think I'll go and see Mr. Black's room before you. George, redirect Mr. Dauphin here to the toilets. Keep an eye on them constable. Which rooms upstairs George?'

'Mr. Carruthers is in 103 Inspector and Mr. Black in 105. Next door to each other they are, in the front.'

'Henri get some coffees for Christsakes while I go and piss. Through here landlord then? Down into an oubliette probably.'

'Right sir, just along that corridor.'

Mr. Carruthers answered the knock on his door and was surprised not to see George.

'Good morning Mr. Carruthers. I'm Detective Inspector Field and I would like to ask you a few questions please.' D.I. Field calmly produced his warrant card and offered it to let Mr. Carruthers examine it. Standing in the doorway Carruthers looked a little lost and flustered. He peered at the identification as if it was something that would bite him and then looked back at the Inspector's face questioningly.

'I might even have found something of yours that you have lost,' D.I. Field added with a smile on his face as he stepped forwards into the room. Carruthers backed up as D.I. Field advanced. Still looking very confused he asked, 'Lost?'

'Yes sir. Don't you own a Leica Reflex with a 200mm telephoto lens?'

'A Leica? I'm not sure.'

'Come now Mr. Carruthers. That's an expensive and powerful camera and you'd certainly know if you owned one. Interesting bruise on your face by the way. Can you show me your hands please?'

'Hands Officer?'

'Difficulty with speech Mr. Carruthers? Late night last night was it? Out to friends you told George and had a little too much to drink maybe? Not much sleep? Looking rather beaten up Mr. Carruthers? Do you want to sit down sir? And the hands? My, rather torn. Scratched I see. Why don't you tell me who you are Mr. Carruthers and where you're from? After that we might get into where you have been? Which friends you visited like? Just a few simple questions sir.'

Mr. Carruthers shuffled his feet and wrung his scratched hands together. Rather disjointedly he tried to gather his thoughts and work out what to say. With so little sleep after a very tiring yesterday his mind was not geared up to sensibly answer police questions – even so-called simple questions.

'I'm down here on holiday Inspector and wanted to see the forest that supports this special Education Centre. I'd heard about it from a friend and thought I should come down and see it.'

'Down from where sir?'

'London.'

'Big city Mr. Carruthers.'

'I live in Canterbury Avenue in Ilford. Suppose it's really in Essex Inspector, but it's all connected now and I.......'

'Work?'

'What is all this Inspector? Why are you asking all these questions? Why should I answer you?'

'Your camera Mr. Carruthers?' asked D.I. Field as he produced the camera from behind his back. 'Your name is on it so we assumed it could be yours, although you're not sure whether you own a Leica. Is there another Mr. W. Carruthers around here? Relative perhaps? Is that who you visited yesterday evening? You were out to see a friend Mr. Carruthers? That's right isn't it? Rest a moment Mr. Carruthers. Sit down and think what you want to tell us. You know, about the camera and where you've been.'

Winston Carruthers took D.I. Field's advice and sat down on his bed. He ran a hand through his dishevelled hair and sighed.

'Tiring walking through the forest isn't it sir? I was just out there, earlier this morning actually. Looks very different when many of the trees have lost their leaves doesn't it? Bit muddy too in places. Are those your shoes sir? Not very clean for a visit to a friend's house now are they? Wonder if the leaf mould on your shoes would match the leaves at the scene of the crime?'

'Scene of the crime? What crime?'

'And that is the question Mr. Carruthers, isn't it? What crime? Well is could be murder Mr. Carruthers. Simple straightforward murder and a very dead body in the forest. Recently dead Mr. Carruthers, like in the past twelve hours you know. Where have you been over the past twelve hours Mr. Carruthers? Did you say this was your camera? We haven't developed the film yet but that will get done later today. What will I see on the film Mr. Carruthers?'

'No Inspector, nothing. The camera flashed and then nothing. It was chaos. I never realised there were so many people. There were so many people and it was dark. People were hitting people, screaming, falling over and it all was supposed to be beautiful. They were supposed to be pretty and ......it was so ugly.'

'This is your camera sir?'

'Yes officer.'

'Right Mr. Carruthers. I'm going to ask you to get properly dressed and then I'm going to take you down to the station for a serious conversation. Wait for me downstairs with my constable. I have one other task to do up here. Whilst getting dressed Mr. Carruthers think very carefully what you are going to tell me. Tell me why you are here and what you have been doing since you came here. I will be down in a little while Mr. Carruthers but don't be too long sir.'

D.I. Field left the room and shut the door as he looked along the corridor for Room 105. He knocked, firmly. There was no answer, no response and no sound from the room. Turning the handle Terence found the door was locked. He quietly descended the stairs and obtained the keys from George.

'With me George if you please. Got your coffee I see Mr. Dauphin?'

Upstairs Terence knocked again and had George unlock the door. The room was empty – of people that is. The bed was undisturbed but clothes still hung on the hangars and a case stood open at the foot of the bed. Terence did a quick but cursory check on the clothes and case. There were no papers, no identification, and no obvious explanations. There was no supposed half-written book.

'Well George. Has our Mr. Black done a runner for whatever reason or has he gone walkabout?'

'Buggered if I know Inspector. He seemed an okay sort of bloke. In his forties I suppose and quite chatty with it. My best guess is that he came from London Inspector. His accent was more Midlands but the address he gave was London. He was going bald – sort of thin on the top you know.'

'Had hands and feet I suppose?' asked D.I. Field somewhat obtusely.

'You kidding me?' asked George. 'Of course he had hands and feet. Drove here didn't he. Some flashy motor. Hands and feet? Normal he was. Well dressed, polite and paid his bar tab.'

'Cash George?'

'Yes, he paid cash.'

'How was he going to pay for his room? Cash or credit card?'

'Dunno. We never got that far. Was going to settle up when he had finished his investigations he said. About three of four days he reckoned.'

'George, lock the room for me can you and if possible keep it locked. I'm going to send one of my people down here and do some searching. I need to keep the room free from other people. Understand?'

'Yes Inspector. He a suspect Inspector? That Carruthers looks more the type though. Something shifty about him Inspector. Asking after the reverend he was. Said a friend in the village had told him about our reverend. From his attitude he seemed keen to know about the reverend but I'm not sure whether it was a friendly query.'

'I assume you mean the Reverend Gabriel and not Peter Masters?'

'Aye, s'right. I think Carruthers went to the church yesterday, for the morning service you know. He was out in the morning. Come to think on it he wasn't in for lunch either – took sandwiches he did. I had to make them up special so he must have been out all day.'

'Thanks George.'

D.I. Field and George descended the stairs and found Mr. Carruthers sitting in a corner looking less dishevelled but decidedly pale and wan. He was nursing a coffee.

'Shall we go Mr. Carruthers?' asked Terence.

'Where's Bernard?' demanded Henri. 'What have you been talking about with Bernard?'

'With who Henri?' asked Terence

'Bernard, Bernard Black of course. Our friend in Room 105. Come on Leslie, we'll go up and find him.'

'I think you'll find the room is empty but locked Henri. I've ordered it locked and George here has instructions not to let anyone in that room.'

'Is he there then? Is he dead in there?'

'Why should he be dead Henri?'

'No, no reason Terence. Just we were looking for him and we're surprised he is not here.'

'Special friend is he?'

'No, just someone in which I have a financial interest. I told you, we have put some money into his book, his research. Just anxious to make sure it is money well invested you know.'

'Sure.' Terence turned to PC Goodfellow and the pale Mr. Carruthers. 'Well sir, shall we go?'

After they had left Henri turned to Leslie. 'Now what? Where is he?' Henri turned to look at George. 'He didn't leave any message George? Didn't say when he'd be back?'

'No sir. Just said he'd be late. Don't wait up he said.'

'Henri, a word. Over here.'

'What now Leslie? You got any ideas?'

'Maybe a visit to my source. He may know what's going on, or what's gone on. He may know something. Come on, let's go knocking on doors.'

At the police station D.I. Field led Mr. Carruthers into an interview room and asked whether he needed another coffee, or a tea perhaps, which might be safer on the constitution than the station's coffee? Carruthers shook his head and looked down at the table.

'Well sir. Just sit down and we'll have a more formal dialogue. You've had time to think what you are going to tell me. Let's start with who you are, what you do, where you live, and then why you are down here shall we? My constable and I here will listen patiently and then ask you to write it down for us. Just a reminder Mr. Carruthers, a reminder that we are investigating a murder, so please be quite truthful in what you say. You are?'

Winston Carruthers slowly and rather hesitantly explained who he was, what he did, and so on as D.I. Field requested.

'So you know Tom Daley?'

'Never met him, but I contacted him through the internet. We exchanged emails but I don't know him. Don't know anything about him,' emphasised Mr. Carruthers rather insistently.

'Continue.'

So the story unfolded how Carruthers had heard about the reverend and his special ceremonies, including the initiation of new angels.

'And you wanted to photograph this special religious ceremony?'

'Yes.'

'But you didn't ask the reverend whether you could? You wanted to do it sort of incognito?'

'It was a personal project and I didn't want to disturb the realism of the ceremony.'

'Anything else you wanted to do with the reverend? Did you want to talk with him? Do you approve of what he is preaching or is that irrelevant and your interest is primarily with the angels?'

'I don't know him Inspector. My friend said he was controversial but I wasn't really interested in what he was saying.'

'So you don't bear any grudges against the reverend? You aren't upset about this so-called angels' ceremony?'

'No.'

'But the angels' ceremony excites you – hence the camera?'

Mr. Carruthers hesitated.

'Your camera Mr. Carruthers. The one containing photos of the angels' ceremony perhaps? Going to sell them Mr. Carruthers?'

'No. No. They're for me. Only for me.'

'So just a voyeur Mr. Carruthers eh? Just a personal project you said?'

Mr. Carruthers shifted his weight on the hard wooden chair and looked down at the table.

'You said earlier it was supposed to be beautiful. In the dark, in the forest, in the rather cold forest, it was all supposed to be beautiful but then it went ugly you said. People everywhere. Several other people interrupted this rather revealing exhibition before you could capture it on film?'

'My flash went off and then all hell broke loose.'

'And what happened to the reverend and the angels?'

'It was dark Inspector. Pitch black and people were everywhere. It was brutal. I dropped my camera and tried to hide. Someone found me and flashed a light in my face. They hit me and then dropped me. I managed to wait until it got quiet and people moved away. I slowly moved to my car and drove back to the pub. I was exhausted, battered, and very confused.'

'What did the people say who found you, who hit you?'

'Nothing. They just flashed the light and then I was hit.'

'No words, no questions, no comment?'

'No Inspector. Whoever they were after it wasn't me apparently.'

'They were after someone Mr. Carruthers? How do you know they were after anyone? Perhaps they were just there poaching? Maybe they wanted to disturb the ceremony?'

'No, no Inspector. They were searching for someone but luckily it wasn't me.'

'True Mr. Carruthers, too true or we wouldn't be having this conversation. Okay, you write up what you have told us and we'll run you back into the village. For the moment Mr. Carruthers you are free to return home but settle up with George first please.'

'Yes Inspector, yes of course.'

'We've taken the film for developing Mr. Carruthers but here is your camera. When we've finished we'll send you the negatives; for your personal project.'

The two police officers left Mr. Carruthers putting pen to paper.

'So constable, what do you think about our "on-site witness"?'

'Voyeur of some kind sir that was in the wrong place at the wrong time. I'll check with the MET and maybe the Essex police to see whether our Winston has a record. Why are we taking him back to the village sir?'

'Friendly gesture as we are going back to the village constable to visit our old friend Tom Daley. Leslie Dauphin was working on some story about the Reverend Godschild and wanting to embarrass the Lord family somehow. He and Henri Lord went to hear the reverend's sermon yesterday in the village and they were quite enthused about some of the words. I don't think our Leslie is likely to turn to murder. Somehow I believe he thinks the pen is mightier than the sword. Now that Henri's living in London he isn't very familiar or up-to-date with village affairs. However, although they got invited down for Christmas the fact that they have a "friend" staying at the George is a little suspicious and it's my bet that Tom Daley may know our Leslie Dauphin as well as Mr. Carruthers. We'll take young Wilkinson if he's around because he's supposed to be a hacker of repute if I hear the canteen gossip right. Go and look for him for me please constable while I check our Winston is making progress on his life's story.'

'Morning Tom. You've met Henri here?'

'Is it? Is it morning? Christ – what time of day do you think this is? Henri you said. Is that Henri Lord by any chance? Small world. Suppose you'd better come in.'

'Sure Tom. Mind if I open a window or something? The aroma's a little heavy.'

'Whatever man. Want a toke?' and Tom lit up a rather irregular-shaped cigarette.

'Tom my man, what's going on in this village? We know what should have happened but what has really happened?'

'Nothing on the electronic world Leslie. Quiet for the past twenty-four hours or so. Some people checking how other people are but that's all normal. Over this festive time people space out, loose track of where they are, and then come back to this world paranoid about where they've been or what they've done. Quite normal man. Why, what should have happened? Say, have a toke man.'

'Thanks but no thanks Tom. You told us the reverend was planning a little initiation last night. Same time, same place you said.'

'So?'

'Did it happen?'

'Fucked if I know. I certainly wasn't there.'

'Where's the reverend now?'

'Jesus. What is this? Twenty questions? Relax man. I surf the net. I troll a little. Hack here and there, but I don't keep tabs on all the folks in the village.'

'What about the disciples?'

'This is doing my head in you know.'

'Something has happened Tom, something big, something serious. Someone found a body in the forest last night.'

'Cool. A body eh? In the forest you say? Well there's no picture on the web man so I don't know who the fuck it is. You think it's the reverend? Several people here want to shut him up. Run him out of town like. All sorts of folk think he's full of shit. Think he should be tarred and feathered or whatever. Parents think he's corrupting their kids. Funny really 'cos there are other people thinking he's for real, especially those little angels. Man must have some silver tongue. Maybe he's offering me competition with the brain candy but I haven't heard that. What body?'

'Where's he live? Where's the reverend live Tom?'

'And that is just the question I was going to ask,' said Terence as he came into the room. 'Door was open Tom and my constable and I needed to pay you a visit. We've also brought another friend. This is PC Wilkinson as well as PC Goodfellow who you know from before.'

Terence turned from looking at Tom to cast his eyes on Henri and Leslie.

'Mr. Dauphin and Henri, I suppose this is no real surprise that we should meet again and here in this cosy house. Now Tom, you were about to answer Mr. Dauphin's question, about the good reverend that is.'

'Smells like good grass bro,' said PC Wilkinson as he came further into the room and comfortably sat down in a sagging armchair.

Tom Daley toked on his cigarette and Henri turned to Leslie. 'What are we doing here? We don't need to be mixed up in this. We've got to find Bernard.' Henri turned to D.I. Field and said, 'Inspector, Terence, we may need to report a missing person. No-one has seen our friend, my investment you remember?'

Terence looked at Henri. 'Since when Henri?'

Henri turned and looked at Leslie. 'We saw him yesterday morning, after the church service.'

'Not quite twenty-four hours Henri, but keep me posted will you?' Terence turned back to Tom. 'Now Tom, we've worked together before remember, and I want you to let our mutual friend PC Wilkinson here check on a couple of things in your computer. You may want to help him, like last time. While you and Wilkinson are digging around on the web perhaps you'd answer Mr. Dauphin's question. I'm sure we'd both like to go and visit the good reverend. You never know, perhaps Henri will find his good friend having tea with the vicar. Writing a guidebook you said Henri and the reverend is surely a character of renown and fame in the village: worth a word or two as a local attraction?'

D.I. Field turned back to look at Tom Daley with an interrogating look on his face. Just over five months ago Tom and his computer's contents had revealed rather relevant pieces of evidence in the missing persons and assault case involving Gary Templeton. The case that ultimately turned into murder – despite a lack of body. Tom was in no position to shout privacy invasion, search warrant or any other obstruction and so he resignedly pulled a chair up for PC Wilkinson in front of his monitor.

'We'll be back Wilkinson. Try and keep to the relevant items lad. I know you'll find a few naughty pictures but we're looking for recent information exchanges regarding village activities son and not so concerned with the goings on in Thailand.'

'I'm cool Inspector.'

D.I. Field laughed as he left the room and out into the clean, clear, smokeless sunshine of the village street. 'Yes constable, I expect our young Wilkinson is cool in such an environment. With his skin colour he fits in there better than he would out here on the street don't you think?'

'That's racist sir,' said PC Goodfellow, but he laughed as he said it. 'He's a good lad Inspector, and he certainly has some skills and contacts we don't.'

D.I. Field turned from listening to his constable and looked at Henri and Leslie.

'Are you two going to follow us to see whether your friend is with the good reverend? Maybe your good friend was out with the reverend last night? I heard from Mr. Carruthers that a lot of people were out with the reverend last night. Gallivanting around Fotheringham's forests by all accounts too. Sort of close to where we found the body you might remember.'

Henri grabbed Leslie's arm. 'We can't go with them.'

'Come on constable. They can follow as they see fit. Maybe we can find some angels with the right reverend.'

The reverend's house was shut up tight and no amount of authoritative knocking produced a response. The policemen circled the house but all the doors and windows were locked. There were no lights on and no smoke from the chimney.

'No car constable.'

'Our holy man has flown sir? Ascended? Up and away with the angels maybe?'

'Maybe constable, just maybe, but the question is why?'

'Lot of people quite outspoken against him sir. You said the Lord family were thinking of ways of banning him from speaking at their Education Centre. Told me that yourself sir.'

'If what Carruthers told us is close to the truth constable then this is all a bit sudden. Successful, rousing sermon yesterday morning and a youthful baptism ceremony planned for yesterday evening. Things were looking good constable yet the supposed fracas in the woods sounds like it was planned. Someone had a plan that preceded yesterday's rousing sermon. Perhaps we should find some of the flock if we can't find the good shepherd. Wilkinson will have found who are the closest disciples of our absent reverend, and we can follow them constable. Perhaps we can follow the true path, or path to the truth. We can always return and look inside the cottage if that proves necessary.'

The car radio squawked into life and PC Goodfellow listened carefully before he replaced the receiver.

'That was the lab sir. Doctor there has a funny sense of humour. Doing that kind of job must warp the mind somehow. Dead bodies seem to lead to sick humour.'

'Constable, I'm assuming something relevant was said, apart from sick jokes.'

'Yes sir. Sorry sir but seems a bit gross.'

'Constable!'

'Yes sir. Well, our corpse has no special marks except an old appendix scar. Has small feet too Doc says, which may or may not be relevant if we ever find the hands. Not a fit man Inspector, and a drinker too. No obvious drugs in the system but it's too soon for a complete analysis.'

'And? Your concern over sick jokes?'

'He has a tattoo sir.'

'What where constable, or is it too sick to describe? Should I call the lab to offset your sensibilities?'

PC Goodfellow sat up straighter in his seat and looked out of the windshield down the quiet village road. The view looked pretty, conventional, English and clean. 'He has a tattoo of the male symbol sir.'

'And constable? Or perhaps where?'

'On the underside of his penis sir but the doctor said he didn't see it at first. It wasn't until he inflated the corpse's penis that he saw it properly. Said he couldn't imagine how the tattooist managed to do the job without Viagra or something. In an exciting array of colours too sir.'

'So we have a chubby mid-life male with a penis fetish minus head and hands. What do you think of that constable?'

'Someone was trying to send us a message sir. A man can't preach without a head sir. Lose the head and you lose the ability to speak, to listen, to taste and to smell. Take away the hands and you lose the ability to touch so it's a message. No more laying on of the hands.'

'And the penis tattoo?'

'Earlier life? If the attacker or attackers had known about that they might have castrated him as well as beheaded him sir.'

'Mmm. Let's find the disciples constable and see whether any of them know the reverend that intimately. Small feet remember. We may need to break into the house and find a pair of shoes.'

Terence and his constable returned to Tom Daley and discovered three names and addresses. They spent most of the afternoon interviewing the three men. Their story coincided and corroborated the tale spun by Winston but none of them knew of the whereabouts of the reverend. Estimates on shoe size varied and Terence could see the need to revisit the reverend's house. None of the three had ever attended an angels' initiation before so they had no knowledge of any tattoos.

'So has he run off with one of the angels then Mr. Kershaw? Who were they? Did you say who they were?'

'One was Mandy Ricks and the other was young Pauline Abbott. Both of them are orphans and they live with Keith Mount and his missus. They get some form of foster grant or something from the government. Listening to the two girls though, overhearing them like, I reckon they just wanted to get away. I never heard all the details but there was some abuse there officer. Can't say 'cos I don't know but the two of them were keen on the reverend. They thought, perhaps they hoped he could help them.'

'Did you see the reverend after the break up of the ceremony: after the flash?'

'No. Confused weren't we? Blinded by the light. Didn't know what was going on. Whether that was all part of the ceremony and the reverend never explained. Then people started hitting.'

'No noise? No words?'

'Lots of yells and screams Inspector. Could hear people getting hit. I recognised a couple of voices. Heard Ted shout and then young Grant hollered in pain. I couldn't see anything so I legged it.'

'Where does Mr. Mount live Mr. Kershaw?'

'Leslie, why are we still here? Buzz isn't here. Shit, this is going from bad to worse.'

'Henri my dear, try and stay calm. Although our friend Bernard isn't physically here, it is possible that Mr. Daley, who is here, and his capable friend PC Wilkinson can find where our friend might be inside that magic box.'

Leslie turned to Tom. 'Well Tom, what has our boy in blue found?'

PC Wilkinson turned and looked at Leslie. 'You get off on some of this stuff do you sir?'

'I thought you were supposed to be tracking emails constable? Looking for the action in this village I thought your Inspector said?'

'Well your Mr. Black was fairly chatty for a while but since yesterday the well has gone dry. The last word infers that he's going hunting. Talks of a rendezvous though but doesn't say with whom, where, or when. End of story.'

'He could be anywhere Leslie.'

'Did you ever read Baroness Orczy Henri?' asked Inspector Field as he came back in through Tom Daley's front door.

'Who?'

Leslie laughed and quoted, 'They seek him here, they seek him there, the Frenchies seek him everywhere etc. Inspector. In heaven or in hell? Elusive too but we're not looking for the Scarlet Pimpernel Inspector, we're looking for our friend.'

'How well do you know this friend Mr. Dauphin? Describe him to me please.'

'Fat and forty I suppose,' laughed Leslie.

'Leslie he's not. He's not fat.'

'How would you describe him then Henri? Well-built, trim and forty? Big man, small man? Hands of a blacksmith or dainty jeweller? Drinker, smoker, heterosexual or .....?' and Inspector Field let the questions hang.

'Jesus Christ Inspector, you can be pretty crude at times. He was, no is my friend. A good friend.'

'A very good friend Henri? Know about the tattoo do you?'

'What tattoo Inspector?' asked Leslie, suddenly looking sharp and attentive.

'We're trying to identify our corpse Leslie and the doctor has just added some information to our earlier limited knowledge.'

'If you let us look at the body we can tell you whether it is our friend or not. No, no, it can't be. Why would anyone kill Bernard? He's a guidebook writer.'

'Has small feet doesn't he? Neat, tidy dapper man. Manicured nails but drinks a lot.'

Henri turned to Leslie and grabbed his arm. 'Leslie, we've got to see him. We've got to see this body.'

Inspector Field turned to his constable flicking his fingers over the keyboard and pasting one window over another.

'Wilkinson, have you anything of note to tell me? Does the reverend preach very much on the web?'

'He has his own website sir. Schedule of events and message for the day kind of stuff.'

'And what was the good reverend doing today Wilkinson?'

'Nothing sir. Last night's event was posted but there's nothing for today.'

'Seem to remember he is about forty, well-built, small hands, neat and tidy face. None of the good disciples know much more about him.'

'You think it's the reverend Terence? You think the body in the forest is the reverend? Why?'

'Gets mixed reviews Henri. You should know. Anthony and Sylvia aren't fans and Daniel was looking for how to ban the good reverend from promoting himself at the Education Centre.'

'But the Lord family didn't kill him Terence. That's ridiculous. They were as surprised as we were when those two wildlifers came barging in.'

'Were they Henri?'

'Christ Terence they're family, your family.'

'Puts a stop to the reverend though doesn't it? Sort of permanent ban.'

'You're warped Terence. It certainly couldn't have been the family.'

'Right Henri, certainly not directly but what about a contract?'

Henri looked at Terence as if he was mad. Leslie watched the scene and wondered what game Terence was playing. Terence turned to look at PC Goodfellow.

'I think constable we might eliminate one possibility with a joint visit to the morgue. Wilkinson, wrap up what you have found and come with us. Henri, you and Leslie here seem so concerned about your investment friend that we should have you come with us too and eliminate one possibility. Your friend Henri has suddenly gone very quiet and that interests me. Follow us in your car will you please?'

The two cars pulled up at the morgue and Inspector Field buzzed the front door. He turned to Henri and Leslie.

'This is partially to satisfy your curiosity and partially to help me eliminate a possibility. I don't want any questions but I do need to determine whether you can identify this body. Do we understand each other?'

'Yes Terence. Thanks. We'll be relieved if it isn't our friend.'

'But he'll still be missing Henri.'

'Yes, yes of course. Please show us.'

The Inspector left Wilkinson inside the car as the constable hesitantly explained he wasn't keen on dead bodies, especially this one. Leslie glanced at the constable after he said this but nothing further was forthcoming. The four men trooped inside the building and the Inspector led the way down a corridor through the swing double doors. The smell hit them and Henri almost gagged. True it was only the disinfectant smell but it was strong, and the brain realised that the strength was necessary to mask other odours.

'Inspector. Come to see my puzzle have you?' and the doctor moved over to a table covered by a sheet. The Inspector put out his hand and stayed the doctor's next move.

'Judiciously I think doctor. My two civilian companions are not so familiar with autopsy rooms and dead bodies can be disturbing. This may be a friend of theirs.'

The doctor looked at Henri and Leslie and back to Inspector Field and nodded slightly. He carefully parted the sheet around the midsection and pushed the upper part upwards over the stomach and chest leaving it bunched below the shoulders. The lower section he pushed downwards to the foot of the table. Henri gasped and reached out to Leslie beside him for support. Leslie visibly paled and staggered with the shock and with Henri's unexpected weight. Suddenly Henri reached over the body and grabbed the far arm. He held it up.

'Where are his hands? Why did you cut off his hands?' he shouted. Leslie's knees buckled and he fainted onto the floor. PC Goodfellow leant over and pulled Leslie's body away from the table. Finding a chair he hoisted Leslie onto it and bent him over so his head was between his knees.

'Just breathe easy sir: slow breaths like. Take it nice and slowly sir.'

Terence looked over at his constable and saw that all was under control. The doctor looked at Terence and an understanding passed between them.

'Henri. Henri, look at me,' said Terence. 'There were no hands Henri. We suspect that someone in the forest cut them off. Both of them,' he added somewhat un-necessarily. 'Now, are you okay to stand or do you want a moment to sit and breathe? It's a shock I know. I'm assuming from the reaction you both know this man?'

'It's Buzz,' whispered Henri. 'It's Buzz.'

Terence looked a little puzzled for a moment. 'This is Bernard Black, your friend?'

Behind him Terence heard Leslie try and speak but the voice came out stifled, garbled and breathless.

'It's Buzz Haas Terence; a good friend, no a very good friend,' and Henri let go of the arm he had tried to lift.

'Henri. I'm sorry but this is very serious and very important. I do need a positive identification. I need you to be sure you know who this is. Can you tell me who this is with certainty? Take a moment please.'

Henri stood up straight and Terence could see him brace his shoulders. Calm now on the outside but emotionally torn apart inside

Henri looked back at the Inspector and then at the doctor. 'This is Mr. Buzz Haas Inspector,' he said very formally. 'I can positively identify him, as can Leslie if necessary.'

The Inspector looked at Henri very carefully. 'Mr. Buzz Haas Henri, and not Mr. Bernard Black? I want to make sure we all heard you correctly.'

'Can we get out of here? I don't want to be here. I don't want to see him like this. He was our friend. Can't you understand Terence; can't you understand what I am saying? He was a special friend to both of us. Let me out of here. I can't stay here any more,' and Henri wheeled away from the body and rushed out of the swing doors.

'Thank you doctor,' said Terence. 'It's a start to know who he is. By the way doctor, any further ideas on time and cause of death?'

'Sometime around midnight Terence, give or take a little.'

'Cause?'

'Bit more difficult with missing parts, relevant missing parts. There are no bullet wounds on the corpse, no knife punctures, and no obvious signs of asphyxiation or poisoning.'

'So a blunt instrument to the skull is still a possibility and maybe a distinctive wound so let's take the head. How was the head severed?'

'Something like an axe, not a saw. Same with the hands. Just hacked off.'

'Alive?'

'Not sure but possibly. If already dead then the parts were hacked off straight away. Should be a fair amount of the blood at the site. Certainly where the hacking took place.'

'Thanks doctor. Time to detect I think and we'll start with the friends.'

Henri and Leslie sat on conventional uncomfortable chairs in the office of the morgue. PC Goodfellow had found some tea for both of them. Leslie still looked like he would keel over at the slightest push but Henri had become more controlled. Interesting thought Terence as he walked into the office and looked at the two men. Wonder exactly what the relationship was. Samantha did confirm the obvious that Henri is gay and so is Leslie if I'm not mistaken. Wonder if this was a jealousy thing gone wrong.

'Henri I need to ask some questions. Are you and Leslie here up to that? I should mention that the sooner I learn a little more from you the sooner I can start to find the perpetrator.'

Henri took a deep breath and sat up straight on the hard chair and looked at the Inspector.

'Why didn't you show us his face?'

'Because it isn't there,' said Terence. 'Like the hands, the head had been severed and it was not found. It had been carried away or carefully hidden. The same is true for all the clothes. Perhaps the perpetrator wanted to make the identification difficult for us. Take away teeth and fingerprints for example.'

'Bastards, bloody bastards,' said Henri and he turned to Leslie. 'This is a message Leslie, a message for me.'

'Henri can we start at the beginning please? You and Leslie here seem to know a lot more than we do. You said the man is Buzz Haas and you both know him. Can we go from there? What does Buzz do, where does he live and why is he here for starters?'

Terence looked carefully at both men because he still didn't know whether this was a jealousy thing gone wrong. Either Henri or Leslie could be the perpetrator – even if the actual killing was done under contract. Unlikely though thought Terence given the where, when and the whole process. Still, one step at a time and assume nothing.

Slowly Henri explained the background of Buzz Hass, aka Bernard Black, and the whole story of getting a newspaper article on the Reverend

Godschild. During this explanation Leslie stirred a couple of times and tried to interrupt but Inspector Field wasn't having his storyteller swayed in mid flow.

'Your turn will come Mr. Dauphin,' the Inspector said. 'Continue Henri. Buzz was there to take photos of the initiation ceremony.'

'And afterwards Terence, in the cottage. We'd heard there was likely to be something else in the cottage.'

'Do you know Gloria Manson?' asked Inspector Field. He watched the reaction which answered the question. 'Still see her up in London do you? Back working at the Oasis isn't she? She still with the rest of her friends, Lola, Gina, Sheena and who, who was it constable, the young one?'

'Belle sir, Belle Katz.'

'Right constable. Yes, Belle Katz. So you do know them Henri? Never mind. Carry on with your story with Buzz taking photographs in the cottage. Shades of déjà vu constable.'

'Yes sir.'

'And Buzz and Leslie here would produce this embarrassing story for the tabloids?'

'Not embarrassing Inspector, just a factual account of a Lordly family permitting the confusion and distortion of young minds in their infamous Education Centre. A simple story of abuse, mental abuse by a powerful family,' said Leslie.

Terence thought of a comment about how to win friends and seek for money but kept the thought to himself. Why state the obvious he realised.

'Message Henri, you said earlier that this was a message. Can you explain that comment please?'

Leslie put his hand out quickly to grab Henri's arm. 'Shut it, shut up you fool. You'll get us all killed.'

'Bit melodramatic Leslie,' said Terence. 'Who would want to kill you? Have you really annoyed the reverend or any of his followers? Your friend really messed up their party last night. I can imagine the reverend was quite frustrated not being able to initiate his sweet young angels. Didn't the good man say "Vengeance is mine said the Lord"?' Inspector Field looked carefully at each of the two men.

'Did either of you go out last night?'

Henri gasped and went red. He stood up and aggressively moved towards the Inspector. 'You think we did it? You think we killed our friend? You really think we killed Buzz and cut off his hands and his head? You're crazy, absolutely mad.' The emotion suddenly drained out of Henri and he sat down shaking and wringing his hands. 'He was our friend,' he whispered, 'our friend.'

Leslie had slumped back into his chair and looked defeated. Something had left him and he just looked shattered.

'Who wants to kill you Mr. Dauphin? Who sent you this message? Cutting off the head and the hands was a message right? Your friend, the photographer has taken one photograph too many and pissed someone off. Take away all the senses, sight, touch etc. and you can't communicate. Your line of business isn't it, communications? You and Buzz together and now someone sends you a rather crude and pointed message.'

Terence paused and listened for a reaction. He let the silence lengthen but Henri and Leslie both appeared to be genuinely shocked by what they had seen and learnt. But messages thought Terence and more likely a London thing than the reverend.

'London Henri. This is all about London isn't it? I don't quite see our missing reverend as part of any such message. Not quite his style somehow. I can't imagine his ceremonies include an axe or large sacrificial knife and the weapon was on site. Comments?'

Like Leslie Henri seemed to have collapsed. The strength had gone out of him and Terence watched him shudder as if a threat had crossed his mind. Terence waited again and patiently watched the two men. PC Goodfellow had worked with his Inspector for some time and he knew that he too was to stay still and silent. The clock on the wall ticked steadily and the noise seemed to increase as the silence lengthened. Slowly Henri brought himself back together and it was as if his body gradually filled more of the chair thought Terence. Realisation and living for tomorrow is coming back to him. Resilient. Samantha told me he had been a strong and powerful climber. Had seen some dead bodies in his time. Witness to death. Had done some hard routes too, and when she says that you can bet she means really hard routes. So the man has some backbone and inner strength. Let him get himself back into reality.

'Message from whom Henri?'

'Another story Inspector,' suddenly and unexpectedly interrupted Leslie. 'Another expose as you put it.'

'So you know who did this to your friend?'

'Given what they did I've got a good idea. They'd threatened us before but we thought we had a good story and threats are part of our lives. Buzz and I live in a world of threats Inspector. It's part of our working environment and you learn to live with it.'

'Mr. Dauphin this is becoming a little more serious and formal. I think we all should move from here and go back to the police station. My constable in the car will begin to think we all have this fascination with dead bodies. It will bother him. Let's go.'

SUSPECTS

WHEN THEY WERE FOLLOWING THE police in their car Henri told Leslie that he was going to tell the Inspector everything, well almost everything. Buzz had been his friend. Buzz had been a friend to both of them, a loved one.

'This is war Leslie. Before, you and Buzz might have had a story that could threaten them but now this has become more serious, more personal. I know they think they have a hold over me but this has become more brutal.'

'Henri they do have a hold over you my dear, a one hundred thousand pound hold, not to mention those photographs they talked about.'

'Leslie my only hope is through the police. We can't hope to get those animals off our backs on our own. We need the police to smash them, arrest them, whatever.'

'Well you certainly do Henri.'

'Oh no Leslie. I'm not alone in this. You and Buzz have been in their faces for a while now. When you hinted about your story and going to the tabloids you raised the ante on your head too. No Leslie, it's not just me that's in danger.'

Back in the police station Inspector Field sat Leslie and Henri down in an interview room, and once PC Goodfellow had attended to their need for coffees he started his investigation of "messages" in severed hands and head. The four of them sat peacefully in the overheated room while Terence quietly leafed through some of his notes before he turned to look at Henri and Leslie.

'London? You've annoyed someone I take it if this is a message?'

'Inspector, it's complicated. I suppose there are two parts to this story,' started Henri. 'I can tell you my involvement and then Leslie can tell you his. You need to know the whole story if you're going to stop these animals. And we need you to stop them or likely we'll be next.'

Terence looked across the table at his far-removed in-law relative. Bit melodramatic Henri thought Terence, but then Leslie isn't his usual obnoxious self so this message is blunt enough. It's certainly got their attention.

'We're listening Henri. Been going on a long time or is this just recent?'

'Inspector, Terence, I don't know what you know, what the family has told you, but I've got a gambling habit, and a drug habit too I suppose.'

PC Goodfellow looked at his boss but Terence kept quiet.

'I gambolled and for a while I lost. I borrowed. I kept on borrowing and these people bought my I.O.U.s. I didn't know who they were but I needed to get out from under. You can understand surely? My luck had to change eventually and so I continued. I owe them a lot of money and I don't have it. I have to pay by the New Year and I can't. They killed a friend of mine to tell me they were waiting.'

'Rather over the top Henri, just for a gambolling debt. And for the record, how much?'

'Over two hundred thousand and I haven't got it.'

Leslie suddenly sat up straighter on his chair. 'Two hundred thou…….' but Terence held up his hand to quieten Leslie.

'Yes, two hundred thousand. That's why I was asking the family for help. That's why I need Anthony to change his method of inheritance. Why I need Peter to let me have what is mine. It's crazy what they do. All of the rest of the family think it's cruel. Ask Samantha. She'll tell you.'

'Were you supposed to pay earlier?'

Henri shuddered. 'I was supposed to pay it all before December but I couldn't. I was supposed to pay last July but I couldn't. Every month I was to pay but I've missed them all.'

'And the interest is piling it on?'

'It's killing me. There's no way I can pay. They'll kill me.'

Terence sat and thought about that. What was it Matthew had said about the Lord family looking out for each other? Wonder what might happen? Perhaps another prod might be in order to see whether Henri has anything else to confess.

'Drugs Henri? Do you deal as well as use? Have you upset someone dealing? Have you sold something and not paid? Is there more to this story because trying to find a murderer for what happened out in the forest is not going to be easy. Likely the person or persons directly involved were not the someone who is personally looking for you, if you know what I mean. The actual murderer was probably a bit player and you need protection from the boss if I understand you correctly.'

There was another pause. Leslie fidgeted and rolled his coffee cup around in his hands. Henri looked at Leslie but for once Leslie was quiet.

'Yes,' said Henri.

'Cocaine?' asked Inspector Field. While he waited for Henri to answer Terence thought over the implications of this complex murder case. It was rapidly spinning out of his control as the likely perpetrators were London-based and involved in gambolling, drugs, extortion and likely other things like money laundering. This was going to be a MET case or even some special squad. He'd lost track of the various organisation shuffles that happened up in London as they struggled to combat organised crime.

'Yes, and some heroin too. Not much, only a little. I don't myself. I really don't.'

'Anything else I should know about you Henri?'

'No, that's everything.'

Maybe thought Terence, but maybe not.

'Why here Henri? Why at Fotheringham and not up in London? I would have thought these people would feel more at home in the city. Did anyone know you were coming down here? And you came down here as two separate groups so someone must have been tracking you. Were you thinking of doing a runner Henri?'

Across the table Henri looked stunned, shocked. He shook his head. Terence let it drop for the moment but it was still a question. He changed direction.

'You still haven't told me who this anonymous faceless threat sending you messages actually is now have you? Does it have a name, or names?'

'They're Europeans, East Europeans. I'm not sure from where. I don't know the language but they're rough.'

'Know where in London?'

'I don't where they live but I suppose I got started through one of their clubs.'

'And this might lead into your friend's involvement? Leslie, you've been very quiet, which I appreciate, but now it might be time for you to speak. How have you and Mr. Haas antagonised these E.U. members?'

'They're smuggling people into the country Inspector. Girls. Girls for drugs and prostitution. Girls for couriers too probably. They buy and sell people. They're slave-traders.'

'Interesting Leslie. You have evidence? Did you see or hear something or is this just imagination and supposition? I've heard that you write for the tabloids and a fair proportion of that is inflammatory fiction, sometimes libellous fiction. You have evidence?'

'Buzz has some photographs, photographs of girls, photographs of rooms of people.'

'Which include some of these East Europeans? Not family members over on vacation? What is special about these photographs? What is incriminating? What is hard evidence Leslie?'

'I've got tapes. I've got copies of emails. The language is Serbian. I've had some of them translated.'

'You never told me,' cried Henri. 'You've never said you knew who they were. You never said that you knew their names.'

Inspector Field looked at the pair of them. Love, trust, belief, sharing all seemed stretched and contorted in this relationship but so what as this is rapidly becoming not my case.

'I'm going to ask both of you to write up what you have told me. Then you can leave but I can assure you that we will be back for further discussions. Constable, I think it is time to collect some paper and pens for our two informants here. When you're back I'll go and make a few phone calls.'

Having written their stories Henri and Leslie left the police station. Dusk had already fallen.

'Now what? Now where? I feel drained and exhausted Leslie. Thinking over what they did I'm sick.'

'It's too late to drive home. Let's go and collect Buzz's things. I don't think we'll be welcome back at Fotheringham so we can stay at the

George. We can stay in Buzz's room and remember him. We can get drunk and remember Buzz Henri.'

'What if they're still around Leslie? Have you thought of that? They could come looking for us next. Should I go back and warn Terence?'

'Henri, forget it. They've sent their fucking message. Back to George, now Henri.'

'George will be happy if we settle up Buzz's account.'

'Fuck him Henri. Fuck them all. Let's go and get absolutely pissing drunk. I need to get drunk and then I can think how to get even.'

Back in the police station Inspector Field made several phone calls. His boss wasn't pleased being called on Boxing Day but he did understand the reason. Yes he agreed, this was going to be passed to the MET but he told Inspector Field he had better go with the evidence and be involved. He said he would phone his Chief Constable and then the right people in London. Terence phoned Fotheringham and spoke with Sylvia and with Daniel. Last of all he phoned Samantha.

'Poor Henri Terence. He must be devastated. The three of them were all so close, truly close Terence. Giselle was telling me about the relationship. She was really worried about her brother. Have you called Marcel? He and Marie went home this evening, back to Dartmouth. Have you called Giselle?'

'No love. I've taken care of the official calls but the only family I have called were Daniel and your mother. I called them first.'

'That was thoughtful Terence. Mum would appreciate that. Look, I'll call Marcel and then I'll call Giselle. I'll tell them to keep it to themselves at the moment shall I? I'm assuming this is just the start of your work?'

'Samantha darling, you amaze me. Here I was expecting something quite different from you.'

'Like what Terence? I've changed my love. Working with Janet has taught me better manners and a greater appreciation of knowledge, public and private. At the moment this is classified as private, for your eyes only kind of stuff. Can Marcel and Giselle call Henri though? Where is he by the way? Mum banished the pair of them so they've either gone back to London or they're down at the George. Anyway, can they call?'

'Yes Samantha. As they were all there at Fotheringham when this was found they can all know that we have identified the body, but, as I told Sylvia, keep it to the family and no repeating it elsewhere. You're right though, this is just the start and I may have to be away from tomorrow onwards as this develops.'

'Holiday or no holiday?' said Samantha. 'James will miss you. I will miss you. Me and the baby will miss you.'

'Yes love I know. Both our jobs are good news/bad news stories but I love you Samantha, I really do.'

'You home tonight?'

'Yes love, I'll be home in the hour. You can call Marcel and then Giselle. She's with Stephanie still isn't she?'

'And Christina Terence? I almost forgot Christina.'

'I told Daniel to do that for me and be discreet about it. I know Christina gets emotional and I didn't reveal all the details of the body rather deliberately at Fotheringham. Daniel will be sensible I'm sure.'

'See you soon love.'

'In the hour,' and Terence hung up.

Samantha briefly told Janet who whistled and looked quizzical.

'Pretty clear message Sam. I wouldn't want to be in your cousin's shoes right now, or his partners for that matter. What'll happen next?'

'Terence said it'll become a MET case but he'll have to go up to London too. His boss told him he needed to be there as he knew most of the background details. So he'll be away again.'

'You sure you want to stay working Sam? Why don't you go up to London with him? Your family could look after James. Katya would love to have him and James could enjoy his Christmas present. He's always talking about Dainty.'

'Thanks Janet but Terence will be busy in London. I'd sooner be doing something other than just sitting around waiting for the odd moment with him. No, I've a meeting in two days time with some clients. I'm meeting them in Bristol and then we're off around Chipping Sodbury. Katya will get James anyway.'

'She's happy Sam, with her baby I mean.'

'Yes Janet. It's just a shame that dad is so sick. Normally with two new children coming into the family he would be over the moon. He loves children, he really does but now he has difficulties.'

'Growing old's a bitch Sam. Don't go there though. You and Terence are wonderful and now your brother is doing his bit too.'

Samantha laughed and lightly punched Janet on the shoulder and then hugged her.

'Two hugging hot women,' exclaimed James as he came running into the room. 'What's for dinner? I'm hungry.'

Samantha separated from Janet and it was Janet who scooped James up off the floor and turned the pair of them into a merry-go-round.

'Faster, faster.'

'I'll go and phone Marcel,' said Samantha.

Phoning Marcel was straightforward, although Marcel didn't sound all that sympathetic. He and his brother were quite estranged thought Samantha. Shame, but then they really are different. Funny really because Daniel and I are quite different and we love each other very much. Strange world. She phoned Stephanie.

'Samantha, Giselle is not here. Thank you for telling me what has happened. It really is rather gross but I'm glad to hear your Terence has found out who it is, the body I mean. Now I suppose he's got to find out who did it. Anyway, I'll tell Giselle but she's had to go to work. She briefly explained there was something special on but then you know her. She'll never tell you anything about what she really does. Take care Samantha love; take care of yourself and your baby. Good night love.'

'Good night auntie.'

Giselle had left Fotheringham right after Terence's briefing. She had dropped off her aunt and taken Matthew back home to London.

'You say you're going to work Giselle?'

'Yes Uncle Matthew.'

'Bit far from Bristol?'

'And you're too inquisitive for your own good.'

Matthew laughed and looked at Giselle. 'Did I ever tell you what I did in the war?'

'No, never. You've always been quite reticent. We all know you were some kind of expert. Something to do with radar or communications but I've never heard the details. Auntie Stephanie doesn't know, or she wouldn't tell me.'

'Loose lips lose ships.'

'That's long before my time uncle.'

'And I know better than to ask you why you're working in London.'

Giselle quickly glanced across at Matthew as they sped up the Motorway. 'Let's just say it's a special op,' she said.

'Enough said,' said Matthew and he settled himself more comfortably in his car seat.

'You ever think of marrying Giselle?'

'Where did that come from?'

'Well, Marcel married, Henri married, sort of, and you are a very gifted and attractive young woman.'

'And you're a clever old man and you never got married. You're one to talk.'

'Wasn't attractive enough was I?' said Matthew and he laughed. 'May have been gifted but just wasn't attractive.'

'Auntie Veronica told me you were always taking things to pieces. Drive a woman mad that would. Bits everywhere. Actually though, Henri is quite happy with his partnership. In fact it is an interesting and unusual relationship because there are three of them all living together. Henri tells me it is very loving and friendly. That's one part of his life that seems to have stabilised and become happier. When he was younger he was really confused about his sexuality. Tried both ways you know.'

'Yes Giselle. I know a little about it. Stephanie told me quite a lot about Henri. She used to tell me a lot about all of you. I have always admired Stephanie for what she did for the three of you, but then she really loved your father. A strong and supportive family member is Stephanie. Still, she tells me she is worried about other parts of Henri's life. He has an obsession for money. Apart from the fracas over this past couple of days Henri has asked me for money on a couple of occasions. I'm not averse to giving Giselle as I have little use for it these days but I never got good answers to my few questions. I don't like throwing good money after bad. I'm old, and old-fashioned. What's Henri really into?'

Giselle sighed. She glanced at the clock on the car dashboard. 'Let's get you home and I'll spend a few minutes to explain. It's complicated and the traffic is getting heavy. By the way, you'd better make sure I find the right way home. I'm not that familiar with West London.'

After Giselle had got her uncle home, and given him a thumb nail sketch of Henri's apparent dilemmas, she wished him good night and drove further into the West End. After some uncertain navigation she successfully found herself driving down Whitehall and turned in to New Scotland Yard. There she checked in to the front desk and someone came down to take her to her meeting.

Monday, December twenty seven dawned clear and frosty, and people were on the move. Sylvia had the doctor come out as Anthony had had a troubled night. Very deliberately Sylvia had not told Anthony any details of the body in the forest and Anthony had not asked, which in itself was not a good sign. Daniel and Katya made sure the small full-time work crew had a clear understanding of their work for the next week and Daniel told Bob Edwards about the taped off crime scene near the Ferris cottage. Bob Edwards in turn echoed Detective Field's earlier thought about bull-dozing the place and letting nature heal the area.

As soon as Daniel and Katya were back at the Big House Samantha arrived with James. Despite admonitions from Sylvia the noise level did increase somewhat. Katya promised she would take James out, and James promptly demanded a visit to Adam and Storm.

'Please Katya? Adam would love to see us and I haven't seen Storm for ages. Adam's mummy makes delicious cakes. She says they are good for me. Orgassic or something. Scrumptious and I haven't eaten since breakfast and that was ages ago. Please?'

Katya laughed and told James she would drive with him in the Landrover and visit the Entwhistles.

'Why can't we ride? I need to get comfortable with my new saddle. We could both ride and I can show Adam how Dainty does tricks.'

'James MacRae, we will go in the Landrover and politely visit with Adam and Storm. We will also ask whether there is anything we can do for Mrs. Entwhistle. You're old enough to start learning about responsibilities. My father would insist you learn how to behave as a gentleman.'

'But he's not here,' said James. 'How will he know what I do?'

Katya looked at James and smiled. 'And when we are in the Landrover you can tell me the names of the various trees we see. That way we have learning as well as being a gentleman. It's what special friends do James, and I'm your special friend. Isn't that right?'

'Okay,' said James, 'just this once, but I'll need at least two cakes if I get them all right.'

While Katya took James one way Daniel took off to visit Christina and check her comfort with the story of the body in the forest. He also wanted to talk with Enrico about a piece of plantation history, and check that Peter and Tony didn't start amateur sleuthing.

Away from Fotheringham, at the George, Henri and Leslie slumbered on. Several empty bottles littered the bed as the two men had had a personal wake for Buzz. Inspector Field had phoned George the previous day to give him a few details and to expect a clearing up of Mr. Black's room.

Earlier that day, Terence himself said his goodbyes to Samantha and James, and said he would phone. Samantha reminded him that she too would be out that day and the next couple of days. She gave him a list of numbers. Call me she had said as she drove over to Fotheringham with James.

'You off too Janet?' asked Terence.

'Sure am Terence. Like Sam, I've got clients, but they're up in town. Look, thanks for having me. It's been a usual Lord family gathering where something always happens. Remember the first time we ever met? When I claimed my M.O.T. wasn't up-to-date? That was a chaotic Lord family get-together too.'

'So, should I banish you from Fotheringham Janet?' asked Terence.

'No way Inspector. I wouldn't miss the excitement for the world. My best friend and I here thrive on excitement.'

'Well don't excite her too much for the next little while Janet, please?'

Janet suddenly went serious and looked back at Terence. 'No Terence, I won't. Sam told me the history and I know how much the pair of you want this baby. I'll try and keep her from doing anything crazy. She's desperate this goes okay for you, for the pair of you.'

'Thanks. Now I've got to go and join the rat race in London.'

'Me too.'

Having wisely left her car at New Scotland Yard Giselle walked from her hotel to her briefing that morning. Early in the day the London air was still relatively crisp with a nip in the air. She had left her hotel deliberately early and Giselle walked a little of the way along the Thames Embankment. The tide was close to full ebb and the shingle shore was visible in a few places. A few tugs were busy and Giselle noticed that the river looked clean. She thought about her brothers. Marcel would be leaving today, off to another series of races in the Caribbean. He loved the life, the camaraderie and the competitiveness. Like our parents Giselle thought, even though Marcel said he never wanted to be like them: competitive and bold, just a different natural environment. And then Henri. Oh Henri, what have you got yourself into brother dear? Where did you go wrong? You were a good climber, a great climber yet you got lost somewhere. You've got a good brain and you were so confident and sure of yourself when you first started work in Bath. We all thought the move to London was for the best. Always the highs and lows though Henri. Somehow stability isn't in your nature. Leaving the changing river and putting aside her swirling thoughts Giselle walked through to New Scotland Yard and found her way into the reception area. It was time for Giselle to concentrate on her own rather disturbing world. A young WPC came out of the lift and walked towards her.

'Miss Lord, we're waiting for you. Come with me will you please?' and she led Giselle back into the lift, and away to see the WPC's boss with some other police inspectors and a Superintendent. Also in the room was a young girl, about fifteen. The men introduced themselves and a lady Inspector, Brenda Dawson. It was Brenda who introduced Giselle to the young girl, even though she knew that they had met before.

'I'd like you to meet Janice Krass Miss Lord,' and Giselle shook hands with the girl who was dressed in a High School dark navy skirt and white shirt. Long white stockings and black boots like Doc Martins completed the ensemble. It didn't come as a shock to Giselle when the girl smiled at her as she shook her hand and said, 'Good morning Auntie Giselle,' as she said it in Serbo-Croat. Giselle smiled and quietly replied, 'and a fine morning it is to be sure,' in the same language. The two of them winked at each other.

'If we can all be seated,' said Superintendent Ralston. 'By the way, I've coffee and tea coming at ten. My secretary has also promised me biscuits, but she said that I should abstain so all the more for the rest of you. Now, thank you for coming and I'll let Inspector Dawson introduce our two new ladies. I know some of you know a little about both of them but Brenda here will give you the background so you understand exactly what Operation Tito is all about. Brenda?'

Inspector Dawson looked at each of the individuals around the table. She passed out a couple of biography sheets to each person. When everyone was settled she began.

'First, I'd like to introduce Giselle Lord. Giselle comes to us from her office in Bristol. Welcome Giselle. Miss Lord comes to us fluent in many European languages including Serbo-Croat, which is what you just heard by the way. She has been working for the government for over ten years now involved in smuggling, especially people-smuggling. Over the past three years Giselle has been directly involved with sex-trade smuggling, particularly from Europe and western Asia. Some of that has been from Turkey, some from the Ukraine but also some from what was Yugoslavia.

It appears there are still people who want to perpetuate the atrocities of the unrest in Bosnia, Serbia, Croatia and Montenegro of the early nineties. We have identified a pipeline of people coming into this country from Bosnia, most of whom are Muslim women being kidnapped, transported, sold and/or used by Serbs. Miss Lord has personally seen parts of this pipeline in Serbia, in Bosnia and in Croatia. She has also observed parts of the process in their crossing from Europe into England. We know a little about the destinations in London. There are three night clubs, one official casino, and several illegal establishments, brothels in fact. It's been hard to tie all these parts together and collect solid evidence for any prosecution. We now have most of the pieces and we think we are close to the whole story. Giselle has worked with us and seen several of the parts and together we think we have a possible way to collate the evidence. As part of the job for her office Giselle has worked underground. Her boss, Mr. Tallin, is here to confirm that and to provide other information and resources as required.'

'We'd like to do all we can to stop this trade in humans,' said Mikel Tallin. 'I can understand people wanting to get into this country to better themselves. That's just what I did. However, I get sick to my stomach at the thought of the fate of the girls being brought here. I know some of them actually believe they are coming to secretary jobs, hospital jobs, even modelling jobs. The flow from my home country, the Ukraine saddens me. We would like to reduce this activity as much as possible. I realise we will never eliminate it but we think we can stop part of it. I can bring other people to this operation as required.'

'Thanks Mikel. Unfortunately we need people who can think like these animals. We need people who can operate like these people. People who can hide or even disappear,' added Brenda Dawson. 'With that thought in mind I'd like to introduce our other lady guest and she also is someone special. Janice Krass was christened Djardjica Krasic and she is just fifteen. However, in those few years Janice here has managed to experience a lifetime of events. By the way, Janice is here after some long and detailed discussions with her mother. Janice's mother is Croatian from Sarajevo but her father was Serbian. In that rather infamous but beautiful city they fell in love at the wrong time and in the wrong place. As most of you know people in that part of Europe don't always take kindly to people marrying out of their nationality or religion. Janice's father was killed by some ultra-patriotic Serbians. Janice's mother managed to escape and after nearly a year of hiding in different parts of Europe she and her daughter reached friends here in England. She changed her name from Krasic to Krass, and she changed Djardjica to Janice, but she never forgot what had happened and what she saw in her travels.'

Brenda paused and looked at Janice. 'You okay Janice? Your mother assured me that this was something you had discussed and knew about. Can I continue?'

'Yes Inspector. It's done and nothing can change it. I want to help things in the future. I want to help other young people, people like me. Things are better here. Not always sure. There are still people here who hate, who torture, who kill but overall things are better here.'

Several of the people around the table looked at each other and they all thought about the work they did. Most of them were not so sure that things were all that better here. Still, perhaps the work they did exposed them only to the nastier parts of life. Janice looked at Inspector Dawson and nodded her head.

'We know that some of the girls come in as part of a school party. In the party are several girls who are bona fide schoolgirls but there are usually one, two or maybe three girls who are not. We think the party is organised in Bosnia to include the official schoolgirls through bribery, extortion, or maybe even ultra-patriotism. These girls come and return and the trip is paid for by the smugglers masked through a travel agency and bank. We aren't really concerned with how that part of the group is organised 'cos it is the "cargo" being carried by this innocuous group that interests us. The "cargo" manages to get lost somewhere on this trip in England. Girls run away we get told. Girls get lost. We want to track the "cargo" all the way across from Europe to its destination in England, in London. As I said before Giselle has done part of this and we know that parties often come across from Holland to Harwich on the ferry. The Hook of Holland boat train whisks them down to Liverpool Street and then they disappear.'

'And Operation Tito will make sure they don't,' interjected Superintendent Ralston, who wanted to make sure everyone knew who was really running this operation.

'Yes sir,' confirmed Inspector Dawson, and she paused to see whether her boss would add any other words of wisdom. When none were forthcoming she looked back around the table. She continued.

'There will be three parts to the operation. We've had some good information of an expected party coming across in four day's time, New Year's Eve. The party are booked to catch the midday ferry and they have seats booked on the train from Harwich. According to the booking there are eight girls and two minders, or supposed teachers. We think one or two of the party are "cargo". Leastways, that is our information. The first part of the operation involves Giselle and Janice in the foreground and a couple of our people in the background. You probably didn't catch it when Janice here first met Giselle but she called her Auntie Giselle 'cos Giselle will be Janice's aunt for the ferry trip. They will catch the boat in Holland and make the crossing. Somewhere, somehow with the language, Janice and/or Giselle will strike up an acquaintance with one or more of the girls. Our background people will observe who else has an interest in the party. We're pretty sure these groups travel with support personnel in the background.'

'Who else knows we're doing this?' asked one of the Inspectors, an officer from the Drug Squad, who was not directly involved in the people smuggling operations. 'You said that Miss Lord has been involved in this for some time. Seen most of the pipeline you said. So who else knows about this?'

'About this operation no one,' said Inspector Dawson. 'Right now we're just observing in Europe and on the ferry. Right now no one outside this room knows,' she added.

'Stays that way Tom,' emphasised Superintendent Ralston. 'If this is successful we might consider involving some of our friends across the Channel if we repeat this.'

Once again Brenda Dawson paused to make sure her boss had finished.

'Phase two takes place on the train. This is non-stop from Harwich to Liverpool Street, which is good news and bad news. Still, cell phones help these days. Again, Giselle and niece Janice are booked on the train and in the same compartment as part of the school group. The ten of them have booked a compartment and a bit. We don't know how they will split up the minders but during the course of a two hour train ride Giselle and Janice will try and find out who are the cargo. They won't necessarily try and make contact with them. We expect these two girls will be frightened out of their wits and/or drugged, probably the latter. Giselle has several tracker buttons and she will try and slip these somewhere onto the cargo. One or two of them are innocuously concealed in address notes or exchange gifts.' Inspector Dawson didn't add that Giselle also had a couple of other devices on her person, including a miniature camera and tape recorder to capture audio and visual images. Janice needn't know all that she had decided.

'Again, on the train, we have our background people plus a couple of new background people who will join the train in Harwich. If Giselle has identified the cargo by this time one of our background people may bump into the cargo or something and slip a tracker on her. We're not sure exactly what kind of luggage the girls will have. Our people on the train are well trained and we'll have the cargo identified by the time the train arrives in London.'

'And if not? What if this goes wrong or doesn't work? What if the girls don't get on the train at Harwich? What if there is an emergency stop of the train?'

Superintendent Ralston shifted his considerable weight in his chair and looked down the table. 'Colin, you always are a miserable bastard – pardon my French Miss.'

'Come on Bob. These ops have a tendency to go tits- ….. go wrong.'

'Inspector Lutz, we've thought through such contingencies, including the ferry being hi-jacked by pirates.'

Everyone laughed. Brenda Dawson continued. 'Giselle and Janice will do everything they can to identify the cargo on the ferry, including add trackers. In fact we've got our people brushing up against all members of the party during boarding so by the time the ferry docks, provided it hasn't been sunk by the odd floating mine, we'll have tagged the entire group. We will be very careful with the minders though. Then, if they don't get on the boat-train we can still track them as a party. That contingency is covered. Now, on the train we will almost certainly have delays, unexpected stops as this is an English train.'

Everyone around the table dutifully laughed.

'So, we have people travelling by road on the A12 in case there is another unscheduled hold-up. You with me so far Inspector Lutz?'

'Come on Brenda. You've made your point.'

'Okay. More serious now, in fact much more serious now we'll get to phase three. Giselle and Janice fade from the scene. They're going to stay with relatives somewhere in Wimbledon and they hope the girls have a good holiday. Bye and the best of luck. Exit left and our people take over.'

A knock came at the door.

'Come,' boomed the Superintendent, as it was his office.

The young WPC entered the room wheeling a tea trolley suitably cluttered with tea pots, coffee pots, jugs of milk, bowls of sugar, spoons and the "not to be touched sir" plate of biscuits.

'Thank you Susan,' said Superintendent Ralston. WPC Susan Hughes looked at her boss with a smile and a quick nod at the plate of biscuits. She shook her head, negatively. Turning on her heel she quietly left and closed the door behind her.

'Caught that look did you Bob?' asked Inspector Lutz. 'Clear message I think. Bourbons I see, and chocolate digestives. Suppose rank does have its privileges.'

'Let's take a break before Brenda describes phase three.'

Henri stirred. His tongue felt furry and his throat was like the bottom of a parrot's cage. Rolling over he felt Leslie's inert body beside him. Sitting up in bed Henri groaned and felt his head.

'Jesus, I've a thirst. Where's George with a cup of tea?' Henri slowly swung his legs over the side of the bed and stood. He staggered a little as he made the effort to pick up some clothes. Finding a pair of trousers he tried to slide one foot down the legs. Like a felled tree in the forest Henri toppled over and fortunately found the bed, sprawling clumsily over Leslie's feet. There was an instant cry of pain. 'Shit, my foot, my foot. Christ, my head. Get off Henri. Get off for fuck's sake man. You've broken my ankle you stupid bugger.' Henri rolled off and ended up kneeling on the floor. He wriggled into the trousers and rushed to the door. He made it down to the end of the hall and into the lavatory before erupting in a great flood of piss. He felt so sick as he hung over the toilet bowl. 'Good morning Mr. Crapper,' he managed to utter.

'You've broken my bloody ankle,' said Leslie when Henri came back into the room. 'Get some ice before it swells up. Shit, I feel like death. Henri go and get some tea for God's sake. Over there, over there pour me some water. My throat's like......'

'Good morning gentlemen,' said George as he knocked at the open door. 'Heard someone mention tea. Well here we are then. Nice fresh pot and breakfast in half an hour is it? By the way, Inspector Field telephoned and told me to tell you they will be keeping the body of your friend at the morgue. Said he would contact you when they release the body, for burial that is gentlemen. He said he expected you'd want to have your friend moved up to London. Gruesome business it is to be sure. That cottage sure has a history.'

'Landlord,' said Leslie, trying to stem the flow of George's monologue. 'Thanks for the tea and yes breakfast in half an hour. Don't suppose there's a doctor in this god-forsaken village as Henri here has twisted my ankle. Feels broken.'

'I can get some ice sir. Wrap it up good and tight with ice in the bandage.'

'Thanks George,' said Henri. 'Thanks for the tea and I'll come down for some ice in a minute. We'll be down for breakfast in half hour as you say.'

An hour later Leslie was still muttering in his foul mood.

'Henri I can't drive with this ankle.'

'Leslie, you've turned into an old woman this morning. George fixed the ice bandage and you'll survive until we're back up in town. Doc Munro can see it there. I'll drive. My head still feels like shit but I'm starting to recover from Buzz's wake, and I'm starting to feel revengeful.

306

I feel like kicking someone's face in Leslie. Buzz needn't have died like that. That's just vicious. That's just inhuman.'

'But that's what they are Henri. You didn't see Bosnia. You didn't see what they all did to each other over there. Didn't matter who was who but neighbours massacred neighbours. I still have nightmares of what I saw over there. One reason Buzz was so wound up about those illegal girls was because of what he had photographed in Bosnia. You don't want to know Henri. Now help me move. You get the bags and you can drive. Fuck it, I'm sure it's broken.'

Henri collected all the bags, including the stuff belonging to Buzz, and packed the car.

'Where's Buzz's car Henri? It's not here so he must have left it somewhere in the forest.'

'Inspector Field never mentioned anything about the car. Guess you're right. I'll phone Daniel as he's sure to find it being the bloody boy scout he is. His sister can drive it up. She is supposed to be coming up to London sometime soon. No, she said she was going to Bristol. Shit!'

'Henri just phone for fuck's sake and then let's go. I want out of this bloody village. I never want to see this place again. Phone.'

'Okay Brenda, let's hear about phase three. Do we still need Giselle and Janice with us or can they go and do some shopping or other?'

'No sir. That's a good idea.'

Inspector Dawson turned and looked straight at Giselle. 'Why don't you take Janice somewhere nice and get to know each other a little better? I know you've met before Giselle, the couple of times with her mother but it would be good if you both had a chance to exchange experiences: would be less chance for any slip ups between you. We'll meet again in a day's time, just before you catch the train to go to Holland.'

Giselle stood up. 'Thanks Brenda. That okay with you sir?' asked Giselle of Mikel Tallin.

'Yes Giselle. Sure. Makes sense. Go and buy some ear muffs or something. Holland is always such a windy place I find.'

'Go and look at the Millennium Dome or that giant Ferris wheel thing just outside my window,' suggested Superintendent Ralston. 'I'll bet both of them are on the schoolgirl's agenda. If they're here for the Millennium celebrations then they'll want to see both of them. Get to know the area and the details. Good background that. Good work. Yes, good work the pair of you.'

Giselle said a general thanks to the people around the table and smiling at Janice she said, 'Shall we go then niece?' in Serbo-Croat and Janice's face broke into a big grin.

'It's nice to hear the sounds again,' she replied. 'Perhaps we should continue to speak only in Serbo-Croat for a while, for the whole day perhaps. Would be good practice auntie.'

The pair of them left the room and WPC Hughes escorted them back to the entrance hall and out past reception.

'This going to work Janice?'

'Yes auntie, this is for my dad. Mum and I agreed we're doing this for my dad.'

During part of the rest of the day Giselle gently explained the previous boat trips she had made with another Croatian girl. She described the process and what they had done.

'But why me if you've done this before with this Letti?' asked Janice.

'New face Janice. I'll look different when we do this too. We don't want the fox frightened out of the chicken coop do we? We have to be very careful and smart how we do this but your mother told me you like acting. You'll have the leading role in this stage play my love. Anyway, let's go and see the Superintendent's tourist attractions shall we? For once it's clear in London and the sun is shining.'

As predicted Daniel found Buzz's car, well away from the crime scene taped area. He drove across to PC Goodfellow who was supervising the various experts still combing the area.

'We're nearly finished Mr. Lord. Can turn the forest back to you pretty soon. We've been careful with the badger run and his gate. Neat that is. Never seen the likes. Hope we've not disturbed him too much.'

'Not likely constable,' said Daniel with a smile on his face. 'Our brock is very much a creature of habit and nothing disturbs his routine – hence the gate. By the way I've found a car that doesn't belong to us. It may be the victims, Henri's friend Buzz whatever.'

'Have you sir? Well, suppose the Inspector might want that for evidence so I'll arrange for it to be transported out of here Mr. Lord. You show me where sir and we'll shift it. The forest will be all yours by tomorrow morning sir. Inspector Field's keen on moving that cottage too sir, if you know what I mean. I think he'd like to bury it somewhere Mr. Lord. Says he's seen it too many times. Sort of bad luck charm he thinks it is. Says you were thinking of bulldozing it sir?'

'Maybe constable, just maybe. Trouble is my wife thinks it suits the scenery. It does fit into the location really well but it does carry a lot of baggage. We'll see. Thanks for dealing with the car. Just hope we don't find any more bodies out here.'

'There's still Freddie Dunster somewhere sir. We never did find his body you know.'

'Hopefully not out here constable. Hopefully there are no more bodies in this forest,' and Daniel thought reflectively on the remains of Senor Mendoza buried just a couple of kilometres from here. 'Bye constable, although I'll probably be over this site again tomorrow. Thanks for everything. Hope you catch whoever.'

'Inspector Field's in London sir where we're certain the real culprits are. Not a local thing at all really.'

With a firm admonishment from his boss that this was their case, their murder, D.I. Field drove quietly up to London listening to traditional jazz. Unknown to many people Terence's father had been a clarinettist in his early days, around the fifties when traditional jazz swept across much of England. Terence had been brought up listening to the music of Chris Barber, Humphrey Littleton and the like. His dad had even played records of Kid Ory, Bix Beiderbecke and Louis Armstrong. As a clarinettist his dad really liked Johnny Dodds and the soprano sax of Sidney Bechet. Much to the surprise of his peers, who were brought up on Rock and Roll, this kind of music had stayed with Terence Field. As the kilometres sped by under his wheels D.I. Field travelled to New Orleans, Bourbon Street, St. James Infirmary, and St. Louis before he rambled with the muskrats. It helped pass the time and Terence realised the thinking part would start when he got to London. No doubt someone in the MET would have very clear ideas what they would do next whether it was Terence's murder case or not.

Not quite so quiet was the car trip up to London that included Henri and Leslie. Whether it was to overcome his shock, or maybe fear after seeing what they had done to Buzz, but Leslie complained almost non-stop about his ankle. He made Henri stop soon after they passed Bristol to go and get some more ice. As this was England, and Motorway Restaurant Services provide a limited supply of options, ice was not readily forthcoming. After some sweet talk Henri managed to get one of the girls to scrape around the inside of the ice-cream freezer and pack the shavings in a plastic bag. She even suggested he buy several ice lollies and wrap them around the whatever. Henri thought about it but decided that Leslie would argue over the flavours he had bought so he bypassed that option.

'Right around the ankle Henri. Shit, that hurts. Don't press so hard and it doesn't bend that way. Now tie it on with something. Your handkerchief will do. Good job you don't work in a hospital. Patient could die in the time it takes you to strap me up. Okay, so lift the leg back up again, slowly. Slowly Henri!!'

Henri's emotions were a mix of fear and worry over money gradually being overwhelmed with a feeling of anger and the need for revenge. He bound up Leslie's leg with his mind in automatic mode. He didn't hear Leslie and as soon as he was back in the driver's seat he took off at speed.

'Slower Henri. I want to arrive in one piece. I don't need the other leg smashed up as well. You did a good enough job leaping on one foot. You're not back in the office today. We don't need a speeding ticket. It's my car remember. Ease up.'

Henri glanced at Leslie. How did he really feel? How did he really feel about Buzz? We've lost our friend and lover – a part of our family and all he does is whinge about his bloody foot. Me, me I feel mad. I'm torn apart with sorrow and disgust, but I'm also feeling we need to kick back. I'm not going to be walked all over. Fuck it. This is my country and a bunch of bloody immigrant peasants think they can call the shots. Time to fight back. Henri's foot pressed harder on the accelerator and Leslie closed his eyes.

Later that evening, with Leslie still nursing a bandaged ankle but re-assured of a doctor's appointment tomorrow first thing, the telephone chirped into life. Henri lifted the receiver.

'Hello, Henri Lord speaking. How may I help you?'

Henri carried his office's telephone spiel home with him. He listened carefully. There was a long silence but eventually a guttural voice said, 'Friday evening Mr. Lord, bearing gifts.'

Henri was about to say that he wasn't Greek but the line had already gone dead. 'Bastards,' he said as he put the phone down. 'Murdering bastards.'

PLANS FOR REVENGE

THE CLEAR FINE DAY OF yesterday changed as the weather in London turned cold and sleet slanted down as Henri walked to work in the city. The office was virtually empty as many of the staff took the Christmas to New Year's period as an extended holiday: most of them preparing for the new millennium. At his computer terminal Henri calmly assessed the status of the various accounts he managed. Yes, it was as bad as he remembered and somehow the shit was going to hit the fan come New Year. No matter how he juggled things Henri was going to get caught with his hands in the cookie jar. Suddenly Henri had a thought. Buzz, what about Buzz? He never said, but he made good money and he never spent anything thought Henri. Wonder who is the executor of his will? Must be Leslie. Henri phoned but the phone at home rang and rang. Shit, that's right, he had to see the doctor about his bloody ankle. Looking back at the screen Henri juggled a few things around which looked better, but not if you probed too deeply. Any auditor worth his salt would soon unravel Henri's efforts at masking the true state of affairs.

'It's sprained Mr. Dauphin. Painful I know, but it is a sprain and not a fracture. Here, the x-ray clearly shows there is no break.'

'I don't want to see it doc. I just want it fixed,' growled Leslie.

'That's easy,' said Doctor Munro. 'And cheap,' he guffawed into his wild red beard. 'Aye mon, reet cheap and that's the way I like it too.'

'Trouble is you're not,' complained Leslie. 'How? What magic pill are you going to prescribe, cheap or not?'

'Time laddie, merely time. Rest it. Keep off it. It'll mend itself.'

'Christ, I could have told you that. Why did I bother to come in?'

'Professional advice my dear man.'

'But it hurts. I need something for the pain. Wrap it up or something can't you?'

Doctor Munro sat up straight in his chair and looked pointedly at Leslie. 'Mr. Dauphin, your body is telling you to keep off that foot. The pain is to remind you to keep off that foot. If you keep off that foot it will heal itself. The swelling has gone down, the tissues are fine and wrapping it will only make you think it is okay to walk on. Rest man. If you want a pill for the pain, have a whisky. I can recommend a very good single malt. Pay my receptionist when you leave. She will call you a taxi. Rest it man.'

Leslie went home in a taxi feeling pissed off about paying for common sense. The message recorder light on his phone was blinking as he hopped into the sitting room and sank into an easy chair. By professional habit he picked up the receiver.

'Dauphin,' he barked down the line.

Leslie listened to Henri's terse message. "Call me. Immediately. Henri."

Having found himself a prescribed single malt Leslie sank into the chair and as there was nothing special to do he phoned Henri.

'Leslie I've got it. I've got an answer to my problem at work. In fact you've probably got the answer to my problem.'

'My ankle is fine thank you Henri. I'm glad you asked. The doc says it's not broken, despite your efforts, and he told me to just rest it. Oh, and he charged a bloody fortune for his cheap advice. Harley Street quacks have obviously got high rents. Still, the doc probably spends it all on whisky as all he recommended was an expensive single malt.'

'Yes, sorry about the ankle Leslie. Glad to hear it isn't broken.'

'Painful though Henri, still bloody painful thanks to you.'

'Listen up Leslie. I want to ask you about Buzz's will. You must be the executor. That's right isn't it? And we know he's got no family. Doesn't support any cat or dog's homes and he was never religious. So, he's left us all his money right? I can use my share to cover most of my losses. I can top up my client's accounts Leslie. It's brilliant. It's so bloody timely.'

'And Buzz lost his head over it Henri you callous sod. What makes you think Buzz left you any money anyway?'

'Shit, he must have. Who else was he going to leave it to?'

'And why should Buzz have any money?'

'What else did he do with it? No matter Leslie, I need it. It's an answer to my present prayers. How much is it?'

'Jesus Henri, the poor bugger isn't in his grave and you're scrambling all over the corpse ripping off his rings and flogging his watch. You're a ghoulish bastard at times Henri. Is this a climber's thing? Every time you watch a mate fall off the cliff do you all rush down to divvy up the gear? You'll be thinking of breaking my other ankle and running off with my assets next.'

'Stuff all that Leslie. Now listen up. Go look. Look at the will. Phone his solicitor. Find out the details, the timing. I need it this week at the latest. Call you later. Bye.'

Leslie dropped the receiver onto the cradle and collapsed back in the armchair. Rest he thought. Christ, just when we've got a story to put together, and either print or threaten, this has to happen. And photographs, yes pictures, but the bloody police must still have Buzz's cameras. He must have had them with him out in the forest and around that cottage but that Inspector pompous Field never said bugger all about any cameras. Perhaps those animal bastards who caught Buzz took them as well as his hands. Shades of what we saw in Bosnia Leslie thought. Someone needs to string them up. And now, all Henri can think about is his bloody money. Leslie stretched out his legs and looked around the room for a pouf for his foot. Not obvious. He looked across the room at the liquor cabinet but that was too far away to go looking for some more pain killing scotch. He was about to curse at the room, the flat, and life in general when the telephone rang again.

'No I haven't phoned the bloody solicitor yet. Oh, it's not you Henri. Inspector, yes good morning. No, actually it's fucking not a good fucking morning. I've a sprained ankle which hurts like hell and Henri is doing my head in. You what? When? Henri's at work all day. He'll be back around five, probably. Both of us? Okay, see you about six then. You know the address? Bye.'

Shit, I should have asked about the cameras. Never said where he was did he so I can't contact him. What a fucking day.

Terence turned to Sergeant Barry Gates and Inspector Darlene Lane. 'This evening at six,' he said. 'You think it's the same club?'

'We've had our eye on it for some time Terence. Remember that little caper last summer down your way? What did you call it? Call-girls in the country cottage or something equally corny? Anyway, one of your village girls was up here and I recognised her. Remember I came down to see you and we talked with what's her name? Gloria Manson, yes that's who. We'd had a murder up here a couple of weeks before she left remember and I came down to talk with her.'

'Yes, but then Gloria left again. I've not seen her or her friends since the clearing out of the cottage. You know that it's the same cottage, or close by that this murder of mine happened? Keep telling the owner, my brother-in-law actually, to bulldoze it. Anyway, you think Gloria's involved in this?'

'No Inspector,' said D.I. Lane, 'not directly.'

'It's where she works Terence,' said Barry Gates, 'or rather where she used to work. She's back at the Oasis and another couple of clubs but she's not working at the Exotica any more. Can't say I blame her from what we know of the Exotica.'

'Let me get this straight,' said Terence. 'Gloria and her bunch of sensual friends, Lola, Gina and the other two worked at this Oasis and the Exotica, and you think it is the people from the Exotica that are the likely perpetrators of my murder? I know from Leslie Dauphin and Henri Lord that they were writing a newspaper article, an expose I suppose of the activities associated with the Exotica. Dauphin was inferring that many of their activities are illegal. I also know that Henri Lord is in deep debt to someone and he believes the people behind the Exotica are the holders of his markers. He's been threatened several times now and his ultimate payment date is January 1. He and Dauphin are convinced Buzz Haas's murder was a simple message from these people.'

'Terence, we're trying to bust up the activities of these same people. We know they are a bunch of Serbs and they run several clubs and a variety of other rackets. As you asked we've scanned miles of CCT images and it appears some of this group was stupid enough to use their own cars going down to see you. On December 23rd we've identified the car you found in the forest, the Haas car, plus the car belonging to Mr. Dauphin, and three cars belonging to our Serbian brethren. It looks like the three Serb cars played follow-the-leader behind Dauphin. Periodically they changed the lead car but they all three tailed all the way. That confirms what you told us about the timing of the visits. We've also got the same three Serbian cars coming back to London early on December 26th, morning of the murder you said. I know it's circumstantial but so far it fits.'

'Can you seize the cars? Have you seized the cars?'

'No D.I. Field. Until your boss phoned we had no cause. We didn't know they had left town,' said Inspector Lane. 'It was only after you'd talked with Gates here that we checked the tapes.'

'You looking for a head Terence?'

'For starters Barry. Would certainly help. An axe would also help, complete with Mr. Haas's blood on it.'

'When we go round tonight we should get Henri to visit on New Year's Eve and pay his debt. Perhaps he could ask for his friend's hands and head in exchange? Maybe the silly bastards will have the head mounted on the boss's desk as a reminder to future debtors. Sort of "look what happens if you don't pay" reminder.'

'Sergeant you've a warped mind,' said Inspector Lane.

'No Mam, just thinking out loud and positively for Terence here.'

Henri's evening was a busy one as Terence and Barry Gates were round at six as planned. The two policemen wanted to know more about Henri's plans for paying off his debt. Henri however was very cautious about explaining his possible ideas. At this stage he wasn't going to share them with the authorities. Now that Leslie was out of the battle Henri had something else in mind. He thought he could take the fight to the enemy but he wasn't going to share those plans with anyone yet. After an hour Terence and Barry left with a statement they would keep Henri informed of any further developments. Leslie remembered about the cameras and Buzz's car. Terence told them the car was down at

Fotheringham and being inspected for any useful evidence. He would tell them when it could be released.

'And the cameras?' asked Leslie. 'They are part of Buzz's property and as I'm the executor of his will I should have those,' he said. 'Also, some of the images will be useful for my article on the good reverend. Have you found him by the way?'

'Not yet Mr. Dauphin but I've no doubt he will turn up somewhere. His reincarnation may not reveal itself as a reverend but he'll show sometime. We think he's run off to heaven with one of his new angels but Saint Peter may bar their entry and force them back to earth. We've copied the images from the cameras and so we can return those to you. You want them sent here I suppose?'

'With the images still intact Inspector if you don't mind. I'm assuming none of them showed anything relevant to Buzz's death?'

'No sir they didn't.'

Terence and Barry had no sooner left when the telephone rang.

'Henri, is that you? It's Giselle. I'm in town and thought I'd call. Look, I'm not doing anything this evening. Could we go out for a drink somewhere? I'd like to talk to you. I don't know London very well as you know but I'm staying up in the West End. Why don't you drop by and we'll go out somewhere? In about an hour? Okay?'

Henri held the telephone to his ear and thought for a moment. Leslie and his bloody ankle are a pain and all I'll get is abuse this evening if I stay in. And he thought, I need to check something out.

'Sure Giselle. Sounds good. I'll come by around eight to eight fifteen. I'll take you somewhere different, somewhere nice.'

'Henri I'm not into gay bars love. I just want a quiet drink and a chance to talk with my brother. Can you handle that? I may have some ideas for you. Help for you actually.'

'Always come up trumps don't you Giselle? Fine, about eight. Bye.'

Putting down the phone Henri looked at Leslie.

'Any news from the solicitor? About what I mentioned earlier today?' he added when Leslie looked blank.

'Look Henri. This is a bit risky isn't it? You sure you're not just pouring good money after bad?'

'Leslie I'm not investing or gambolling with this money. I'm just filling up coffers that are supposed to be full already. Once the Year End audit is over I can retrieve it and give it back. If it ends up being mine when you've finished your thing with the will then I might try and be more inventive, but for the moment it will keep the auditor off my back.'

'Give me an estimate and I'll sort it out tomorrow.'

'The numbers are all in the office Leslie. Look, I'll call you back early tomorrow morning from the office and tell you the numbers. Then I can get the books and accounts all fixed and looking proper before the end of the month.'

'Christ you sail close to the wind on occasions Henri.'

'No Leslie love, that's my brother. I just climb on the edge of all things. By the way, that was Giselle on the phone and she wants me to go out for a drink. She doesn't know her way around town and so I'm going to pick her up around eight. Think I'll show her some of the nightlife she doesn't get to see in Bristol. Don't wait up.'

'Get stuffed Henri. Go and get pissed. I've got to rest my bloody ankle thanks to you. While you're prancing about get me that bottle of whisky down from the cabinet. At least I can dull the pain. Both of us might as well get pissed I suppose. Get lost then. Out!'

'What is this place Henri?'

'In this dangerous little part of the world Giselle, in this desert of godless people this is the Oasis.'

'Henri pull the other one. You're full of it. This is Soho and this is some seedy club. Looking around me it is not even a gay club unless you've found some incredibly unusual transvestites. Tell me they're not girls?'

'Gloria, my sister's concerned. She's not sure whether you are a girl or a man in disguise.'

Gloria looked at Giselle. 'Suppose you are another Lord but you look like a lady to me.'

Giselle looked up at Gloria and smiled. 'Touché. Point made. Henri, I'll have a vodka and orange please.'

'Make mine a scotch please Gloria,' Henri said, 'and a quick word when you've got a moment. I'll come over to the bar when you've brought the drinks.'

Gloria left and Giselle looked at her brother. 'Henri, how deep in trouble are you really? I realise you've got money problems but then you've had money problems for a long time. What else is there I should know?'

'Thanks Gloria,' Henri said as the drinks arrived. 'Cheers Giselle, here's to you. No, here's to us,' and he clinked his glass against Giselle's.

'Henri!' said Giselle. 'Perhaps I can help.'

'The message was pretty clear Giselle; the message with Buzz.'

'Henri that was gross. These people are…well I don't know what. I assume you owe them?'

'That's part of it but Leslie and Buzz had a story going on them too. They had tapes and photographs and were going to publish it. They're into everything. Look, some of the girls who work here know a bit about them. Gloria you just met was one of the girls Daniel chucked out of the cottage at Fotheringham.'

'Oh, she was part of that little enterprise earlier this year? I never did hear all the details but Daniel and Aunt Sylvia broke up some brothel or other in the forest. Wasn't Terence part of that too? Is that how you know them?'

'That doesn't matter, but through Gloria and some of the other girls here, Leslie found out a lot more about the people holding my markers. They don't own this club but they do own several others. As I said, they're into gambolling, money-lending and therefore extortion as well as sex activities.'

Giselle sat back in her chair and sipped her drink. 'Know who they are Henri?'

'I don't know them personally but I do know where they have one of their clubs. It's called the Exotica and it's not far from here.'

The darkness in the club hid the expression that passed across Giselle's face and she looked at her brother. What did he know? What should she say? These were people her brother should avoid.

'Henri, listen to me and listen carefully. Pay these people. Pay these people and don't look back. Whatever you do don't get any further involved.'

'You sound just like Gloria here,' said Henri. 'She and some of the other girls here used to work at one time at the Exotica. They won't go back there again. Gloria says it just freaks her out and she's not easily frightened. I've only been there a few times and it's like here really. Same sort of drinks, floor show and opportunities for experiences in back rooms. I can't see it's any different although Leslie and Buzz thought there was much more to it. I never did see Leslie's article or Buzz's photos so I'm not sure what they found.'

Giselle sipped on her drink and thought fast how this could play out.

'What do you need? How much do you need I suppose I should ask? What will get them off your back? Isn't your deadline the first of January? A "Welcome into the New Millennium" gesture or something?'

'Fifty thousand would probably get them off my back,' said Henri, 'although that's not the whole amount.'

'Shit Henri. You really have gone wild this time. No wonder you were so desperate.'

'It's the interest,' said Henri. 'I couldn't find the money anywhere and the more I delayed the more the interest piled up.'

'You know I came up with Matthew Henri? I drove him home from Fotheringham after Christmas. I talked with him Henri and he was prepared to help if you were really desperate. He said he didn't want to throw good money after bad but I'm sure I can persuade him to help if this stops Henri. I mean it. Clean the slate and walk straight. Just this once Henri do as I ask, please.'

Giselle leant across the table and touched her brother's hand. 'Do it for mum,' she said. 'You always respected her and her advice. When you were growing up and really into climbing you were always quoting her advice. Do it for our mother Henri.'

Henri looked around the room. Sheena was dancing. Giselle followed Henri's gaze.

'She's not your type Henri.'

Henri laughed and turned his hand over in Giselle's. 'No she's not,' he said with a chuckle, 'but she's a wonderful dancer nevertheless. She's really fit you know. Jogs almost every day she told me.'

'Money Henri,' exclaimed Giselle.

Henri looked away from his sister and focussed on the girl dancing. Giselle turned to see where Henri was looking.

'Where's she from Henri?'

'Sheena's from Eire Giselle, and she claims she's not part of the IRA so you can relax.'

'And her?'

'Which one?'

'Either of them?'

'The shorter lady is Lola. She's probably Gloria's best friend and occasionally she's been my friend too,' added Henri.

Giselle's eyebrows lifted and she looked at her brother to see whether he was joking.

'Lola is originally from Spain but she's been here since she was a little girl. Gina, the taller of the two is Italian. She told me her parents were Sicilian but then she told me where she was from.'

Henri laughed.

'So where Henri?'

'From Wapping. From the backstreets of the East End. She's a real Londoner.'

'Stunning girl though Henri.'

'Want to meet her?'

'Henri, I came here to talk some sense into you and maybe help. I didn't come here to socialise. This isn't really my scene, although it is a little interesting. Now, let me tell you what I think I can do if you promise me to end all of this. End it all as soon as possible, like tomorrow or the next day Henri. I will talk with Matthew tomorrow and then see you again tomorrow evening. This is Tuesday and I think I can get you the money by Wednesday or Thursday at the latest. Paid by Thursday and you're in the clear. What do you say?'

Henri looked around the room again. What did he want to do? He could use the money to sort out his problems in the office. But then Leslie could help there. Well he said so. Could use the money to recoup my losses gambolling. Could use the money to pay off some of the debt. I haven't told Giselle the whole story Henri thought. Could I stop? Shit, after what they did to Buzz I need some sort of revenge and not just a wimpy payment. The money might open some doors though – might get me closer to the chief bloodsucker.

324

'Henri?'

'I'll order you another drink. I've got to go and have a quick word with Gloria. Just watch Sheena for a moment.'

'Christ Henri, you'd try a saint. Go on then, but we can fix this you know. Fix it for ever.'

Leaving Giselle to nurse her drink and watch Sheena Henri walked over to the bar where Gloria was resting between orders.

'Got a moment?'

'Briefly Henri. Supposed to be serving drinks and not chatting up customers.'

'What do you know about the Exotica?'

'No way am I going back there Henri.'

'No, no Gloria. I just want to know a little more about their set-up, where everything is. Back behind the club room itself there has to be other rooms. In fact I know there are other rooms 'cos I've been in one with Lola. What else is there? Is there an office back there, along that corridor with the bogs? I've never been down that corridor but it goes back a ways.'

'No Henri, don't bother. Those are just rooms for…well let's say other services. Perhaps like you and Lola. Remember the fire escape door just before the loos? Well, that's not any fire escape but it does go to the boss's office. It also leads to the room where they gambol. There's a staircase and it goes up to a floor above the corridor. From the top of the stairs you go through the gambolling room and the boss's office is beyond that.'

'But he must have another exit Gloria? That's too much of a dead end.'

'I've only been in there once Henri so I'm not sure 'cos that was a long time ago now. You're right though. There's probably an exit to a real fire escape or out onto the roof but I don't really know.'

'Who would? Would Lola or Gina? Lola worked there I know. Who knows the boss?'

'We all knew the manager Henri 'cos it's the same bloke as here – it's Vince Tobin but I never knew who the owner was. Think he and his main mates are European – Polish, Russian or something. Look, I've got to go. Ask Lola, she might know. See yer.'

Henri looked around. Sheena had finished dancing and little Belle Katz was slowly twisting around wearing her specialised gymslip. Giselle got up from her table and walked back to her brother.

'Time to go Henri. I've work to do tomorrow. I'll get a cab but remember I'll call you tomorrow. Finish it Henri. Night.'

'Giselle wait. I'll just be a moment and I'll take you back to your hotel.'

'No Henri. You sort out what you've got to do and I'll phone tomorrow. Thanks for the entertainment but it's really not my scene. I'll be fine,' and Giselle walked out.

Henri felt bad for the moment but suddenly felt arms travelling up his back and around his neck.

'Can't resist can you Henri? You just like to be dominated and I hear you were asking for Lola. Despite being a lot smaller than Henri Lola spun him round to face her. She waggled her whip in his face and gently drew the handle down the side of his cheek.

'Going to cost you Henri love. Shall we go somewhere quieter?'

'Lola I just need some information.'

'No you don't Henri, you want the full treatment.'

'Lola cut it out. Just for once I need information.'

Lola pouted and flicked her whip about. 'Like the last time I gave you information?' she said and flicked the whip about some more.

'Yes and no,' said Henri. 'I do want to know more about the Exotica but not about the people but about the club itself. Leslie and Buzz found out their bit thanks to you but I need to know the layout of the place.'

'Thinking of a raid Henri?' said Lola, and she laughed. 'You, that Leslie and Buzz – that the army is it? Darling you might need some more troops.'

'Buzz is dead,' said Henri sharply. 'They killed him.'

Lola placed the stock of her whip firmly on Henri's chest and looked up at his face. 'Whoa darling. Be careful what you say. Quietly now. Who's dead and who are you accusing?'

'Our friend the photographer, Buzz Haas,' said Henri. 'They killed him over Christmas.'

'Not in the papers Henri. Not done up here or have the fuzz buried it somewhere?'

'No Lola, it was down on my family's estate. Done in the forest and they just chopped him up.'

'What do you mean chopped him up? How do you know this anyway? I've not seen it on the news or heard anything about this.'

'Lola, Leslie, Buzz and I were all down at my family's house for Christmas. Leslie and Buzz had some other story they were on down there but they caught Buzz and killed him. Leslie and I have seen the body. It was horrible. They chopped him up.'

'Henri if they chopped him up how the fuck do you know it was Buzz?'

'They just cut off the head and the hands. It was a message, a message to Leslie and Buzz to back off. It was also a message to me 'cos they did it at my family's home. The bastards killed our friend Lola. They butchered him.'

'Who's they Henri, and be quiet about it?'

327

'The people at the Exotica Lola. Leslie told them he was going to print their story and I know Buzz had some pictures. Also, I owe them some money and I haven't paid.'

'What story Henri? And what money?'

'We'd found out about the girls there and some of the other activities. Leslie had also followed some of their people and found another couple of places, private places. He'd taped some conversations and Buzz had managed some revealing photographs. They were going to print the story in the New Year.'

'Jesus Christ Henri. Do you know who you're messing with? They'll fucking eat you alive darling. Leave alone Henri. Let it be and tell Leslie not to be such a stupid prat. You'll both end up with your heads on poles somewhere.'

'Bugger that Lola. I want to know about the Exotica. I've got to go there and pay anyway. I just want to know where everything is. Gloria said there is an upstairs. How do you get in and out of the office? There has to be a back door somewhere?'

'You didn't hear this from me Henri. Got that? Christ you're playing with fire.' Lola spent ten minutes with Henri until he felt he knew enough for the time being. He paid Lola and left the club. No time like the present Henri thought and he walked through the crowded streets of Soho. Although it was midnight a noisy jostling crowd of folk walked from venue to venue taking in the variety of entertainments on offer. It wasn't far and Henri was soon looking at the entrance to the Exotica. So Henri said to himself, how do we get in and out? Fire escape stairs, roofs, windows and they all lead where pondered Henri. Just another urban rock climb. Bring some gear and maybe come across from the next door building – it's higher. Henri moved across the street and investigated the next door building. The lowest level was a shop front but there was a door and presumably a staircase behind the shop that led to the upper floors.

Tenements thought Henri or maybe offices. What about the back? For the next hour Henri carefully and quietly investigated his new climbing challenge. An alley at the back let him discover a way up to the flat roof of the adjacent building. He looked down at the roof of the Exotica. As Lola explained it did have a crude fire escape which led to a small enclosed yard closed off with large double gates. This little yard probably served as the service entrance thought Henri – can bring in supplies. Can bring in and out whatever he realised. So if I get in and do my thing they'll think I go out that way. But, if I go out and up they'll never think of that. So, how do we get back up here? Quick jumar up a standing rope. Could rappel down, do the business and leave by coming back up the rope. Henri let ideas run around in his head. There were several skylights on the roof. Wonder whether any of them lead to the toilets 'cos that would be a good way in. Quietly in that way and then surprise surprise. Lola said there was another bathroom off the main gambolling room on the upper floor. After an hour Henri realised he needed to make a recce inside the club as well but he could do that tomorrow. It had been a long day. Need to get it right he muttered to himself.

'Leslie, you still up?'

'What's it look like Henri. Ankle's throbbing something awful. Can't get comfortable.'

'Been taking your pain killer?'

Leslie brandished the empty bottle. 'Don't think much of Doc Munro's prescriptions. Bloody Scottish quack. Man's a fraud. I should write him up and have him struck off.'

'You ever get through to that solicitor of yours?'

'I told you I'd sort that out tomorrow. Christ, don't you ever listen? How's your sister by the way? What did she want? Nosey bitch on occasions Henri that sister of yours. She asks too many questions and never tells you fuck all. What does she really do?'

'Giselle's fine Leslie. She cares. She wants to help.'

'Got a million pounds has she? Going to wave some magic wand and make the bastards at the Exotica turn into straw men so we can burn them. I need Buzz's photos. I need to publish that story and make the bastards sweat.'

'Lola said we're playing with fire. She told me to back off.'

'Henri when will you ever learn? Women don't know fuck all. It's us men that call the shots and we're going to do more than play with fire. We're going to fight Henri, fight the bloody bastards. Fight fire with fire.'

'With your ankle Leslie?'

The telephone rang and interrupted Leslie's response. Henri lifted the receiver.

'Hello, hello. Who's there?'

Henri nearly dropped the receiver and gasped. Shakily he put the receiver down and broke the connection.

'Well?' said Leslie. 'Who the fuck was that disturbing our peace at this time of night? I assume it wasn't my good doctor wishing me good night?'

'Just a reminder Leslie. Someone wanted to remind me about... well about the money.'

'What are you going to do about that? You still haven't got it have you? Suppose we could always mortgage the flat or something if you got that desperate.'

'Shit Leslie, I am that desperate. Still, hope may be on its way as Giselle offered to help.'

'You said that Henri but I don't see any money in your hands. Got it stuffed in your pockets have you?'

'She said tomorrow,' said Henri.

'Sure lover, she said manana. That means maybe, and maybe later, and maybe not at all.'

'No Leslie. Giselle does what she says. She talked with Matthew.'

'What, that old wizard we saw at Christmas? You said he was a scientist or something Henri. Didn't you tell me he made computers? Makes money now does he? His precious computers print out bank notes? All with different numbers I hope Henri.'

'I'm off to bed Leslie. You're not making any sense. I'm going in to the office tomorrow. Phone that solicitor and get the will thing sorted. At least I can arrange to keep the auditors off my back. Do that for me will you? Night.'

'Pass me another bottle before you go Henri. Thanks, and now sod off.'

Lying in bed that night Henri slowly and carefully went over his plan of action. Finish it Giselle had said. Well maybe this would finish it with some honour. Yes mother, we'll do it right Henri dreamed.

Wednesday dawned grey, slate grey, and the continuing rain tried to become sleet as the temperature hovered around freezing. Henri had wet feet by the time he reached his office. The market hadn't changed much overnight and so the financial situation was still as dark and dank as the weather. Henri fiddled around on his terminal and started to seriously look where he could patch holes and fudge gaps. Starting with a specific fictitious amount of money Henri simulated a series of actions of what to do if we had so much and what else to do if the amount increased. It all depends on Leslie Henri thought. He was tempted to phone but that wouldn't achieve anything other than piss Leslie off. Henri knew that Leslie would phone as soon as he could. That's what lovers are for he thought.

331

Families look after each other Giselle reasoned as she called Matthew. Now that her plans for the end of the week were settled she told Janice she would see her and her mother later that afternoon to go over some personal details.

'Matthew, how are you this dreary morning?'

'Better for hearing from you Giselle,' chortled Matthew. 'How are you today my dear?'

'Worried Matthew if truth be told. I'm at a loose end this morning but I have a problem that I would like to share with family. Actually, I have two problems and I hope that you can temporarily solve one of them.'

'Intriguing Giselle. I love problems. Knowing you and a little of what you do I'm assuming this is not mathematical or computer oriented?'

'No Matthew, although probabilities may enter into it.'

Matthew laughed. 'Good job it's not computers as I have forgotten all those things.'

'I'll be round in about an hour. Thanks for sharing.'

'Family you said? Maybe I'll speculate while you drive over. Work on some probabilities as you suggested. See you soon.'

'Terence, something new has just come up. My Inspector has discovered we have mutual friends with other parts of the MET. My D.I. would like us to meet with her and another couple of people. The meeting's over at the Yard. Given the weather we'll grab a taxi. I for one don't want to arrive in that prestigious building looking like a drowned rat.' Efficiently the taxi took Sergeant Gates and D.I. Field to New Scotland Yard and by ten o'clock they were ushered into a cramped but tidy office. Detective Inspector Lane was already there with another woman.

'D.I. Field I'd like you to meet D.I. Dawson.'

Terence shook hands with Brenda Dawson and noticed the smart crispness of the uniform that went along with the tidy office. Definitely her office thought Terence.

'I hear you've had a rather brutal murder down your way Inspector. I also hear you think that the killers are from London. Can you tell me why?'

Terence smiled and remembered the words of his boss as he left Somerset. 'Your murder son and don't you let those lazy buggers in the MET steal it from you.' Succinctly Terence explained what had happened where, and the conversations he had had with relevant parties.

'And the direct and/or indirect culprits are part of the family running the Exotica, amongst other places?' asked D.I. Dawson. 'Or so your sources think? Bit tenuous isn't it? Doesn't your part of the world also have some rapists and knife-slashing fraternal murderers? In fact D.I. Lane here tells me you have quite an array of unfriendly locals so how come we've got your murderers?'

Terence and Barry Gates broadened their explanations describing the antics of Gloria and her friends and the activities of Buzz Haas and Leslie Dauphin.

'Well we may be able to help. We may be able to apply a little pressure to your possible culprits. We are planning to pay them a little visit over another but possibly related matter. Some of the things your Buzz Hass and Leslie Dauphin unearthed are about to reach a climax. Perhaps the new millennium will bring us all some new beginnings. I make no promises as the people under discussion are a particularly unpleasant and hard crowd. There's a very strong ethnic loyalty about them which is partly their strength and their weakness. Did Darlene explain anything about our planned activities?'

Terence spent the rest of the morning listening and learning.

'We can give you a crack at some of the bastards when we bring them in if you like,' Brenda offered. 'We can soften them up with all sorts of charges and then you could twist knives and see whether you can pry one of them away from the national motherhood. You're going to need a lot more than the suspicions you have to date.'

'Thanks,' said Terence, 'but I have a question. I don't want to interfere in your Friday night visit but do you have anyone inside? If the place is as well organised as you say the more of our people inside the better surely? Contrary to popular belief I don't always look and sound like this. Right from the start of my career I was undercover because of some talents I have.' Terence laughed and Barry turned to him and grinned.

'You're not going to tell them about the conference party?' asked Barry. 'That'll go down in history but most of us keep it quiet. Embarrassing that was.'

The two female D.I.s looked at Terence and Barry.

'Okay, a brief outline,' said Terence, and he told the story of a senior officer's conference where he had masqueraded as a waiter and taped the supposed private conference unknown to any of his superiors.'

'So,' said Brenda Dawson. 'Not that embarrassing, just clumsy.'

'No,' said Barry, 'it's what happened afterwards that's embarrassing.'

Terence continued to explain about the very private party the officers held with a stripper and a supposed sex act.

'And you were directly involved? You were taking photographs? Nude? And no-one knew? Jesus, that's pretty brazen. Surprised no-one fired you after that. How come no-one recognised you with that kind of disguise?' and Brenda Dawson laughed.

'No-one at the conference had met me face to face.'

'Or face to something else,' chortled Brenda.

'So I'm thinking of being a customer,' said Terence, serious for a minute. 'I'm not known in London. I'm certainly not known at this club. I could be wired and in the loop.'

'Tell them why Terence. It's personal but not directly personal.'

Both ladies raised their eyebrows. 'No conflicts of interest I hope sergeant,' said D.I. Lane. 'We don't want country vigilantes.'

Terence was quiet for a moment and let the words settle. Then he explained that Messrs. Lord, Dauphin and Haas were a threesome, a family. Terence paused.

'Henri Lord is a once-removed brother-in-law,' and Terence explained the relationship. 'The murder took place on my in-laws estate and therefore I have a stronger than usual motivation to resolve this murder.'

The two lady D.I.s looked at each other.

'I'll have to take this up with my boss,' said D.I. Dawson. 'Superintendent Ralston may see this differently. Did I hear you say Lord Inspector Field? Any relationship with Giselle Lord from Bristol? I met a Giselle Lord the other day but she and her boss are very tight-lipped about everything.'

Very quickly Terence spun a few things around in his mind. He wondered what Giselle had or had not said. He also wondered how she was involved in any of this because she worked for some translation service in Bristol. Was she involved because she was Henri's sister?

'I know Giselle Lord and she is Henri Lord's sister.'

D.I. Dawson looked at Terence and then she looked at D.I. Lane.

'I'll take that under advisement too Inspector,' she said. 'Thank you for your time. I hope we can help each other. I'll get back to you with comments from my boss. I can reach you at D.I. Lane's office can I?'

Henri picked up the telephone and said, 'Dalston Investments Limited, Henri Lord speaking. How may I help you?'

The receiver hung there mute in Henri's hand and he suddenly realised that it was his cell-phone that was ringing. Crashing down the receiver Henri guessed it must be Leslie, Leslie with the news, the good news!

'Leslie how much?'

'You're still a callous sod you are Henri. Buzz's money and all you can think about is how much. Cheap. Anyway, probably enough you sexy loser. And Henri, my fucking ankle still hurts so thanks for asking.'

'How much?'

'There's a quarter of a million for you, give or take.'

'Thank god for that. How do I get it?'

'In pound coins, in a suitcase delivered by an ice cream truck driven by the tooth fairy Henri. How the fuck do I know?'

'Leslie I can't put promises in the computer. The auditor needs real numbers. How is the ankle by the way? Do you need any more scotch? So can I get a bankers draught or something? Anything that's real?'

'I'll get back to you. Bring me two bottles of scotch though. Now fuck off.'

Henri watched the connection break. Saved he thought. One down and one to go. Back at the computer Henri checked his life-saving strategy. Deep into money manipulations Henri almost ignored his insistent cell-phone. Leslie again being a prick he thought. The persistent ringing eventually stopped Henri flicking money about and he pressed receive.

'Henri, you asleep wherever you are?'

'No, no, I thought you were Leslie.'

'I'd have to grow a little hair and put on a few pounds for that Henri. I'd also have to lose a few years. By the way, I've had a visit from your sister. She tells me the family should help one another. I'm offering to help Henri. From what Giselle has told me you've promised to clear this up once and for all. I'm prepared to accept your word on that Henri. The word of a Lord and a gentleman Henri. Do we understand each other?'

'Yes yes, but how can you help? Giselle didn't say.'

'Because Giselle didn't know Henri. She merely came to me and asked me to help. Now my boy, I have two things you might find useful. Learning a little more about your friends and the ultimate fate of one of them caused me to rethink how I might help you. Come round tomorrow afternoon, about four and we'll talk.'

'Uncle Matthew it's not talk I need, it's money.'

'Tomorrow Henri, around four and we'll talk.' The connection was severed. Shit thought Henri. I don't have time for Matthew's stupid games. He's too intellectual and wants to play bloody mind games. Wonder what Giselle actually told him?

Having taken two bottles of Scotch home for moody Leslie Henri felt at a loose end. Then he remembered he had a job to do that evening. He dressed in a black turtle neck, black pants and reached in the cupboard for a dark reversible ski jacket. He stuffed a watch cap in his pocket along with a torch. Searching through the various shoes he found a pair of old scuffed sneakers. He looked at the soles. They'll have to do he thought.

'You look a right disaster,' said Leslie. 'You'll never get a decent dinner reservation dressed like that. Pass the bottle.'

'Where I'm going this is fine.'

'Where?'

'To look at the lay of the land and find weaknesses.'

'You're fucking weak in the head if you go where I think you're going. Didn't you say you'd pay the bastards? Get it done Henri, once and for all.'

'Now you sound like my sister. Everyone's telling me to get it done. Shit Leslie, those bastards killed Buzz. You keep reminding me about

Buzz. Well I'm going to sort it. I'm going to make good use of the money he left me. Now, I'm off. As they say in all the best family movies "don't wait up". Goodnight.'

Henri put Leslie's fancy trilby on his head and walked out of the door.

Inside the Exotica the lights were low and visibility was further restricted with the pall of smoke that drifted around. Henri found a table near the wall and looked around him. Doorman, two bouncers, barman and two or three girls distributing drinks but they all looked normal, or English, although one of the bouncers could be Eastern European. Leaving his hat and coat on the chair Henri slipped up the corridor to the gents. There was no-one in the corridor and Henri did a quick check in the ladies but that was conventional and had no windows or other exits. He slipped back into the gents. Three stalls and two cubicles but no vents, windows or anything useful. The corridor was still empty and Henri quietly cruised up the length of it. Three doors but they were all locked except one. There was no different sound along here and the music from the main room thundered around the poor acoustics. The room was empty but there was another door on the far side. With his ears tuned to anything alien Henri walked quietly across the room to the far door. His hand slowly turned the door-knob and very very carefully Henri eased the door open. It opened inwards. Real fire hazard Henri thought and then he stopped. Jesus he said to himself. He stood in the doorway and let his eyes gaze around the room. The ceiling was high and even if he jumped Henri couldn't reach it despite his six foot six frame. Lights were set into a mirrored ceiling and the ceiling itself curved into the mirrored top of the walls. Partway down the walls the mirrors stopped and a black sort of rubbery compound covered the walls to the floor. Henri banged it with his fist. It gave and there was no sound. He hit harder and the wall just absorbed his fist and no sound came back. The floor was another mirror. Scattered around the room were shapes like chairs all covered in the black absorbent materials of the walls and one shape that was bed size Henri realised. Seeing there was no other exit from this room Henri turned and nearly shit himself. Standing behind him was a grinning man.

'Looking for something special are we friend?'

Henri frantically pushed the sunglasses firmly onto his nose and let go of the doorknob.

'Wouldn't let go of that mate. You might have noticed that there isn't any handle inside the door. Once inside you might never come out. Well, until we want you to come out.'

'I got lost. I came out of the gents and must have turned the wrong way.' Henri tried to slur his words as if he was drunk and he staggered forwards out of the frightening room.

'Lost eh?'

'Shhurre,' Henri whispered out of the side of his mouth.

'So you don't fancy an evening of fun and frolic with D in there mate?'

'Don't know any D,' said Henri, trying to move away from the door, but the grinning man wasn't moving anywhere.

'Okay Vlad?'

Henri heard a new voice but couldn't see past the grinning man's bulk.

'Right boss. Friend here couldn't mange to jerk off in the bog and so he thought this playpen would heighten the senses.'

The hidden voice laughed and Henri heard another door open. A hand grabbed his collar and twisted him towards the corridor. Henri played limp and staggered his feet after the hand pulling him away from the special playpen. He was out in the corridor and pushed back to the club room.

'Next time just ask one of the girls mate.'

Henri slumped back at his table and gulped his drink. He shuddered and then almost jumped when one of the girls tapped him on the shoulder.

'Heard you were looking for something special?' she asked. Tassels twirled a little from her nipples and just to add to the offer she spun around and bent over. Henri gulped at his glass but it was empty.

'Just a drink please,' he managed to whisper.

'You sure darling? Heard you were the adventurous type. Liked to look in exciting places. I've got some very special exciting places love. You could do more than just look. Big man you are love. Big hands, big tongue and big….'

'Just a drink please.'

'You'll regret it,' but she waltzed away to the bar.

Having paid for his drink Henri looked about again. He'd wanted to try the fire escape door in that corridor, the one that led upstairs Lola said, but after his last encounter he didn't think he could run that risk again. The voice behind the grinning ape sounded like the voice on the telephone. The voice reminding him about the money. He'd have to come back tomorrow night with some gear and try another way. Finishing his drink Henri waited until the floor show had livened up a little and most people were looking at the two girls on the stage. Attention demanding if you're into that kind of thing but not Henri's preference. Now if they were males but… and Henri slipped out of the club. He pulled the hat down over his head and huddled into his coat. The rain had stopped but as the temperature had dropped a thin sheet of ice glazed the road and pavements. Placing his feet carefully Henri crossed the street and slid into a dark doorway. He looked back at the Exotica and that side of the street. Tomorrow he thought and we'll find another easier way. Bastards. He spat in the gutter and went to find a taxi home.

PAYBACK

ON THE THURSDAY A COLD easterly wind blasted through the streets as Giselle and Janice boarded the ferry in Harwich, along with several other unknown but interested people. The watchers had strict instructions not to lose their target and the group Giselle and Janice might meet. In London several people were anxious that this operation went off successfully. They wanted to permanently dismantle a very obnoxious form of immigration. The high pressure in Europe brought clear skies, lower temperatures and a severe head wind for the ferry as it battled its way across the lower North Sea to Holland. Several of the passengers succumbed to the rolling motion of the ship as it cleared the protective breakwater and most people stayed below decks. Giselle and Janice made themselves comfortable in the lounge and quietly discussed life in England, but speaking Serbo-Croat the whole time to brush up on their language skills.

During the morning Henri managed to work in a three-ring circus of telephone calls, transfer arrangements and money manipulations with Leslie and Buzz's solicitor. By lunch time Henri was exhausted, but his unauthorised use of client's money was now covered up, at least temporarily. After going out for a celebratory lunch, and staying longer than he should have, Henri came back to his office mid-afternoon feeling sleepy. With his feet on his desk he was about to doze off when his telephone jerked him back to the real world.

'Henri, an update.'

'Oh, yes, Terence, an update. Well, Leslie and I haven't done anything. I've…'

'Henri, it's me with the update. We're closing in on the murderers. Don't go out of town. We may need you and Leslie for some identification in the next few days. Okay?'

'Sure Terence. I'll let Leslie know. You've found them have you? You're going to arrest them? It's all sorted? When? When are you closing in Terence?'

'I'll call you if and when we need you,' said Terence.

Henri's mind moved back into gear fast enough to realise he needn't tell Terence what he had been doing. No point in saying anything Henri thought. I'll do it my way and Terence can do what he likes. Henri heard the line click dead and he replaced his receiver. And I'm closing in too thought Henri.

'Henri, come in come in. It's good of you to visit and see an old man. Nobody followed you I hope?'

'Followed me? Why?'

'Can never be too sure Henri. Nasty people everywhere in this world. I used to have secrets you know. I always watched to see who was following me, in person and on the computer Henri. Clever people out there these days too. Some clever nasty people. Hear you've found a few. Giselle was telling me some of the details. She asked whether I could help. Well in a way maybe I can. This is family help Henri, and one good deed gives rise to some obligations. So, as I told Giselle, I'll help you but you in turn have to help your sister.'

'My sister? How can I possibly help Giselle? She's so organised and always has everything under control. She doesn't need any help.'

'Sit down Henri. Relax a little boy. You look all tense. You also look shagged out to use an old expression. Is being queer as tiring as being heterosexual? I can't remember ever looking quite as haggard as you look now.'

'Matthew, I am who I am,' said Henri sharply. 'Being gay is perfectly normal and everyone realises that now. It's not a perversion, a crime, or even a hidden situation this day and age. You should really get with it.'

Matthew chuckled, and muttered he would get with it, as he looked at Henri. Slowly, running his eyes up and down Henri's rather tense frame he said, 'Possibly Henri, possibly, but then you're the one in trouble. I just think you don't look in top form my boy. However, enough of all that, so let's get down to the business at hand shall we? Giselle is worried about you. So, responsibilities and obligations Henri – repayment if you like. I help you and you help Giselle. Is that a deal or not?'

'What do I have to do?'

'Not quite the right words Henri. Not quite the right frame of mind. Not the right question. You don't have to do anything, and then again, neither do I.'

'Christ Matthew. Giselle said you would help me and all you want to do is play word games.'

'I'll make it simple for you Henri, although I always thought you were an intelligent young man. Perhaps growing up became too much for you. Listen. I will give you one hundred thousand pounds. Giselle mentioned you told her the amount was fifty thousand pounds but that wasn't all of it. She also mentioned some other blackmail stuff they were holding so I've made the amount double her number. Clean it up Henri. And in answer to your question about what do you have to do for her it is simple. Just do it completely and stop. End of story and Giselle will feel happy again. Right now she's quite worried about you and she doesn't want to feel that way. Family obligations Henri. Understand?'

'Yes. Sure. But Giselle said you could help in two ways. What's the other?'

Matthew sat back in his chair and looked at Henri. He tried to breathe normally but at eighty five it was a rasping kind of action. Closing his eyes he thought back over the Lord family history. He was the fourth child and his elder sister Harriet, his parent's second child had been a rebel, had burnt out at age twenty-one and committed suicide. Henri's father Charles had also been a second child, as was Henri. Anthony's second child Michael had been a handful and then he got killed, shot to death. What was it with this family he thought? We are so different. Matthew opened his eyes and looked at Henri. Henri was sitting opposite looking at him. He was wringing his hands and Matthew could feel the frustration and anxiety.

'In my day a man did what he had to do Henri.' He handed Henri a gun and a package. 'This was a war trophy from Veronica's husband. As such it is untraceable and the package contains ammunition. I'm assuming you know how to use this kind of thing?'

'Yes,' said Henri, 'yes I think so.'

'Henri, both of these items are important. Here's the money and here's the gun. Use them both and get this stupidity over for all time. Do we understand each other? This is family Henri and we've always been bold and decisive. We haven't always done legal things but we've always got it right when it came to family honour. English honour Henri. Your great grandfather, your grandfather, Veronica and I all served this country Henri and we were proud to do what we could. I understand from Giselle these people are not English, some peasants from Eastern

Europe, some obnoxious peasants. Sort it out Henri. Now go and let an old man rest. I don't need thanks boy. I just to want to hear you helped your sister. She loves you. Go.'

Henri took the packages. He retrieved his coat and left. Christ he thought. One hundred thousand pounds! What he could do with that. He placed the gun and the ammunition on the seat beside him. Untraceable he said. Shit, it's time to revisit the Exotica. Not like this though he thought. Change of clothing, some climbing gear, headlamp, gloves and a degree of skill. Time to take the fight to the enemy's camp for a change.

Across town Darlene Lane walked into Barry Gates's office and looked at Terence with a resigned look on her face.

'D.I. Field, I've just heard from D.I. Dawson and she's says her boss says it's a no. Everything is under control and he doesn't want to change the plan at this stage.'

'Thanks,' said Terence rather formally to D.I. Lane. 'I appreciate the information,' and understand that they don't want a country yokel buggering up MET internal politics and relations thought Terence. Well, we'll see about that. It's still my case and I'd like to see it through to the end.

'So Terence, looks like we're on the outside mate, as usual,' said Barry Gates.

'Aye Barry, but we can still be there for the kill. Nothing the brass says can keep us off the streets of Soho is there?'

Sergeant Barry Gates looked at his friend. They had been together as young cadets and had stayed good friends even though their careers had taken them miles apart.

'Are you thinking what I think you're thinking?'

'That's an awful lot of thinking Barry.'

'Maybe, but then you always were the one for listening and thinking weren't you?'

Terence smiled. 'Isn't there a stupid saying about "the heart doesn't grieve over what the eye can't see"?'

'Something like that, and I'm assuming, rather than thinking you'll note, that the MET's eye won't see you?'

Terence's smile broadened. 'We'll see, and then again perhaps we won't see. Just as an aside it is wonderful what you can learn from children's books.'

'Okay Terence,' said Barry, 'I'll bite. What have you learnt from these educational children's books?'

'I bought my son a copy of the "Just so Stories" for Christmas.'

'Kipling?'

'Yes, and the story of how the leopard got his spots.'

'Where the zebra and the giraffe keep disappearing instead of being breakfast?'

Terence laughed and clapped Barry on the shoulder. 'The benefits of an educated childhood prove valuable at the oddest times. Yes my friend, a little camouflage is in order.'

After seeing Matthew Henri went home and rethought his original idea. He could still go in the way he planned. He could still pay off his debtors. He could finish it as Giselle wanted but now he had a gun. What could he do with the gun? Matthew talked about honour, family honour and using the gun.

'Henri I want to go with you. I want to go when you pay off these fuckers. I want to see their faces when I tell them about the story.'

'Leslie forget it. First of all your ankle is crippling you so you're a liability. Secondly, I don't want you telling them anything, story or no story. Whether you publish or not is up to you but I don't need them pissed off in my face thank you.'

'It's not for you to tell me whether I can publish or not you stupid wanker. This is my story, mine and Buzz's. Bugger you Henri, I'll go anyway. You can't stop me.'

'Leslie this is not the time for any confrontation. My sister and my uncle want me to end this – end it once and for all. I don't need you stirring up trouble.'

'Weasel, wet wanking weasel, weak and family-whipped. Jesus Christ Henri, for once in your life be a man. We need to make these bastards realise we aren't going to take Buzz's murder lying down. We don't just roll over and pay. We make them pay.'

'Fine words Leslie, but then you are a man of words aren't you? You've never climbed at the edge: you've never stood there on the edge of all things: never felt the thrill and absolute fear and excitement of climbing up something at your limit. No mate, you've sat in your chair and written about it. You tell me the pen is mightier than the sword, or some such old cobblers, but my family, the Lord family, is more about honour through action Leslie. We do things.'

'And look where that's got you.'

'Go write your memoirs Leslie. I'm going to bed. Fuck you.'

The return ferry crossing from Holland to England was delayed that Friday afternoon because of the threatening rough seas so the party of school girls were disappointed they may not make it to London for the midnight millennium celebrations. Eventually the ferry pulled out from the Hoek van Holland dock and set about clearing the harbour walls. Rough seas churned up the shallow North Sea and very few people ventured on deck. The wind whipped spray across the windward side and Giselle and Janice sat and talked on the leeward side.

'Have you seen them?'

'I think so but I wasn't close enough to hear anything for certain. The clothes look right though, as did the faces.'

'There are supposed to be eight girls and the two minders. Perhaps they took a cabin?'

'One or more of them might be sick. They've probably never been on a boat like this before.'

'We'll split up Janice and start at the bow. I'll go down one side and you the other but be casual.'

'I can disappear Giselle,' said Janice. 'Mum taught me how to disappear. She said she and dad used to practice that a lot. They had to.'

Yes thought Giselle. I'll bet they did but they still found your dad love.

'Okay Janice, but no contact until we've met up. I don't want you disappearing for real. You understand?'

'Yes Giselle.'

'Good love, then let's go hunting.'

Terence sat in the office with Barry Gates and thought about various tactics for this evening. Barry idly leafed through some paper work but watched his friend.

'You're still thinking of a way in?'

'Mmm.'

'You need a face with you, a face to open doors.'

'Don't think you fit the bill Barry. I'd guess your face is too well known.'

Barry laughed. 'Unfortunately too true.'

'The idea is good though Barry, actually maybe very good. What would interest that mob? What face would open doors? What about a new face, a face and maybe a new body, a new entertainer, a new performer for them? How about I take them a possible new recruit?'

'They'd be suspicious Terence. They'd need to check out who you were and who she was.'

'But I'd get the door open in the process. I'd get further into the club than just the ballroom so to speak.'

'Got any volunteers?'

'Got any European WPCs?'

'Jesus, you're asking a lot.'

Terence laughed. 'Just joking Barry. I should have thought of this earlier. Poor planning but I could do with a key.'

'How well do you know those girls at the Oasis? Didn't you tell me you got to know all of them after last summer's circus down your way?'

'A thought Barry. Trouble is some of them have worked at the Exotica and they're known there. I may go and find Gloria though. She might have an idea. She hates that lot at the Exotica.'

'Know her address?'

'As it so happens I do. Remember me telling you about this Toby the Fixer?'

'The promoter? What did you say he does now – he's a negotiator? What the hell does he really do?'

'As the word says Barry he negotiates: he helps parties settle disagreements and apparently he's quite successful. In his early days he managed bands, organised gigs and the like. Anyway, after last summer's "circus" as you called it they all moved back here to London. Gloria and her mother moved in with Toby. So yes, I have the address and I'll give them a call.'

'Think Gloria can help?'

'Out of all the girls I met there was one who I know didn't work at the Exotica Barry. She'd be a good candidate if I can find her.'

349

'And persuade her to do something dangerous Terence. Where you're going ain't no tea-shop. These are nasty people mate, real nasty. Remember, they chop off people's heads you told me?'

'Just have to hope that the cavalry can recognise the good guys Barry,' said Terence.

'Well I'll be in the cavalry Terence so keep your head on until I get there mate. Anything else I should know? I'm asking 'cos I don't expect you'll look like you do now. Will I know you? Actually, more seriously for any future such stunt should I know you? Would it be better if you get swept up in the haul?'

Terence thought on this question. 'Not sure. Really I'm only here for the murder. I don't have any further agenda. Still, probably for the best if you haul me in as a suspect. That way my assistant's face doesn't get tied in as a friend of the cops. She stays untainted.'

'Untainted!' Barry laughed. 'There ain't any such animal in this city who's untainted Terence. We're all villains of one sort or another. You stay in your nice clean countryside mate. I know you have murder, rape, as well as cattle stealing and broken windows. You told me all that, but some of the people down there seem to be nice people. No mate, we're all tainted up here. Okay, we'll pull you and your face in for questioning. Good luck.'

Having decided he'd sorted the accounts out as best he could Henri left the office. Shit, it was New Year's Eve and if he stayed any longer he'd likely bugger something else up. He was so nervous and kept going over and over the plan in his mind. He tried to think about the evening as if it was a big climb. Preparing for that was much the same he told himself and you could do that. Get the gear organised: get the route sorted in the mind: check the weather: get the team psyched up. There is no team Henri, get a grip. This is a solo thing. But I don't do solo climbs. Well this one is solo Henri. You and you alone mate; the big one. Henri looked at his hands. They shook. I need something thought Henri, but not a drink. Alcohol and climbing don't go. I need a high.

'Success,' said Janice. 'I was right Giselle. Two of them are real sick. One of the older women has two of them outside, leaning over the rail. They're as pale as can be. One of them can hardly stand but I heard the women speaking to them.'

'See the others?'

'No, they must be inside.'

'Okay, show me the sick couple. I may be able to offer some help,' and Giselle smiled. 'You okay Janice?'

'Bit scared, but then I keep thinking of my dad and I feel stronger.'

Giselle put her arms around Janice and hugged her. Together they went back inside the ferry and slowly made their way to the place where Janice had seen the two sick girls. The ship rocked and rolled with the violent sea motion and walking was a little precarious. Most of the passengers were sitting huddled up and looking anxious. A few hardy souls were sipping drinks. A bunch of young lads were actually out on the windward side of the ship dodging the spray that occasionally cascaded this far aft.

'Outside now auntie,' Janice whispered in Serbo-Croat. Giselle glanced out of the somewhat steamy windows. With a close to freezing temperature outside and a snug warmth inside there was a lot of condensation on the glass.

'Poor girls,' Giselle replied in the same language. She squeezed Janice's hand as she glanced around her. There were several family groups scattered in the lounge. People returning from Christmas with their relatives in Holland or Europe Giselle thought. She could hear a smattering of non-English voices.

Toby Dobbs, or Toby the Fixer, sat and listened to Terence Field. Gloria, and Tilley, Gloria's mother, also sat in the living room and listened to the story Terence spun.

'Why should we help Inspector?'

'I thought I'd heard these people really frightened you Gloria? Wasn't there some story of murder? Didn't you tell Gary or someone about girls getting killed?'

'But you just want a face as a key Inspector?' asked Toby. 'You just want an excuse to get to the office; get to see the main man? Then what? Knowing that kind of set-up there will be layers of people and lawyers lurking behind every door, not to mention goons.'

Fortunately Tilley and Gloria got into the conversation with questions of their own and Terence could draw breath for a moment and just listen and think. He wasn't going to explain that a raid was planned.

'You know Henri Lord is trying to find out more about the Exotica?' said Gloria. 'Earlier this month he and his two friends have been at the Oasis. Seems that the words man, Leslie something or other, wants to write about the girls there. Henri was in again just recently to find out more about the Exotica. Not sure why 'cos he's been there several times before. Has this got anything to do with Henri and his loving friends? Actually Inspector, isn't Henri married to one of those friends?'

'Married? What do you mean Gloria?' asked Tilley. 'How can two men be married to each other?'

Gloria giggled and held her mother's hand. 'Mum this is London. We do things differently up here. Toby love, explain the new facts of life to my mum here.' Gloria turned back to Terence. 'How dangerous Inspector? Sure, I'd like nothing better than to see that lot carted away. Most of them and their poxy clients are animals. 'Bout time someone cleaned out the scum but I don't want any of my friends getting hurt Inspector. That's a dangerous place with some very nasty people.'

Terence looked at the three of them and thought about what to say. 'I'm not going there as me,' he said, and then he surprised the three of them by speaking the next sentence in Russian. The two women just looked confused but Toby lifted his head and smiled. He replied in Russian and it was Terence's turn to smile. Half an hour later Belle Katz came knocking at the front door and the discussions continued about faces and perhaps other body parts to unlock doors.

While Giselle talked with the minder Janice gently spoke with the two sick girls. Digging around in her purse she found some pills that eased the stomach she said. She offered them the whole packet. During the conversation Janice discovered that both of them were legitimate school girls but she did find out who were the two late additions to the group. When one of the sick girls had to go to the bathroom Janice offered to go too. The minder hesitated and Giselle quickly commented how sick the second girl was and that she should stay out here on deck, with the minder she added. Over the next thirty minutes, and meeting the rest of the group inside the saloon, Giselle and Janice managed to pass tracking buttons into the clothing pockets of the various girls. As a safeguard Giselle managed to get another device into the shoulder bag of one of the targeted girls, but one never knew whether the accessories would be dumped somewhere along the way. Even tracking devices on the clothing were no guarantees of success but Giselle had instructions to keep the encounter as short and casual as possible. Just a chance passing, a friendly gesture and an exchange with someone speaking a foreign language.

The ferry docked with some difficulty and most of the passengers boarded the train. It was a fast run across the flats of Essex to Liverpool Street station and the lights and excitement of London on Millennium Night. On the train the senior watcher approached Giselle and they had a brief exchange of information. As a safeguard the planners had booked seats for Giselle and Janice in one of the two compartments reserved for the group from Serbia. If contact on the boat had failed this would have been another chance to identify who was who. However, given that Giselle and Janice had already done that and attached trackers, it was decided not to push their luck and occupy that compartment. Too many coincidences and suspicious people start to get antsy so Giselle and Janice sat comfortably in a second set of reserved seats. A young couple with a baby occupied the seats with the school party and inevitably the young girls wanted to hold the baby. The young couple were also watchers but they appeared to speak only English. Everyone enjoyed the more relaxing train journey after the upheavals crossing the North Sea. Everyone except the two young girls sitting in the compartment with the senior minder and three other schoolgirls. They stayed pale, frightened and silent despite the excited buzz of chatter all around them.

At Liverpool Street station Giselle and Janice waited until most of the other passengers had left the train and passed into the concourse. Everything was in place and the watchers carefully tracked the bunch of schoolgirls with their two minders. Two men met the party and the police promptly had their images checked with headquarters. In addition to the watchers on the train there were four additional police staff at the station. They watched to see who else, either from the train or in the concourse, was paying any attention to the crowd of schoolgirls. It was assumed by the authorities that the smugglers would also be remotely tracking their package. Surrounded by adults the eight girls trooped down the passages leading to the Tube. Discreetly watchers followed, paying particular attention to the two special girls. One of the two men who met the group purchased tickets and the twelve of them proceeded down to the platforms.

It was a Friday evening. The evening to end the millennium, and in London that meant partying. The entire city was going to party. The Tube was packed with people milling about and coming in and out at every station. It was hard to see who was who and where anyone was. A watcher with a hidden tracking device got out at every station as quickly as possible to see who got off and then jumped back on again if it was a false alarm. Communications with Inspector Dawson at headquarters were curt and tense.

Giselle had already decided that she and her boss had their own agenda. Although the pair of them were not officially part of the team to raid the Exotica they both thought they should be there at the kill – well just afterwards if truth be told. Very quickly Giselle had taken Janice safely home to her mother and left straight away to find Mikel Tallin. They had a quiet meal together in Giselle's hotel and discussed the timing of their visit to the Exotica.

In the early part of the evening Henri wandered rather aimlessly around the flat.

'For Christsakes stop muttering to yourself Henri. You're driving me nuts. Fetch me another bottle. I need to toast the New Year in. If you're buggering off somewhere tonight, as I think you are, then I want to get blind drunk before you leave. I want to enter the new millennium in the right frame of mind. Where are you going by the way?'

'Leslie I'm going to pay off those bastards at the Exotica. I told you. I've told you a hundred times. That's what the money is for.'

'I thought the money was to cover your unprofessional use of client's assets somewhere in your accounts. All that stuff I did for you from Buzz's slush fund was to doctor the books for the year-end audit you said. Take care of embarrassing things at the office. Where did the money come from to pay those dogs at the Exotica? I thought we agreed we weren't going to pay them. I told you we would pay them back. Make them pay for a change after what they did to Buzz. Christ Henri, you're not going to give them money surely?'

'Leslie, what they did to Buzz was a message, a warning if you like. I've had them phoning me for the past few days reminding me that tonight is payback time. They've threatened me.'

'And you've put your tail between your legs and peed your pants,' said Leslie. 'Pass me the bottle. I need to drown my sorrows. I need to quietly fade out of this world and re-enter in the brand new year of two thousand to start again. I'm not sure I want you back here Henri if you going to give those bastards any money.'

Henri popped another pill. He passed a full bottle to Leslie sprawled on the couch resting his damaged leg and looked at his friend, his significant other, his lover. Sitting up straight and taking a deep breath Henri looked calmly at Leslie.

'I'm going to give them some money Leslie, and then, just as they are about to take it, I'm going to take it back again. I'm also going to make them pay for what they did to Buzz. I had a long talk with my Great Uncle Matthew and he explained in very simple words all about family honour and obligations Leslie. I'll remind you that I come from a long-lived family of traditionalists and we Lords have honoured our family and our friends for many years. Matthew made me realise my family obligations and he provided the wherewithal to make it happen. Remarkable man my great uncle Leslie, quite remarkable.'

'Crap Henri, utter bull-shit. You're an investment counsellor and not some fucking knight in shining armour. What're you going to do – offer to invest their money in some off-shore groundnut scheme? I can do them more damage with my words than you can do with your family obligations. Maybe I'll write another article to get the authorities to close them down or something. Doesn't have to be about any girls, just rats in the kitchen or e.coli in the tap water.'

Henri looked at his watch. 'I'll go and get ready.' Leslie turned the cap on the bottle and generously splashed scotch into a glass. 'Get some ice on the way will you? Just dump some in a bucket or something and leave it here. Go and get ready indeed.'

Quietly Henri tumbled some ice cubes out of the fridge and into a bucket. He carried it back to Leslie and put it on a side table. 'Anything else my lord?'

'No Henri, no, not at all. You're the Lord remember. You just told me all about family honour and payback. Well go and do it for God's sake and let me get drunk.'

It didn't take Inspector Field very long to go through Belle's wardrobe and work out what she should wear, although Belle kept making unnecessary suggestions.

'Belle, this is serious and not some night of fun and frolic. I'm really glad and grateful that you agreed to this but I'm sure Gloria told you that these people are brutal. If we do this right there will be no danger but this isn't the place to improvise. I want you there as an assistant and not a liability. Gloria tells me you are a right charmer and you can look very young and that is just what I need. So, minimum make-up, no smart-arse remarks, and looking pale and frightened. Put on those clothes and then we'll go to my hotel and I'll change.'

'What do I get out of this Terence? In all honesty why the fuck am I doing this?'

'Thought you were a friend of Gloria's and Lola's?'

'So?'

'The people at that club gave both Gloria and Lola a rough time. Several people around this city want those animals off the street and without going into details that's what we're going to do. You helping helps Gloria, your mate.'

'I'll tell the silly cow she owes me one.'

'Good. Grab your coat and let's go and get me dolled up.'

Henri changed into black clothing: smart black shoes and socks, sharp creases down his dress pants, polo necked stylish sweat shirt, and covered with a buttoned blazer. In his hand he was carrying a small dark rucksack. Leslie peered at him over the rim of his amber-filled glass. 'Behold, the man in black. You're too young to remember Valentine Dyall. Are you Zorro, the fox? Perhaps the elusive pimpernel? Which character are we playing tonight Henri at this fancy dress party at the Exotica?'

'Funnily enough Leslie I'm going as me.'

'What's in the sack? Toys for the children? You've missed Christmas Henri if you were thinking of going down the chimney.'

Leslie laughed into his drink and then tipped up the glass and drained it. 'Another,' he said imperiously. 'Pour me another you strange fellow and get you gone.'

Silently on his rubber-soled shoes Henri walked across the room and filled Leslie's glass.

'The sack does contain some gifts if you must know,' said Henri. 'It also contains some props to go with the "character" as you put it. Ways and means to help me get in and get out.'

'You got an Uzi in there Henri?' laughed Leslie.

'No Leslie, something a little more subtle than that. Don't wait up.'

'Very funny Henri. Before long I shall be pissed out of my mind. Go and play Lordly honour and obligations. What do I care? I miss Buzz. Fuck you Henri. Just fuck off,' and Leslie threw the glass at Henri before slumping into a heap on the couch.

Picking up his rucksack Henri walked over to his friend and made him more comfortable. He picked up the glass and placed it on the small table. Kneeling down by Leslie he gently lowered his head until he could kiss his friend goodnight. 'I shall return my dear friend when honour is satisfied. All will be well. Bye my love.' Taking one last look at his friend Henri swung the sack onto his back with both arms through the shoulder straps and left the flat.

Fortunately it was cold that night, cold enough for the two girls to keep their coats on and the watchers could follow the tagged clothing on their monitors just in case anyone lost sight of the quarry. Two men and the two special girls got off at Holborn on the Central Line while the rest of the party went on. Four watchers had got off too and they independently walked towards the exits while the two men waited on the platform holding the two girls. Two of the watchers out of sight quickly reversed their clothing, changed hats, found a walking stick and re-appeared as new arriving passengers to wait for the next train. They boarded the next train along with the men and the girls. Communication was difficult with headquarters and D.I. Dawson sat with the headphones plastered to her head while contorting her face with anxiety. She didn't need to say anything 'cos everyone on the op knew this was serious and big-time. Two stations later, at Oxford Circus, the procession left the train and made its way into Soho and the Exotica. Watchers dutifully reported, as did the watchers following the official school party to Marble Arch, and D.I. Dawson breathed a loud sigh of relief. Phase three was halfway home and everything should be in place for the grand finale. Time to check all the players are waiting in the wings ready for their cues.

Black as the night and keeping in the shadows Henri silently walked around to the back of the Exotica and the next-door building. From his rucksack he brought out a black mask and slid it over his head. Just need a broad-brimmed hat Henri chuckled to himself and I could be Zorro. He wore tight-fitting black gloves on his hands and now the only parts of him easily visible were his eyes. Should I bother with mascara on my eyelids he asked himself or is that going overboard? Fuck it, too difficult to apply right now so leave it. Looking up Henri scanned his line of ascent. Just like a rock climb he muttered to himself and he automatically adjusted the harness he was wearing and settled the sack snug on his back. Within minutes he was on the roof of the adjacent building and looking around for a suitable tie-off for the rope. Using a series of slings and a solid screwgate karabiner Henri rigged a bombproof anchor and then he uncoiled the dark rope from his sack. Making sure he had the jumars to re-ascend the rope afterwards Henri abseiled down the single rope to the roof of the Exotica. In the rucksack he still had the money, the gun and some more equipment if needed.

After her dinner Giselle decided to telephone Matthew. She thought she should find out whether Henri had actually gone to see him and what had been said.

'Giselle my dear, I gave Henri the money as we discussed. I told him it was an exchange. I gave him something and he in turn has to give something back.'

'But he doesn't have any money,' explained Giselle. 'That's why I asked you uncle. He can never pay you back. Well, not for some time. Years maybe.'

Matthew chuckled down the telephone. 'And I haven't got years now have I Giselle? This old man doesn't have many years left in the bank now does he?'

'That's not what I meant.'

'No no Giselle. I didn't tell Henri to repay the money. Like you suggested it is an investment in the Lord family name.'

'How did he react?' asked Giselle.

'In his usual somewhat remote way. But I did offer him something else Giselle. Something in addition to the money. I gave him.....' and Matthew paused.

'What uncle, what did you give him?' said Giselle when there had been a long silence down the telephone.

'No matter. I just told him to do the honourable thing and make you happy. Told him to repay me by making you happy. Less worried perhaps. Yes, that would be a better thought.'

'But I am happy uncle. How could Henri make me happy?'

'By giving you less worries my dear. By changing his life such that you don't have to continually look out for him. You do you know. You're like Veronica was with Harriet, although Harriet was a far harder and far younger case than Henri.'

'But he needs help uncle. He's so unsure of himself, even at his age. In so many parts of his life Henri's not sure which way to go. It's only when he's climbing, when he's in the mountains that he seems to find direction.'

'Yes,' said Matthew, 'a little like his parents but that wasn't the answer either was it?'

'Will he be alright uncle? Did he seem settled in what he had to do? Did he have a plan?'

'He muttered something about taking the fight into the enemy's camp,' said Matthew.

Giselle looked at the telephone in her hands and wondered what Matthew had said and what Henri meant. 'Thanks uncle. Thanks for all your help. I'm sure everything will go well. Happy New Year. Welcome to the new millennium. Good night.'

'Good night Giselle. All my love.' The line clicked and Giselle slowly replaced the receiver. Mikel Tallin looked at Giselle.

'All is well?' he asked.

'Maybe,' she replied, 'and then again maybe not. I think it's good that we are going to visit that place. In fact we had better get going as it's gone eleven. If I remember correctly Brenda Dawson was going to raid the place five minutes before midnight. Just when everyone would be getting ready to welcome in the New Year. Come on Mikel. Grab your coat and let's find a taxi.'

Terence had padded out his clothing, worn high heel boots, made-up his face, changed the colour of his hair and kept muttering under his breath in Russian. At his side Belle looked like a little doll. She too was into acting and appeared fearful to the doorman and the bouncers. Coming in Terence had asked to see the Manager, but only after he'd had a couple of drinks. The question had been voiced in a mixture of Russian and broken English and he'd had to repeat it a couple of times to make himself understood. They will remember me thought Terence and the word will get passed on. Grabbing her by the arm Terence half-dragged a reluctant Belle into the Club. He growled at her and she cringed. Terence turned to look at the doorman and he grinned.

Henri quietly crossed over the roof of the Exotica and looked down through one of the skylights. He had already decided that the fire escape that came straight out of the boss's office only opened outwards and as he was no locksmith it was in through a skylight. Sliding down another piece of climbing rope he had taken from his sack Henri found himself in an empty bathroom. Looking around he decided to stash the rucksack and just take the essentials, like the money and the gun in his pockets. He could get the job done, retreat to the bathroom and lock the door, jumar back onto the roof and up again to safety. Easy. Quietly and cautiously he opened the door and peered down the corridor. He was on the upper floor like he planned, but he'd better make sure he could safeguard his position and retreat.

Mikel and Giselle had come into the Club along with another two couples as if they were all part of a large group. They stayed with the other two couples and everyone ordered drinks. The music that accompanied the movement of the two girls on the stage drowned out any cross table conversation so Giselle could easily whisper to Mikel.

'Do you want me to explore a little – go to the loo and get lost a little in the back corridors?' Mikel looked around the room surreptitiously and decided it wasn't crowded enough. He took Giselle's hand and leant a little closer.

'Wait until there are a few more people. It's too easy for the staff to see the gaps and we're not sure where the police will try and enter. I don't want you getting in any cross-fire Giselle.'

'You think there'll be any firing? This is England remember Mikel.'

Mikel chortled. 'Sure, and you're a peace-loving country with bobbies with truncheons. Wait a while. It's only eleven thirty.'

Sitting in the boss's office Terence glanced at the clock on the wall before refocusing on Nemanja Makavejev sitting opposite him.

'I've come to trade,' he said in Russian. 'I've come to offer you a titbit for the table,' and he laughed as he lifted Belle's chin and then slid the back of his hand down her slender throat. He stood quickly and yanked Belle upright off her chair. With his two hands he pulled the coat roughly off her shoulders, bent her over his outstretched knee and spanked her bare bottom and then stood her upright again. 'As I said, a titbit. Dress her up in a transparent burka and men will have their tongues out. People could lose their heads over her. A new sensation. Just imagine.'

Although Makavejev sat quietly across the desk with an impassive face the heavyweight behind him could hardly keep still. Somewhat unwisely he put his hands on his boss's shoulder and leaning forward he whispered, 'She'd be a sell-out boss. People could really lose their heads over that one,' and he laughed. It happened in a flash, and even Terence was taken somewhat by surprise as Makavejev twisted suddenly in his chair and grabbed the hand of his minion off his shoulders. Pivoting he slammed the man's hand down on the desk and snapped the wrist with his other hand chopping down hard. He didn't say a word as Dusan Tadic screamed with pain and grabbed at his broken wrist.

Terence took the opportunity to thrust Belle behind him as he appeared to stumble and knock against the side of the desk. The box on the corner fell on the floor with a thump and suddenly Makavejev was still again. Wincing with pain Tadic looked even paler as Terence bent down to pick up the box.

'Souvenir?' he asked, shaking the box. 'Gift for a friend perhaps? Could be what you might want to trade for my titbit here?' Terence started to open the box when Tadic shouted, 'Stop, stop him boss. That's for Henri Lord. For Henri Lord when he comes to pay tonight. He'll come boss. Don't you worry. We've been reminding him every night this week it's tonight or else. Should make a nice gift for him. Face to remember,' and again Tadic laughed as he held his broken wrist.

'A gift for me? How nice,' said Henri as he quietly entered the office. 'And, as your threatening piece of shit keeps telling you I have come to pay tonight.' Henri advanced from the doorway across the room towards the desk. Terence quietly and slowly moved backwards keeping Belle behind him and almost out of sight. Fortunately Henri had his eyes focussed on Makavejev.

'So what is this gift?' he asked.

'Money tosser,' growled Tadic coming round the desk towards Henri and holding out his hand. Henri reached into his jacket pocket and pulled out a wad of notes. He slapped them down on the table in front of Makavejev completely ignoring Tadic. Reaching into his pockets again he pulled out another wad of notes and slapped it alongside the first pile. Without taking his eyes off of Makavejev Henri said to Tadic, 'Count it peasant, if you can count that is.' Suddenly Henri straightened up and turned to Tadic. 'No,' he said loudly. 'No, I'll have my gift first. Open my gift. Oh dear, you can't can you as you've hurt your hand? Well then I'll open it,' and Henri ripped the top off the box.

'Stop,' shouted Makavejev in a voice that completely filled the room and Henri just held the box. 'That's not enough,' and Makavejev slowly rose from his chair to dominate the scene.

'That's what I owe you,' said Henri, 'eighty thousand pounds. Get your peasant to count it.' Henri looked inside the box and gasped.

'Another twenty thousand Mr. Lord. You owe one hundred thousand,' thundered Makavejev.

Henri stood by the desk looking stunned as his eyes were fixed on the box. Everyone in the room was silent and for a moment it seemed that the world stood still until Tadic laughed, Henri dropped the box, and Makavejev held out his hand.

'One hundred thousand Mr. Lord, by midnight we said. In six minutes time,' he added as he glanced at his watch.

Henri sighed and let his shoulders sag. He reached into his pocket as if to find another wad of notes and let the gun fit snugly into his hand. Slowly he straightened up his body and looked across the desk at Makavejev.

'I assume this is my friend in the box? This gift is my friend?'

Tadic laughed again and Henri turned and shot him straight in the chest. Without warning all the lights went out and the rooms downstairs exploded with sound. Terence grabbed Belle and thrust her down on the floor in a corner well away from the door. The fire exit door suddenly crashed open inwards and three or four armed men with torches and loud voices jumped into the room. Henri didn't hear, or perhaps didn't heed the shouts of 'Flat on the floor, flat on the floor,' and the torchlight caught the weapon in his hands. 'Drop the weapon,' came too late as in the wavering torchlight Henri shouted 'Payback' and shot at Makavejev two, three, four times and saw his body slump to the floor. A further single shot flashed across the room and then the lights came on. More people poured into the office and voices shouted at each other.

'Henri, why couldn't you wait?'

Giselle lent over her brother's dying body as Henri tried to speak. Blood flowed out of his mouth.

'Only the first Lord,' he whispered, 'only the first Lord in this family can afford to wait.'

CAST OF CHARACTERS

The Lord Family

George Lord   Born 1880. Died 1946
Eldest son. Soldier in WWI. Married Virginia Milne in 1908 at age
of 28.

Virginia Milne   Born 1883. Died 1966

George and **Virginia** have four children: **Desmond, Harriet, Veronica
and Matthew.**

Desmond Lord   Born 1910. Died 1968
Eldest son. Pilot in WWII. Married to Rosamund DeWinter in 1938
at age of 28.

Rosamund DeWinter   Born 1912. Died 1987
Only daughter of French parents. Dies 1987 at age 75 slightly gaga.

George and Virginia also have:
Harriet   Born 1912. Died 1933
Veronica   Born 1913. Died 1999
Matthew   Born 1914. Alive 1999

Desmond and Rosamund have three children: **Anthony, Charles and Stephanie**

Anthony Lord   Born 1940. Alive 1999
Marries Sylvia Trelawney in late 1964. Anthony and Sylvia start their own company in software development called Brainware. Head of the family at Fotheringham Manor

Sylvia Trelawney   Born 1942. Alive 1999
Daughter of Cornish family in the China clay business.

Charles Lord   Born 1941. Died 1966
Meets **Helene Forcier** (age 18) in Chamonix, France. Have three children, **Marcel, Henri** and **Giselle**. Charles and Helene are killed while mountaineering in 1966 at age 25.

Stephanie Lord   Born 1942. Alive 1999
Trained as a vet. Works on genetic research in sheep at Home Farm at Fotheringham Manor. In 1966, when Charles and Helene killed, Stephanie takes on the adoption of Marcel (6), Henri (5) and Giselle (4).

Anthony and Sylvia have 4 children: **Geoffrey, Michael, Samantha, and Daniel.**

Geoffrey Lord   Born 1965. Died 1990
Marries Christina DeLucci in 1988 and have son Peter, born late August 1989. Geoffrey dies in climbing accident in 1990 leaving son Peter heir to the Estate. *(Details in novel Michael).*

Christina DeLucci   Born 1965. Alive 1999
Born in Italy. Son Peter born 1989. Somewhat emotional and very family oriented. Lives on Home Farm at Fotheringham with son Peter. Adopts Tony, Michael and Danielle's son in 1998.

Michael Lord   Born 1969. Died 1991

Second son and resents Lord family policy of primogeniture. Michael killed 1991 but has a son with Danielle Made called Tony (born August 1989). (*Details in novel Michael*).

Danielle Made   Born 1970. Dies 1998

Born in Mozambique. Came to England in 1989. Has son Anthony (Tony) born August 1989 with Michael Lord. Lives in London 1989-1998 when she flees down to Fotheringham. Killed 1998 at Fotheringham. (*Details in the novel Samantha*).

Samantha Lord   Born 1972. Alive 1999

Grows up a tomboy with two brothers. Marries Andrew MacRae 1993 and has son James. Moves to Canada in 1996. Returns from Canada in September 1998 with son after husband Andrew MacRae killed. Joins old school friend Janet Donaldson in Heritage Adventures Company. Marries Terence Field in July 31, 1999. (*Details in novel Samantha and novel Daniel*).

Daniel Lord   Born 1974. Alive 1999

Receives Forestry degree in 1996 and is in charge at Fotheringham Manor Estate. Meets the Howard family and daughter Katya. Marries Katya in July 31 1999. Birthday Oct. 24. Lives at Fotheringham. (*Details in novel Samantha, novel Daniel and novel Gloria*).

Charles and Helene have three children: **Marcel, Henri and Giselle**

Marcel Lord   Born 1960. Alive 1999

Born in France. Adopted by Aunt Stephanie in 1966 when parents killed. Marries Marie in 1980 and have sons Jean and Philippe. International competitive yachtsman. Wife Marie lives in Dartmouth with the two boys.

Henri Lord   Born 1961. Alive 1999

Born in France in June. Adopted by Aunt Stephanie. Grows up to be a climber like his father. Moves to Bath and works in financial planning and investments. Moves to London. Marries Carol Matlock 1989. Divorced

1991. Has a "partner" Leslie Dauphin, who is a spiteful journalist who resents Anthony/Sylvia Lord family and its traditions.

Giselle Lord   Born 1962. Alive 1999

Born in France. Never really remembers her parents and is brought up by Aunt Stephanie. Develops a talent for languages. Goes to University from 1982 to 1985 with a First in Modern languages. Speaks Italian, French and Spanish and works as an interpreter for a Government office in Bristol.

Other Lord offspring include

Peter Lord   Born 1989. Alive 1999

Born late August. Son of Geoffrey Lord and lives with mother Christina DeLucci at Home Farm, Fotheringham Manor. Heir to the Lord family estate after death of his father in 1990.

Tony Lord (Made)   Born 1989. Alive 1999

Born in London in August. Mother was Danielle Made and father was Michael Lord. Lived in London with his mother most of his life. Adopted by Christina Lord after his mother killed in September 1998 and lives with Christina and Peter at Home Farm. Keen on football and swimming.

James MacRae   Born 1994. Alive 1999

Born August. Son of Andrew MacRae and Samantha Lord. Raised by Anthony and Sylvia Lord for most of his first year. Went to Canada with parents in 1996 and returned with Samantha in 1998 to Fotheringham.

Jean Lord   Born 1981. Died 1990

Born in Devon. Elder son of Marcel and Marie Lord. Keen to sail like his father but afraid. Dies from drowning while out sailing with Michael Lord in 1990.

Philippe Lord   Born 1982. Alive 1999

Born in Devon. Younger son of Marcel and Marie Lord. Goes to Bristol House School with fees paid by Stephanie Lord.

Henri's friends and relations

Leslie Dauphin

Free-lance journalist friend and marriage partner (1995) of Henri. Lives in London

Buzz Haas

Paparazzi photographer and lover/friend of Leslie and Henri in London

Carol Matlock

Society girl in the Arts world who can climb. Henri's wife from 1989 in London. Divorced 1991

Henri's friends

David – first friend. Fell off cliff in Cheddar Gorge and died
Darnley Cheevers – High School friend, cross-country runner, climber in Rockhoppers. Not as good a climber as Henri but could out-run him. Gay lover. Killed in gay-bashing brawl
Ralph Beckham – climber, instructor in Rockhoppers. Introduces Henri to sex
Justin Tyndall – University male friend of Henri. Long-distance runner until leg broken.

Highland Finance and Investment Company

Duncan MacKenzie	Born 1920. He has stroke and dies 1985
Alan Gray	Born 1921. Dies 1984
Robert Knox	Born 1925 and retires in 1990
Sandy McNeil	(aka Bert Gauge) employee of H.F. & I. Eight years older than Henri
Malcolm MacDonald	ex Glasgow successor into Highland Finance. Married. Two children.

Rory MacDonald   brother of Malcolm. Single. Gay. Systems
                   Manager for Highland finance.

Other Characters at Fotheringham

Enrico Branciaghlia   Born 1922. Alive 1999
Born near Cortina Italy. With brother trained as a forest worker. Well
respected on the Estate and in the village. Carves wooden toys for
children. Stays on in Estate cottage living alone after brother killed in
1990. Retires in 1997. Moves into Home Farm in 1998. (*Details in the
novel Daniel*).

Terence Field   Born 1966. Alive 1999
Detective Inspector in 1998 at time of Samantha/Daniel. Regional Crime
Squad investigates September incidents at Fotheringham. Becomes
friend of Samantha. City born and bred. Unfamiliar with country.
Marries Samantha Lord in July 1999. (*Details in novels Samantha,
Daniel, and Gloria*).

Katya Howard   Born 1977. Alive 1999
Only daughter of Delaney IIIrd. and Deidre Howard from Jackonsonville,
Florida. In 1998/9 is studying Forestry at Oxford University and in her
final year. Special friend of James MacRae and girl friend of Daniel Lord.
Marries Daniel on July 31, 1999. Birthday in January.

The Reverend Gabriel Godschild (aka Alan Briggs)
Preacher in the village and at the Fotheringham Education Centre.
Believer in instant humans and the need to save the world through God's
word. Converter of the heathen and initiator of angels. A fraud.

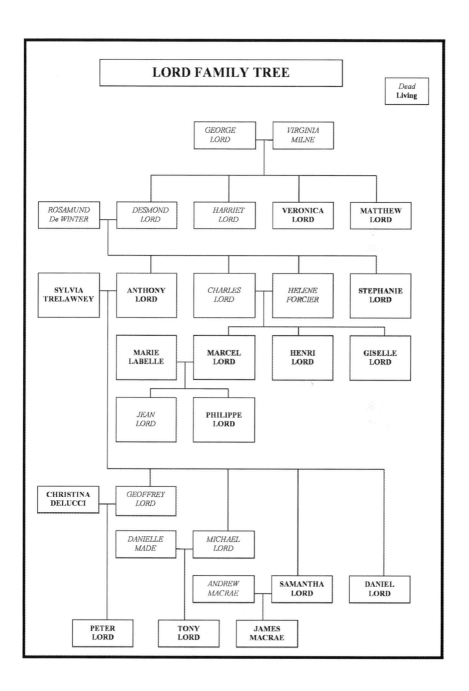

LORD FAMILY TREE

Dead
Living

GEORGE LORD — *VIRGINIA MILNE*

ROSAMUND De WINTER — *DESMOND LORD* | *HARRIET LORD* | **VERONICA LORD** | **MATTHEW LORD**

SYLVIA TRELAWNEY — **ANTHONY LORD** | *CHARLES LORD* | *HELENE FORCIER* | **STEPHANIE LORD**

MARIE LABELLE — **MARCEL LORD** | **HENRI LORD** | **GISELLE LORD**

JEAN LORD — **PHILIPPE LORD**

CHRISTINA DELUCCI — *GEOFFREY LORD*

DANIELLE MADE — **MICHAEL LORD**

ANDREW MACRAE — **SAMANTHA LORD** | **DANIEL LORD**

PETER LORD | **TONY LORD** | **JAMES MACRAE**

373

ABOUT THE AUTHOR

JOHN OSBORN WAS BORN IN 1939 in Ipswich England but grew up in the East End of London where he learnt to sail. In North Wales he graduated as a professional forester and rock climbed three days a week. After working as a field forester for three years in Australia John went to Vancouver, British Columbia for postgraduate studies and the Flower Power movement of the sixties. While working for thirty years for the Ontario Ministry of Natural Resources, both as a forester and a systems analyst John sailed competitively, climbed mountains and taught survival and winter camping. He finished his professional career with three years consulting in Zimbabwe, walking with the lions. Now retired, although working part-time at the local Golf Club, John lives with his wife in Kelowna, BC where he hikes and x-c skis from his doorstep.